SERAPHINA GREY SUMMONS A DEMON

GREY SISTERS SAGA
BOOK ONE

CRISTINE COURCY

SMASHED HOUSE PUBLISHING LLC

WWW.CRISTINECOURCY.COM

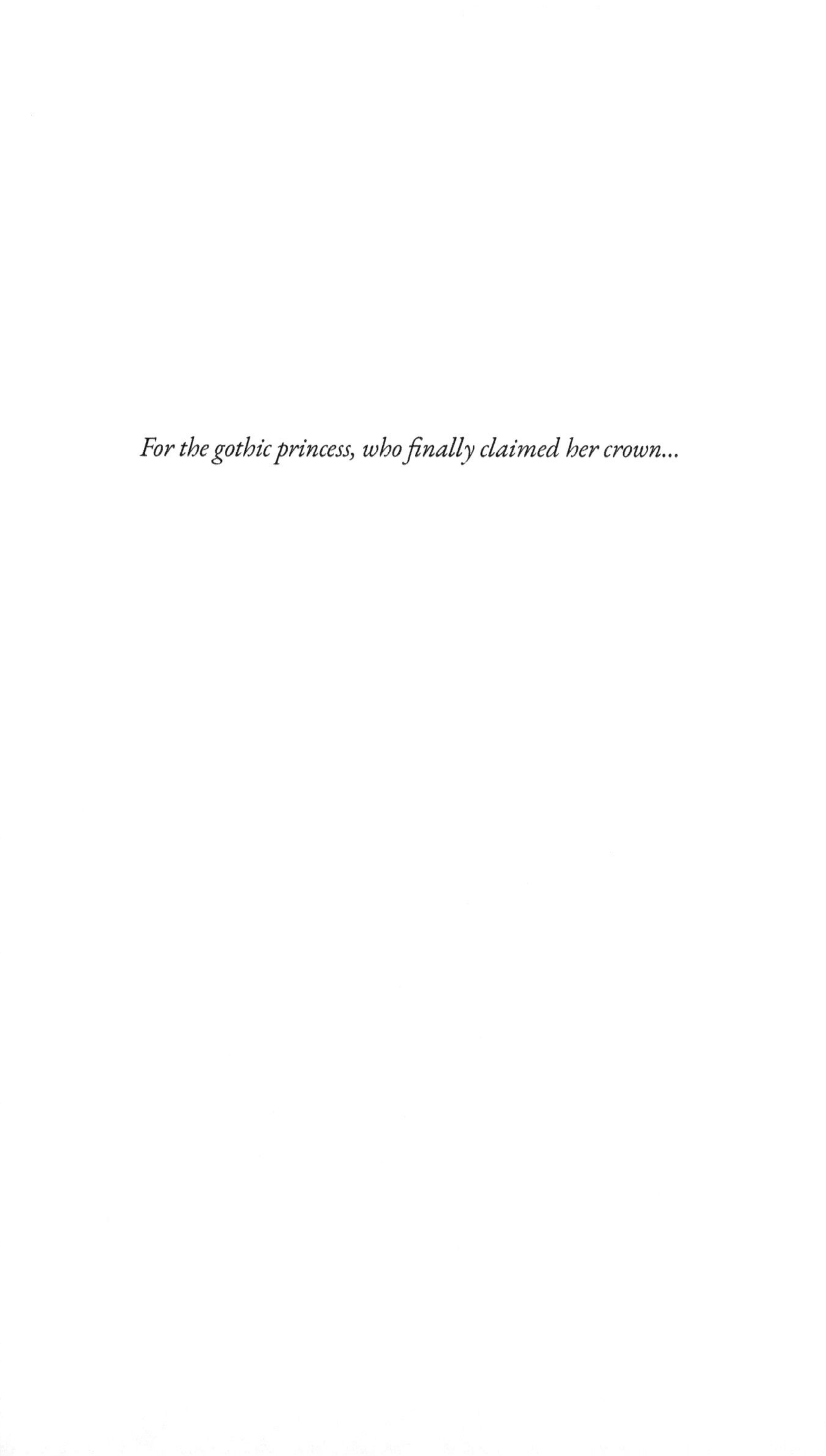

For the gothic princess, who finally claimed her crown...

CONTENTS

FAILURE BY DESIGN

Phoenix reached for my hand, but I slapped her away.

It had to be a bad dream. This wasn't happening. There was no way this could be real.

Whispers hissed in the darkness all around me.

Seraphina can't conjure.

She can't cast.

How embarrassing.

It's like she isn't even a witch.

What's wrong with her?

Phoenix could do it, and she's her twin.

I bit down hard on the inside of my cheek. I blinked slowly, forcing my eyes to remain dry. They shined silver in the firelight.

Don't cry.

Do. Not. Cry.

Phoenix reached for me again. I closed my hand into a tight fist. I moved away from her. The simple gesture of comfort made the blood burn in my veins. It wasn't Phoenix's fault, of course. It was mine.

I'd just failed the most important test of my life. In front of my entire family. In front of the whole coven. And with the Wand Forging, there were no do-overs.

I stood there, in the middle of the circle, unmoving and unsure what to do next. The weight of dozens of eyes pressed upon me. This wasn't supposed to happen. The Forging Ceremony wasn't something a witch could fail. At least, it hadn't been until now. I swallowed thickly, my tongue dry in my mouth. No one spoke up. The awkward silence was laced with poisonous murmurs.

The cauldron didn't glow.

The fire didn't burn.

The metal didn't spark.

Seraphina couldn't forge her wand.

What does this mean?

I flinched as Mama's hands rested gingerly on my shoulders. "Come on, Seraphina."

And with her arm wrapped around me, she led me away from the cauldron, out of the circle, and across the field toward Blackwell Manor, the whispers hissing at our heels like snakes in the dark grass.

It was quiet in Blackwell Manor. No one had returned from the circle yet. It was just me and Mama as we waited in the library of our ancestral home.

I used to love that room. It was a pleasant mixture of comfort and sophistication. Dark wood finishes, coupled with warm accents of reds and golds splashed around the curtains, the lampshades, and the plush chairs and couches. The walls were completely hidden behind floor-to-ceiling bookshelves, stacked and overstuffed with hundreds and hundreds of books. It was the perfect place to both research and relax, whatever mood struck you at the moment. But now, it would be forever stained by this memory—the worst night of my life.

I stared into the flames as they flickered in the giant fireplace, casting dancing shadows on the large rug. I didn't dare to speak. I had too many questions I didn't want answered.

Mama went first. "You don't have to worry, Seraphina. It'll be all right. We will get through this together. Like everything else."

I tried to nod, but all I could manage was a stunted twitch.

Icarus, Mama's familiar, was the first to enter the room. He padded softly across the floor and leaped gracefully into my lap. His claws kneaded my gown as I instinctively stroked his soft black fur.

The coven elders came in shortly after. Mama and I stood quickly. Icarus dropped from my lap with a disgruntled yowl. We bowed our heads respectfully as they entered: first my grammy, Nancy Grey, High Priestess of the House of Grey, followed by her brother, my Uncle Richard Blackwell, and her sister, my Aunt Cordelia Blackwell.

Aunt Cordelia stood tall beside the couch, too stuck-up to sit down. Beneath her periwinkle pointed hat, her white and gray hair twisted into a thick braid down her back. She smoothed her matching powder-blue robes with her round nose high in the air. Uncle Richard leaned against the mantel over the fireplace, his eyes crinkled in the corners from the kind smile half hidden beneath his wild gray beard. Grammy stood between them with an uncharacteristically stoic expression on her normally animated face as she studied me for a moment.

"Seraphina, you may grab a plate in the Great Hall until we call you back...there are things we must discuss with your mother before—well, before we discuss your...situation."

She didn't need to ask twice. I stood, bowed respectfully, and hurried from the room.

As I shut the door, I lingered for a moment in the dark of the hallway. The last place I wanted to go was the Great Hall, where I would be forced to face the insincere sympathies of the entire coven...namely, my hag cousins.

I considered sneaking down to the lake, but then the

murmured voices of the elders began to rise, and I paused to listen, lurking at the door, hidden in shadow.

"The High Council has requested it, Charlotte." Aunt Cordelia sniffed. "You can't refuse them."

Mama answered in a voice that wavered with waning patience. "I have three girls to care for...they can't possibly—"

"It's your responsibility!" Aunt Cordelia snapped. "Or at the very least as good as, after Alice—"

"Enough," Grammy murmured coolly.

A loud silence rang in my ears as I tried to quiet my breathing and listened for someone to break it.

Uncle Richard spoke first.

"The signs are clear, Lottie." Uncle Richard's voice was gentle and soft, so much so I leaned into the door to hear it. "She has returned."

Another silence followed.

"Fine." Mama's voice was sharp and crisp. "I will leave in the morning. But Fawn must stay here at Blackwell Manor with you, Mother."

"And what of the twins?" Grammy prompted.

"What of *Seraphina*?" Aunt Cordelia asked dryly.

"The girls I trust to stay at Grey Cottage until I return," Mama answered, ignoring Aunt Cordelia. "They will be safe there."

Aunt Cordelia scoffed. "You really think it best for Phoenix to be holed up in that old hut? My dear Charlotte, Phoenix could be a rare talent. Why, in all my years, I haven't seen a Forge so impressive. She should be at Stone Point—at the very least while you're gone. She can board throughout the week and visit Fawn on the weekends. Take the opportunity to try it. I know the headmaster personally. He would no doubt jump at the chance to enroll my grandniece."

"That won't be necessary, Aunt Cordelia." Mama's voice was cold. "Fawn will be able to pass through the portal between Blackwell Manor and Grey Cottage at her leisure, and the girls need each other. Now more than ever."

"But what of *Seraphina*?" Aunt Cordelia clipped. "To fail the Forge—it's unheard of...a complete disgrace! A stain on the House of Grey! It is clear she has no magical ability...why, one might even question if she is in fact a witch at all—"

"Cordelia!" Grammy said sharply.

Aunt Cordelia continued as though she didn't hear, not pausing to take a breath. "But it's not like you could send her off to school with *ordinary* children. After what happened with Charlotte and—"

"Aunt Cordelia..." Mama interrupted. "Seraphina's knowledge of the craft is extraordinary." Mama's voice came strong and controlled. "She is skilled in her potions as well as geology, herbology, and astronomy. She may not be a Natural, Aunt Cordelia, but with more time and a mentor, she could become a proper mage."

My eyes burned and blurred with shame. I bowed my head as I gripped the door.

Cordelia snickered darkly. "A *mage*? Really? The family has sunk so low? A priest has almost as much power in prayer as a mage has in practice...this is your alternative?"

A tear slid down the bridge of my nose. I'd heard enough.

I hurried down the corridor as though I could leave my shame behind me, the tap of my boots echoing loudly in my ears.

Phoenix spied me the second I'd slipped through the Great Hall doors. "Are you okay?" She scooted up beside me. "Mama made me wait here with Fawn...I wanted to come with you but—"

"I'm fine, Phoenix." I sighed impatiently. "Just grabbing a plate."

Phoenix touched my arm. "I'm sorry about—"

My eyes narrowed, and I rounded on her. My temper snapped, just like my voice. "It's not your fault, Nix, all right? Just...I don't want to talk about—oh, *great.*" I cursed silently as a group of teens encircled us.

I forced a smile.

Phoenix, on the other hand, didn't bother to hide her displeasure. She threaded her arm through mine. "We were just grabbing plates, so if you'll just—" Phoenix shooed at them.

The group didn't part for us and instead stood their ground, like a wall between us and the buffet tables.

"Seraphina," crooned Tabitha. "I can't believe it. I'm so *embarrassed* for you. What are you going to do? Did Aunt Nancy tell you what to do next?"

My nostrils flared. I gritted my teeth in an effort to stop the words from slipping off my tongue.

But Phoenix shot the words I'd held back. "No, Tabitha. Did she tell you?"

Tabitha crinkled her nose, but pretended like Phoenix wasn't there. "It's fortunate you're *homeschooled* on that island of yours. If word got out at Stone Point, you know, the *witch academy*—that something like that had happened to *me*...I'd never be able to show my face at school again! I'll bet you're grateful to be stuck at home all day with your twin."

Cecily nodded solemnly. "Yes. I still can't believe the cauldron wouldn't catch."

Ronald smirked. "Well, it's no surprise, really. Sera's always had trouble with magic, haven't you, Sera?" He gave me a hard slap on the arm. "And let's face it, wand forging isn't something you can learn from a book." He put his hand on his hip and waved the other to illustrate his point. "You're obviously well read and knowledgeable, but..." He shook his head and clicked his tongue against his teeth. "When it comes to actually *applying* the knowledge, you just can't manage it, can you?"

"Mother says this hasn't ever happened before...no witch can *fail* to forge a wand," Cecily murmured, her blue eyes wide.

Ronald nodded and smiled as though enjoying a pleasant joke. "So, you're kinda not even a witch, huh? I mean—"

"Ronald." Tabitha shook her head but didn't bother to hide her indulgent smile.

"Are you going to like—have to go to school with *ordinary* kids?" Cecily shivered. "I would be so embarrassed!"

"And with *island* kids, no less." Tabitha stuck her nose high as she winced. "I do feel for you, Sera, having to live on that lame Martin Isle, so far away from—everything." She laughed airily.

"Hey, hey!" Ronald held up a hand excitedly. "What do you call a witch without magic? Seraphina Grey!" Ronald doubled over with laughter.

I jutted my chin out and narrowed my eyes to hold in the tears. Before I could think of a retort, Phoenix shoved him. Hard. Ronald cried out as he stumbled back.

"Oops. Excuse me." Phoenix pushed by the rest of the girls. "We're getting food. Maybe you hags should try it and stuff your big fat mouths."

My eyes burned as I hurried after Phoenix, leaving them staring and muttering behind us. "Nix, you shouldn't have said that..."

"No." Phoenix grabbed a plate and passed it to me. "*They* shouldn't have said that."

I gripped the plate in both hands and blinked back the tears threatening to spill. Then Phoenix snatched another plate for herself and heaped food onto both of our plates as we moved along the table. "They've always been hags. You know that. I'm just sorry they showed their warts tonight."

Phoenix led me toward a table that was empty save for our eight-year-old sister Fawn, who had her nose buried in *Harry Potter and the Sorcerer's Stone*. She was spooning mashed potatoes into her mouth, her eyes never leaving the pages, and hadn't yet realized her spoon was empty. She dropped the book flat on the table as we took our seats and tossed her spoon onto her plate with a clang. Then she leaped from her seat and threw her arms around me in a tight hug.

I smiled despite myself and squeezed her back. Her tawny hair filled my face, and I breathed in the calming woodsy smell of her. Somehow, Fawn always smelled of the forest and rain. Though, it was probably because she spent half her life slipping between the trees.

"I'm sorry it didn't work, Phin," she said in a small voice.

I pulled back from her and smoothed back the curls tumbling from her plait. I looked deep into her big honey-brown eyes, and I found a smile just for her. "Don't be."

Fawn blinked, her warm eyes shining in the candlelight as she searched my face. "Are you okay?"

This time my smile touched my eyes. "Yes, Fawn. I'm more than okay."

Her little hands found mine. "Maybe Grammy will let you try again?"

I swallowed the lump in my throat and bit my lip to keep it from trembling. I squeezed her hands. "Maybe, but you know what? If not—I'll *still* be okay." I smiled a watery smile.

"More than okay?" Fawn prompted, her brow knitted with concern.

I gave her braid a gentle tug. "Yes. Now get back to your book. I want to know how it ends!"

Reluctantly, eyeing me suspiciously as though she didn't fully believe me, Fawn settled back into her chair and picked up her book again. She cast me one more piercing, dubious glance before she disappeared within the pages.

The smile faded from my face as I poked at the pasta on my plate. Phoenix was watching me. I could feel her. I looked up as I dropped my fork. "What?"

Phoenix met my withering stare with patience. "Do you want to talk about it?"

I studied Phoenix for a moment. How different we were, in

both looks and temperament...it was almost stereotypical. She was short and dark-haired and playful. I was tall and blonde and studious. And that was fine; I *wanted* to be different from Phoenix. But the cruel irony of my existence was that Phoenix—for all her disinterest and refusal to apply herself to her studies—had magic, and I didn't. And I knew it wasn't logical or fair, but sometimes I blamed her for it.

I frowned. The most frustrating part was that Phoenix took it for granted, her magic and her talent. My eyes moved to her dark scarlet hat, discarded on the table with her newly forged wand tucked lazily into the burnt-orange ribbon that encircled it above the brim. She wasn't even bothering to keep her wand on her, let alone her hat. My jaw tightened. I had had Mama sew a special wand pocket into my gown for tonight. It was stupid of me, really. I'd never shown any hint of magic before. Why did anyone expect me to suddenly, *magically* be able to cast tonight?

A joke.

I was a joke.

What do you call a witch without magic? Seraphina Grey.

"Well?"

I'd forgotten her question. I stared back down at my plate. "I'm fine."

"What did Grammy say?"

I looked at her again. "They're calling me back after they talk to Mama."

"Mama?" Phoenix made a face. "Why are they—"

"The High Council wants her for something."

Phoenix's amber eyes grew large.

I nodded slowly. I'd been so wrapped up in myself, I hadn't registered it yet. But the High Council calling on Mama was a huge deal. Almost as big as being the first witch in history to fail her Forging. I winced at the memory and massaged my temple as though I might erase it. "I couldn't hear everything..." I added dryly. "They started talking about it as soon as I left the room."

Phoenix snickered. "Seraphina Grey—listening at keyholes? I'm shocked."

I frowned. "Unlike *you*...who makes a hobby out of eavesdropping and shoving your nose into everything..."

Phoenix shrugged and popped a grape with a pleased smirk. Then she shook her head. "*The High Council.*" She popped another grape and sat back in her seat in disbelief.

I leaned toward her and lowered my voice. "Do you remember Mama mentioning anyone named Alice?"

Phoenix scrunched up her face for a moment and then shook her head again. "Why?"

"Mama didn't want to do it—whatever they were asking of her. Then Cordelia harped on Mama about it being her responsibility because of 'Alice.'"

Phoenix scowled. "Hag."

I nodded. One thing the two of us could agree on: Cordelia Blackwell was a hag.

Phoenix tossed a baby carrot into her mouth and crunched loudly. "Well, the High Council—that's like a huge deal...end of the world stuff."

"Shh!" I jutted my eyes toward Fawn, who was hidden in her pages and again shoveling air into her mouth.

Phoenix rolled her eyes impatiently. She leaned into me and whispered loudly, "What do you think they want?"

I nudged her back into her seat. Phoenix had all the subtlety of a hex to the face. "It's not our business. It's Mama's business. Whether or not she tells us is up to her."

The High Council was in charge of overseeing, and sometimes policing, all the witches of the world, from covens to solitary practitioners. That's all we knew about them, anyway. Mama tended to keep things on a need-to-know basis. Cordelia called us "sheltered," but I disagreed. I trusted Mama. If she had reasons for not telling us something, that was all I needed to know.

Phoenix scoffed. "'Not our business.' You made it our business when you leaned in to listen. Plus, if Mama has some kind of assignment, that concerns us, too."

I was quiet for a moment. "She's leaving in the morning."

"*Leaving*?" Phoenix grabbed another carrot and crunched loudly.

I glanced over at Fawn and whispered, "Fawn's staying here with Grammy."

Phoenix's eyes narrowed. "Why? We can watch her—"

"Mama requested it specifically." I glanced sideways at Phoenix. "Then Cordelia argued that you should be sent to Stone Point."

"What!" Phoenix demanded incredulously.

"Mama said we're staying at home."

Phoenix tore off a bite of baguette and munched. "She must be planning on being gone for a while."

Icarus jumped onto the table. His green eyes regarded us reproachfully. His tail flicked back and forth. Clearly, he disapproved of our discussion. Then his eyes rested on me. "They're ready for you."

I opened the door and walked inside the library. My heart pounded with each brisk step. The three of them—Grammy, flanked by Aunt Cordelia, and Uncle Richard—stood in a neat line before the fireplace. Mama stood a bit off to the side, as close to the elders as her coven rank allowed her. I stopped halfway across the room.

"The House of Grey acknowledges Seraphina Grey. Please approach the elders."

Obediently, I stepped forward, stopping a few feet from Grammy, giving her the space demanded by her position. I removed my hat with a flourish as I curtsied low. "High Priestess."

As I came back up, I held my head high, keeping my eyes on my grandmother and pointedly ignoring my Aunt Cordelia. I gritted my teeth, inhaling deeply through my nose as I steeled myself. I didn't even dare pray for a second chance. And I would not let Cordelia see me cry.

"Seraphina Grey." Grammy's voice was cold and formal.

I flinched. Out of the corner of my eye, I saw Cordelia smile.

Grammy continued, strong and impressive and impossibly final. "The elders have concluded, taking past magical precedent into account, that the results of your Forge must stand."

My heart dropped like a stone in my stomach. Do not cry. I lifted my chin a bit higher.

"As such, while you will, of course, retain the title of Witch, an earned ranking title will not be accompanying your name."

"High Priestess Grey has spoken," Uncle Richard and Aunt Cordelia murmured together. "So shall it be."

Official business thus concluded, Grammy turned to Cordelia. "Please, excuse us. I wish to speak with my granddaughter alone."

Aunt Cordelia sniffed indignantly, her nose impossibly high in the air. Without a word, she marched out of the library, her robes and skirts swishing noisily behind her.

Uncle Richard stepped toward me, put a gentle hand on my shoulder, and gave me a squeeze. "Good evening, Witch Grey." He bowed his head to me. "Have courage. Keep heart. And don't be a stranger." He gave me a wink. Then there was a whoosh and a flutter as he disappeared into a stream of smokey gray color that seemed to be sucked upward as it vanished into the air.

I always liked watching the elders disappear. But not everyone could master it. Aunt Cordelia couldn't do it. It was a rare skill, for it wasn't easy changing from a solid to a gas and then vanishing into the sky, only to appear somewhere else in a whoosh of cloud that quickly morphed back into a solid. The more powerful the witch, the more variation and control they had on their disappearance. Mama vanished in a whisp of blue light. Grammy, on the other hand, disappeared in a burst of black glitter.

As my thoughts continued to wander, I glanced at Grammy. She eyed me closely as she pursed her lips. She closed the distance between us and rested her hands on my shoulders. Like Mama, I had inherited her height. Grammy met my gaze easily. But unlike Mama, and the rest of the family, I was the only one who had inherited her striking silver eyes, a distinct trait of the House of Grey. Eyes. The only thing I had inherited from a long, proud line of witches. Pathetic.

"Hush now." Grammy smoothed her thumb underneath my leaking eyes. "You have inherited the strongest heart of all the House of Grey."

I blinked back at her, unmoved by her words and ability to tap into my thoughts. Whatever anyone said, I was the weakest witch in the history of the House of Grey. A witch without magic. Without power. Pathetic.

"Power doesn't always mean magic," Grammy scolded me gently. "There are so many more ways in which you are powerful, Seraphina. You need to understand that sometimes, the weakest are those who rely on magic instead of on themselves."

I took a shaky breath. "Why didn't it work, Grammy?" My voice thickened with emotion as I broke. "It was supposed to work."

Grammy's forehead creased as she looked at me with sad, stormy eyes. "You aren't the first witch to struggle with her craft..."

"So, what?" I shrugged as I looked away from her and stared blankly into the fire. "I just have to come to terms with the fact that I can't cast? I won't ever...it won't ever happen for me?"

No one said anything. No one knew what to say. There was nothing to say.

"I don't understand." I shook my head, numb with disbelief. "Why can't I do it? *What's wrong with me?*"

Mama spoke softly, almost hesitantly from behind me. "I know you don't like the sound of it, Seraphina, but a mage is a very respected—"

My whole body stiffened. No. Not going to happen. I wasn't going to listen to this. I stepped away from them, flinching away from their touch, and bowed my head respectfully to my grandmother, High Priestess of the House of Grey. "Please, excuse me, High Priestess."

I hurried from the room, despite their protests, and I didn't look back.

I'M NOT OKAY (I PROMISE)

And I didn't head back to the party.

Instead, hat still in hand, I made my way outside, through the night, and across the grounds, away from the chatter and cackles of the family, and down to the steps cut into the side of the granite cliff that led down to the lake. The skirts of my gown swished through the dark, wet grass, picking up leaves and mud as I passed. My feet moved fast. I didn't even bother to lift my hem. In the darkness, with the full hunter moon at my back, I felt my way down the steep stone stairs. My fingers gripped the sides of the granite as I descended lower to the rocky beach.

I breathed in deeply, filling my lungs with the cold, damp air. The breeze billowed about me as it left the lake and pressed against my skin, calming me as quickly as it cooled me. Something about the nearness of the lake always brought me comfort. Tonight was no different, and for that I was grateful. The sculpted staircase curved at the lower part of the cliff, turning along the base and leading toward the black water. The lake was quiet tonight.

The ripples along the surface rolled toward the shore and

lapped lazily against the rocks as I made my way down. I moved my boots carefully along the bottom few steps. The green mossy algae made the stones dangerously slick. One wrong stone could mean a cracked skull.

My feet left the last step, and my boots teetered unsteadily on the pebbles. There was no sand on the beach; instead, only more and more stones littered the shore. Some might find it unpleasant, but I loved a rocky beach. Often, those were the most private and secluded, not to mention they had a countless selection of skipping stones. I dropped my hat on the ground and sat on a wide, flat rock, close to the water's edge, so close that the waves tumbled and spilled onto the points of my boots and my skirts soaked up the subtle spray as I hugged my knees into my chest.

I closed my eyes then and allowed myself to get lost in the rhythm of the water and the cold smell of the lake. There were legends of witches born of a rare talent—woods witches, sea witches, and mountain witches; I knew I was a lake witch. In my heart, I knew that's what I was, formed of fresh water and granite and moss...or I would've been, if I had been able to forge a wand. My body tensed at the memory as it flashed through my mind like lightning over the lake. It had always been obvious that my talent was buried beneath the surface, but until tonight, I hadn't realized it was simply not there. I had nothing inside. No power. Nothing.

Sera can't conjure. She can't cast. *How embarrassing.* It's like she isn't even a witch. *What's wrong with her?*

I felt empty inside.

Like a piece of my soul was missing.

Something warm pressed against my side. I didn't bother to open my eyes.

"Don't waste your time trying to make me feel better, Icarus." I reached out a hand and stroked the black cat as he rubbed against my hip. With a weighted sigh, I peeked into the cat's green lamp-like eyes.

He pushed his way into the space between my chest and my knees, forcing me to cross them instead as he curled confidently into my lap. I stared out across the lake at the tiny pinpricks of light studding the thin strip of land on the other side. The mountains in the distance were like black shadows against the horizon, and the only way to tell they were there at all was the small line of lights from the secluded state prison. I frowned thoughtfully as my eyes scanned the distant horizon for Bird Island. It was so dark, I couldn't make it out.

"Phoenix is coming," Icarus purred without opening his eyes.

My frown deepened, and I stared down at him accusingly. "Did you tell her where I was?"

"By the lake? Seraphina, no one needs to be told that." He nestled deeper into me, soaking up my warmth and hiding from the wind.

I stood abruptly. Icarus slid off me and nearly tumbled into the water. He mewed angrily. Then he slinked back up the steps with a furious flick of his tail. I snatched up a stone and chucked it into the lake.

"You know, it helps to have a light hand with that." Phoenix chuckled as she emerged from the darkness and stumbled over the stones toward me, one hand on her hat, her boots unsteady on the bumpy shore. Phoenix plucked up a rock. She rubbed her thumb along its surface and skipped it effortlessly across the waves, sending it so far it disappeared into the dark before it sank beneath the waves.

I chewed on the inside of my cheek as I glared at the water. "I know how to skip a rock, Phoenix."

Phoenix glanced at me as she skimmed another stone over the lake. "Well, duh. I was just—"

"Kidding. Right, yeah. I know." I rolled my eyes. "I'm heading back."

"I wouldn't," Phoenix warned.

"Then don't."

I pushed past her and was almost on the first step when Phoenix added, "They're having a casting contest..."

I let out a hiss of frustration as I froze, unable to decide which would be more annoying: staying on the beach with Phoenix or standing around like an idiot while everyone showed off their magic.

"Fine." My anger leaked out of me with a heavy sigh. I turned back and stood with Phoenix. Silently, we stared out into the night.

"Can you see Bird Island?"

I shrugged. "It's dark."

Phoenix took a deep breath, apparently over the small talk already. "It's not the end of the world, Phin."

"Easy for you to say," I snapped. "*Everything* is easy for you. I try so hard. I study. I practice. Nothing. But you? You don't even have to think, not even twitch your nose, and—"

"It's not that big a deal, Phin. So, you don't have a wand. Who cares? We don't even use them anymore!" She reached up into her hat and tugged her wand out of the ribbon. She held it up with a dismissive shrug before shoving it behind her ear. "Nobody even bothers to learn how to use them!"

I crinkled my nose in disgust. "You don't even realize how lucky you are, do you?"

"Lucky? To what?" Phoenix jutted her chin out in challenge with a sarcastic smirk. "Be a witch? Wake up and smell the potion." Phoenix snatched her hat off her head and flung it out to the lake like a skipping stone. "You're a witch, too!"

"Just in name," I countered. "Tonight proved it. Not a drop of magic in my veins."

Phoenix groaned. She shook her head in disbelief. "Oh, my God, Phin, you seriously need to get over it. Your mom's a witch. *That makes you a witch*. It's basic biology. Even I know that, and I slept through most of that class last year."

"Don't patronize me, Phoenix. I'm warning you, don't you dare." I pointed a finger at her heart. My silver eyes blazed.

Phoenix held her arms out wide, welcoming the challenge. "The only one who cares about any of that is you."

I scoffed incredulously. "Of course I care about it." I shrugged. "It's all I care about. Magic matters to me. It's important to me. And no matter what I—"

"And all I care about is *you*," Phoenix said sadly. Her arms fell limp at her sides. "You need to rethink your priorities, or you'll end up just like Dad—"

I flinched. "Don't—"

"Abandoning your family because you're too selfish to see past yourself."

I scowled through the darkness at Phoenix as the guilt ate away at my insides. Instinctively, I grabbed the pendant hidden beneath the bodice of my gown and squeezed it tight. I didn't remember much of him. He left well before Fawn was born. The memories that remained were really just shadowy snippets of a figure looming tall above me, or a phrase from an indistinguishable voice. Nothing solid. Nothing really real. The iron amulet at my neck was the only concrete thing I had of him. He'd given it to me the day he left. He had made me swear never to take it off. Not for anything. And I hadn't. He hadn't given Phoenix anything. But she didn't care. I did. "Don't talk to me about Daddy, Nix. Ever."

"Fine. Whatever." Phoenix shrugged and turned back toward the water. "Be mad at me. I'm used to it."

"And don't make this about you."

The silence hung between us as the shoosh of the waves splashed against the rocks.

"I'm not trying to fight with you," Phoenix murmured.

I took a deep breath and tried to exhale the anger and resentment that had risen to the surface like hot steam. "Of course I care about my family, Phoenix. That's why I'm so upset. You didn't just mess up your whole life! Don't you remember when we were little?

All we ever wanted was to forge our wands, live up to the Grey name. Well, congratulations, you've done it. But where does that leave me? Aunt Cordelia was right. I'm an embarrassment. A witch without magic?" My voice broke as my eyes blurred. "It doesn't even make sense."

"A mage is—"

"A joke," I snapped. "An insult. I can't believe Mama even suggested it." Phoenix reached for my hand but I folded my arms, leaving cold lake air between us. "And Cecily was right."

"I'm sorry..." Phoenix stuck a finger in her ear and twisted. "Did you say *Cecily* was right?"

"I'm going to ask Mama if I can go to school on the mainland."

Phoenix recoiled. "What?"

I turned away from Phoenix then, to stare back out at the lake. "I can't stay at home, Phoenix. I don't belong there anymore."

"You don't belong at *home*?" Phoenix demanded incredulously.

"You know what I mean. I'm not going to study magic anymore. There's no point. It's over for me."

"You can still do spellwork with meditative practice," Phoenix protested. "It'll just take a bit longer...just because you didn't forge a wand—"

"I'm not going to settle for becoming a mage. I'm just going to be an ordinary teenager. I already am anyway."

Phoenix shook her head, her expression hidden in the darkness. "That's the most ridiculous thing I've ever heard. You're a *witch*, Seraphina, whether you feel like one or not. You can't just *decide* to be ordinary!"

"Who says?"

"Forget it. Fine. You talk to Mama. See what she thinks. I know what this is really about." Phoenix turned and stomped back toward the stone staircase, her boots teetering on the uneven stones.

"What is that supposed to mean?" I demanded, my voice raised to be heard across the growing distance.

Phoenix didn't say anything. She didn't even turn around. She disappeared around the bend and up the staircase back to the house, leaving me standing alone in the darkness.

BOULEVARD OF BROKEN DREAMS

Phoenix didn't talk to me the rest of the night.

Neither did Icarus.

By the time we got back to Grey Cottage, the dark had faded to a blue twilight, and Fawn had fallen asleep on her broom, with Icarus curled up asleep on her back. Phoenix hopped off her broomstick, hitched it over her shoulder, and stalked swiftly into the house. Mama stroked Icarus awake. He leaped to the ground and rubbed affectionately against her skirts before bounding into the house after Phoenix. I lifted Fawn up off her broom and hugged her close as I carried her little lanky frame inside, with Mama behind me. She bolted the door and propped the brooms neatly in the corner. We wouldn't touch them again until the next coven ceremony.

I brought Fawn into her room and tucked her into her canopy bed. Then I carefully undid her braids, pulling out each ornamental gemstone and bead in turn and placing them one by one on her nightstand. I swept the tawny curls from Fawn's face and gingerly touched my lips to her forehead. Despite my horrible evening, I couldn't help but smile at the little girl snuggled in her heap of blankets, framed by the rich emerald curtains of her bed.

"Come on, Phinny."

I turned at the sound of Mama's whispered words and hurried from the room. Phoenix was already in the kitchen, pacing while she waited for the cider to brew. She'd already changed out of her ceremonial gown into her dark-red flannel pajama bottoms and an oversized Lacuna Coil T-shirt, and her hair was back to normal, swept up in a dark topknot, the burnt-orange tips sticking out like flames, but this time held in place by her wand. Her face was lined with a scowl. My face slid into a frown to match my sister. Did she have to shove the stick in my face like that? She didn't even look at me as I sat at the table. Instead, Phoenix crossed her arms and leaned against the counter, her eyes on Mama.

"Okay. Phin's here. Are you going to tell us about the High Council now?" Phoenix asked flatly.

I couldn't help but think Nix's bad attitude had more to do with our argument at the lake than with Mama.

Mama's soft expression flickered at Nix's tone but recovered quickly. She sighed heavily and massaged her temple as she went to pour the cider into three mismatched mugs. Icarus mewed and jumped onto Mama's shoulder, sliding beneath her thick, blonde braid to curl around her neck. "The High Council...has requested a meeting with me. I will be leaving within the hour. Fawn will be staying with Grammy after this weekend."

I watched Mama as she passed the mugs to us and then took a seat at the table. Icarus, still on her shoulders, snuggled his face against Mama's cheek as she drank deeply from the still steaming cup.

"Why?" Phoenix's voice echoed inside her cup as she came up for air.

Icarus gave a low warning chirp as he slipped off Mama's shoulders onto the table and sat up straight beside her like a sentry, staring disapprovingly at Phoenix.

Mama swallowed her cider slowly. "Fawn will be staying with Grammy, but will be using passage candles to come back and forth." Mama gave me a warm smile. "She wouldn't want to miss her potions with you, Seraphina."

Phoenix scrunched her nose dubiously. "You still haven't—"

"I will expect the two of you to behave yourselves." Mama set her mug down gently and licked the warm, sticky froth from her lips. "And remember that you're a team..."

I put down my mug, untouched.

"Why?" Phoenix repeated.

"Icarus, of course, will be watching...I don't know how long I will be gone...I will be Unreachable—"

"What?" Phoenix stared, mouth agape.

"Seriously?" I cocked an eyebrow as I studied Mama. Unreachable meant just that—magic enchantments so intense nothing could get through...least of all, communication.

"But if you need anything, Icarus can help." Mama nodded to the cat, whose eyes half closed in pleasure.

Phoenix and I stared at her.

Mama shifted in her seat underneath the weight of our silent stares. Finally, she said, "As an adult, I have responsibilities that I need to take care of..."

"Right, but what responsibilities are they?" Phoenix stomped over to the table and dropped into the empty seat beside me. She thumped her mug on the table, leaned back in her chair, and crossed her arms.

I took a deep sip of my cider.

Still, Mama didn't answer.

"And we know it's not private tarot readings..." Phoenix quipped.

Mama sighed and pushed her mug to the side. "You know I do my best to protect the three of you. To keep you safe. I am honest with you. I don't lie. But there are some things that you just aren't ready to hear—"

"Mama, we're almost seventeen, for Fay's sake!" Phoenix

righted her chair and stood from the table. She stomped to the cupboard and snatched a brown sugar donut.

I glanced sideways at Phoenix in a mixture of amusement and annoyance as she dropped back into the seat beside me, dunked the donut into the mug of cider, and took an obnoxiously big, soggy bite.

Mama covered her face. Her fingers massaged her forehead. She sighed again and dropped her hands into a prayer position, pressing them against her lips. "I need to meditate on this before I discuss any more of this with the two of you."

I chewed on my tongue to hold in my questions. I trusted Mama. Besides, I had a more important question I was saving…

"'Ee can't go uh sheep now!" Phoenix mumbled through a mouthful of soaked donut.

Mama held up her hand and shook her head. "I'm not saying anything more."

The silence settled around the table, humming low with frustration.

I finished a small sip. I couldn't help myself. I had to ask the question Phoenix had forgotten. "Who's Alice?"

Phoenix looked at me with her nose crinkled in confusion and popped the final bite of the drenched donut into her mouth.

Mama pulled out her tarot deck and began to shuffle in the way she did when she was upset about something. "Who?" she asked, stalling for more time to think.

I frowned. It was one thing not to tell us something, but another thing entirely to hide things. "I heard Cordelia. She said because of 'Alice,' the High Council's request is your responsibility…"

"That's right!" Phoenix snapped her fingers as a thought came to her, sending sparks of orange magic scattering around the table. "Who's Alice?"

Mama slapped her deck down at that and slid them angrily across the table, fanning them out in front of her. "Enough!" she snapped. "I'm not discussing this anymore." She flicked her finger at a card, and it floated through the air into her hand. "Until I've had time to think."

"Seraphina has something else to ask..." Icarus murmured. His green eyes glowed disapprovingly at us.

Mama's eyes shifted from the card to the cat and then to me. "What is it, sweetheart?"

I swallowed thickly, instantly uncomfortable and hating Icarus for calling me out.

Phoenix scoffed in disgust and gulped loudly from her mug.

"What is it?" Mama repeated, a hint of an edge in her voice.

I cleared my throat. "I was going to talk to you about it in the morning...but since you're leaving..."

Phoenix shoved away from the table and dropped her mug loudly in the sink. "She wants to go to Mater Christi High School on the mainland."

I shot her a murderous glare, but Phoenix didn't flinch. She stared back at me as she leaned against the counter, her arms crossed once more. Then she shrugged. "What? It's true, isn't it? Now, I'm curious, are you going to board all week like the other island kids do? Why not...I mean that just means less time with the family, and that's what you want, isn't it? Or is it just *me* who bothers you?"

I shook my head in frustration and rolled my eyes. I looked back at Mama, who slipped the card back into the deck and began to shuffle them again.

I licked my lips and took a deep breath, ready to explain myself. This was my moment. I wanted to get it right.

"No," Mama said shortly. She didn't even look up from her cards, now a blur in her hands.

"But Mama!" I stared, wide-eyed as she shuffled.

She shook her head and shuffled harder. The cards made a loud shlooshing sound every time they slapped against each other. Magic glowed around her hands like blue pixie dust, shimmering over the deck. Icarus began to lick his sleek black fur with a tiny smirk on his furry face. Phoenix plucked up Mama's empty mug and dropped it happily into the sink. My blood simmered as I clenched my fists underneath the table.

Mama looked up, sensing my anger, and cocked an eyebrow, mild-tempered annoyance lining her face.

I looked away, unable to stand against the weight of Mama's stare. My eyes burned and blurred. "We can't even talk about it?"

Silence hung around the room, suspended by awkward tension. Phoenix leaned against the sink a little to the side of Mama, literally backing her up.

Mama slid the cards across the table again in a wide rainbow. "I was hoping we'd discuss your magical studies after tonight's... results..." she finished delicately, her words full of warmth and compassion as she stared at the backs of the cards.

I scoffed. "And set me up to be a mage? A *mage*?"

Mama arched an eyebrow. "A mage is a very respected position in the magical community."

I clenched my fists tighter, digging my nails in my palms. I wasn't listening. I was too focused on controlling my anger...but I lost it.

"How could you let me do it?" I snapped loudly.

The whole kitchen was stunned into silence by my outburst. But I couldn't stop.

"Mama, how could you put me in that position! You set me up for failure—my whole life! Building to this moment, when everyone—*everyone*—knew that I wouldn't be able to do it."

Mama blinked as though I'd slapped her. "No one could have predicted—"

"And now you want me to continue! You expect me to keep my head down, power through, while Phoenix just skips along to success...and I'm reduced to nothing more than a glorified librarian!"

Mama frowned. "Whatever your magical abilities, you have worked too hard in your studies to throw them all away."

I scoffed and glared down at the cider in my mug.

"Whether you like it or not, Seraphina, you *are* a witch. It is your heritage. And not just any witch. An heir to a Hallowed House. And as for my expectations? I expected you to keep your head held high and remember yourself. I did *not* expect you to give up, to turn your back on us and run away like—"

My eyes darted to meet Mama's; the normally warm blue eyes were cool as a fresh spring morning. Like Daddy. She didn't need to say his name; we all knew. My fingers snatched at the pendant at my neck and squeezed.

Phoenix looked awkwardly at the ceiling.

Icarus mewed, jumped from the table, and disappeared from the room.

I opened my mouth to speak several times, but nothing came out. Hurt swelled in my throat, blocking my voice. Instead, I pushed back sharply in my seat and hurried from the room, shedding tears as I went.

I threw the bedroom door wide and burst into the room. Icarus sat expectantly in the dark on my bed, waiting for me. I glared at him through shining eyes.

I held the door and jerked my head. "Out."

Icarus simply blinked, calm in the face of my temper.

"*Get out!*" I stomped my foot, hating myself even more for behaving like a bratty child.

Icarus didn't move.

"Fine. FINE!" I screamed.

He didn't even flinch.

I let out a feral shriek of frustration and slammed the door. I winced at the sound and my own impulsivity. Guilty that I may have scared Fawn awake, and furiously blaming everyone else, I threw my hat on the ground and with shaking fingers, ripped through my braid, furiously unraveling the ribbons and tearing out the stones so carefully and lovingly woven by Mama just hours before.

I dropped down onto the bed, grabbed Icarus around the middle, pulled him into my arms, and cried noisily as I buried my face into him. He stayed with me, patient as I hugged him to me. Hot tears spilled onto his fur. And, all the while, he purred softly and soothingly into my ear.

By the time I had quieted, the door opened.

I didn't bother to look up. I didn't say anything either. I had nothing left to say.

"I'm so sorry, Phinny," Mama whispered into the dark.

My face still buried in Icarus's fur, my words were muffled. "It's fine."

"No, it's not fine, and we both know it."

My ears prickled as Mama exhaled deeply. "You had an awful night on what was supposed to be the best night of your life. I can't even imagine how you must be feeling..."

I scoffed loudly.

Mama continued, her voice gentle. "You deserve to be heard and make your case before I make a decision like that. It's always been our way, and I'm sorry I didn't let you speak."

I lowered Icarus into my lap and slowly turned to look at her. She stood in the doorway, framed by the light of the hallway like an angel in the darkness.

"Thank you," I said in a small voice.

Icarus slipped down onto the floor and quietly left the room.

Encouraged by my response, Mama quickly sat beside me and wrapped her arms around me in a firm hug. She smoothed away the wetness from my cheeks and held my face in her hands as she looked deep into my eyes. "I am so sorry things didn't work out the way we wanted them to tonight. And I am so sorry you had to go through that so publicly."

I shrugged as I pressed my lips together in an effort to hold in fresh tears.

"And I am so proud of you and the way you handled yourself in an impossible situation." Mama gave me a gentle shake for emphasis.

My anger melted away in the warmth of her words. "Thank you, Mama," I whispered. We both smiled weak, watery smiles, and then I tried again. "So, can we talk about it?"

Mama's smile wavered ever so slightly, and my smile slipped into a frown.

"Or not..."

Mama took a deep breath. "When I was a little younger than you...I asked Grammy to go to Mater Christi with the other Nile kids."

"Mama..." I groaned.

"I know—I know you know this story, but please...you have to understand. The kids, their parents, some of the teachers even, tormented me the entire time. At first, they will love you, flock about you, soaking up your light...and then they will turn on you when you least expect it. Islanders have never been kind to the Greys. The hatred they hold for us has been passed on through each generation...from the time of the founding and the hangings and burnings on Bird Island, it has been so..."

"Then why do we still live here? Why did you move back to this cottage?"

Mama smiled patiently. "Because the island loves us...you've felt it in the granite and the lull of the lake. It's our home...whether the islanders want us here or not. Nile isn't Nile without the House of Grey."

I didn't argue. I couldn't.

"And..." Mama took another shaky breath. "One story I haven't told...haven't *wanted* to tell...but I feel like you now need to hear it..." Mama's voice trailed off and was lost in the dark.

I nudged her gently.

"You asked about Alice..." Mama cleared her throat. "A long time ago, a young witch—" She bit her lip.

"Alice?" I prompted.

Mama swallowed. "She had trouble with magic...not unlike yourself." Mama took my hand and squeezed it hard. "Her struggles with her craft became an obsession that led her down the path of the dark arts. You see, dark magic is always easy because the cost is so high. She lost her way...and I just..."

I stared as Mama's eyes filled.

She shook her head and looked toward the ceiling as though gravity might force back the saline filling in her eyes. Then she looked at me, spilling tears onto a rueful smile. "I just don't want to see you lose your way, too."

I gave her hand a reassuring pat. "But, Mama, that's just it...I don't have any way. I'm done with magic. I tried so hard to fit in. To be a great witch. But it was all a fantasy I made up in my head. And I'm done pretending—" My voice faltered as Mama's face creased with concern. "I'm done pretending to be something that I'm not."

Before she could contradict me, I shook my head. "Mama, please." I cleared my throat and continued, my voice strong once more. "If I go to school with ordinary kids, I'll be able to get on with my life, instead of being stuck watching Phoenix rub her wand in my face."

"Seraphina." Mama frowned. "You know that's not—"

"It's what it feels like...I'm just tired of being inferior to her. You may not compare us, Mama, but I do. I can't help it. I need to get away. I need this, Mama, please."

She brushed a thumb underneath her eye and smoothed away the tears. She looked at me with sad eyes and the weakest of smiles. Again, she squeezed my hand so hard I winced. "Seraphina, you are so talented, in so many ways. I think it'd be a great disservice to yourself if you were to give up...but if you want to try it...you should."

My heart swelled, and my shoulders straightened as the weight of my own expectations lifted from me. "Really?"

Mama nodded vigorously as she shook my hand in hers. "But you must promise me that you'll be careful. I'm trusting you, Seraphina Grey."

I nodded, barely able to contain my smile. I threw my arms around her and hugged her tight.

Mama left quickly after that, and I didn't see her again.

ST. CLAIRE AND A SEMESTER ABROAD

"Curse it, Nix! Look what you made me do!" I grabbed for a dish towel and mopped up the mess of potion and shattered glass. "It took me all morning to brew this doctrina! I needed it for school."

Phoenix jumped off the counter and tossed her half-eaten apple in the trash. "All I was trying to say is that you need to work on your concentration. It's not my fault you dropped it."

I rolled my eyes as I slapped the towel in the sink. "Anything to keep me trapped here with you…"

"What was that?" Phoenix crossed her arms and stared up at me. I easily towered over her by a good couple of inches.

"Forget it." I stalked out of the room.

"It wasn't my fault!"

I ignored her and didn't stop until I got to our room. Fighting the urge to slam the door in Phoenix's face, I threw my Book of Shadows onto the floor and kicked it underneath my bed. Then I dropped onto my bed, snatched my book from my nightstand, and buried my face behind it. I could feel Phoenix standing over me, but I didn't look up. It was the only time she could ever look down on me.

"Hey."

I ignored her and flipped a page.

"Hey." Phoenix slapped the book down, revealing my fuming face.

"Leave me alone, Phoenix." I pushed her back with my foot.

Phoenix shook her head. "No. Nuh uh. What is your problem?"

Maybe it was the ruined potion, maybe it was the way Phoenix had slapped at my book, maybe it was the way Phoenix stood there: hands on her hips, chin stuck out. Maybe it was the fact that no matter how hard I tried, I was always coming up short...or more than likely, it was the fact that I was a bit nervous to be going to school. But whatever it was...that was it. And it might not have been fair, but I unleashed all my anger onto Phoenix, because in that moment, it *was* all her fault.

"You. *You're* my problem. I worked so hard on that potion, and you just couldn't keep your comments to yourself!"

Phoenix frowned, hurt etched in her face. "I was just trying to help, Phin. I didn't—"

I pushed off the bed. I stared down at Phoenix, using my height to my advantage. "Yeah, right. Help. That's laughable. You don't want to help me. You love the fact that I can't—" I couldn't say it out loud. "Whatever. It doesn't matter. You win. I lost. I'm going to school with the rest of the ordinary kids on Monday."

"*You're* the one who makes everything a contest," Phoenix pointed out angrily. "If you'd stop trying to compete with me all the time, you wouldn't always feel like you're losing!"

I shook my head in disgust. "Just leave me alone, Phoenix."

Phoenix blew her black bangs out of her face, the burnt-orange tips flickering like fire. Her brown eyes burned bronze. "You blame me for everything! It's not my fault you can't cast. If you'd just—"

My gray eyes narrowed. Line crossed. I pushed past Phoenix and marched back out of our room. The cottage was too small to contain my anger. I stomped down the hall, grabbed my bag off the hook, and headed for the door. I heard Fawn call my name from the couch, and I hesitated just a moment to shoot over my shoulder, "I'm going for a walk."

I yanked open the door.

My breath caught.

"Jinx it, Cole!"

Cole St. Claire stood in the doorway, his hand raised as though he had just been about to knock on the door. Cole was one of our only friends. It was hard for us to make friends on the island. It was a small town, and the rumors whispered about our family didn't help any. And, unlike most witch families, we didn't attend the witch academy, so no friends there either. Mama didn't want us to be a part of a student coven due to the cattiness and competitiveness that tended to happen when you threw a bunch of witches together. But I suspected it was a bit more than that: Mama didn't want me to be uncomfortable or teased about my lack of abilities.

The homeschooling of young witches was standard, of course, for obvious reasons. Not only to foster magical skills and learning, but to keep our skills a secret. No one wanted a repeat of the Salem witch trials. And in this town? It could happen.

Sometimes when I went to the store, or when we stopped at the tiny one-room library, I could feel the eyes on us, scurrying over us like beetles. It sent shivers down my spine. Like our ancestors were warning of the danger islanders posed. The only reason we were even friends with Cole was that he showed up on our doorstep on a dare: Ding Dong Ditch the Wicked Old Witch Down Old Grey Lane. It was a favorite pastime of the Nile kids... but none of them usually made it down Grey Lane, much less up our porch and to our doorstep. But Cole had.

He'd also nearly jumped out of his skin when Icarus bounded out of the dark, spitting and hissing like a cat out of Hell. The other boys had booked it back up the lane, disappearing into the night, but Cole had been pinned against the door by the cat.

Phoenix and I had opened the door, and he'd fallen inside, scared half to death.

That was four years ago. We'd been best friends ever since. Now, finding him at our front door was a commonplace occurrence, especially in the summer when he wasn't at school. Because there wasn't a high school on the island, the island kids were able to pick one of the mainland high schools to attend, and most of them, Cole included, selected the private school, Mater Christi, due to its optional boarding program. The ride across the lake to the mainland, coupled with the drive into town, made the five-day boarding an appealing choice. Plus, most of the island kids had unhappy homes they were more than willing to escape. That day, being Saturday, Cole was home for the weekend, and his first stop, as always, was Grey Cottage.

Usually he was a welcomed sight.

Not this time.

"Jinx it, Cole," I repeated. My heart hammered hard against my chest.

Cole blinked his deep-brown eyes in surprise and shook his dark hair out of his face. "Nice to see you, too. You all right?" His hand came up to grip my arm with a comforting squeeze.

I couldn't ease the scowl from my face. I didn't bother trying to argue against the obvious. "Phoenix is inside. I'm leaving." I sidestepped him, but he held me fast.

"Whoa, wait a minute."

I groaned and gritted my teeth as Phoenix came up behind me.

"Cole, would you please tell Phin to—"

My eyes blazed. I rounded on Phoenix. "Why don't you—"

"Hey, hey!" Cole pushed his way between us, a brotherly hand on each of our shoulders. "Looks like I came just in time. Rachel is waiting for us at the Tracks, but I say let's head into the kitchen, so I can snag a cup of Ms. Grey's world-famous cider, and then we'll head out, yes?"

Phoenix shrugged off her anger and tension like a Labrador

shakes off the lake. Her easy smile slipped back onto her face. "Sounds good to me."

I continued to glare at her. That was another thing: Phoenix never cared enough about anything to stay upset for more than a few minutes. I, on the other hand, could hold a grudge firmer than granite.

"Come on, Phin, fall's in the air!" Cole clapped me on the back and led me back into the cottage and toward the kitchen.

"Hey, Cole!" Fawn chirped happily from the couch. Her long, little limbs were tucked neatly under her as she looked up from her book as they passed her. Icarus was curled up in her lap and opened one eye at the disturbance.

Cole smiled at her, and he plopped down on the couch beside her to peek at what she was reading. "What you got there?"

Icarus gave an irritated chirp in Cole's direction, jumped down, and left the room. Maybe it was due to their first encounter, or because Cole behaved like a shaggy dog, or because he smelled like his Golden Retriever, but Icarus couldn't stand Cole. Fawn loved him, just as much as we did, and maybe even a little more. She smiled at Cole, her warm honey eyes filled with humor as she held up the book. "Harry Potter. It's *hilarious*."

Smirking and dark eyes glinting, Cole flicked one of her thick, tawny braids. "I love that one...what are you? No, wait, lemme guess..."

Fawn sat up straight. Her eyes glittered, and her smile beamed.

Cole scrunched up his face as he studied her. "You'd have to be Slytherin..."

Fawn giggled. "You're Hufflepuff, easily."

Cole scoffed. "How'd you know?"

"Come on, Fawn." My anger melted away as I watched them. A small smile tickled my lips. "Time for cider."

Phoenix was already in the kitchen, filling four mugs to the top with frothy amber goodness. The crisp apple smell filled the air and followed the four of us as we filed out of the kitchen door onto the back porch, the cool new October air pressing goose bumps into our skin. I tilted my face to the gentle sun, and my smile broadened at the sight of the trees, their leaves slowly burning red and gold at the edges. We all dropped down on different steps and sipped our cider in silence, all of us basking in the sweetness of an early autumn afternoon.

Suddenly, Phoenix broke the pensive stillness. "Thank God you showed up." She slapped Cole's leg cheerfully as she eyed me. Her lips pursed in a weak attempt to hide a grin. "Seraphina was about to run away."

I frowned. "Why? Why do you have to keep pushing? Can't we just sit here and enjoy the sunshine?"

"Forget the sun!" Cole smiled slyly over his mug. "This cider is the only reason I ever come over here..." Cole laughed as Phoenix punched him playfully.

Fawn giggled. "Cole is scared of the Nile Witch!" She wiggled her fingers at him like she was casting a spell.

Cole was the only person, the only *ordinary* person, who knew our family's secret...for sure, anyway. The rest of the island town of Nile had their suspicions and their whispers, but Cole had first-hand knowledge, knowledge that he'd take to the grave.

Cole grinned. "Who wouldn't be? She's really tall...where is she, anyway?"

"Mama got called away—"

"On a secret mission for the High Council!" Fawn finished eagerly. "It was so important, she had to leave in the middle of the night."

"High Council?" Cole raised an eyebrow.

I nodded grimly. "It's like the witches' version of the UN."

Cole whistled. "What'd they need her for?"

I shrugged. "She wouldn't tell us."

Phoenix put her mug down on the deck and checked her watch. "We better hurry if we're going to meet Rachel..."

"Yup." Cole nodded over the top of his mug before drinking deeply.

Fawn edged closer to Cole, bouncing in place, her mug cupped in both hands. "Oh, show him, Nix. Show him!"

"What?" Phoenix cocked an eyebrow, a slight pink burning her pale cheeks.

I looked away and stared into the trees.

Fawn continued to chant "Show him," over and over.

"Oh, okay, okay," Phoenix grumbled. "I'll show him. Here."

I glanced sideways at Phoenix as she reached behind her head and pulled the wand out of her hair. Instantly, her thick, black hair fell down her back, the orange ends flickering like flames. She handed it over to Cole. A modest blush colored her fair face and a small, sheepish smile set her dimples in her cheeks.

"I didn't want to be nosey and ask...but what took you so long to show it off, Nix?" Cole fingered the iron wand and gave it a wave through the air. "Sweeet." Cole dragged the word out like a California surfer, but as he continued to admire it, he nodded seriously. "It's beautiful, Phoenix. Excellent work."

"Thanks, bruh." Phoenix took it back, twirled her hair into another knot, and stabbed her wand in the middle, magically holding it in place. Literally.

I chewed the inside of my cheek. I hadn't even asked to see Phoenix's wand. I'd been so caught up in my failure...and then excitement about starting school. Guilt twisted knots in my stomach. I probably should've shown an interest...at least congratulated Phoenix. Had I at least done that?

I glanced at the wand as it poked out of Phoenix's hair. It was a deep blood red, so dark it was nearly black, with orange and gold markings swirling and twisting around the shaft. It was beautiful. I frowned at Phoenix as she shrugged off the whole thing, how she feigned innocence, as though she *hadn't* been itching to show it to Cole the second he walked in the house.

Cole nodded at Phoenix again, his appreciation and admiration clear on his face. "You have to hit a certain level of witchyness to do that, right?"

Phoenix shrugged, and her eyes flicked awkwardly toward me.

Cole followed her gaze and instantly shifted uncomfortably in his seat. He took a big drink of cider.

Phoenix blew her bangs up as she tried to blow off the conversation, but Fawn answered Cole eagerly as she slapped at his shoulder. "The first hunter moon of her sixteenth year, a witch forges her wand from magical metal and fire and earns her ranking title. It's a *huge* deal. We had a party with the whole coven—like a hundred witches all in one place!"

Her honey-hued eyes were big from behind the brim of her mug as she gulped down some cider, which left a glistening, sticky mustache above her grin. "You should've seen Phoenix smash that thing! Bam! BAM! She hammered it like crazy! There were sparks of magic and everything."

"That's awesome, Pheeny." Cole tugged at a strand of her black and orange hair. "What do—"

"How's school, Cole?" I interrupted. I wasn't about to sit there like an idiot and listen to how awesome Phoenix was. Plus, I didn't like it when Cole used Mama's matchy nicknames for us. Phinny and Pheeny. Ick. I tolerated Mama using them...Cole using them was maddening, in an obnoxious, dress-your-twins-alike kind of way.

Cole glanced up at me and back at Phoenix, who frowned down at her mug. "Uhh, it—"

"She made a fire *tornado*!" Fawn piped.

"Uh, good. School's good...Rachel is expecting us at the Tracks today since we missed her last...uhm..." Cole rambled awkwardly.

Fawn threw her arms wide. Her mug sloshed cider on the steps. "It *exploded* into the sky! It rained fire! Magic fire bits! Some landed on Narcissus and burnt his robes!"

I gritted my teeth at the memory.

"Now she has a title and everything—Phoenix the Red. Isn't that cool? Phoenix Grey, the Red Witch. Ha! It's so perfect."

"Uhh, yeah—"

I couldn't take it. "Mama said I can go to school with you," I blurted without thinking, my words coming out loud and sharp, almost angrily. My cheeks burned at my tone. "I start on Monday," I finished softly.

Phoenix didn't say a word.

"Really?" Cole said, surprised.

"*What*?" Fawn demanded, her eyes wide, confused and hurt.

Jinx it.

"You're going to school with Cole?" Fawn's words, high and panicked, pierced my ears. "That's a *boarding* school... You...you aren't going to be home anymore?"

I opened my mouth but couldn't find words. I reached out to pull her into a hug, but she flinched away from me and slammed her mug down on the steps. Then she jumped to her feet and ran inside the kitchen. The screen door banged behind her.

Phoenix glared into her mug. "You couldn't have told her better than that?"

"Well maybe if you weren't bragging about your precious wand, I wouldn't have snapped!" I cried defensively, my eyes welled up with shame. I jumped up from the porch and hurried inside after Fawn.

I caught up with her in the living room as she headed for the door. "Fawn, wait—"

"I'm going for a walk." Fawn grabbed her backpack off the hook. The front door flung open with the force of her magic, almost exploding off its hinges to let her through. She stomped outside, Icarus yowling after her. The door then slammed so fast and so violently, it almost caught his tail, but he was able to slip out just in time. Copper magic sparks flared around the doorframe and fizzled away.

I stared at the door in disbelief. The sudden silence was loud in my ears. How had things gone so wrong? Why did I have to open my big mouth? And why couldn't everyone just be happy for me?

"So, Tracks are out," Phoenix snipped snarkily from behind me.

I turned to see the two of them lurking in the archway. Cole at least looked properly guilty for having been eavesdropping.

"We can take Fawn," I snapped. "It's not a big deal. She loves it when we bring her with us."

Phoenix cocked her eyebrow and smirked. "Good luck finding Fawn in the forest."

My heart sank even lower. No one could find Fawn in the woods if she didn't want to be found. Like her name suggested, she could slip through the trees and cover her trail better than anyone.

Cole ran a hand through his dark hair and pulled out his phone. "I'll text Rachel it'll just be me…"

Phoenix slapped a hand on his shoulder. "And me. I'm coming."

Cole hesitated. His eyes moved back and forth between us. "Uhhh…?"

"You're just going to go without me?" I crossed my arms and glared down at her.

Phoenix shrugged, her face stoic. "You made the mess, you deal with it. Come on, Cole."

I shook my head incredulously and watched wide-eyed as the two of them crossed the room and headed toward the door.

Cole gave me an apologetic, sheepish look. "Do you want me to stay with you? I could tell Rachel—"

I forced a smile for Cole's sake. "No, Cole. It's fine…you go on."

Cole nodded. "Okay, well…can I pick you up for school on Monday?"

I brightened a bit at that. "Absolutely. I can't wait to get out of here."

"Sounds about right," Phoenix muttered from the front door.

"Oh, put a potion in it, Nix. You're the one who's leaving now, so I don't want to hear it."

Cole hurried out the door with a quick wave.

Phoenix paused and shot me a final scathing stare. "You don't need me, remember?"

I flinched as the door slammed, and I was left alone...again.

5

DEAR MATER [CHRISTI], COUNT ME IN

Monday morning was slow to dawn. I'd spent the rest of Saturday tracking down Fawn. She'd shown up just after dark, dirty and disheveled and unwilling to talk. Not even Phoenix could get her to speak. Without a goodbye to anybody, Fawn grabbed a passage candle and disappeared through the back door to Blackwell Manor.

Phoenix didn't say much to me either, the whole time silently fuming as she stomped around the house. Not even Icarus acknowledged me the rest of the weekend. It hurt, but I tried to shake it off by spending Sunday organizing my outfits and gathering things I might need.

I went to my cabinet for a few potions and my peony pouch for good luck. The only magical things that could be useful in the normal world. Potions weren't really magic, anyways...more like medicines. And as for the peony pouch, charm bags, and the like... those were...well, science...botany. They didn't make me a hypocrite. Not really. And come Monday morning, with my backpack stuffed with a sage bundle, a peony pouch, and a tiny bottle of bamboo essence, I left the house before the stars left the sky.

Cole had stressed the pickup time for several reasons. He had to pick up Rachel, he needed to stop for coffee, and it was almost an hour-long drive into town; given that we would have to make it in time to catch the ferry to the mainland, everything had to be timed perfectly.

Rachel was our other best friend—only, unlike Cole, she didn't know anything about magic or witches. Cole had introduced Rachel to us shortly after he'd stumbled into our house all those Halloweens ago. Rachel and Cole were cousins, although unlike Nix and I, they actually could have passed for twins. Rachel was dark-haired and doe-eyed, with sharp cheekbones and full rosebud lips, set against an almost ghostly white complexion, in an angular, square face. Exactly like Cole, give or take several extra inches of hair.

I ran through the dying night to Cole's old van and yanked the side door open. The van—Cole babied that thing. And he should, considering how much work he put into it after his dad junked it to him with the condition he could have it as long as he got it running again. Oh, he got it running again, and worked all summer down at the ferry docks to pay to completely renovate the interior. He even had the Nile mechanic, Edwin Martin, give it a final look. If Edwin Martin said it was good, then it was good. And it was. The last thing he did was work up the courage to ask Phoenix to paint it—whatever she wanted. And Phoenix, being Phoenix, she painted fire. Dark, blazing, beautiful fire, engulfing a phoenix made of flames. Now the van had brand-new bench row seating just behind the front seats where Cole stashed his guitar, Jean, and an empty back that Cole used for his air mattress when he went on long snowboarding treks in the mountains.

I jumped inside the van, backpack slung over my shoulder, breathless, bright-eyed, and more than ready for the day. Cole, red-eyed and sleepy, turned around in the driver's seat, his black hair falling into his face. "Morning," he grumbled.

"Good morning, Cole!" I beamed underneath the yellow van light.

He mumbled snarky comments under his breath about early risers as he put the van in reverse. I laughed, shaking my head, and looked back at my sleepy little cottage with a broad smile on my face.

A faint glow of red-gold sparkled in the dark from my bedroom. Instinctively, I pressed a hand to the van window. Phoenix was doing the same, without question, leaning against the windowpane, watching me disappear into the woods and down the lane.

For a brief moment, my heart ached. I'd been unfair. All weekend. It wasn't Phoenix's fault that I was a horrible excuse of a witch. I almost told Cole to stop, to go back, to let me out.

Almost.

By the time we'd loaded a yawning, stumbling Rachel into the van, the glow of the sun peeked over the mountains across the lake. Rachel rubbed the sleep from her eyes and blinked stupidly at me. "What are you doing here, Phin?"

I smiled. "I'm—"

"And where's Phoenix?" Rachel peered around the empty passenger seat as I pursed my lips in an annoyed pout.

"Phin wanted to experience Hell on Earth," Cole muttered as he pulled the van into the parking lot of the only gas station on the island. "Phoenix had the good sense to stay home.

"Speaking of Phoenix..." Cole adjusted the rearview mirror ever so slightly. "I didn't want to bring this up in front of her... when...you know, she was a bit..."

"Insane with burning rage?" I suggested with a smile.

"Right...well, are you boarding? Because, since Rachel and I board, you'll have to take the bus back and forth to the islands..."

My heart dropped a bit as I remembered.

"Uhh, well..."

"You can change your mind, you know." Rachel placed a reassuring hand on my shoulder. "Not all the island kids board. And they let you switch if you decide it isn't working for you...whatever that is..."

Cole put the van in park and both of them stared at me, waiting for my answer.

I'd seen the island bus. It was a tiny purple contraption that looked like something you'd ride up a mountain to go skiing. Occasionally, it oozed blue smoke. Other times, it let out angry bangs as it putted along the highway that cut through Nile. Cole had said it even caught fire once. The idea of taking the bus all the way home made my stomach squirm.

"The bus will be fine." I smiled with forced enthusiasm.

Rachel gave me a reassuring pat on the knee. "I knew you'd say that." She flashed a bright grin. "Going from homeschool to boarding five days out of the week would be a pretty extreme switch."

Cole nodded. "Too much."

My smile faltered just a bit. "Right."

Cole pulled the keys out of the ignition and caught my eye in the rearview mirror. "But, no bus today. I'm bringing you home, since it's your first day and all."

I hesitated. "Are you sure? I don't want you to have to—"

Cole waved away my concerns.

"I'm just surprised Charlotte let you out of the house, let alone start school." Rachel frowned thoughtfully.

I looked at her, eyebrows raised.

Rachel stifled a yawn. "Not in a bad way...just because of what happened over last week...the whole, well...you know."

Still confused, I shook my head.

Cole winced. "A couple was found dead in their house off East Shore."

My stomach twisted uncomfortably. "What happened to them?"

"Murdered."

Cole gave her a sharp look. "Rach—Sheriff Vantine hasn't released any details yet."

"They were murdered, Cole. Courtney heard it from Joey. He was on the scene, and just because his daddy didn't make it public yet doesn't mean it isn't true."

"A murder—a *double* murder in Nile?" I breathed. Things like that didn't happen in our small island town. And why hadn't Mama said anything about it...especially when she was leaving us home alone? "What did he say happened?"

"They were ripped apart," Rachel blurted before Cole could stop her.

"Rachel!" Cole glared at her.

"I wasn't able to sleep much last week. I knew them...their daughter and I were really close, and..." Rachel trailed off, her face sad and disturbed. Then she added quietly, "They were shredded to pieces."

"Do they know who did it?" I demanded. A twinge of fear spread in the pit of my stomach. I glanced around the van at all the different cars coming in and out, the dozens of people walking to the store and leaving it.

"No idea. And that's the scariest part..."

"Oh, don't even—" Cole rolled his eyes.

"Joey said there was no sign of a break-in, no sign of anything... like the killer just magically appeared inside their house."

My eyes darted to Cole, who shook his head and met my gaze pointedly. "Joey also thinks the moon landing is fake, and the Earth is flat. The only reason he became a cop is because of his dad. Nepotism can overlook dumb. And isn't he related to Lacey McGregor? Not to be mean, but there's a reason they call her Spacey Lacey..."

Rachel rolled her eyes at Cole but didn't deny it.

I breathed a bit better. Obviously this Joey guy was prone to insane theories, and his judgment was highly questionable. But with Mama gone to some secret meeting at the request of the High

Council, and an almost magical element to a double homicide...it made my stomach hurt.

"Anyways, enough depressing talk. You want anything?" Rachel yawned again as she climbed out of the van.

I took a deep breath and agreed. No more murder. I pushed concerns of killers and questions about why Mama hadn't told us out of my mind. This was going to be a good day.

"No, thanks. I'll sit tight here...just hurry, you guys!" I shooed them away with a grin. "I don't want to be late!"

And we weren't late, but just barely. The ferry was moments away from pulling out from the dock when Cole revved the van up the ramp and parked among the other dozen cars. Luckily, the line hadn't been long...it seemed we were on the last load to the mainland for the morning commute.

The drive in was full of loud music and fun conversation. Both Cole and Rach were still groggy, but they managed to come out of their fog enough to perk up about me attending the school. Cole made a point to warn me about certain guys, all the while giving me sharp stares through the rearview mirror, to which I, smiling, rolled my eyes in response. I had no interest in dating, so therefore had no need to make a list of potential heartbreakers and troublemakers.

"I'm actually looking forward to making *friends*, Cole. Maybe you've heard of them?"

Rachel furrowed her brow as she considered the concept. "There aren't that many good friend options either..."

Cole chuckled. "Agreed. But, if you try out for a team or join a club, it's like a guaranteed group of friends...for better or worse."

My eyes shined with amusement, and I shot Rachel a sly sideways smirk. "I still find it hard to believe you're on the basketball team, Cole. A cool, punk rock, loner dude like you? No way."

I saw Cole's cheeks flush in the mirror.

"You forgot to add 'short.'" Rachel snickered.

Cole scoffed. "Hey, at least I'm not a pom-pom shaking bimbo like some people..."

My jaw sagged, the smirk still lingering in the corner of my lips. I rounded on Rachel as she punched the back of Cole's seat. "Rachel St. Claire, you're a *cheerleader*?!"

Rachel glared at Cole, who fixed his eyes on the road and turned the music up a bit louder. "Thanks for that, cousin."

I shook my head, my cheeks aching from my broad smile. "How on Earth did that happen? You're like, the least peppy person in the world." I gestured to Rachel's *Devil's Rejects* T-shirt and black pants crisscrossed with chains.

Rachel snorted bullishly and crossed her arms. "It's a long story," she mumbled moodily.

I gave her a playful nudge. "Does Phoenix know this?"

Horror blanched Rachel's face whiter than usual. She grabbed my arm. "You can't tell Nix. Please, please, *please* don't tell Nix."

I chuckled. "Okay, okay. But I don't see what the big deal is... why keep it a secret? And seriously, what made you decide to be a cheerleader?"

"All the hot sweaty dudes," Rachel retorted flatly.

I took the hint and dropped it. Still, the idea of Rachel smiling and jumping around cheering for a team in a skirt made me feel warm and fuzzy inside.

"Maybe I'll be a cheerleader with you!" I gave Rachel a playful nudge. "It seems easy enough, right? I don't know how to do anything else..."

Cole grinned. "No skill required for the bimbo squad."

Rachel's eyes blazed, and she gave Cole a swift smack on the side of the head.

"Oi! Okay, okay."

"Actually," Rachel answered loudly, "there is quite a bit to it... but there are also plenty of beginners who join the squad...so that would be really cool…" she added, slightly embarrassed. "If it's your thing…"

"It sounds fun!" I looked from one St. Claire to the next. "Is there anything else I should know before I walk through those doors? No one is secretly a chess champion or mathlete genius?"

Rachel grinned. "You'll learn fast."

The rest of the ride went quickly. I sat up straight, almost nose to the window, when Cole announced our arrival. The van turned down a side street through the woods and bumped over the railroad tracks that seemed to act as the boundary of the school, separating it from the outside world.

I'd never been to the high school before, and my eyes widened at the sight of the sprawling campus emerging from the forest. It was massive, like a college or university, with numerous brick buildings dotted all over, all connected by smooth, narrow black roads.

Rachel perked up a bit in her seat and pointed out all the different buildings and explained their uses.

"I'm never going to find my way around all of this…you didn't tell me it was as big as a town!"

Cole burst out laughing.

"You say 'high school,' you think a building or two…but this—this is a village!"

"Stick to your map," Rachel quipped brightly.

"I'm going to get lost!" I cried, the humor fading to an insecure panic.

"Nah, it's not that hard to navigate." Rachel waved a nonchalant hand, as Cole pulled up to one of the smaller buildings that resembled a modest two-story house.

"Do you mind if we stop at the Martin House real quick before classes start? We have just enough time and that way you can see my dorm room." Rachel shrugged sheepishly.

"Sorry, Phin." Cole glanced back at me with a wince. "I forgot to mention, boarders usually stop by their dorms first. Check in and get their stuff situated for the week..."

"I'd love to see your rooms!" I grabbed my bag and hopped out of the van.

The two of them got out behind me. "Just mine. Girls aren't allowed in the boys' dorms. And believe me, you do not want to get on Sister Francis's bad side." Rachel gave a shiver. "She's the dorm mother from He—"

"This is the Martin House..." Cole interrupted. "So called in honor of—"

"Martin Isle!" I guessed excitedly as we approached the building.

I took in the deep-red brick and the ivy draped over the sides like thick curtains. The windows were old and fogged with age, and in the gray, cloudy morning, it seemed a bit forbidding. Like an old haunted house from a ghost story. As we climbed the handful of concrete steps, Cole took out a keycard and held it to the door. It was an old door, and possibly the original, but the doorknob had been replaced with a modern steel handle, coupled with a keypad and a sensor.

Cole pulled the door open for us as it buzzed, and we went inside. It opened up into a small common area, full of plushy couches on top of lush rugs, and side tables stacked with books and forgotten coffee mugs, and a modest fireplace with a small fire snapping in the corner. It was like we'd stepped into the coziest of bed-and-breakfasts. At the back of the room, there were two small, darkened archways at opposite ends of the wall where identical staircases jutted upward into the shadows.

"I'll meet you both back here." Cole gave us a little wave as he headed toward the left staircase.

"Come on. The girls' dorms are up here." Rachel led me to the one on the right.

I gripped the strap of my bag tightly and hurried after Rachel, my eyes moving around the common room, trying to take everything in at once. As soon as I passed under the archway, a steep staircase was at my feet. As Rachel trudged up the stairs, I eyed it uneasily before I took my first step.

The staircase was ancient—more ladder than staircase, as it was more vertical than slope. There were rubber tracks on each stair, evidently to prevent slips, which made sense considering how steep it was. Thankfully a railing had been bolted to the wall for balance. It felt like the stairs went on forever, each one creaking slightly, and my stomach quickly grew queasy from the sharp ascent.

"This is pretty steep..." I clenched my hand tightly around the rail.

"Yup," Rachel called from above me. "They say a girl tripped and cracked her head open in the '50s, and you can still see the brain stain underneath the carpet."

Ew.

"That's when they added the rubber and the rail."

I could hear the smirk in her voice.

Suddenly, as sharply as the stairs had begun, we were on a landing, which tumbled out into a narrow hallway on the right side. But, I noticed with curiosity, the stairs also turned to the left and stopped a few steps higher at a second landing, and a door. A black door, bathed in shadow.

Creepy.

Rachel had started to head down the hallway, but I stood rooted to the spot. "Rach, what's that door lead to?"

"Hmm?" Rachel glanced back and waved off my question. "Oh, that's Sister Francis's room. Hurry up, or we'll be late."

I tore my eyes away from the ominous-looking door and jogged after Rachel.

"Do you have a roommate?"

The hallway ran the width of the House, ending in a long window that stretched from floor to ceiling. Several doors were on either side of the hall, all with brass nameplates on them.

"Nope. Some girls do, but it's random, I think...depends what rooms are available when you enroll. This House, the Martin House, is just for island kids...so, there's not many of us." Rachel stopped at a door on the right and pulled out a set of keys.

I bit my lip; a rush of excitement set my fingers tingling. Just the idea of having a room, a space, all to myself was thrilling. I'd been stuck sharing my personal space since before I was born.

A door farther down the hall, right next to the window at the end, opened and a girl came out. She was tall, almost as tall as me, with long, dark hair that cascaded in waves down her back, tied with a headband made from a scarf. She was dressed in layers, looking extremely polished for a high school student, as though she'd just stepped out of a fall fashion shoot rather than a girl's dormitory.

She was clearly a mainlander. Island girls came in two varieties: those who longed to fit in, but just couldn't quite manage it, and those who stood out, a little bit extra on purpose. But either way, both kinds stood out equally as an "other." Not this girl. This girl didn't just fit in—she made the mold.

I smiled in her direction, but she didn't bother to look at me. Instead, she walked with her chin held high, her heels clicking smartly on the wooden floor. She bumped me hard as she passed. Then she stopped abruptly and turned to look at me. I thought she was going to apologize, but instead the girl just stood there, regarding me with an odd expression, before smiling coolly.

Rachel lowered her keys.

"Good morning," the girl murmured in a voice as cold as her smile, her eyes so deep a brown they were almost black, focused solely on me.

I hesitated underneath the weight of the girl's stare.

Rachel spoke first, with emphasis and sarcastic cheer. "It was."

The girl's dark eyes stayed fixed on me, her mouth in a cruel smirk. She continued to stare as though she hadn't heard Rachel. As though Rachel didn't exist.

"You're new here."

I frowned. "Yes."

The girl smiled. "Be careful."

I raised an eyebrow and opened my mouth to say something, but before I could, the girl laughed and walked away, disappearing down the staircase.

"Scurry along," Rachel muttered as she returned to her keys with a shake of her head.

"Thank God, I don't have a roommate." Rachel flicked her keys to find the right one.

I nodded, still unsettled by the girl. "Who was that?" I stared after her, completely forgetting the reason we were in the hallway in the first place.

"Daphne Collins. Weird, right? She doesn't dorm here, thank God."

"Then what was she doing here?"

Rachel shrugged and nodded toward the door Daphne had come out of. "That's Aubrey LaMothe's room. Let's just say, Daphne likes to bother her..."

Rachel stabbed her key in the hole and unlocked her door as she changed the subject. "The front door of the House got a high-tech lock upgrade. But the dorm rooms are still stuck in the 1800s."

She pocketed her keys and led me inside, slapping on the light and washing the room in a warm glow.

I blinked.

Rachel held out a hand. "Make yourself at home. I'll be quick...just gotta put my stuff away, get my things ready, all that."

I nodded, but I wasn't really listening. My eyes flickered around the room in envious admiration, the awkward encounter with Daphne erased from my mind. There wasn't a window, but Rachel's room didn't seem to need one; there was already so much to look at—almost too much.

The room was exactly like Rachel: warm, edgy, and artistic. The walls were black, and I didn't believe for a second that they had been that way before Rachel got there. But, despite the deep color of the walls, the room didn't feel dark. She had dangled strings of lights around the ceiling in low hanging loops that reminded me of Mama's room. Rachel's bed was pushed up sideways against the back, with an empty easel wedged between the foot of the bed and the wall. She'd plastered the black walls with band posters, movie posters, and tiny canvases of her own art. A bookshelf, overloaded with books stacked too many ways, was pushed against one side of the room, with a cushy armchair and vintage lamp beside it. On the opposite side was a desk littered with sketches, more books, crumpled paper, and an old soda can. I saw with amusement a pair of green and silver pom-poms stuffed underneath it, half hidden behind a backpack. Rachel's dresser was on the left side of the doorway with a bulletin board hanging over it.

My heart warmed at the sight of the pictures pinned into the corkboard: Many of Cole, Phoenix, and myself—mostly of Phoenix, though—and a few of some other girls I didn't know, and one of the Mater Christi High School cheerleading team. And there was Rachel in the front, a grin on her pretty face and an emerald bow in her dark hair. I stepped back from the board with a slight smile. Then I noticed a bright-orange toolbox, so big that it came up to my elbow, on the other side of the door.

I turned to Rachel, who was bent over her backpack and stuffing the last of her stuff inside it. "What's with the toolbox?"

"What else?" Rachel tugged her backpack onto her shoulders, walked over to the toolbox, and pulled out a drawer. "Paint supplies."

I laughed, and we left her room, Rachel locking it behind us.

"You always lock your door?" We headed down the stairs; our pace slowed as the steps shifted dramatically downward.

"Everybody does. But it doesn't really matter," Rachel replied dismissively. "There's a set of keys for every student's room in the dorm office room...it's down the hall, right before the library."

"You have a library here?"

"You didn't notice the big red doors when you came in?" We both stumbled a bit on the bottom steps and found ourselves in the common room again. "There's a kitchen, too."

Cole was plopped lazily in a huge squishy chair, hugging his backpack to his chest like a pillow. And just behind him and off to the side was a pair of large crimson doors, right beside the House entrance.

I felt like an idiot. "Oh...those doors." I smiled sheepishly as Rachel kicked Cole awake.

The three of us left the House and loaded back into the van. And, as the van pulled away from Martin House, I stared after it. How cool would it be to have a room all to myself inside it...

It only took a minute or two for us to pull up to the main school building. Cole shut off the van in the school parking lot, and all my initial excitement returned, along with a fresh batch of butterflies. I slung my book bag over my shoulder and waved a happy goodbye to Cole and Rachel, before hurrying into the school in search of the principal's office. Mama had left a message for the principal of the school, Father LaValley, somehow setting up my enrollment without issue. I couldn't imagine how Mama knew a priest, let alone had such a personal relationship with one who she could call and pull strings, but I didn't bother to question it. As long as I had a seamless entry into the private Catholic school, I didn't care about any of it.

I found the office quickly enough. The secretary told me with a cheerful smile that Father LaValley was in a meeting at the moment, but he had left a welcome packet for me with everything I'd need to have a successful first day.

"Now." The secretary smiled sweetly as she pulled out a packet. "We have your room all set, and your name plate has been ordered. Your roommate has already been informed...the only thing..." She pushed her bedazzled spectacles up the bridge of her nose and squinted through the papers she was shuffling. "I don't seem to have your signed permission slip from your parent or guardian..." She licked her thumb and swiped a few papers from the stack and tucked them into the packet, before passing it to me with a bright smile. "Extras. Just in case. You get one of those permission slips back to me or the guidance counselor down the hall, and we can hand you your key."

"Uh...no. There must be a mix-up...I'm a day student." I smiled ruefully as I tucked the welcome packet into my backpack.

The secretary nodded, still smiling. "All right, well, in that case, you are all set. You have the slips if you change your mind." Gingerly, the woman placed her index fingers on the frames of her bedazzled glasses and pulled down her spectacles, so she could peer over them at me as she whispered loudly, "It happens all the time."

I gave her an incredulous grin. Then I glanced down at the map of the campus and then my class schedule. I thanked the woman and told her to give Father LaValley my best, before I disappeared back out the door.

New school.

New me.

New life.

I was ready.

LIFESTYLES OF THE WITCH & FAMOUS

O r not.

It didn't take long for the whispers to start.

As soon as my math teacher announced my name to the class in first period, the news spread like wildfire. The stares were the worst. And by lunch, I was seriously considering just walking out.

Then, in line for a carton of French fries at lunch, a girl touched my arm. "Are you Seraphina Grey?"

Inwardly, I groaned as I tried to maintain my temper. At least this girl asked me personally. "Yes."

The girl seemed so small and frail, a wisp or fae creature. She was easily almost a foot shorter than me. Her features were angular and delicate in her diamond-shaped face. I was almost surprised her ears didn't end in points in the same way her tiny nose did. Even her outfit was elven: a soft, flowery, flowy dress straight out of Woodstock. The only thing that seemed out of place was a heavy, clunky tarnished locket dangling from her neck on a thick chain.

She smiled kindly. "I thought so...everyone's talking about you..."

I frowned and turned back to the lunch line.

The girl picked up her tray and cut in beside me. "My name's Aubrey...LaMothe. It must be hard starting a new school, especially after it's already started."

I nodded as we moved slowly through the line.

"I just started boarding this week, myself...I was homeschooled for a while, too...until eighth grade. My dad left, and my mom had to get a job for the first time in...well, anyways—sorry. I tend to ramble..."

I glanced down at her from the corner of my eye.

Her cheeks blushed prettily, and she shrugged. "I just wanted to let you know—you aren't alone."

I raised an eyebrow.

Aubrey bit her lip and tucked her yellow hair behind her ears. "The rumors...they'll talk about you for a bit and then they'll move on to someone else...that's the way it is here. Trust me. I've had my share of whispers."

I smiled. "Worse than 'witch'?"

Aubrey didn't smile. "Kids can be cruel. They used to go after my best friend and me pretty ruthlessly. To the point that we stopped being friends. I'm sorry you had to come here."

I scoffed with a small smirk. "Believe it or not, I wanted to come here."

Aubrey's soft blue eyes widened. "Why?"

I laughed. "Honestly, after today, I have no idea what I was thinking."

Aubrey smiled at that. "Well, if you're looking for a friend, I'm happy to help."

I inclined my head as I studied her for a moment. "Thanks. I'd like that."

We took our fries from the counter and filed out of the kitchen line into the cafeteria.

"Do you want to grab a table?" Aubrey asked brightly.

I scanned the room for any sign of Cole or Rachel but couldn't see either of them. "Sure."

We took seats at one of the dozens of large round tables scattered around the room, dropping our backpacks into the empty chairs beside us. I sat up straight, hyper aware of the eyes continuously flickering toward me.

"What class do you have next?" Aubrey took a fry and dunked it into a paper cup full of mayonnaise.

I pulled out my schedule. "Study hall..."

Aubrey smiled. "Nice. What a great way to end the day, huh?" Her smile faded quickly as she spied someone in the crowd. "He's new..."

"Who?" Instinctively, I glanced over my shoulder and scanned the crowd.

But before Aubrey could answer, two girls dropped their trays on our table and took seats between us. Ignoring me, they both focused their attention on Aubrey.

"Hey, how are you doing, Aubs?" the girl with the golden-honey braid draped over her shoulder murmured, clearly concerned.

Aubrey tucked her hair behind her ears and nodded. "I'm fine. I'd rather not talk about it, if you—"

"Of course!" The girl with the black locs held out a hand, her perfectly manicured nails shining under the harsh fluorescent lights. "We totally get it," she added breathlessly. Her smile was bright but almost over-exaggerated, as though her nerves were getting the better of her.

The blonde eyed her friend warily, as if willing her to calm down. "We were actually wondering if you wanted to have a sleepover this weekend? We thought it'd be good for you..."

I watched them curiously. They were like Barbie and Christie... same girl, different version.

"You can come, too..." The blonde turned to me then, her polite smile fading slightly. "Oh my God, you're—"

"Seraphina Grey." I nodded with an awkward frown.

The brunette snapped her head to look at me, her warm, brown eyes wide. "Holy...*whoa*."

"Morgan!" The blonde nudged her and then smoothed a fallen honey curl behind her ear. "Sorry, Seraphina—it's just...you're like a legend..."

The brunette—Morgan—nodded furiously, her eyes still huge. She pointed to the blonde and blurted, "Courtney's mom loves your mom!"

I blinked and smiled despite myself. "Uhh...thanks?"

Courtney blushed prettily as she rolled her eyes at Morgan. "Thanks, Morgan, for that..." Then Courtney turned back to me, her dark-blue eyes sparkling with amusement. "My mother's a customer...swears by her love potions. I'm on my fifth stepdad thanks to her." Courtney held up her soda bottle in toast.

I laughed. "Uh...happy to help...?"

"You should totally come this weekend...what do you think, Aubrey?"

Aubrey had sat quietly, watching the exchange with a small smile. A pretty pink bruised her cheeks as the table's attention turned back to her. She tugged at the necklace at her throat, sliding the locket back and forth along the chain. "I don't know. My dad might not want me driving into Nile—"

Morgan let out a little mortified gasp; her dark skin paled. "Oh, no—"

"We were thinking at *your* house...Dad's house..." Courtney added quickly.

Aubrey nibbled on her lower lip. "I guess...if Seraphina comes..."

I blinked in surprise at the sudden ultimatum. I'd never had a sleepover before...the idea was exciting and nerve-racking at the same time. Courtney and Morgan looked at me expectantly.

"Uh, my mom doesn't—" I mumbled without thinking. "I mean, I'm not so sure—"

Courtney and Morgan both grinned knowingly, and together

they picked up their trays and stood from the table. "See you guys this weekend! Friday night?"

And then they disappeared into the crowded cafeteria.

"Sorry about them…" Aubrey mumbled. "You don't have to come if you don't want to…I was just kidding. They probably won't even come; just trying to help me feel better—"

"No, it's okay…"

Aubrey took a deep breath. "See, I just moved into my dad's house last week…and it's been a bit of an adjustment."

I nodded sympathetically, but before I could reply, a girl with deep-red hair and a worried smile hurried toward our table with her tray of food.

"Hey, Aubrey…" The girl hesitated, standing in front of a chair, unsure whether she should sit down. I looked from Aubrey to the girl, trying to gauge the awkwardness of the situation. The girl was clearly uncomfortable. Her brow furrowed as she continued with a shy smile, "We missed you at practice last Friday…"

Aubrey looked down at her carton of fries. "I know, I—"

The girl cut her off, emboldened by Aubrey's voice, and she hurried on in a rush, breathless and desperate, "We really want you back, Bre…it's not the same without you. Will you come to prac-tice today?"

Aubrey tugged on her locket again. "I don't know…"

"Who's your friend?" The girl smiled warmly at me. "She could come too! Taylor would appreciate an extra…"

I gave her a polite smile.

Aubrey nodded in my direction. "This is Seraphina Grey…"

The girl's hazel eyes widened. Then she looked from me to Aubrey and then back to me. "Oh, wow!" The girl dropped her tray onto the table and sank into a seat. "Everyone's been talking about you…but I didn't realize…wow." She blinked her big eyes. "I'm Cheryl Bradbury…I'm not technically a local islander myself, so I wasn't like *raised* on the stories, you know, but—I can't believe the things they are saying. Rachel's trying to keep them quiet, but gosh, you're practically *famous*, huh?"

"It's my mom, really…" I muttered awkwardly, increasingly uncomfortable with this conversation.

Cheryl nodded, her eyes still wide and her mouth slightly open. "Kaitlyn pulled up her YouTube channel in class…the tarot thing? Peter Blanchard says she's the real deal. Is it like a Wiccan thing, or *The Secret*, or something?"

I hesitated. "Uhh…well, not really, no…"

"Wow." Cheryl shook her head with an impressed smile. Then she leaned into Aubrey with an amused smile. "Daphne is *furious*."

I stared between them, trying to keep up with the switch in the conversation.

Then Cheryl's attention was back on me. She gave me a rueful smile. "I would *not* want to be you right now."

I crinkled my forehead. "I'm sorry?"

Cheryl looked at Aubrey, who shrugged and nibbled on a French fry. Then Cheryl turned back to me. "You know Daphne Collins? Aubrey's stepsister? Let's just say—she likes to be the center of attention around here…" Cheryl's voice trailed off as her eyes caught something behind me. Her face blushed almost as red as her roots.

I glanced up. Daphne Collins towered over my chair with a face as hard and beautiful as ice. Her eyes were on Aubrey.

"Hey, Daphne…" Aubrey gave her a small smile.

Daphne didn't smile back. "I need to talk to you."

Aubrey audibly gulped. "Uh, sure…I'll see you guys later…" Aubrey grabbed her things and followed Daphne out of the cafeteria.

Cheryl let out a sigh of relief and gave me a smile. "Speak of the devil, huh? Well, I gotta get going…it was nice meeting you."

"You too." I forced a smile and watched her leave.

I sat alone at the table, lost in thought, and flinched as the bell rang. I scooped up my backpack. One more class and then I could go home. Holding my map out in front of me like a hiker trekking through the forest of students filing into different classrooms, I searched for study hall.

It was a labyrinth. So many twists and turns and stairwells and hallways...I somehow even stumbled upon an enclosed courtyard that, judging from the sunlight streaming in through the trees, had no ceiling and simply opened right up to the sky.

By the time I made it to the classroom, the halls had emptied, and my heart dropped.

The door was shut.

Class had started.

Jinx it.

"It's okay," came a soft voice behind me. "I'm usually late, too. A lot of kids are. Mr. Blake doesn't mind. It's just study hall."

I turned, my hand falling away from the doorknob, to see a girl with long, dark hair that framed her face. She smiled kindly with hazel eyes that seemed a bit sad.

"Oh, well, that's good..." I replied awkwardly.

The girl was...odd. She was dressed in all black, but not in a goth or punk kind of way like Rachel or Phoenix...she was dressed up. Like formally. Black dress pants and shirt, complete with a sharp black blazer that had large silver buttons down the sides, and lapels decorated with silver embroidery that swirled all down the arms. Her sharp clothes contrasted with her features, which were round and soft, from her full lips to her big doe eyes. She gripped a leather duffel bag in one hand and a Spiderman backpack was slung over her opposite shoulder.

The girl smiled shyly and shifted underneath my stare. "Should we head inside? There's no assigned seats, so you can just sit wherever... I can go in first, if you like? I know it's hard being new..."

I hesitated. This was the first interaction I'd had with someone who hadn't stared at me like the freak of Nile. My cheeks burned as I realized this time it was me who was staring. A slow smile slid onto my face. I nodded. "Thanks."

"No problem. I'm Maddie, by the way..."

"I'm—"

"Seraphina...I know." Maddie gave me an almost sympathetic smile.

"Oh..."

"I'm actually your new roommate," she added brightly.

I blinked. Before I could correct her, she opened the door and led the way into the classroom.

It may have been normal for kids to arrive at study hall late—but that didn't prevent anyone from looking up and staring as we walked in. And just like in every class before this, every eye in the room found me, following me to the back of the class as I grabbed an empty desk. There were murmurs and even a gasp from somewhere in the room as I pulled out the seat. Doing my best to ignore it, I dropped my bag to the floor, sliding it neatly under the desk and out of the way.

As I went to sit, my eyes locked with the guy seated behind me. He was leaning lazily back in his seat, so the chair was supported by only its back two legs in a manner I was sure every teacher had chastised him for in the past. His hands were threaded together behind his head. His eyes moved over me in a way that made my stomach clench. I smiled uncomfortably, but before I could turn back around in my seat, the guy jutted his chin in my direction.

"I was hoping I'd see you again."

I raised an eyebrow, but couldn't think of anything to say to that, so I just gave another awkward smile and quickly turned back around in my seat, staring wide-eyed at the whiteboard, hoping he'd leave me alone.

But he didn't.

Behind me, he leaned forward, the chair dropping back down to the floor. He tapped on my shoulder. I whirled around to look at him.

He smiled again. "I've seen you around Nile. What took you so long to come to school?"

My cheeks heated, and I felt with slight panic that I might start sweating. "You've *seen* me?"

He nodded, his thick black hair falling a bit into his ice-blue eyes. "I'm Damien Barrow. My friend Elijah—he's a Grunvald, graduated from Ethan Allen High last year—he has a boat, and we go out a lot. I've seen you at the access a few times...well, around the corner from the access. Plus," he added almost shyly, "you must know your family's famous."

My stomach knotted. Yes, I knew. This guy clearly was used to charming people...but I couldn't imagine how; to me, he came off greasy and shallow.

I frowned. "Right."

A slick smirk slid across his face. "Oh, not like that...I didn't mean..."

"It's fine," I murmured coolly, turning back around.

He grabbed my arm. "Hey, listen." His grip on me was tight.

I looked back at him, eyes narrowed.

He released me, but irritation lined his face. "I only meant that island off the sandbar...and then the street named after you. I wasn't talking about...anything else."

I scoffed, raising an incredulous eyebrow. "Right. I'm sure you weren't one of the guys papering our house on Cabbage Night... too afraid to ding dong ditch, though, I bet. Too scared to make it up the steps."

He opened his mouth to protest, but I cut in. "Excuse me, I have work to do."

And with that, I turned in my seat and pulled out my math homework.

My ears prickled as the guy hissed behind my back, "Witch."

I didn't take the bait.

Maddie, who'd taken the seat next to me, passed me a note:

Nice.

I glanced at her sideways and smiled, but before I could scribble a reply, the door opened and my heart dipped.

In walked Daphne Collins, the heels of her designer shoes clicking crisply on the linoleum floor. Her eyes met mine. She flashed a snide smile as she slid into the last empty seat in the classroom, directly behind me and right next to the jerk Damien Barrow.

I could hear them whispering. My face burned, and I dug inside my bag for a pencil.

I felt something hit the back of my head.

And again.

I didn't turn around.

I glanced at the teacher.

Mr. Blake had his back to the class as he hunched over at his computer, tapping incessantly away at the keyboard. He'd be no help.

Then there was a scrape of the chair against the floor, and Daphne pulled her seat up next to mine. She leaned back and crossed her legs over the top of my desk, the heels of her shoes tearing my notebook page.

"So, how was your first day?" She kept her eyes on me as she took a sip from her water bottle.

I regarded her coolly. "It'd be better if you got your feet off my desk..."

As if sensing the tension, everyone (except for Mr. Blake) slowly put down pencils and put aside books. And one by one, they all turned back in their seats to watch us.

Daphne gave a sarcastically sheepish shrug as she twisted the cap back on her bottle. Then she removed her feet and sat up straight, before resting her elbow on my desk instead, her raven hair spilling over my work. "You know, I've heard a lot about you... you're all anyone can seem to talk about." Daphne's black eyes never left mine.

"Is that so?"

A frown flickered across her fake smiling face for just a moment and then it was gone. "My stepsister sure seems to think you're special. I hear you're coming to my house this weekend even..."

I didn't answer. Instead, I regarded her with as much disinterest as I could manage.

Daphne bit her lip as she smiled like a cat cornering the canary. "Do you know what they're saying?"

"I honestly don't care...and if you don't mind, I have math to do, so—" I waved her away.

"Sure..." Daphne hesitated a moment. "I just have to ask..."

I raised an eyebrow.

Daphne leaned in close to me.

I could smell her perfume and fought the urge to pinch my nose.

"Is it true?"

"What?"

Daphne smiled as she slowly unscrewed her water bottle. "Do you melt in water?"

Before I could respond, she jerked her bottle up, splashing me with a face full of water. Laughter, muffled by hands and hidden behind backpacks on desks, vibrated around the room.

"Oops." Daphne's dark eyes glittered as she grinned. She tossed the empty bottle onto my desk. It bounced off onto the floor.

I blinked through eyelashes thick with water droplets. I smoothed back my wet hair from my face.

"Guess everybody's wrong..." Daphne stood easily from her chair, looking down on me with a satisfied smirk. "There's nothing special about you after all."

Then she scooped up her bag and left the classroom, the tapping of her heels echoing from the hall. She didn't seem to care that there were still forty-five minutes left of class.

. . .

After school, I stood in the courtyard between the two school entrances, scanning the students for any sign of Rachel or Cole. I was ready—more than ready—to get home. A full day of being ogled at by every single person in school, on top of being hazed, was too much. As my eyes moved from face to face, my eyes locked on a guy leaning lazily against the brick wall of the school. And his eyes were on me. I did a double take. Unlike all the other kids rushing away from the building—some toward the parking lot, some heading down either direction of the sidewalk, and even more hopping into awaiting cars—this guy was frozen in place.

Staring at me.

Watching me.

7

CHECK YES, SERAPHINA

"Phin!"

I tore my eyes from the guy and turned just in time to see Rachel shoving her way through the throng of students. Rachel had changed into her cheer uniform and the difference was striking. With her dark hair pulled out of her face, and her head topped with a cute bow, and her raccoon eyes wiped clean with a sprinkle of glitter on her cheeks, she was a whole other version of herself.

"I've been looking for you all day!" She elbowed a boy as she forced her way next to me.

"Where's Cole?" I looked over her head but didn't see him anywhere. "After the day I've had—I really don't want to ride that bus..."

Rachel waved away my question. "He forgot he has basketball practice, but that's okay, becauseee—" Rachel gave me a sly smile as she threaded her arm through mine and led me toward the left entrance in the direction of the strange guy, who I realized with a jolt, was *still* staring at me.

"You're coming to cheer practice with me!"

I wasn't listening. I leaned down toward Rachel's ear and muttered, "Do you know that guy?"

Rachel's eyebrows knitted together as she craned her neck to see over the sea of students. "What guy?"

I looked back and nodded toward the brick. I blinked. He was gone. "Uh, never mind..."

Rachel shrugged and tugged me toward the sidewalk.

What she'd said began to register. "Rach, when you said... coming to cheer practice... You mean, just to watch, right? While I wait for Cole..."

Rachel looked up at the sky with a Cheshire cat grin. "Weeellll..."

"Rach—I don't know anything about cheerleading!"

Rachel laughed. "That's okay. We aren't like all-star or anything...it's very laid-back. You just need to try out—no, listen! It's only a formality, I swear," she added hastily as I paled. "You're guaranteed the spot; no one else has signed up... The coach just needs to see where your skill level is...the tryout is this weekend. But, this way, you'll be able to watch, get a feel for it now, and hang out with the girls before—"

"My skill level? It's nowhere! Did you tell her that? That I've got no experience whatsoever?"

Rachel chuckled and gave my arm a squeeze. "You'll be fine. You wanted friends...and I told you—this is the quickest way to instant friendship."

I frowned thoughtfully. "After today, I'm not so sure..."

Rachel looked up at me with a sympathetic smile. "How was your first day, anyway?" Then she frowned and studied me curiously. "What happened to your hair?"

I shrugged, ignoring the last question and addressed the first. "The classes were fine...but I didn't realize—"

"How popular you'd be?" Rachel quipped with an eyeroll.

"Yeah. I mean, how am I supposed to make any friends when everyone is talking about me behind my back?" I shook my head.

Rachel winced. "No standouts so far?"

I sighed. "Well, this girl, Aubrey...and another girl, Maddie?"

Rachel nodded appreciatively. "Both cool girls...but—"

"What?"

She hesitated, as though suddenly uncomfortable. "Nothing. It's just...they've both had a really hard year. You'll be good for both of them." Rachel scoffed with a rueful smirk. "Aubrey's actually been my best friend since we were like five. She's..." She scrunched up her face and searched for the right words.

I stared down at her as the sidewalk stopped, and we headed left down a black back road that ran along the far side of the school grounds. Then I remembered. "Aubrey invited me to her house for a sleepover."

Rachel looked up at me in evident surprise. "She did?"

I nodded. "But after learning that Daphne Collins is her stepsister and *lives* with her, I don't know if I want to go—"

Rachel snorted. "Understandable...although, like I said, Aubrey and I have been best friends forever...and believe me when I say, her friendship is worth putting up with Daphne Collins. Only—you have to promise you won't miss tryouts..." She gave me a playful pinch. "We'll get you in your new cheer uniform, complete with built-in best friends, and everything will get better."

I smiled. "If you say so..."

Rachel glanced at me curiously. "I thought you guys weren't allowed to sleep over?"

I shrugged innocently. "Mama hasn't ever told me 'no sleepovers'...I mean, not technically. Although, I guess I've never really asked her before—"

Rachel chuckled and gave me a little nudge. "Well, if she changes the policy, let me know. I've been trying to get Nix to spend the night for years."

The subject changed to the upcoming Apple Fest as the two of us continued the long trek down a few narrow black roads to the practice field, with Rachel occasionally muttering curses at the basketball team for taking up the gym and forcing the cheerleaders to practice outside in the cold.

"This is Amber…" Rachel pointed to a tall, tan blonde seated at a long folding table. "And that's Taylor." Rachel jutted a thumb toward the girl with black feed-in braids and loose curls framing her dark face, seated beside Amber.

Both girls smiled and gave little waves. "Hi, Seraphina. Thanks for volunteering to fill the spot."

I stood in front of the table, keenly aware of the other girls grouped off to the side and watching. I shifted my stance and tugged at my hoodie, shivering slightly from the cold. "I don't know if you'll thank me for trying out when you see I have barely any coordination…"

Amber grinned and exchanged knowing looks with Taylor. "That's fine. Trust me, without you, we weren't going to have enough girls to compete."

"Compete?" I repeated, my voice high and thin. I looked at Rachel, whose guilt was plain on her too-wide smile as she shrugged.

"Here." Taylor passed me a packet across the table. "These are different cheer moves and poses that will be important for you to memorize as soon as you can. Rachel…" She side-eyed Rachel, with an amused smirk playing at her lips. "Will be responsible for your success. So I'm sure she'll give you extra practice sessions."

Amber and Taylor pushed out from the table and stood up at the same time. "Your uniform is there." Amber nodded toward the folded green and silver bundle. "And Rachel has extra bows…why don't you both head to the locker rooms and make sure it fits?"

Rachel gave a bobbing nod as she stood from the table and waved me over to follow her. I grabbed the uniform and pom-pom set and started after her.

"All right, ladies." Amber addressed the squad. "Go get changed. Practice tomorrow, same time, in the Abernathy Gym."

I followed Rachel and the other girls to the small building off to the side of the bleachers. We all filed inside, and I picked a stall to change, while the other girls went to their lockers and started to strip in the middle of the room.

"How's it fit, Phin?" Rachel called through the door.

"It's good." I pulled the uniform back off and tucked it, along with the pom-poms, back into my already overstuffed bag.

When I exited the locker, the girls were all sitting around on the benches, talking. They turned to stare at me with polite smiles.

"I'm so glad you came!" A girl with deep-red hair jumped up to give me a hug.

"Oh, hey, Cheryl, right?" I smiled awkwardly as she released me and hopped back to her seat on the bench.

"I wish you'd have convinced Aubrey to come, too...maybe you can get her to tag along to tryouts this weekend. You're going to do great." She smiled broadly.

I felt my cheeks burn. "Thanks..."

Cheryl nodded, still smiling so big it looked like it hurt. She pointed a finger at the girl next to her. "This is Kaitlyn...she's sort of an islander, too..." She rested her hand on Kaitlyn's shoulder.

Kaitlyn rolled her dark eyes. "Part-time islander. Divorced parents." Kaitlyn shrugged, and she flipped her dark, shiny hair over her shoulder. The green glitter sparkled on her sepia cheeks.

"She boards in Martin House, too," Cheryl added helpfully. "You already know Amber and Taylor," she said brightly as both girls walked into the locker room.

"Our squad is on the smaller side..." Rachel explained.

"Which is why it is so great you're here," Amber offered, sliding out of her uniform and pulling on a fresh change of clothes from her locker. "When Aubrey decided to quit on us, I didn't know what we were going to do."

"Seriously, I can't believe she did that," Kaitlyn muttered.

I shifted where I stood. I didn't want to talk about Aubrey behind her back. Maybe it was because she was the first person to reach out to me and make me feel welcome, but I felt a strong sense of loyalty to her.

"Ditching us for Damien? Blech." Amber stuck out her tongue in disgust.

Kaitlyn crinkled her nose. "And then that whole Bird Island thing with—"

Rachel cut off Kaitlyn quickly. "Aubrey's dealing with a lot, okay? I get it." Rachel frowned reproachfully at the lot of them.

The girls all mumbled in reluctant agreement.

"I had lunch with her today..." I blurted before I could stop myself.

The girls turned their attention to me.

I cleared my throat and continued with a one-shouldered shrug. "She seemed pretty sweet to me. And it's got to be hard for her with her stepsister and all..."

"Understatement." Taylor scoffed, and Kaitlyn nodded grimly.

"Who's going to the Apple Fest this year?" Rachel asked randomly.

The girls all stared.

Rachel sighed. "What? It's next week...I'm done gossiping..."

"Did you find out any more about the Rousseaus?" Taylor looked at Rachel expectantly.

Rachel frowned. "No...and if I did and I told you...that'd be gossiping."

"Well, you know how it's a complete mystery how the killer got inside?" Kaitlyn asked in a hushed, excited tone. "Brentley told me that he heard from his sister, Lauren, that this has happened in Nile before."

Cheryl gasped and turned toward Rachel, who was pointedly ignoring them as she tugged on her baggy black pants over bright-orange underwear.

"What do you know about it, Seraphina?" Amber nodded toward me.

"Uhh, I haven't heard of anything like this before..." I murmured uncomfortably, wishing I had more to share.

Rachel's voice was muffled from inside the hoodie as she pulled it over her head. "Who's going to Apple Fest?"

"Doubtful anyone will go with a psycho on the loose," Kaitlyn pointed out. "Lauren said like twenty years ago these island kids started messing with satanic stuff and a girl *died*."

Kaitlyn nodded solemnly as Cheryl made the sign of the cross.

"If it wasn't an island thing, I would say it was Daphne...she's definitely into Satan..." Cheryl's eyes were wide as she looked at each of us in turn.

Amber kinked an eyebrow in skeptical amusement. "If it was twenty years ago, how would Lauren know? She just barely graduated."

"Did you ask your dad about it, Kaitlyn?" Taylor asked.

"He wouldn't know anything. He grew up in Montreal, remember? Anyways, Lauren heard it from a friend or something who had an older sister who knew the kids...or something." Kaitlyn waved a hand dismissively. "It doesn't matter. The point is...it's happening again. There's no other way to explain it."

"Uh huh..." Amber exchanged identical smirks with Taylor.

"Well, we've heard all about the Nile Witch," Cheryl murmured quietly.

My heart stumbled in my chest, quickening its pace as it tried to recover. I glanced quickly at Rachel, who shot me an apologetic look.

"Michael said the Nile Witch married the Devil and dances naked under the full moon..." Cheryl whispered, as though she were afraid to speak.

Kaitlyn elbowed Cheryl sharply in the ribs. Cheryl whined, but at the sight of Kaitlyn's face, she bit her lip, her cheeks burning bright red as her hair. She looked at me with big, tearful eyes. "Oh, gosh, I'm so sorry, Seraphina...I forgot that—well, that you—"

Kaitlyn cut in defensively, "It's just a silly Nile legend...for fun, you know?"

"It's okay. I get it." I forced a smile.

The girls all eyed one another awkwardly, before Amber said, "Listen, Seraphina, we know the rumors aren't true...and we're all going to make sure to shut people up when we hear them talking."

Everyone nodded in agreement. Cheryl was so enthusiastic in her agreement she looked like a bobblehead.

"Thanks. I appreciate it." I forced another smile but couldn't hide my discomfort.

"And Michael is a moron," Rachel snapped angrily.

We all stared at her.

She shrugged sheepishly. "Who's going to the Apple Fest?"

The girls groaned through indulgent grins.

Rachel shrugged. "Well, it's next week, we need to make plans..."

"Fine. Apple Fest plans...and go." Amber looked pointedly around the room.

"Are you going to the Apple Fest, Seraphina?" Cheryl asked with a sweet smile, as though I'd completely forgotten that she'd accused my mother of dancing around naked.

I glanced at Rachel before I took a deep breath and answered vaguely, "My family actually has a stand...so I'll be there."

Kaitlyn and Cheryl exchanged knowing glances. Every islander knew what stand the Greys put up for the Apple Fest. But before Amber or Taylor could ask what kind of stall, Rachel and I said polite goodbyes, and Rachel led me out of the locker room.

Cole was still in basketball practice. Rachel, reluctant to leave me, decided to sit with me in the main lobby, just outside the gym doors. After about a half hour of waiting, Rachel jumped to her feet and headed into the gym to get a time estimate, grumbling about homework and much-needed sleep.

I smiled after her as she left. I stared around the deserted hallway, gripping the wooden bench on which I sat. All in all, I was happy with the day. Sort of. It may have started off rocky, and ended horribly thanks to Daphne, but between Aubrey and Maddie, and the girls on the cheerleading squad, overall it'd been okay.

My ears prickled at the sound of boots clicking down the hallway. I looked up as a girl, clearly upset and crying, stalked into the lobby. Ignoring me, she dropped down on the bench opposite mine. She muttered down at her phone clutched in her hands. Her dark hair hid her face as her fingers jabbed at the screen. She wore black slacks and a black dress shirt. She'd dropped a duffel bag at her feet. It was Maddie, the girl from study hall. I didn't recognize her right away without her stitched blazer...well, that and she was a complete distressed mess.

"Maddie?" I spoke without thinking.

Startled, she looked up from her phone. She brushed her hair back from her damp cheeks as she forced a smile. "Oh, hey, Seraphina..."

She sniffed softly and stared back down at her phone.

I hesitated, unsure what to do. I didn't want to bother her... but she was obviously upset. I went with my instinct and stood from my bench and made my way across the room to hers. I sat next to Maddie and nudged her gently. "Are you okay?"

Maddie sniffed again and scoffed. "Yeah...I'm fine."

I nodded, accepting her answer. "What are you doing here so late?" I inclined my head toward the clock on the wall. "It's almost six."

"Oh, I had practice..."

I raised an eyebrow as I glanced down at her duffel bag. "Like band practice? Or..."

"No..." Maddie's flushed face burned a deep red. She rolled her eyes as she kicked her duffel bag. "It's stupid...you don't want—"

I frowned. "No, it's not. Tell me. I'm honestly interested."

Maddie tucked her hair behind her ears as she shrugged. "I'm a magician."

"Oh." I blinked. Although that was the last thing I expected her to say, now her outfit made sense. "Like..."

"Like illusions and tricks..."

"With doves and—"

Maddie nodded without bothering to meet my gaze. "Yeah. I know, it's lame."

I smiled, genuinely impressed. "No, it's not. That's so cool!"

Maddie glanced sideways at me with a small smile. "You really think so?"

I nodded eagerly. "Definitely. When is your next show? I'd love to watch."

Maddie's smile warmed her face. "I was thinking about getting a stand at the Apple Fest next weekend..."

I grinned and gave her a nudge. "You should totally do it."

Maddie scoffed shyly. "Well, it wouldn't be half as popular as your mom's tent. My mom and my sister, we usually have an art tent, but..." Her face slowly fell and her eyes dropped back down to her phone.

I frowned. "I know you don't know me too well, but I'm here if you want to talk about anything."

Maddie sighed heavily. "Thanks...that means a lot."

There was a moment of silence in which I gave her time to think it over.

Then she looked up at me. "So, what are *you* doing here? I thought you'd be back at Martin House by now."

I inclined my head curiously, and then my eyes widened with understanding. "Oh, right. I didn't tell you—I'm not boarding at Martin House...there was a mix-up with my paperwork."

"Oh." Maddie sighed again, clearly disappointed.

I lightly touched her shoulder. "Trust me, I'd love to be your roommate, but there's no way my family would go for it."

Maddie nodded with a rueful smile. "I get it...my mom didn't want me to board either, but I had to get out of the house."

I bit my lip. I felt that. No one knew that feeling more than me.

We both looked up instinctively at the sound of footsteps in the hallway. Aubrey came around the corner, carrying a large stack of books that almost hid her from view. She peeked around the stack, watching her step. Her eyes widened with pleasant surprise at the sight of Maddie and me seated on the bench.

"Hey!" She hurried over to us, dumping her books onto the bench, some of which tumbled onto the floor. "What are you guys doing here? I thought you'd be at Martin House..."

Maddie sniffed and hastily pushed her palm into her cheeks, clearing her face of any remaining tears. "Seraphina's not boarding."

"Oh, I thought—" Aubrey's face fell, but she recovered quickly. "Well, that's okay... You're sleeping over this Friday, right?"

Before I could answer, Aubrey continued to release a happy bubbling stream of babble. "I just texted Cheryl, and she's coming with Kaitlyn...oh, and I'm so sorry about Daphne..."

Maddie glanced at me sympathetically. My face burned as I remembered the entire study hall had witnessed my humiliation; it made sense word would spread fast. "It's not a big deal..."

"It is!" Aubrey exclaimed. "I shouldn't have left you like that just because she wanted to talk."

I blinked. Then I realized Aubrey was talking about lunch. I relaxed a bit.

"I didn't mean to be so rude...she just—we have a *difficult* relationship, to say the least..."

My forehead crinkled, and I gave Aubrey a sympathetic smile.

"If you want to talk about it, I've had my share of strained sister experiences."

Aubrey tugged on her tarnished locket. "It's just hard. I never got to see my dad often. So, I'm left out a lot."

I nodded. "I could see how that would hurt."

Aubrey bit her lip. "When Dad moved from their two-bedroom apartment to their bigger house, I didn't even get to have a room because Daphne needed the extra space. And don't get me started on my stepmom."

"They wouldn't let you share? Wait—they gave her an *extra* bedroom?"

Aubrey blushed prettily as she shook her head, her brilliant, blue eyes shining as she tried to shrug it off. "She has a YouTube channel...so she uses it for like a studio kind of thing..."

"So, where do you sleep?" I cried, aghast at the idea of a parent not even making space for their child.

Aubrey hesitated, her cheeks pink with her embarrassment. "On the couch...but it's no big deal. Like I said, I didn't go there often...then I started boarding, so it didn't really matter."

I blinked incredulously. "I'm so sorry...I thought I had it bad competing with my sister in—" I caught myself and corrected mid-sentence, "competing in our schoolwork...I can't imagine having to compete for a *bed*."

Aubrey laughed lightly. "Don't get me started on competition...but—I got to get all these to the library..." She stood from the bench and then froze, fixing me with an anxious smile. "You *are* coming to the sleepover, right?"

"Uhh—" Instantly, I thought of what Rachel had said about Mama. "I'm not sure if—"

Aubrey bit her lip as she watched me hesitate. "Please? It would be so fun."

I scrunched up my nose as I thought it over. Whatever Mama had said to Phoenix, she'd never told *me* no...although, I'd never actually asked. But still, if Mama had meant no, then she would've said no to me. Made it clear.

Aubrey smiled. "Maddie can come, too."

Maddie looked up in surprise. "Really?"

Aubrey's smile brightened. "Sure!"

Maddie peeked at me with hopeful doe eyes.

Maddie looked so excited, I spoke without thinking. "Okay—but I have cheer tryouts on Saturday, so—"

Aubrey waved a hand as she bent to grab her stack of books. "Pshh. You'll make it. And with Morgan and Courtney coming, it'll be like a real party!"

"Do you want me to help you with those?" Maddie offered.

Aubrey's smile crinkled her eyes. "Sure."

And I watched as the two of them split the books between them and headed out of the school, my stomach knotted with guilt.

By the time Cole's practice ended, it was past six.

And by the time we made it onto the ferry and through Nile, back to Grey Cottage, it was nearly eight o'clock.

And Fawn was already back at Blackwell Manor.

And Mama hadn't called...at least, that's what Phoenix said without looking up from her book on the couch, her wand stuck in the top knot on her head and her hand stroking Icarus, who blinked reproachfully at me as I walked inside.

Whatever.

And Phoenix...well, I didn't bother trying to make Phoenix talk to me. Instead, I headed to my...*our*...room.

I scowled and dumped my bag out onto the bed. Then I sorted through my school stuff and got to work.

It was even later when Phoenix finally came into the room. Her face was stony as she grabbed her pajamas and left the room to change. When she returned, she dropped her wand on her nightstand, flopped onto her bed with her book, and buried her face behind it.

If Phoenix didn't want to talk, that was fine with me. A silent Phoenix was a pleasant change.

Of course, she could only last a moment. A snort came from behind her book.

I pursed my lips on an impatient frown. "What?"

"Nice pom-poms." Nix snickered.

My heart dipped in my stomach as my cheeks burned hot with embarrassment. I grabbed the cheerleading uniform and pom-poms and shoved them under my bed.

Phoenix mumbled something under her breath.

I glared at her. "Do you have something to say?"

Phoenix didn't bother to look up from her book. "I just can't believe you actually signed up to be a cheerleader." She shook her head as she slapped at a page and continued in a bored voice, "Congratulations, you're officially a walking stereotype."

"How does being a cheerleader make me a stereotype?" I demanded, fighting the urge to blurt out Rachel's secret. No wonder Rachel didn't want to tell Phoenix. Judgy much?

Phoenix turned a page so violently it almost ripped. "Now you just have to start dating the captain of the football team and you'll be a cliche."

My blood burned, but before I could fire back, Phoenix looked over at me, her caramel eyes cold. "Fawn was really hurt when you didn't come home."

Phoenix shut her book and snapped her fingers. Her lamp went out with a little pop. Then she rolled over and went to sleep, leaving me speechless and shamed, and with a ton of homework left to do.

I had to take the bus that morning. I'd nearly forgotten and had to run out of the house with wet hair and untied laces. It was nearly a forty-minute walk to the Corner Stone, which was where the "bus stop" was located, and I had just enough time to make it. Although, by the time I did, I was flushed and sweaty despite the cold. Luckily, there was no one else there to see me.

The tiny purple bus shuddered to a stop with a loud bang from its back end. The driver, a man who could easily have been mistaken for a stinky mall Santa Claus, cranked open the door for me. I hesitated only a moment before ducking inside.

It was cramped. I had to bend over almost double as I made my way down the aisle and took one of maybe ten seats. All were empty except for one in the back, in which a guy was slumped over, asleep, his face smushed against the window, his breath fogging up the glass.

The bus made two more stops before shuddering up the ferry ramp, picking up a rather grumpy-looking girl with a squished nose and another girl with a dreamy gaze, wearing a lumpy home-made hat with googly eyes stitched on top.

To my increasingly awkward discomfort, she took the seat beside me with a smile. "I know you."

"Oh, hi." I tried to smile, but it came out as an uncomfortable wince.

"You don't know me," the girl replied simply.

"No…" I agreed.

"My name is Lacey McGregor. This is my last day at school."

I blinked. "It is?"

Lacey smiled serenely up at me. Her hat sagged a bit underneath the weight of a large googly eye. "I'm going to homeschool from now on."

I inclined my head and a genuine smile warmed my face. "That's great! My sisters homeschool."

Lacey nodded eagerly. "I'm very excited."

"What made you decide to switch?" I watched her pull a yellow thermos out of her shoulder bag.

"Would you like some soup?" She held up the thermos. "I made it myself."

"Oh, no—that's okay…"

Lacey continued to smile politely at me, her eyes wide and curious. "You should be careful."

"Why?"

"There are brindycaps buzzing around your aura."

I crinkled my nose with a bemused smirk. Had I heard her right?

Lacey leaned in to whisper. "They attract ghosts."

"Oh…" I smiled kindly as Lacey drank her soup. Then I quickly pulled a book out of my bag and buried my face behind it.

Once we made it into the mainland, the bus driver dropped us off at the public bus stop beside the train tracks…a good hike away from the school. The kids headed right, in the direction of the public school, Ethan Allen High, but not before Lacey gave me an enthusiastic wave that stretched high as her arm could reach while she bounced on the balls of her feet. Then she turned and skipped away, the other two kids keeping their distance from her as they followed. Smiling slightly in amused disbelief, I took a left toward Mater Christi High School.

It wasn't hard to find. The tracks ran right past the campus, so I really just had to follow them for a bit and cut through the small stretch of trees at the right moment. And as I neared the entrance, hair limp, shoulder aching underneath the weight of my bag, and back cold with sweat beneath my jacket, the idea of boarding five days a week was incredibly appealing. I definitely didn't want to do this every morning, let alone again in the afternoon. But did I really want to bring up that argument with Phoenix? No. I really didn't.

My second day at Mater Christi was considerably better than the first. The whispers stopped and were instead replaced by a polite interest, and I couldn't help but wonder whether the cheerleading squad had already gotten to work squashing the rumors. MCHS had a block schedule, so, although the classes were twice as long, we only had four each day. (A days and B days, they called them—creative, huh?) Today's classes were not only in different parts of the school than yesterday, they also had completely different kids in them. But I was pleasantly surprised to see that I recognized a few of the kids from yesterday. And I was extremely excited when I realized I had all the girls from cheerleading scattered throughout my classes.

The only downside to the day—I had to wait for lunch to see Rachel and Cole, for unluckily, I had no classes with them at all.

"How's it going?" Rachel asked around a French fry.

"Great!" I grinned so big it hurt. I looked pointedly at Cole. My silver eyes sparkled. "Absolutely nothing out of the ordinary."

Cole gave me a warm, brotherly smile. "Glad to hear it."

Rachel grabbed another fry. "How's Nix doing? I called the cottage, but she didn't pick up. You know, it'd be nice if you guys had phones. Nobody has house phones anymore."

I fought the urge to roll my eyes. "Phoenix is fine."

Rachel crinkled her brow at my brevity, but she didn't press the issue. "Any new friends yet?"

I smiled as I stole a fry off Cole's tray. "Actually, yes. Aubrey and Maddie, both from yesterday. I haven't seen them today, though. I should've asked for their class schedules..."

"Another reason a phone would be good. You know, so you could enter the twenty-first century with the rest of us—constant connection, instant interaction, all themes of this generation," Rachel teased.

"I'll make sure to ask my mom next time I see her." I gave her a cheeky wink. But I knew the answer to that question already. Mama was of the firm belief that cell phones interfered with magic. She didn't even like them in the house, let alone in our pockets.

Rachel reached for another fry as a comfortable silence settled around our table. Then she glanced at me sideways. "I heard about Daphne."

My smile slipped, and I gritted my teeth.

Rachel's dark eyes were soft and serious. "Are you okay?"

I nodded and shrugged it off. "It wasn't a big deal."

"I wish you would've told me yesterday," Rachel mumbled moodily. "I could tell something was bothering you…"

"It's fine." I waved a hand. "I'd rather just forget it."

Rachel exchanged looks with Cole but didn't say another word.

"And please don't tell Nix, okay, Rach? She'd never let me hear the end of it." I stared down at my fries, appetite gone.

Rachel frowned. "You don't have to be embarrassed about it. Daphne is always doing dumb stuff like that. Did Aubrey tell you what Daphne did to *her*?"

I hesitated. "You mean about her bedroom and—"

Rachel shook her head, chuckling darkly. "No. It was a lot worse than that. You should ask Aubrey about what happened on Elijah Grunvald's boat…"

"Well, I plan on avoiding Daphne as much as possible. Although with the sleepover, that might be hard—"

Rachel's frown deepened. "And your mom's okay with it?"

My cheeks burned. "Mama never said no."

Rachel shrugged. "Don't let anyone talk you into doing anything you don't want to do…that's all I'll say about that."

Before I could respond, Rachel grabbed her carton of fries and slung her backpack over her shoulder. "I gotta get to class. I'll see you after school?"

I cocked an eyebrow, as I double-checked the clock. Lunch was far from over. But Rachel gave me a small wave and walked away.

I scoffed. What had just happened? I stared at Cole in disbelief.

He shrugged sheepishly. "I think Phoenix may have said something to Rachel down at the Tracks...about you being desperate for friends." He winced as he curled his lip and scrunched his nose. Then Cole scratched his head as though digging for the memory. "Something about doing anything to fit in, keeping an eye on you..."

My eyes widened as my cheeks burned. I sputtered, speechless and embarrassed.

Cole touched my arm. "I know it's not like that. I get what you are trying to do. I do, Phin. And Aubrey and Maddie definitely could use a good friend right now..."

I stared down at my fries, stomach soured. "Why's that?"

Cole sighed heavily. "Well, first off, Maddie's little sister was in a car accident..."

Startled, I looked up from the table, searching Cole's sad, dark eyes.

"She's been in the hospital for like two weeks. I heard from my nana that they might take her off the machines soon...and Aubrey, well..." Cole frowned ruefully and gave me a slap on the back. "Let's just say, whatever Nix and Rachel may think—I get it."

I winced as the bell rang. I would never get used to the sound.

Cole squeezed my shoulder. Then he grabbed his stuff and headed out of the cafeteria. I stayed seated at the table, trying to process my thoughts. My eyes stared unseeing ahead of me as kids passed through my vision, cutting between the lunch tables and ducking past empty food trays.

Then it was as though time slowed and sound stopped, and I found myself staring straight into sharp, narrow eyes.

It was the guy from before, watching me. Again.

My heart hurried, harried in my chest as my breath caught uncomfortably in my throat. Before I could decide what to do, a group of giggling freshmen passed in front of me, and he was gone.

And I was left wondering whether he'd really been there at all.

8

FAMOUS LAST WORDS

I got home late again. Aubrey and I had stayed in the library for a while after school, and then I had to wait for Cole's basketball practice to get out because I'd just barely missed the bus.

Cole didn't mind taking me back, though. He'd take any excuse to drive the van around Nile, and for that I was grateful. But the morning commute was a definite no. As early as I had to wake up to even *catch* the bus, Cole would have to wake up even earlier to drive all the way to Nile and then back. I wouldn't ever ask him to do that, but I also didn't know how much longer I could stand taking that awful purple bus either. And by the time I walked through the front door of the cottage, I was seriously considering forging Mama's signature then and there to spare me the nightmare in the morning.

The cottage was quiet in a sad, lonely way that was unnatural in our home. Usually it was filled with noise. Lots of noise, from laughter to potion bangs to cat yowls. But tonight there was nothing, only a ringing silence that hurt my ears.

I headed into the kitchen to grab a quick bite before bed, hoping Phoenix was already asleep. Nope. I halted awkwardly in the archway at the sight of her munching on M&Ms while reading at the table, on which Icarus sat, back straight and green eyes staring right at me.

Phoenix didn't bother to look up.

I hesitated only a moment before hurrying to the cabinet for an apple cider donut. Jinx it. No more donuts. Awesome. I'd have to settle for crackers and cheese.

"You missed Fawn again..."

I glanced over my shoulder at Phoenix. She still didn't look at me. Instead, she turned a page in her spellbook with unnecessary force that crinkled the paper. I frowned and collected my sad excuse of a dinner.

"Mama called," Phoenix muttered as I headed out of the kitchen.

I froze in the doorway. I backed up and slowly placed my plate down on the table. I studied Phoenix. She glared down at the spellbook and slapped another page, before tossing another candy into her mouth.

I watched her for a moment, waiting for her to speak again.

Scowling, she scribbled a note in the margin of a page. She smacked away the page to read the next one, muttering angrily at the text.

My impatience got the better of me. "Well? What did she say?"

Phoenix made another note and grabbed more M&Ms. "She's going to be gone longer than she thought."

My heart sank a little in my chest. My standoff with Phoenix faded from my mind. "What does that *mean*? It's been two days already...no, three, if you count today."

Phoenix shrugged as she popped a piece of candy into her mouth. She still wouldn't look at me.

I gripped the back of the chair. "She didn't say anything else? What is she doing? Where is she?" My voice was strained, breathless with increasing anxiety as I fired off question after question as they came to me.

Phoenix looked up slowly from the spellbook. She studied me critically as she popped another M&M. She continued to stare at me as she chewed, as though thinking something over.

"Well?"

"She said that's all I could say." Phoenix shrugged in a lazy, bored way that made my blood burn.

"'That's all you could say'?" I demanded incredulously. "What the hex does that mean?"

Phoenix frowned, her voice rising with her temper. "I thought they taught grammar at school? Did you not understand the statement? Or were you just not paying attention to me? Mama said *that's all I could tell you.*"

I crossed my arms over my chest to keep me from jumping over the table and shaking her. "So, she told you more than that? Why would she tell you something and not me?"

Phoenix rolled her eyes and blew her black bangs out of her eyes, the orange tips flickering like fire. "Not everything is about you, Phin."

"Right, because it's always about you!"

Phoenix stood from her chair, her hands on the table as the two of us shouted back and forth. Icarus's ears twitched, his tail flicking angrily. "I'm not the one so desperate for attention, I needed to run off to a new school to get it!"

My silver eyes flashed. "I'm sorry for making friends without asking your permission!"

She scoffed with a cruel smirk. "Just because you met someone once doesn't make them your friend."

I blinked, eyes blurred at the truth in her words.

Phoenix winced, then she snapped defensively, "I was here when Mama called; it's not my fault you were at that dumb school!"

I scoffed. "Jealousy clashes with your dye job, Nix."

Phoenix's eyes blazed bronze. "Did it ever occur to you that Mama has real life-and-death issues to deal with, things more important to worry about than making the cheerleading squad or getting invites to slumber parties?"

I flinched, stepping back from the table as though she'd smacked me. Had Rachel told her? Or was she just talking? "You're just jealous."

Phoenix burst out laughing. Like a real, tickled kind of laugh.

It stung.

So I tried again. "You're just jealous because I actually have friends now, and you're alone."

She rolled her eyes, still smirking.

I hit harder. "You can't stand the fact that I finally got away from you!"

The laughter died slowly on her happy-go-lucky face. Guilt twisted in the pit of my stomach. I'd hurt her. Much more than I'd intended.

We stared at each other in silence.

Phoenix's eyes shined as she sniffed and forced a smile. "You know what...you're right. I'd rather be alone than stuck here with you."

And she pushed past me into the living room.

I turned and followed her, trying to think of something to say, but nothing came.

Phoenix grabbed her backpack off the hook, yanked the door open, and slammed it behind her.

The cottage shuddered.

I couldn't sleep at all that night.

Aubrey was waiting for me outside the entrance by the time I made it up the hill to the school. I was just as sweaty as yesterday, if not more so, and incredibly gross and unkempt, in addition to extremely bad-tempered. On top of just barely making it onto the bus, I'd been in such a rush to get out the door, I'd grabbed Phoenix's backpack instead of mine. Although, it was more

Phoenix's fault than mine. For some reason, her backpack had been on my side of the room and in the early morning dark of the bedroom, I couldn't see the difference and didn't notice until I'd gotten on the bus. So not only would all my homework assignments be late, but I had to carry around an enormous spellbook that weighed a ton and whatever else she'd hoarded away in her pack.

"Hey!" Aubrey smiled brightly as she laced her arm through mine and escorted me inside the building, joining the herd of students heading to first period. "Are you okay, Sera? You look a bit frazzled…"

I ran a hand through my wind-tangled hair. "I'm fine, just a long night, and I have to walk a million miles to get here…and my sister is a pain."

"I've been there." Aubrey nodded and patted my arm sympathetically. "I'm telling you, you need to board. Think of the time it'll save! Plus, you can hang out with Cole all the time…"

I stared at her and then laughed as she gave me a sly wink. "Uh, no. Cole is like my brother—that, *ew*, no."

Aubrey laughed. "You have to admit he's hot, though. God, whenever I'd stay at Rachel's house, I'd *pray* he'd show up. He's like a teenage Johnny Depp. And he even plays guitar!" She leaned into me and squeezed my arm as though pretending to swoon.

I giggled despite myself. "Rachel said you guys are friends— why haven't I seen you together?"

Aubrey tugged at her locket and slid it back and forth along the chain. "Oh…yeah, well, Rachel and I…" Aubrey made a face and shrugged. "It's complicated."

"Oh." I hesitated, unsure what to say next.

"We've kind of drifted apart these past few weeks…it's a long story."

"I didn't realize you guys were—"

"Best friends? Yeah…since forever, really." Aubrey looked up at me with a shy, rueful smile. "We make an odd pair, don't we? Most people are surprised..."

I crinkled my forehead and smiled dubiously. "Yeah, just a bit..."

Aubrey noticed something behind me and gave me a small nudge. "Don't look now, but the new guy is totally checking you out."

My eyes widened, and I turned sharply. "What?"

Aubrey squealed and grabbed my arm, pulling me back around, but not before I locked eyes with a guy—the same guy I kept seeing everywhere.

"I said don't look!" Aubrey giggled as she continued to peek at him from around my shoulder.

I wasn't laughing. "I've seen him before." I took Aubrey by the arm and headed toward our Botany class.

"What do you mean—my God, he's staring *hardcore*..." Aubrey turned back around, hopping a bit to keep up with my quick pace. She shook her head, fighting a smile.

"I mean, I've seen him before...staring at me like he's waiting for something... I don't know, it's weird. Do you know who he is?" I bit my lip and tried to remember which way to class, but I was still getting the hang of it.

Aubrey took the lead when I almost missed a turn.

"All I know is he's new...enrolled the same day as you, actually. Maybe he's stalking you."

I looked down at her, eyes wide in alarm. "Do you really—"

"Kidding!" She offered a weak smile. "Like I said, he probably just thinks you're hot, which you are...like a young Taylor Momsen, without the black eyes and icky cigarette smoke." She gave a pout. "Totally unfair."

"Who's Taylor Momsen?"

Aubrey smiled and looped her arm through mine. "Are you excited for the sleepover? I was thinking we'll all meet up for coffee before we walk to my dad's house. Courtney can't come, but everyone else is—"

Before I could answer, Damien, the boy from study hall, followed by a few other guys, sauntered up to us as we made our way around the corner. "Well, isn't this cute? My two favorite girls..."

The boys stopped short in front of us, blocking our path as the sea of students parted around us.

"Hey, Aubrey..." Damien's smile didn't reach his eyes. "You've been ignoring my calls."

Aubrey tensed beside me. I glanced down to see her staring at Damien with the coldest expression I'd ever seen.

There was an awkward silence until it was broken by the taller boy, whose blonde hair fell into his eyes, giving him a striking resemblance to a sheepdog. He leaned around Damien's shoulder. "Well, Day...can't you see she's moved on? After what you did, I don't blame her..." He gave us a cruel smirk as he shook his hair from his eyes. "Aubrey, you're dating the Witch Spawn now? What happened to Rachel?"

Damien shoved the sheepdog, knocking him in the side with his elbow. "Shut up, Brentley."

"I'll see you at lunch, Sera." Aubrey's voice came out in a barely audible whisper before she pulled away from me and hurried away.

The boy, Brentley, dissolved into hoots of laughter as I ran after Aubrey.

"Hey!" I called breathlessly, "Aubrey, wait!"

I could see her tiny frame and wispy blonde hair several students ahead of me, but the hallway was body to body and impossible to push through politely. There was no way she couldn't have heard me, but Aubrey didn't slow down, and I lost sight of her around a corridor.

My heart sank as my pace slowed.

· · ·

I didn't see Aubrey again until lunch. She caught me around the waist from behind, startling me so bad I spilled my fries.

"Oh, God, Sera, I'm so sorry." Aubrey dropped down to help me pick up the mess.

"No—it's my fault; I've been jumpy all afternoon…" And that was true. I was pretty sure I'd seen the stalker dude just as I'd gotten in line for food.

Aubrey smiled a bit awkwardly as she dropped the spoiled fries into the trash can. "I just wanted to apologize…for ditching you with the guys earlier—"

"Oh, you don't have to—"

Aubrey put a hand on my arm. "No, I need to. It was really awful of me. It's just—" She bit her lip and looked up at the ceiling, her blue eyes shining in the fluorescent lights. "Damien and I used to date…for a while—like three years…and—well, I just had to get out of there. He's not a nice person."

My eyes widened, and I nodded emphatically. "Yeah. He's a pretty big jerk. And I've only met him a handful of times…"

Aubrey chewed on her lip and looked at me with anxious eyes. "I hope this doesn't make you think badly of me—"

"Of course not." I gave her a playful nudge. "You're like my best friend."

Aubrey tugged on her necklace and gave me a smile that lit up her whole face. "You're mine, too."

I grabbed a table for us while she went back in line for more fries. ("My treat!") My heart was lighter than it'd been in a while. I'd never had a "best friend." Cole and Rachel didn't count because I had to share them with Phoenix. And if they had to choose, they'd always choose Phoenix. And the idea of having a "best friend" was oddly fulfilling and comforting in a way that made me smile inside and out.

Soon the table filled with Courtney and Morgan, both of whom I quickly recalled from lunch the first day, and even Maddie hesitantly joined the table. I could see Cheryl's red hair at the opposite end of the cafeteria at a table with the cheerleaders. Rachel and Cole didn't have this lunch on A days, so they were nowhere to be found.

By the time Aubrey got back to the table, Courtney was trying to get my thoughts on supernatural activity.

"Have you heard of the Rosecrest House on Apple Shore Drive?"

I tried to keep a straight face, but her enthusiasm made it hard. "Yeah, I think everyone's heard of the Rosecrest House…"

Courtney flipped her thick honey hair over her shoulder and leaned in across the table. "Sure, but see, everyone *thought* it was a ghost, but really it was a—"

"Courtney, can we not—" Aubrey winced as she took a seat next to me and passed me my fries. "I don't want to hear about creepy stuff today."

Morgan and Courtney exchanged almost panicked glances, before Courtney gave her a rueful smile. "I'm sorry, Aubs…I didn't mean—"

Aubrey waved her worries away. "It's fine—oh, shoot. I forgot the condiments." She started to get up, but I held out a hand.

"I'll get them." I grabbed Phoenix's bag and slung it over my shoulder. I'd made a point to keep it close. The last thing I needed was someone snooping through it.

Aubrey smiled gratefully. "Mayonnaise, please."

As I left the table, everyone settled in to discuss the Apple Fest. I weaved my way through the throngs of kids and tangles of tables and chairs to grab two paper cups of mayonnaise. When I turned back around, I saw the guy with the sharp eyes watching me from a few tables away. I frowned. What was his problem? I started toward him to ask him just that, but stopped mid-march as Daphne cut in front of me.

Her black eyes glittered. "Hey…can't wait to see you in study hall."

Instinctively, I backed up a step. "Right." My hand went to my shoulder and gripped the strap of Phoenix's backpack. "Can't wait. Excuse me."

I sidestepped her and headed straight back to our table. I set the paper cups onto Aubrey's tray and dropped the bag at my feet as I took my seat. Then I realized the conversation had stopped. I looked around the table, a quizzical eyebrow raised. Everyone was staring behind me. I glanced backward. And there was Daphne, looming over me like a dark shadow. Awesome.

"What do you want, Daphne?" Courtney asked coolly, her cerulean eyes like stormy skies.

Daphne smiled. "You know, you all should really watch the company you keep. Little Witch Spawn here could be dangerous. And with all the crazy stuff going on in Nile...you can't be too careful."

My nostrils flared as I clenched my teeth tight.

"Daphne—" Aubrey began.

That was it.

Enough.

I pushed back in my chair and stood so fast that it tipped over with a loud smack. A few of the surrounding tables turned as one to stare, nudging one another and muttering excitedly. Ignoring the crowd, I looked at Daphne, straight in the eyes, onyx to silver. I shook my head as I shrugged impatiently. "What do you want, Daphne?" I held my hands out and gestured down the length of me. "I'm right here. *What is it?*"

Daphne fluttered her thick eyelashes and smiled sweetly. "I'm just excited for study hall...that's all. And for the sleepover," she added with mock sincerity. "It's your first one, isn't it?"

I rolled my eyes, temper flaring. "This is getting really old. Look, I understand that it's hard for you that I'm here. But you have to stop."

Daphne's smile slipped. "What—you think I'm *jealous* or something? Who'd be jealous of a freak like you?" She shoved me hard, but I stood my ground. I didn't stumble back.

I wanted to hit her, but I kept my hands balled at my sides, my nails pinched into my palms. I smiled patiently at her. "Did that make you feel better? It certainly didn't change the fact that I'm all anyone can seem to talk about...and that's what really bothers you about me, isn't it?"

"Like you're *popular* or something?" Daphne snickered. "Give me a break. The only reason any of these idiots hang out with you is to ogle you like one of those creeps in the Carnival of Nightmares."

I didn't say anything. I didn't react. I just stood there as calmly as I could.

Daphne stepped closer. We were eye to eye, almost nose to nose. I could see the powder in her eyeshadow and smell the stench of her perfume. Her breath was hot and minty in my face. "You're *nothing*. A homeschooled loser without any friends. These girls? They aren't your friends. They're just here to watch."

I flinched away from her. "To watch?"

"The show." Daphne smiled sweetly. Then she snatched Phoenix's bag off the ground. And before I could react, she unzipped the zipper and dumped the contents on the floor.

9

THE GREAT ESCAPE

It was like the world slowed and sped up at the same time. Several people gasped. The whispers were loud in my ears like a buzz of insects. I watched, heart in my stomach, frozen in horror, as a rock pouch, a tarot deck, a charm bag, and various other herbs and trinkets, along with a giant, ancient textbook dropped to the floor. The spine of the book hit the ground first; the pages splayed open. The old, weathered paper and hand-painted runes, exposed for everyone to see.

I dropped to my knees and snatched the book up to my chest, tears blurring my vision. Over and over in my head, I silently screamed at Phoenix for being so thoughtless, so careless, as to shove such a precious book into a backpack and forget it. But as I grabbed for the book, Daphne kicked at the remaining objects on the ground with her peep toe shoe, sliding cards and stones every which way.

"What kind of satanic crap is *this*?" Daphne squealed in positive delight. "You really are committed, aren't you? Or maybe...you should be? Courtney—maybe you could help her check into the Maple Leaf House...isn't that where Desiree—"

I grabbed Phoenix's charm bag from the ground, and, with the book still clutched tightly to my chest, I jumped to my feet. I dangled the little velvet pouch out in front of her face, like a charmer baiting a snake. "See this?" I snapped in her smirking face. "This is a curse."

Daphne's smile faltered just a bit.

I saw a flicker of hesitation in her face. My eyes narrowed as I lowered my voice to a deep, threatening octave. "If you mess with me again, this'll find its way into your locker..."

"Oh, please—" Daphne scoffed as she rolled her eyes, glancing around at the crowd as though it were a joke.

"Or into your backpack..."

Daphne took a small step back, her smile gone.

I didn't stop there. I closed the distance she'd created between us, the charm bag an inch from her face. "Or maybe it'll find its way into your bedroom Friday night."

"You think you scare me?" Daphne asked coolly, stepping back again.

I lowered the charm bag and shrugged. "Maybe not...but I will. If you don't leave me alone." I shot her one last disgusted look, before I dropped back down to pick up Phoenix's things from the floor.

"You little—" Daphne hissed from overhead.

"That's enough, Daphne!" Aubrey's voice shouted from the table.

Then, before I realized what was happening, Courtney, Morgan, and Maddison were beside me on the ground. And together, we scooped everything carefully, respectfully, back inside the bag.

The bell rang, jarring everyone from the scene.

"See you in study hall, Witch Spawn..." Daphne turned on her heel and marched out of the cafeteria.

I slipped the backpack over my shoulder and stared after her. I wanted nothing more than to go home. The last thing I wanted was to sit in a classroom with Daphne literally lurking over my shoulder for an hour and a half.

Aubrey hurried around the table and gave me a tight hug. "I'm so sorry, Sera. I'm going to go talk to her…"

"No, really, you don't have to—" I stopped mid-sentence as Aubrey ran off after her stepsister. I sighed heavily.

Morgan cleared her throat awkwardly. "Uh, see you later, Sera." Morgan gave a little wave as she tucked a long loc behind her ear. "I'll meet you after school, Court…"

The cafeteria was slowly emptying. I could feel the eyes flickering over me like insect antennas as students passed. Frowning, I shifted the backpack strap higher on my shoulder.

Courtney nudged me lightly. "I don't know about you, but I could really go for a coffee right now…"

Maddie came up beside me and nodded briskly. "Please."

A small smile tickled the corner of my lips. I probably should've thought it over, at least considered the implications of cutting class…but I didn't. "Lead the way."

The three of us loaded up into Courtney's flashy sports car, which was so pink it'd put Barbie's car to shame, and she drove us down a few of the quiet private roads that cut through the woods that covered the grounds to the campus cafe. I'd heard Cole and Rachel mention it before, but this was my first time at…I glanced at the sign as we pulled up.

"Hallowed Grounds?" I asked. The corner of my mouth twitched in amusement. "Seriously?"

"Hey, don't knock it. What did you expect? We *are* a Catholic school, after all…" Courtney beamed as she put the car in park, and we got out. Surprisingly, though fourth period had just started, there were several cars parked in the small dirt parking lot of the cafe already.

The Hallowed Grounds looked like all the other buildings that dotted the Mater Christi campus. It was old, with brown and red bricks draped in thick ivy and two lantern-style lamps shouldering each side of the black front door. But unlike the other buildings I'd seen, this one had string lights with big, chunky bulbs hung in loops below a chic, emerald painted sign that read "Hallowed Grounds: The Green Knights' Favorite Resting Place" and below that, it read, "Roast in Peace," all in silver lettering. I smiled and glanced up at the windows on the second story. There were kids, some reading, some sipping from odd mugs, all seated in plush chairs angled against the fogged glass.

"You ready?" Courtney held the door open as she waited at the top of the steps with an amused smile.

Maddie hurried up the steps and ducked inside, with me close behind.

The atmosphere in Hallowed Grounds was completely unexpected. I had to take a minute, standing frozen on the welcome mat among the coats and hats hung up on pegs on the wall, to fully appreciate it. It was warm and cozy and antiquated, like stepping into the house of a beloved great-aunt. There were oversized couches in rich, warm, paisley patterns and cushy armchairs in deep greens with white doilies on the seatbacks. The tables were low and small with tablecloths of varying patterns, each with three or four mismatched wooden chairs, with seat cushions tied around the backs, pushed neatly underneath them. The place was painted a deep green, save for the gray brick accent wall at the back of the coffeehouse, behind the sleek hardwood counter, presumably to match the school colors. It would've been dark, if not for Victorian lamps with their bright, stained-glass shades and the fire burning calmly in the brick hearth.

"Cool," was all I could say. And it was.

Courtney smiled as she hung up her backpack on a peg. "I know, right? It's not the Honey Bean, but—"

"It's *better* than the Honey Bean." Maddie nudged her playfully. "You aren't at Ethan Allen anymore, you're a Green Knight again, remember?"

Courtney chuckled and led us to a couple of chairs huddled by the fire. "I'll grab the coffees. What's your pleasure?"

"Are you sure?" Maddie mumbled almost anxiously. "I can get it—"

Courtney waved her hand with a cheeky wink. "Don't worry about it—my order is a bit complex..."

Maddie smiled gratefully as she dropped into a chair. I took the one opposite it so that the fire was between us, and we gave Courtney our orders. Hot chocolate for Maddie, and a black French Vanilla for me. Usually, I added hot chocolate to the coffee, but I was too shy to mention it.

As Courtney headed for the counter, I leaned back into the cushions of the chair, sinking into it, and inhaled the rich smells of baked goods and roasted brews. Maddison sat with her back straight up in the seat, looking as if she might bounce up any second. She was nibbling her lip.

She noticed me staring and blushed. "Sorry, I'm nervous." She cleared her throat again and blurted, "Courtney Blanchard...she's a bit intimidating."

I sat up a bit and gave her a curious smile. I glanced up at Courtney, who was now flirting with the cute college guy at the cash register. "Really? She seems nice to me..."

"Oh, she's *so* nice! That's what I mean...and she's *so* generous... but I guess she has the means to be. I mean, you saw her car. The Blanchards are loaded." Maddie leaned in close. "She just transferred back here from the public school. She'd tried it for a few weeks because there was this whole thing with her best friend Desiree last year...people say she was possessed by a ghost or something—"

I raised an eyebrow. "Seriously?"

Maddie nodded, eyes wide. "And with everything that's going on these days...I believe it."

Courtney returned, bright-eyed and rosy cheeked as she passed out our mugs. "God, he's cute."

I smiled at Courtney as she dropped into the empty chair beside Maddie. "It looks like the feeling is mutual." I nodded to the guy who was still watching Courtney through his shaggy brown bangs with a dopey-looking grin on his face.

Courtney giggled, the blush deepening in her cheeks. "Well, he's no Cole St. Claire...but I'll take it."

We settled into our chairs and sipped quietly for a few moments, listening to the murmur drifting down from upstairs and the pleasant crackle of the logs in the fireplace.

"Thanks for getting me out of there... It hasn't been easy." I stared down at the mug in my hands.

Courtney licked the foam off her lip and nodded. "I totally get it. I didn't come back to school at first because of drama like that."

"Maddie was telling me—why did you decide to come back?"

Courtney smiled ruefully. "I actually have been wanting to talk to you about that—"

I paused with my mug at my lips. "Me?"

"My brother and I...well, a few friends of ours got mixed up in...something."

"Something?" I put my mug down at the side table beside my chair.

Maddie scooted straighter in her seat.

Courtney nodded. "And ever since, we've been keeping our eyes out for...for other things..."

I laughed incredulously. "I feel like you're speaking in a code you think I understand...but I don't—"

Courtney flipped her honey hair over her shoulder and gripped her mug in both hands as she leaned toward me. The rosy, flirty air had left her, and she looked at me with wide, serious eyes. "I think there's something evil going on in Nile."

My stomach twisted uncomfortably, and I shivered despite the heat from the fire just a foot away. "Something *evil*?"

Maddie went to take a sip but thought better of it. "Are you talking about—you know...what happened to—well, on East Shore South?"

I remembered what Rachel had said about the murders on East Shore. The locked doors. Cut-up bodies. I drank deeply from my mug.

Courtney nodded seriously. "It's not just the Rousseaus, though...I really feel like something's going on. And Sera, I figured you would know—"

I blinked rapidly in surprise and looked from Courtney to Maddie and back again. "I don't—I mean...I don't know anything about...*evil* things."

Courtney shook her head, and she lightly tapped my knee. "Oh, I didn't mean it like that, Sera. Of course, I don't think you'd —well, it's just, I figured if anyone would know about something supernatural going on in Nile, it'd be—"

I shook my head. "Courtney, whatever you believe about my mother, I'm...not," I finished awkwardly. "I'm just as ordinary and clueless as you..."

"Oh." Courtney's face fell with disappointment. She took a slow sip of her coffee.

Maddie stared down at her hot chocolate cupped in both hands as she murmured, "Creepy things are always happening in Nile...my uncle says the whole town is cursed..."

The door flew open with a creak that made the three of us flinch. Instinctively, we all glanced up to see who had entered. I gasped sharply and looked down at my mug, allowing my hair to fall in front of my face like a curtain. It was the guy from the cafeteria. And the courtyard. And everywhere else I kept seeing him.

Over the top of my cup, I saw Courtney watch him with a small, sweet smile. I glanced at Maddie. She was watching me. As our eyes locked, she raised her eyebrows and mouthed, "What?"

I shook my head and discreetly peeked up at him. He was ordering coffee and what looked like a to-go box of pie. He said something as he passed his card to the college kid, making him laugh as well as the girl cashier, who giggled and ran a hand through her strawberry-blonde hair, batting her eyelashes at him. He nodded in thanks as he took his cup and box. Then he turned and headed up the old staircase, each step groaning slightly underneath his boots. He hadn't noticed me. My heart eased to a steady beat, and I exhaled the breath that had caught in my chest.

"Holy mother...he is freaking *gorgeous*..." Courtney murmured, still staring at the top of the stairs where he'd disappeared. "Who is he?"

Before I could explain, Maddie answered. "He's new. He showed up in my history class on Monday...and my math class the next day. He boards at Martin House, but we never see him... everyone was whispering about it because he showed up right after the—you know, the East Shore...deaths." Maddie drank deeply from her mug. "But then word got around about Seraphina and no one cared about him anymore."

My pulse quickened inexplicably. "What's his name?"

Maddie smiled slightly, encouraged. "Logan. I remember because I'm a Marvel fan," she added, blushing prettily. "He hasn't spoken much...hasn't spoken at all, now that I think of it. He just kind of sits there. And he's into some odd stuff."

My stomach churned uncomfortably.

Courtney went to take a sip but paused. "Odd stuff?"

Maddison scrunched up her face as she tried to remember. "After class, he was on his phone, saying something about demons." Maddie chuckled anxiously at my stricken expression. "I don't know, it was weird at the time. Probably something for Halloween, right?" Maddison forced a smile and sipped her hot chocolate.

Courtney glanced at me. I bit my lip, my eyes drifting toward the top of the stairs.

"I keep seeing him..." I blurted before I could stop myself. "Everywhere," I added with an edge of annoyance in my voice.

Maddie nodded sympathetically. "Yeah, Mater Christi has a pretty small student body, considering its size—"

I shook my head. "No, like, everywhere I go, he's there watching me."

Courtney cocked an eyebrow. "Watching you?"

I nodded, my face scrunched in an irritated pout. "I was going to confront him today at lunch, but then Daphne got in my face."

Courtney set her mug down on a side table with a sly smile lighting up her eyes. "Well, maybe we should do the watching for a change?"

Maddie giggled. "What, like, spy on him?"

Courtney shrugged, her blue eyes glittering with mischief.

I laughed. "We can't—"

"Why not? Could be fun..." Courtney grinned.

I bit my lip in a vain attempt at concealing my smile. "How can we? He went upstairs..."

"He has to come down sometime, doesn't he?" Courtney stood and grabbed our now-empty mugs and brought them up to the counter.

Maddie grabbed her duffel, and I slung Phoenix's bag over my shoulder, and we followed Courtney to the door. She lifted her backpack off the peg and led us outside.

"What are we going to do, wait until he comes out?" I asked as we hurried to her car.

"Yup." Courtney opened her door and flipped the seat for Maddie to get in as I moved around to get in the passenger side.

"You realize your car is bubblegum pink, right?" I laughed.

Courtney giggled. "True...that will make this a bit of a challenge. Which one do you think is his?" She glanced around at the cars parked in the lot.

"Well, let's consider our target..." Maddie mused, leaning toward the tiny window in the back seat behind me. "He's tall. Utility jacket. High and tight..."

Courtney and I exchanged amused looks as Maddie continued,

"With a rucksack instead of a backpack. Looks like he's fresh off an army post or on his way to lumberjack training...I'd say—that truck."

We stared at her rather than the truck, Courtney giggling and me struggling to suppress my grin. Maddie blushed scarlet and tucked her dark hair behind her ears as she smiled, too. "So maybe I read a lot of mystery novels..."

I bit my lip to keep from laughing. "And *what's* high and tight?"

Maddie dissolved into embarrassed giggles. "His hair! My dad's a vet...Mom always cut his hair. That's what they called it."

Courtney burst out laughing. Her laughter was infectious. Maddison giggled, and I snickered.

Suddenly, a shadow passed over my window.

The three of us turned sharply, the laughter caught in our throats in tiny gasps. A guy stood in front of my window, staring into the car.

Before I could react, Courtney blared the horn, sending Maddie and me jumping in our seats, as she yelled, "*Peter Blanchard, you scared the crap out of me!*"

The boy flashed a brilliant smile that set off the dimples in his cheeks. He doubled over with whoops of laughter as he opened my door for me.

"Hey, we haven't met...I'm Peter." He smiled easily at me as he leaned his arm over the roof of the car and ducked his head inside.

"Yes, Seraphina, this is Peter, my knucklehead of a baby brother." Courtney tried to glare at him, but I could see a smile fighting its way onto her face. She shoved her door open and flipped the seat for Maddie.

"Hey, Peter!" Maddie smiled as she hopped out with her, and they made their way around the car.

I got out, too, slinging Phoenix's backpack back on my shoulder.

"I missed you in class, Maddie... Jeez, Court, you've only been back a few weeks and already you're a bad influence." Peter shook his head in mock disapproval, and Courtney gave him a shove, still fighting a smile.

I watched with growing amusement. They looked so similar, both beautiful and blonde with an obvious goodness inside that made them even more so. The only difference between them was their height. Peter was a good inch or two shorter than Courtney. A warmth filled my heart at the sight of them. You could tell how much they cared about each other. It was sweet and made my heart ache ever so slightly at the same time. I pushed thoughts of Phoenix out of my head and tried to follow the conversation.

"We aren't cutting class...it's a mental health break due to hazing." Courtney sniffed haughtily.

Peter's face fell a bit, and he nodded toward me. "Yeah, I heard...Cole's actually looking for you—"

I glanced at my watch. Jinx it. School got out twenty minutes ago. "Can I borrow a phone?" My cheeks burned with embarrassment. What kind of teenager didn't have a phone?

Without any hesitation or awkwardness, Peter pulled his out of his back pocket and started to tap on the screen, before passing it to me with a lopsided grin. "It's already dialing."

"Careful, Peter has a thing for tall girls..." Courtney muttered behind her hand.

Peter made a face at Courtney, and I bit my lip on a laugh as Cole's voice sounded in my ear. "Hey—"

I cut him off before he mistook me for Peter. "Cole, it's me... I'm so sorry. I totally lost track of time!"

"No worries. I see you've met Peter—where are you guys?"

I glanced at the coffeehouse. "We're at Hallowed Grounds, but I'll be—"

"Say no more. We'll be right there."

"Are you sure—?"

"Goodbye, Phin," Cole said with a smile in his voice.

I passed the phone to Peter, and he locked the screen before tucking it back into his pocket.

"Well, now that that's all settled...shall we head in for a cup?" Peter inclined his head toward the building.

"Fine...but you're paying this time." Courtney glanced back at me with a sly smile. "We'll save some seats upstairs..."

Apparently, Courtney hadn't given up on her spying game.

"But you always want a spot by the fireplace." Peter held the door open for us, and we filed in. "Why do you—"

Courtney rolled her eyes and pushed Peter toward the counter. "Just get us a hot chocolate, a French Vanilla, my usual, and a big bag of salted maple cookies." She turned back to Maddie and me with a smirk as she added, "You know Cole's going to bring Rachel...but if he doesn't, maybe he'll bring the whole basketball team with him."

Laughing, we followed as Courtney led us up the stairs. I gripped the banister and tried to be as gentle with my steps as possible, but the wood still creaked ever so slightly underneath our weight. The upstairs was the same as down, but instead of a fireplace it had a desk with an ancient computer on top, and the back wall was lined with bookshelves instead of a coffee bar. The three of us glanced around, looking for the stalker guy—Logan? But there were only four kids, seniors by the look of them, lounging in the plush chairs next to the two tall windows facing the parking lot.

Maddie and I exchanged glances as Courtney headed over to one of the kids. "Izzie, where'd that cute guy go? I saw him head up here..."

"Fire escape boy?" the guy beside Izzie asked with a smirk.

Izzie snickered, nodding toward a door beside the bookshelves. "Yeah, he came up here...but left just as quick down the fire escape."

Courtney looked at me, eyes wide in disbelief that matched my own.

"Why would he do that?" I demanded, almost panicked by the bizarre idea. I leaned over toward the window to check the parking lot. The truck was gone.

The second guy spoke then. "The only time I've headed for the fire escape was to ditch my ex-girlfriend."

"Thanks, guys," Courtney mumbled, before wrapping her arms around Maddie and me and leading us away toward a group of chairs encircling a coffee table. We all sank into chairs with bemused expressions on our faces.

"Why would he do that?" I repeated.

"He said it…" Maddie murmured softly.

Courtney and I looked at her, waiting for her to explain. She cleared her throat and glanced awkwardly at me. "That kid was ditching his ex… Well, maybe Logan was ditching you, Seraphina."

STALKER BOI

By the time Cole showed up with Rachel, the whole place was packed with kids. Apparently, Hallowed Grounds was The Place to Be after school. There was an old jukebox in the far corner upstairs, and some kids were flipping through the CDs for a song. Courtney left us to go hang out with a few of her senior girlfriends in a huddle with Izzie and Fire Escape Boy at the window. Then Maddie got a call from her mom, and her face fell, reminding me of the time I ran into her in the lobby. She forced a smile as she got up to leave and said she'd catch us tomorrow. She wouldn't be boarding tonight.

The rest of us sank into chairs around the coffee table, munching on cookies and sipping from mugs, as we all settled into easy conversation. It'd been awhile since Cole, Rachel, and I had all hung out as a group, and in the warmth of the cozy, crowded coffeehouse, I was grateful. The only difference was, instead of Phoenix, there was Peter, and if you asked me, that was a welcome change to the group dynamic.

"So, why'd you stop homeschooling?" Peter put his mug down on the coffee table with a smirk. "A friend of mine homeschools, and she wouldn't be caught dead in a classroom."

I had to laugh. "My sister feels the same." I took a deep drink from my coffee, wishing I hadn't brought her up. I glanced at Rachel as she stared moodily into her mug. Did she feel that same twist of guilt in her stomach that I did? Or worse, was she wishing Phoenix was here instead of me?

"So, why don't you?" Peter prompted with his easy smile and a shake of his head, tossing his golden hair out of his eyes.

I cleared my throat as I took another quick sip. "I just needed a change, I guess."

"Hey, I'm not complaining..." Peter gave me a sly wink.

Cole smacked him with a chair pillow, and Peter laughed.

Before I could even think of what to say to that, Courtney came over with her friends in tow. She bit her lip on her smile as she stood over me. "Seraphina...some of the girls were wondering if you'd read for them...tarot, I mean...just for fun?"

My eyes widened as my heart stuttered in my chest. I looked from her to the girls gathered behind her. Were they making fun of me?

Morgan pushed her way through the group with an excited grin. "Fun or not, I'd totally pay for a reading!"

I glanced at Cole, who gave me an encouraging smile and an easy shrug.

"Uhh..." I looked up at Courtney as I nibbled on my lip.

Morgan bounced a bit. "Pleaseee. I love this stuff!"

I glanced at Morgan. Her excitement was infectious. I had to smile. "I guess. But just for fun...and no charge."

Courtney beamed and waved the rest of the girls toward the coffee table. They all took seats on the floor, leaning against the chair legs and facing me expectantly.

I swallowed thickly. My mouth had gone dry. I took another sip of coffee, highly aware of their eyes. I put my mug down and unzipped Phoenix's bag. I pulled out her tarot satchel and slid out the cards.

They were smooth and creamy beneath my fingers. It was the

ardor deck. One of Phoenix's favorites. Gingerly, I shuffled them overhanded, one after the other, watching them as they moved through my hands. Dozens of eyes on me, a swell of satisfaction filled my chest and an overwhelming confidence. It wasn't like at home. I was the expert here. And though I didn't have the touch, and no magic dust covered the cards, and no magically divine knowledge would appear before me in the spread, I did know the meaning of each card by heart—and that was more than anyone else here could say.

But I also knew that to use Phoenix's cards—to *touch* her cards—was wrong, and my stomach knotted uncomfortably with the guilt.

I shouldn't have taken them out.

I knew better.

Brow furrowed, I looked up at Courtney.

"Who's first?"

It was dark when I got home—again. I didn't bother looking for Fawn. I knew she'd be back at Grammy's already. So, I hung up Phoenix's bag on the hook and went straight to my room. I pushed open the door, and Icarus blinked at me from her bed.

"Phoenix isn't happy."

I rolled my eyes. I did not have the energy, nor the time to deal with Phoenix. "Is she ever these days?"

A loud bang vibrated through the cottage walls.

And then another.

I flinched at the noise. "What the hex was that?"

Icarus blinked calmly back at me.

"Phoenix?" I rolled my eyes. Shaking my head, I looked around the room for my school bag. I still had assignments to finish. It wasn't by my bed where I'd left it. "Icarus...where's my backpack? I forgot it here this morning...and it wasn't on the hook. Where—"

Another bang. Icarus didn't answer. Instead, he flicked his tail and hopped down from the bed, padding lightly out into the hall.

"PHOENIX!" I tore from the bedroom. It wasn't in the living room. I stomped into the kitchen.

There. My backpack. It was on the table...gutted; its contents were strewn all over. My nails dug into my palms as I stared at the mess of my stuff everywhere.

There was another loud bang like a gunshot just outside. I shoved open the back door and stomped out onto the deck.

The moon was high in the bruised purple sky, illuminating the fields beyond our property, but leaving most of Grey Cottage and the surrounding woods in shadow. The only real light came from the fire pit, where Phoenix stood, apparently practicing a new spell. Her face glowed in the firelight as the flames vanished almost as quickly as they had appeared. Then, in the twilight, she aimed her wand again at the empty pit.

"Surprised you came back," she muttered coolly, not bothering to look up.

There was another loud bang. Light shot from the tip of her wand and hit the pit with a small burst of fire that again disappeared as quickly as it'd come.

I glared at her from the deck and pointed furiously at the door. "What in the hex did you do to my stuff?!"

Phoenix didn't answer. She fired another shot into the pit.

I winced at the sound despite myself. "Unlike you, I actually have homework, Phoenix! Projects, exams, essays to do! I have important stuff in there!"

Phoenix looked up. Her eyes glittered in the dark. "You sure wouldn't want to lose all those boarding forms you've collected."

My breathing came heavy from pent-up hostility. "What?" I snapped.

Phoenix stabbed her wand through her top knot and stomped up the steps, shoving past me into the kitchen. I stalked inside after her and slammed the door behind me. She snatched up a stack of papers from the table and threw it into my chest with such magical force the papers burst apart on contact and flew all over the kitchen.

"Too bad Mama's not here to sign these."

"You don't have any right to go through my stuff," I hissed through gritted teeth and falling permission slips.

"Were you even going to tell me?" Phoenix demanded, her nostrils flaring. "Or was your plan to have Grammy sign it and just not come back at all?"

"You know, you really need to stop nosing into other people's business, Phoenix. Your little keyhole habit is going to get you into trouble one of these days."

"That's not an answer."

I threw up my hands. "For Fay's sake, Phoenix! I wasn't going to board, okay? There was a mix-up at the office, and the woman gave me some just in case."

"Don't try to tell me you didn't think about it..." Phoenix's eyes were murderous. As though the mere thought were a betrayal.

I laughed in her face. "Fine. I did think about it. I've thought about it all week. But I wasn't going to even *bother* asking."

"Why not?" The challenge in Phoenix's voice pushed me over the edge.

"You think Mama or Grammy would let me leave poor, precious Phoenix alone? Fay forbid I'm not here to hold your hand!"

"I don't need anyone around me who doesn't want to be."

"Well, I guess that explains why you're alone all day," I quipped nastily. I heard the words as she did, and I wished I could take them back.

Phoenix flinched as though I'd slapped her. She shook her head. Disgust marred her normally happy face. "You know what, go ahead...I don't care anymore." She flicked her finger at a fallen form and caught it in her hand. Then she took her thumb and slid it across the page, leaving a trail of orange glitter that disappeared as quickly as it'd appeared, before placing it gingerly on the table. Mama's signature was looped neatly on the paper in blood-red ink. "There."

My nostrils flared.

I wanted to scream at her.

Tell her I wasn't going to board at the stupid school.

But Mama's signature, forged so perfectly on the page, made me hesitate. And before I could argue, Phoenix snapped her fingers and all the papers, including the one with Mama's name, flew into a neat pile. The books and notebooks stacked themselves, and everything tucked itself tidily back into my bag and the zipper slid shut.

Then, without another word to me, Phoenix left the kitchen, yanking her backpack off the hook by the front door as I stopped in the kitchen doorway.

"Where are you going?" I demanded, my eyes hot from unshed tears.

"Don't pretend to care now, Seraphina." And with that, Phoenix slammed the door behind her, disappearing into the night.

I couldn't sleep. Again.

I tossed and turned all night.

And Phoenix never came home.

To top it off, I missed the bus. I knew it as soon as I made it to the gas station. I double-checked my watch. I'd missed it by minutes. My speed slowed to a defeated trudge. I came to a stop by the curb and watched the cars rush past on the highway heading toward the ferry. I ran a hand through my wind-swept hair and turned to survey the cars coming in and out of the parking lot.

What was I going to do? I couldn't call the cottage...Phoenix wasn't home. Call Cole? Make him drive out just to bring me back in? I frowned as a car barreled past a little too close. I could feel the island eyes watching me from every vehicle. I gripped the strap of my backpack on my shoulder and headed inside the gas station. As I passed through the glass doors, out of the corner of my eye, I noticed a guy leaning against a truck bed watching me. With a start, I recognized him...it was Logan.

I quickened my pace and headed for the back of the general store, my heart stuttering. Why was he always staring at me like that? And why was I so nervous? I went to the coffee bar and fixed myself a foam cup, half hot chocolate and half black French Vanilla as I tried to think. The bells clanged on the storefront door. I flinched and spilled my coffee down the side of the cup as I attached the lid. I glanced toward the door just in time to see Logan enter the store. I ducked a bit behind a shelf of boxed pasta and peeked over the top of it. I couldn't see him. I hurried toward the cashier's counter to pay for my coffee.

"Keep the change," I mumbled as I pulled out a few crumpled bills from my jeans pocket and left the store. I had no plan. I was literally stranded on an island. And I was hiding from some guy, who might or might not be stalking me. Then I spied the payphone off to the side of the building and hurried over to it, digging my hand deeper into my pocket. Only bills. Jinx it. I should've taken my change. Groaning, I dropped my bag to my feet and, holding my coffee up in one hand, I bent down to rummage through my bag with the other. Nothing. Not a single coin.

"Great," I muttered.

"You need to call someone?" drawled a voice behind me.

I flinched. My muscles tightened, ready to run. I glanced back at the owner of the voice as I zipped my backpack. The hairs on my arms stood on end as goose bumps ran down the length of them.

A lanky man towered over me as I crouched, the weak morning light at his back casting him in shadow. He looked more skeleton than man, with his sunken face, and loose, ashen skin. His eyes seemed to pop from his skull as though there wasn't enough meat on his bones to keep them in place. My nostrils flared. He stunk of alcohol.

"No. Thanks. I'm okay." I tried to smile as I stood hastily to my feet.

"You're Charlotte's girl, ern't ya? You look just like 'er." The man grinned and inched closer.

Too close. I moved away. My back bumped into the plastic siding of the store. I tried to step to the side and grab my bag off the ground, but he moved with me, blocking me.

"I went to school with her for a time...her and Alice, both..."

I didn't answer. My mind racing, I couldn't process what was happening.

He licked his thin lips. "I have a phone you can use...it's in my car."

My heart pounded loudly in my ears. "Uh, no. I don't need—"

"Come on." He stepped closer to me as though he might grab me.

Instinctively, I held my Styrofoam cup out between us and dropped it. It burst open over his ratty old sneakers, splashing his feet and ankles with scalding coffee.

The man jumped back, cursing underneath his breath.

I snatched up my backpack and hurried around him and back to the glass doors, only to come face-to-face with Logan. I froze, eyes wide.

"Problem?" he asked, his eyes narrowed.

I inhaled sharply, my words caught in my throat.

"Nah," drawled the oily voice behind me. "Just offering Miss Grey a phone..."

Logan pulled a flip phone out of his utility jacket and tossed it to me. I caught it in both hands. Just barely. I gripped it tight in my hand. "Looks like she's got one to me. And you look like you need some new pants...why don't you do yourself a favor and go find some."

Logan stared hard just behind me, watching the man, but I

didn't dare turn around. His eyes still staring past my face, Logan said softly, "You need a new coffee. Come on." He jutted his head toward the glass doors.

I hazarded a backward glance to see the gaunt, lanky creep leering at me with pale, beady eyes.

I didn't need to be invited twice. Logan held open the door, and I hurried inside. We walked side by side in silence until we made it to the coffee bar in the back.

"Thanks." I tried to hand him his phone, but he didn't take it.

Instead, he raised an eyebrow as he reached for an empty coffee cup. "You didn't call anyone yet."

My face burned as my heart continued to pound, now from embarrassment rather than mortal terror. "Oh."

I flipped it open and punched in Cole's number.

"I gotta say, you've got good aim...but next time, I wouldn't rely on a cup of coffee to save the day..."

My face flushed, and I gripped the phone to my ear. As I listened to it ring, I frowned, thoughtfully taking in the sight of Logan surveying the coffee machine, a hand in his pocket and a surly, impatient expression on his face. I was tall, towering over most girls and meeting most guys at eye level, if not higher. He was a good two inches taller than me, but he wasn't scrawny or thin. He was strong and built, which was weird for a high school kid. Maybe he was in college? No. Maddie had said he was in her classes. He must work out a lot...but he didn't seem like a gym kind of guy. He was dressed like he was about to go cut down trees or something else outdoorsy. What was it Maddie had said? Lumberjack training? His olive-green jacket was pulled over an open flannel shirt, which was layered on top of a soft black T-shirt, so I couldn't tell whether he had muscles, but based on his broad shoulders, I'd bet that he did.

He looked unlike any of the guys at school. He had a distinct rugged, military look about him. Maybe it was his hair. Maddie said it was a military cut...tall and tight...or whatever. It looked good, anyway. His face was handsome, full of sharp angles, and his striking green eyes were narrow above his high cheekbones. But his forehead had a row of creases in it, like he was in a constant state of curiosity or concerned about something.

"Hello?"

I winced at Cole's voice in my ear. My face burned, and I dropped my gaze. I'd been blatantly staring at the guy.

"Cole? It's me—"

"Phin? Are you okay? Whose phone are you using?"

Logan held the coffee cup up toward me. "What's your poison?"

I blinked rapidly as I struggled to listen to Cole and understand what Logan was asking at the same time.

"Who's that?" Cole demanded.

"Uhh...just this guy—half French Vanilla, half hot chocolate...please," I added hastily, so flustered I barely remembered my manners.

The guy snickered. "Witch's Brew...how fitting."

I gaped at him as he put the cup under the nozzle and started up the machine. "Excuse me?"

He smirked without looking up. He punched the hot chocolate button, humming quietly to himself.

"Phin!"

"Sorry, Cole—"

Logan chuckled.

I scowled at him and waved him away, turning my back to him so I could concentrate. I cleared my throat. "Sorry, Cole—I'm calling because I missed the bus. I was hoping you could give me a ride—unless you know someone on the island who could...I hate to have you drive back and forth..."

"It's not a problem. The Corner Stone?"

"Yeah...I'll be outside by the picnic tables. Thanks, Cole."

"Happy to do it."

I shut the phone and turned back to Logan. "Thanks for that..."

He slapped a top on the coffee and passed it to me. I took the cup and tried to hand him his phone, but he shook his head.

"Keep it."

"What?" I cocked an incredulous eyebrow. He couldn't be serious.

"You seem to need it more than me. It's just a spare." He shrugged. "It's good until the end of the month...take it or toss it. It's up to you." With that, he pushed past me to leave.

I grabbed his arm, holding him back. "Wait, you're giving me a cell phone—just *because*? How does that make sense? You don't even know me."

He raised an eyebrow at my hand on his arm. I released him quickly, face hot with embarrassment.

"I've watched you enough these past few days to know you well enough. And I gotta say, your little Samantha the Teenage Witch act is pretty good...but if I find out you're messing with things you shouldn't—and I mean *anything*—I won't hesitate to grab the quicksilver. Remember that."

My eyes narrowed. "What is that supposed to mean?"

He kept walking.

I hurried to keep up with him. "Wait—"

He didn't. "See you around, Sam."

He slapped a five-dollar bill on the cashier's counter, pointed a finger at me, and then gave the cashier a curt nod, as he headed outside. The bells clanged against the door behind him.

And I stood there, staring after him, coffee cup in one hand, cell phone in the other, feeling extremely flummoxed.

"So, what happened?"

"Phoenix happened," I muttered, staring down at the phone in my hands.

"Explain," Cole replied patiently as he drove the van up the ramp of the ferry and parked.

I sighed. "We had a fight, and she left. She didn't come home all night. So, of course I couldn't sleep...then I had to run all the way to the Corner Stone. Then this creepy old guy tried to kidnap me—"

"What?" Cole looked at me sharply.

"I'm exaggerating, but—" I rolled my eyes and stared out over the lake as the ferry began to move. "It was definitely harassment... he tried to tell me he knew my mom." I made a face. "Then this guy from school showed up and gave me his phone." I held up the phone for Cole to see.

He opened his mouth and shut it again. "Wait—a guy *gave* you his phone? Like to keep?"

I nodded sullenly. "He said he'd been watching me."

"Watching you," Cole repeated flatly. He ran a hand through his hair as he thought it over.

"I know. Freaky, right? This is the first time I've even spoken to him...I don't even know his name, for sure...Maddie said it's Logan and that he just started boarding at Martin House. Have you—"

Cole shook his head. "I haven't seen anyone new. But Martin House is a crash pad. Guys come and go all the time without drawing attention. Did you check the phone?"

I nodded again. "Nothing identifiable from what I could tell... You know I'm no cell phone expert. But no saved contacts. No pictures saved. It's empty."

"Check the call log." Cole jutted his chin toward the phone as he shifted the van back in drive.

I flipped it open and tapped the buttons, pulling up the call history. "Well, this is something..."

Cole glanced down at the phone and back at the road.

"There's only one call. Placed Monday afternoon." I looked up at Cole. "He called my house."

SERA, WE'RE GOIN DOWN

Cole wanted to call Phoenix.

He'd argued with me about it the whole way to school. But I told him I'd take care of it. Made him promise not to say anything. But honestly, I didn't know how to handle it. It's not like I could get Phoenix on the phone and ask her about my stalker from school. She might get paranoid, overreact, and tell Mama or Grammy. The last thing I wanted was for a misunderstanding to land me back at Grey Cottage, stuck watching Phoenix play with her wand all day.

But, on the other hand, what if Logan had actually talked to Phoenix? Maybe *she* told him to follow me? The thought almost made me laugh because it was so insane. For that to happen, Phoenix would actually need to socialize...and she didn't. There's no way she knew Logan any better than I did, if at all.

The phone was heavy in the pocket of my jeans, just as the call to my house was heavy on my mind. I hadn't used it yet. I couldn't even begin to analyze why he would give me a phone. All my energy was focused on the fact that he had called my house on my first day of school.

I was so distracted, at lunch I sat down at our table without having gotten any food. By the time I'd gone through the line and grabbed a carton of fries, Aubrey was waiting for me. Wordlessly, I took a seat beside her.

"Hey!" Her face lit up at the sight of me but fell as she studied my face. "Are you okay?"

I ran my fingers through my hair, squinting as I massaged my temples. "Yeah, I'm just tired...a lot on my mind."

Aubrey laid a light hand on my shoulder. "Sera, I'm your friend. Tell me."

I sighed. "I was late to catch the bus and ran into Logan—remember that guy you saw staring at me yesterday?"

Aubrey nodded slowly as she scrunched up her face to remember. "Okay...what happened?"

I shrugged, struggling with how to find words that would make sense...and not make me sound paranoid. "He's giving me a weird vibe...I keep seeing him everywhere, like he's—"

"Stalking you?" Aubrey's hand squeezed my shoulder tightly.

"I don't know... Yeah, but not like he's trying to hurt me...like —" I bit my lip as I considered how to explain.

Aubrey's face relaxed, and she nudged me playfully. "Like he likes you?"

I shook my head and blurted out the thing that'd been bothering me most all day. "It feels like he's watching me—in case I do something wrong." And hadn't he said as much this morning?

Aubrey's eyes narrowed. She glanced around the cafeteria as she fingered her locket. "Have you seen him since you got to school?"

I craned my neck to scan the cafeteria. "Usually I see him here, though. He has D lunch with us on A days."

"Okay, next time you see him..." Aubrey trailed off as a group of girls I recognized from the coffeehouse huddled almost shyly in front of the table.

"Hey, Seraphina...we were all wondering if you're planning on heading to Hallowed Grounds after school..."

Aubrey raised an eyebrow at me, a smile twitching at the corner of her mouth.

"Uhh..."

Aubrey looped her arm through mine and pulled me into a sideways hug. "Yup. She'll be there!"

The leader of the group smiled, clearly relieved. She gave a little wave. "See you later, Seraphina..." And with that, they hurried away.

"What was that about?" Aubrey released me with a gentle push.

"After Daphne...well, Courtney took me Hallowed Grounds for a pick-me-up, and we kind of drew a crowd."

Aubrey laughed. "I'm glad to see you're finally coming into your own around here! Seraphina Grey *should* be the most popular girl in school."

My cheeks burned. "It's nice to have friends...but sometimes I get the feeling they all just want to gawk at the freak of Nile...you know?"

There was a flash of brilliant red hair in the corner of my eye as Cheryl plopped down in the seat to my right. "Hey, Sera!" Her bubbly expression softened as she looked at Aubrey. "How are you doing, Aubrey?"

I forced a smile. It was hard to focus on trivial high school things when my mind was still wrapped up in the mystery of Logan. "What's up?"

"I just wanted to see if you are going to the football game tomorrow night? Amber wanted me to ask...she and Taylor thought it'd be good for you to scc us in action..."

Confusion clouded my face, and she added hesitantly, "You know, before tryouts on Saturday...and then we can all meet at Aubrey's for the sleepover after the game..."

"Oh, right! I totally forgot about tryouts." I looked at Aubrey. "You want to go to the game with me?"

Aubrey nodded with a small smile.

I turned back to Cheryl. "I'll be there." I gave her a reassuring smile, and she bounced away.

Aubrey glanced sideways at me. "You don't have to try out, you know."

I sighed heavily. "I know, but Rachel really wanted me to do it with her…"

Aubrey shrugged as the bell rang. I winced and scooped up my bag and uneaten fries.

"If you see that guy, text me…" Aubrey gave me a light hug. "I'll see you at Hallowed Grounds." Then she disappeared into the crowd of migrating students, before I could remind her that I didn't have a phone…but then I realized, I kind of did.

I met Rachel and Cole in the courtyard outside school. Rachel had already changed into her cheer uniform and was shivering a bit in the cold autumn air.

"Do you guys want to stop at Hallowed Grounds? I told Aubrey I'd meet her there…"

"I can't. Cheer practice." Rachel waved a hand at her outfit with a small smirk. "But I'll see you tomorrow? And you're going to the game, right?"

"Of course! I can't wait to see you do your thing." I grinned as I gave her a sideways squeeze, and she headed down the sidewalk toward the Essex Field down the road.

Cole led me to the van, which, with its fiery phoenix paint job, was impossible to miss.

"Did you talk to Nix?" Cole asked nonchalantly as we neared the van.

I scrunched up my face at the question, wincing a bit with my guilt. "Nooo."

Cole chuckled. "I knew you wouldn't."

We hopped in the van, and he started it up. Alice in Chains blasted on the radio. "You know I'm just worried about you,

Phin. I'm not trying to nag you or anything...it's just...it's weird."

I groaned. "I know. I know."

"Well? Why didn't you ask her about the call?"

I stared moodily out the window as we headed out of the parking lot and down a side street toward the coffeehouse. "I'll talk to her tonight."

"That's all I'm saying..." Cole nodded appreciatively. There was a pause and then he glanced at me out of the corner of his eye. "I've been looking into it a little bit..."

I looked at Cole with a small smile. "You're the best, St. Claire. You know that, right?"

Cole rolled his eyes as a little pinkish tinge colored his cheeks. "His name is Logan *DeVarney*...he dorms at Martin House, like you said. I haven't seen him there much...like once all week. No idea when he moved in."

"He's boarding in your dorm? How did you not notice someone move in?" I scoffed, torn between amusement and irritation.

"I don't pay attention to new guys. Half the time, it fluctuates. A guy'll board, then he'll stay home, then he'll move back in...I told you, Martin House is like a crash pad with a revolving door." Cole shrugged. "Anyways, after you told me you ran into him at the Corner Stone, I figured Maddison had it right. He had to be a Nile dude. So, I headed back to Martin House during lunch to check. His name is on the sign-in sheet in the office."

A mixture of nerves and excitement flooded my veins with every quick pump of my heart. "Who's his roommate?"

"He doesn't have one...unless someone else moved in, and I didn't notice them, either..." Cole pulled into Hallowed Grounds and shoved the van into park. But before he got out, he lowered the music and looked at me.

My forehead crinkled with amused curiosity at the sight of Cole's serious face. My hand froze on the door handle. "What?"

Cole shrugged. "I'm worried about you."

I wrinkled my nose. "Cole, that guy—I don't think you have anything to—"

Cole smiled and rolled his eyes. "I'm talking about you and Phoenix."

My face fell. I glared out the window, watching the kids file steadily into Hallowed Grounds. "If we don't hurry, we won't get good seats..."

"Phin—"

I groaned. "Cole, I don't want to talk about this right now, okay? I have more important things to worry about—"

"Are you inviting her to the football game tomorrow?"

"What?" I looked at him sharply. "Why would I do that? Phoenix doesn't want anything to do with—"

"What is going on with you guys?" Cole's voice was hard with impatience, uncharacteristic of his easy, laid-back charm.

I studied his face, searching his dark eyes. "Listen, Cole, you don't have to take this on. Phoenix and I will figure it out...it's just been hard since..." I couldn't finish. The lump in my throat was suffocating.

"I know." Cole nodded sympathetically. He rubbed the back of his neck as he struggled to find words. "I know—I can't imagine how it's been for you, but God, Phin...when was the last time you even saw *Fawn*?"

I blinked as my eyes blurred. I sat back in my seat, staring straight ahead.

He'd hit a nerve, and he knew it, but he kept going. "I mean..." He shook his head and waved his arm toward Hallowed Grounds. "Why are you here, meeting up with a girl you've known less than a week, instead of stopping by your grandmother's to check on your baby sister?"

My eyes burned. Enough. That was enough. I shook my head, tilting my chin to hold back the tears. "Just because they don't want any friends doesn't mean I don't want any."

Cole cocked an eyebrow. "And what am I?"

"I'm allowed to have friends who don't include my *twin*." I spat the word out nastily. "I'm allowed to have a *life* that doesn't include my twin." Without waiting for his response, without daring to look at his face, I wrenched open the van door. "Don't bother waiting, Cole. I'll find another ride home."

"Wait—Phin!"

I slammed the door on his words and stomped toward the front door. The van door creaked open and slammed. Cole caught up with me before I made it to the front steps.

He pulled me toward him. "Oi, Phin, listen."

"What?" I rounded on him. A single tear leaked down my cheek. I pushed it away with the heel of my hand as two senior girls turned their noses up at our drama and hurried past us, up the steps, and into the coffeehouse. My cheeks burned despite the cold. I stared past him, eyes glaring at the beautiful red and gold leaves on the trees all around us. I crossed my arms, hugging myself against the wind.

"I'm sorry I said anything, okay?" Cole said earnestly. "You're right. And I'll stay out of it...let you two figure it out on your own. It just—it hurts to see you both falling apart like this."

I inhaled sharply, nostrils flaring. I looked down at him and my anger faded in the face of his sincerity, at his soulful dark eyes and his full lips in a gentle frown. He was like a gorgeous puppy dog. Impossible to hate. I nodded, conceding his admission.

Cole's face broke into a sly sideways smile, and he gave me a little shove. "I love you, Phin, you know that right? Don't hate me for caring." He wrapped his arm around me in a tight, one-armed hug, as he escorted me up the steps.

"You love Phoenix more..." I muttered, only half joking.

"Get inside, you nerd." Cole shoved me away from him, and I laughed.

· · ·

The next day at school, all anyone could talk about was the football game. Apparently, the rivalry between Mater Christi and Ethan Allen High was a huge deal, and the excitement humming in every classroom was palpable and contagious. Kids were loud and rowdy and itching for dismissal. And it was kind of funny to see: a bunch of teenagers with ants in their pants waiting for each bell.

Things had changed for me since the run-in with Daphne in the cafeteria. I was no longer the freak of the Nile, to be whispered about and stared at. Now I was Seraphina Grey, the cool girl from Nile, who'll read your tarot spread for fun. At least, almost everywhere I went. It wasn't until study hall that I remembered what it felt like to be the freak of Nile.

Aubrey and I were walking down the hall toward my classroom, when we were stopped by the sheepdog, Brentley, and some other boys I only knew by sight. They were all dressed up, with long ties tight at their necks. Half of them looked like they'd struggled to dress themselves, with no one to show them how to tie a tie. They were football players, anxious for the game, and looking for trouble.

My heart began to pound, and my eyes darted around, looking for a path through their group, which seemed to be clogging up the entire hallway: guys leaning against lockers, guys with arms crossed standing in the walkway, and Brentley in front, flipping his shaggy hair and smirking.

"Ahhh, it's the Witch Spawn..." Brentley stepped toward us, and together Aubrey and I stepped back.

Aubrey, her arm laced through mine, pulled me tightly to her, rigid and sensing danger.

A guy with buzzed hair pushed off the lockers and came at us from the side. He tugged on his tie, loosening it so it dangled wide around his neck.

Aubrey sidestepped, yanking me behind her tiny frame as he leaned toward us. The stink of his body spray burned my nose.

He smiled wolfishly as he looked from me to his buddies.

"We've been hearing a lot about you this week, and we were wondering—"

Another guy pushed off the lockers and stood next to me. "What will it take for you to go full on *Carrie*?"

They were circling us as curious students parted around the perimeter like the lake circles the island. Aubrey and I tried to push between them, but the wolfish guy lunged for me. He tugged his tie over my head and yanked my neck back, so his mouth was at my ear. "My old man said they used to string up Greys on Bird Island...but then they'd always come back. No matter how long they swung. So, that's when the burnings started."

"Michael! Stop!" Aubrey shrieked. "Let her go!"

He'd only held me for so long because I'd been so stunned. Shocked. Humiliated. It only took me a moment to remember myself. And when I did, my silver eyes flashed as my blood hissed like fire in my heart, igniting every nerve in my body. I snatched the tie off my throat and whipped it at his face. The smack cracked loudly in the hallway as the tie left an angry red welt across his face.

There were loud whoops and laughs from the boys, but they all backed up a pace, as I rounded on them all. My eyes narrowed. I would not let them see me cry.

"Oh, Mikey, here she goes..." Brentley nudged Michael, who held a hand over his face as he laughed.

I stepped toward them slowly. The closer I got, the smaller they seemed. I towered over Brentley by several inches. "If either of you come near me again—I will put a curse on you so dark it'll make your blood run cold, set your skin on fire, and scar you for life."

Michael's laughter died. Brentley's smirk flickered underneath the weight of my stare. I put my hands on his shoulders and shoved him back. Then I forced my way through them, Aubrey hurrying to keep up. As we moved past the tangle of kids who'd gathered to witness the fight, I locked eyes with Logan, who was leaning against the lockers, his arms crossed against his chest, watching me.

For some reason, the sight of him triggered my tears, and they streamed freely down my cheeks, as I shoved and weaved around the kids. A few of the guys called after me. Would they chase me? My anger faded into fear. Primal and ancestral. And I was running by the time I got to the corner. I cut down the hallway and didn't stop. My backpack slammed against my back with each step.

I ran from the school, burst through the double doors, and out into the courtyard. Then I stopped and dropped onto a stone bench. The cold air burned my lungs. I bent over my knees and covered my face in my hands, hiding my tear-stained face. Thoughts raced faster than my heart as I tried to steady my breathing. I barely noticed Aubrey take a tentative seat beside me. I'd known about Bird Island, of course...everyone did. But for him to bring it up, to shove it in my face. For him to grab my throat—

I took a shaky breath as I pushed the tears back with the heels of my hands. I dried my face and nose with my sleeve.

"Are you okay, Sera?" Aubrey put a gentle hand on my shoulder.

I sniffed and stared blankly out at the trees and parking lot across the road. "I'm fine."

"Are you sure you still want to go to the game tonight?"

I nodded grimly. "I told Cheryl I would, and Rachel's excited for me to go, so..."

Aubrey gave me a rueful smile. "You know, Rachel would understand if you changed your mind..."

I shook my head. "I'm not going to let them scare me." A wave of shame crashed over me. I had already, though, hadn't I?

"I'm sorry that happened to you," Aubrey murmured softly, her eyes downcast. "I told Daphne if she gave you trouble tonight, I'd tell Father LaValley about her stealing test answers from the office. She's already got one strike against her...she does *not* want another. Plus," Aubrey added with a sly smile. "You scared her pretty good with that curse bag thing of yours."

I laughed despite myself.

Aubrey wrapped her arm around me and gave me a squeeze. "It'll get better. I promise."

The bell rang throughout the courtyard as a few students hurried inside from the parking lot. I glanced at Aubrey. "You'd better get to class."

Aubrey shook her head. "Not if you don't."

I sighed heavily. "Fair enough." And the two of us headed inside, each of us going our separate ways toward our classrooms.

We all planned to meet at Hallowed Grounds before the football game and then the girls attending the sleepover would walk to Aubrey's dad's house afterward. But we weren't the only ones with that plan. It seemed like the entire school had stuffed itself into Hallowed Grounds in preparation for the football game. Different groups and cliques were huddled together all over the place in a similar fashion to the cafeteria.

Thankfully, Courtney had arrived early and saved as many seats as she could manage by the fireplace. Maddie, Aubrey, and Morgan sank into chairs, while Cheryl and Rachel were herded upstairs by the rest of the cheerleading squad. But Cole and Peter were able to detangle themselves from the rest of the basketball team and sat with us girls, despite the hoots and whistles that followed them.

Cole took out his guitar at Courtney's request and began to play a Sum 41 guitar riff. I fought a smile as I noticed every girl within hearing distance flicked her eyes toward Cole to watch him with a little smile on her face. For a second, I thought of Phoenix and what she would do if she caught them drooling over him. My smile faded quickly. I didn't want to think about Phoenix.

Peter got everyone's order and left to grab us coffees and cookies, his golden head disappearing in the throng of students. The noise was loud and boisterous with that same early morning excitement, amplified by the impending game. And when the door opened and the football team filed in, they were met with cheers and applause as though they'd already won. I looked away quickly, scowling despite myself.

Cole read my face instantly. He slapped his guitar strings still and leaned over to me. "What's wrong?"

I rolled my eyes. "Just more of the same."

Cole's face hardened as he glanced over at the football team. "What happened?"

"It's no big deal, Cole, really. I don't even care," I muttered dismissively.

Aubrey's blue eyes moved between us, and then she piped up, "Half the team surrounded us in the hallway, and Michael tried to choke her with his tie."

"Aubrey!" I cried, eyes wide at her betrayal.

She had the decency to look abashed, her cheeks turning a pretty pink.

"*What*?" Cole demanded, his dark eyes burning black. He stood from the chair, and before I could grab him, he marched over to the football team.

All I could think about was how short Cole was and how big the rest of the football team was, and I jumped from my seat and forced my way through the full house to get to him.

Cole had his arm around Michael; his face was hard, with an ironic smile that didn't reach his eyes. As I got closer, I could tell he was talking to him...and animatedly, with his hand gesturing to Michael, even tapping his finger on Michael's chest, and then waving off in a vague direction. I pushed my way into the circle of rowdy boys and strained to hear what he was saying.

Cole nodded toward me, but didn't loosen his grip on Michael, and it was then I realized he was holding him fast. "Hey, Seraphina, I believe Mikey has something to say to you..."

Michael's face was murderous as Cole released him, and he shoved Cole for good measure. This caught the attention of the rest of the team, who oohed and hooted with laughter at the sight of the scuffle. Michael glanced at Cole and then, without meeting my eye, he mumbled through gritted teeth, "I'm sorry, okay?" He turned to Cole. "Happy now?"

"Not in the slightest." Cole pointed a finger at him. "Remember what I said."

Michael scoffed and mumbled under his breath before elbowing his way out of the crowd and stomping up the stairs as catcalls followed him.

I grabbed Cole by the arm and dragged him away from the football players and toward the front door. "What did you do?"

Cole shrugged. "Told him what would happen if he messed with you again."

I frowned, thoroughly embarrassed. "Why would you do that?"

"It's not like I hit him...although a better man probably would've..." Cole grumbled.

"No, you just made it look like—" I struggled to find the words. But I had none. The only fault I could find in what he'd done was the way it'd made me feel. Embarrassed. Like when Phoenix always tried to come to my rescue with our cousins. I winced and forced her from my mind. Again. "I don't need you beating apologies out of people, Cole, okay?"

"I'm sorry, Phin, I—"

I shook my head. "I need some air, okay?"

I grabbed the door and wrenched it open. The bells clanged loudly in my ears as a blast of cold air blew past me into the coffee-house, fanning my hair. I shut the door behind me, blocking out the shrieks and giggles about the cold, and sat down on the front steps.

The cement was like a block of ice under my jeans. I shivered in the wind as I stared out into the trees. The gray afternoon was bleeding into a black evening. The leaves were dark with old rain, and they shined burgundy and bronze, hanging limp in the cold.

The door opened behind me, and I flinched at the clatter of

the bells and the noise of Hallowed Grounds. I glanced back, expecting to see Cole, but it was Aubrey.

"Hey," she murmured tentatively as she sank down beside me on the steps. "You forgot this..." She slid my backpack off her shoulder, dropping it next to me, and held out a drink carrier with two coffees.

"Thanks." I picked the coffee with my name on it and tucked my bag between my feet on the lower step. I took a grateful sip, letting the rich smell fill my lungs and the warmth flood through me.

"Peter was disappointed that you left...I think he likes you." Aubrey nudged me gently with a hesitant smile and nodded toward my cup.

I looked down and saw a number scribbled on the cup. My heart skipped weakly. I forced a smile, but it came out a wince.

"Are you okay?" Aubrey asked softly.

I took a deep breath, the cold air sharp in my nose. "I'll be fine. Just not looking forward to the game tonight."

Aubrey nodded grimly, sliding her locket back and forth along its chain. We sat in silence for a moment, sipping our coffees in the dreary, late afternoon. "You're a really great friend, Seraphina."

I glanced at her sideways.

"I mean, clearly, the last place you want to be is at a game with the whole school, but it's important to Rachel, so you're going anyway. That's pretty cool."

I nodded uncertainly.

"What?" Aubrey asked, her brow furrowed.

I ran a hand through my hair as it caught in a small gust of wind. I watched the slick leaves slip across the road. "I don't know if I'm going for Rachel, so much as I want to be accepted by the squad. Built-in friends, you know?"

Aubrey scrunched up her face in a contemplative pout. "Well, I do know that being a cheerleader isn't all it's cracked up to be. Having quit the squad, myself. Sure you make friends, but it's kind of forced friendships, based on just being a part of the squad... nothing substantial...you know?"

I bit my lip as I considered this. It made me think of Phoenix and me. Forced friends based on blood, nothing else...was that what we were? Was that what I was most angry about? Was I truly upset because we had nothing in common? Without magic to bind us, we had nothing to keep us together? I took another sip as though it might drown my thoughts.

Aubrey shrugged. "And I also know, if I were you, I wouldn't want to deal with anybody tonight."

I scoffed in agreement.

Aubrey gave me another nudge. "But, hey. At least you'll have your sister with you! I mean, I know you said she was a pain—but maybe everyone will be so focused on her, they'll leave you alone for once." Aubrey winced at her words. "Okay, that sounded a bit bad, but—"

I looked at her sharply. "What?"

Aubrey crinkled her forehead as she gave me an incredulous smile. "Your sister's coming to the game tonight, isn't she? I thought Rachel invited her?"

I gritted my teeth, forcing my face to remain impassive. The last thing I wanted was to have to compete with Phoenix at my school with my friends. Not happening. I turned to Aubrey with a bright smile that didn't touch my eyes. "Let's skip the game and go straight to your house...what do you think?"

Aubrey's sapphire eyes glittered. "I think that's a great idea. I'll text everyone now."

I studied her face as she tapped away on her phone. "Aubrey, why'd you quit? Cheerleading, I mean."

Aubrey flinched, her thumbs pausing briefly over her phone, before she pressed Send and locked it. She tucked her phone back in her pocket. She fingered her necklace as she took a deep sip from her cup, before she sighed and shook her head. "Some people aren't who you think they are."

12

I'D DO ANYTHING

"It's true!"

The room exploded with breathless laughter. I clutched my side as I nearly spat my water. "You really walked in on her when—?"

"Yes, okay! I told you: my mother is an *embarrassment.*" Morgan whined as she struggled between a pout and smile. Her tawny cheeks burned burgundy. "All right, Kait—truth or dare?"

Kaitlyn grinned at the challenge and shrugged. "Dare."

Morgan bit her lip and stared at the ceiling, running her fingers over her locs as she thought. "I dare you to call Cole St. Claire and ask him out."

All the girls *ooooed* as Kaitlyn scoffed. "Too easy."

She pulled out her phone and tapped the screen. I couldn't help but lean forward on my knees ever so slightly to see the number, but Kaitlyn quickly held it to her ear.

"Voicemail." She shrugged again as everyone groaned. "What? She didn't say to leave a message!" Kaitlyn rolled her eyes as we all laughed. "Okay, okay, Seraphina's turn! Truth or dare?"

I glanced around the circle as each girl hugged her pillow, sitting up eagerly in anticipation. Aubrey and I had ditched the coffeehouse and made our way to her dad's house, which was nestled in a neighborhood just over the tracks that made up the west border of the campus grounds. But the rest of the girls shown up later. Morgan had driven Kaitlyn, Cheryl, and Maddie in her car after the game. As soon as they'd arrived, we'd all spent the rest of the evening munching on snacks, reading scary stories, and gossiping—loudly. Then, Kaitlyn had suggested truth or dare...and things had started to get a little crazy. It'd been fun to watch, but now that it was my turn, I felt vulnerable...and insecure.

"Choose or leave, that's the rule." Kaitlyn smirked, glancing sideways at the other girls. "I'm sure Cole St. Claire wouldn't mind showing up to save you..."

My hesitant smile faltered as I regarded Kaitlyn more intently. For the first time, I noticed the glint in her brown eyes, and the hard smile that barely even touched her cheeks. She didn't like me. Not very much, anyway. The thought startled me, but before I was able to formulate another thought or even utter a response, the front door of the house opened and shut. The vibration from downstairs shuddered the bones of the house.

Aubrey flinched, her hand snatching at her locket. She looked at me, her eyes wide and apologetic. "It's Daphne..."

There was a loud silence as we all waited, listening to the tap of her heels on the floor...and then the stairs...and then the hall. The bedroom door opened, and Daphne stood in the doorway, her arms crossed over her chest and her hip leaning against the door-frame. Her black eyes moved over us, taking in the scene, with a calculating coolness. "What are you doing in my room?"

My heart sank. I'd forgotten Aubrey didn't have a room at her dad's house. Hanging out in Daphne's room was like sitting around in a snake pit.

Aubrey seemed to be realizing the same thing as she tucked a strand of white-blonde hair behind her ears and licked her lips. "I thought you were staying at Damien's tonight?"

Daphne sniffed haughtily and marched across the plush cream

carpet. She grabbed a magazine off the nightstand and threw herself onto her bed, her face disappearing behind it. "We got in a fight...so I left with Jack—but God, he's dull...like *really* dull. He may look like Pete Wentz, but he has the personality of Elijah Grunvald. Ick."

There was an awkward silence, and then, to everyone's surprise, Maddie spoke up. "Elijah's really nice..." She glanced uncomfortably around the room, tugging on her dark hair. "He and Peter drove me home once from—"

"That's great, Maddie." Daphne's high voice dripped with sarcastic sweetness as she flipped the page. "It doesn't mean anyone in their right mind would *date* him."

"Actually, I heard he's dating Hannah Green—" Aubrey commented with a kind smile at Maddie.

Daphne flattened the magazine against her chest and looked over at Aubrey. "That freak from the Rosecrest House?" Daphne snickered.

Morgan frowned and flipped her thick locs over her shoulder. "Hannah's pretty cool, Daphne...she helped Courtney through a hard time. You shouldn't—"

Daphne grinned wickedly at that. "Well, *that* I can believe. Courtney has a habit of befriending psychos, doesn't she? How's Desiree doing these days?"

"At least Courtney has friends, which is more than you can say," I snapped.

A sharp silence cut through the conversation.

Daphne sat up slowly in the bed, the magazine falling to the floor as she dangled her legs over the side.

I straightened, gripping the pillow tightly in my hands as we stared at each other, unblinking, onyx clashing with silver.

Morgan glanced at me and then back at Daphne nervously. "Let's keep playing..."

Daphne's eyes slid to Morgan, and she smiled. "Can I play?"

Aubrey took a quick breath, but no one said anything.

My pulse thumped uncomfortably in my throat. Playing truth or dare with Daphne seemed...dangerous.

Kaitlyn looked at me and shoved her elbow into my side. "It's your turn."

Truth was the safe choice. A lie could save you every time. "Truth."

Daphne rolled her eyes, the wolfish smirk never leaving her face. "Figures," she muttered.

Kaitlyn glanced at Daphne and then looked at me with that same smile that didn't touch her cheeks. "Tell us the ingredients to your mother's love potion."

The girls all squealed in appreciative anticipation. Even Daphne looked intrigued despite herself. Of all the truths, I hadn't expected that.

"Ooo, good one, Kaitlyn!" Cheryl, barely containing her smile, bounced on her knees as she hugged her pillow.

Morgan's brown eyes sparkled as she grinned. "Don't even try to deny it, Sera. Courtney's mother's been married like *ten times* because of it—"

"Truth or leave...that's the rule." Kaitlyn fluttered her eyelashes with a satisfied pout.

I bit my lip. "The tonic...it doesn't work the way you think. It's not—"

"Truth...or leave," Morgan repeated.

Daphne eyed me coolly.

I sighed. "Strawberries, hyacinth, vanilla..." I listed off the ingredients, trailing off as I noticed Kaitlyn tapping away on her phone. She was noting everything. Mentally, I made my own note: warn Cole not to accept any drinks from Kaitlyn. I fought to suppress a smile. "You know, there's a lot more to it than just combining the ingredients..."

Kaitlyn pursed her lips and locked her phone. "I know..."

"Don't tell me you're going to corner Cole at Hallowed

Grounds and spike his coffee when he isn't looking!" Cheryl giggled, but Kaitlyn looked increasingly embarrassed.

That was totally her plan.

"Daphne's next..." Kaitlyn blurted quickly. "Seraphina, ask her—"

I looked up at Daphne as she leaned over her knees and dropped her head in her hands. "Truth or dare?" I asked.

Daphne gave me a deadpan stare, her black eyes boring into mine, her dark hair framing her face like a cobra's hood. "Dare."

I swallowed thickly. I had no idea what to make her do. I tried to think. I'd love to dare her to leave. Daphne's smile curved across her face. She glanced at the time on the alarm clock on her night-stand. "Ticktock...you're running out of time."

I looked at Aubrey for confirmation. I didn't realize there was a time limit for coming up with something. I looked back at Daphne.

"Oops, time's up." Daphne smiled, but her voice was low and cold. "That means I get to ask you..."

The girls all glanced uncertainly at me. Aubrey tugged nervously at her necklace.

"And you only have dare left..."

I lifted my chin ever so slightly, preparing myself for the worst. If it was really bad, it's not like I *had* to do it...but then they might actually make me leave...

Daphne bent down and reached for something underneath her bed. It was a Ouija board.

Great. This was not going to be good.

Daphne ran her tongue against her teeth as she smiled wickedly.

Cheryl gasped.

Inwardly, I rolled my eyes.

Morgan bit her lip as she smoothed her hands over her locs. "Daphne, I don't think we should—"

Daphne ignored her. "You know, I've been hearing some weird

rumors ever since you showed up at school, Seraphina. Stuff about witches and Devil worship and—"

"The Devil doesn't exist," I countered quickly.

"That's exactly what he wants you to think..." Cheryl murmured.

Kaitlyn scoffed as she raised an eyebrow at me. "You go to a Catholic school and you doubt the Devil?"

Daphne held the board up for us all to see, like a librarian sharing a picture book. "I dare you to use this Ouija board to summon a demon and sell your soul." Daphne smiled, sweet as poison. "Do it...or leave."

There was silence as all eyes rested on me.

Nobody moved.

"Seraphina, we don't have to play anymore if—" Morgan started.

Cheryl nodded firmly, her eyes darting nervously around the room as she twisted a strand of her cherry-red hair around her finger. "Yeah, let's just—"

Aubrey's eyes flickered toward me and then back to the Ouija board.

Daphne continued to watch me, a hungry glint in her eyes.

Maddie finally found her voice. "That's not what a Ouija board is for—"

Daphne's eyes slid over to Maddie. "Haven't you ever heard of a crossroads deal?"

"Sure." Morgan cocked an eyebrow. "But this isn't a crossroad—"

Aubrey fingered her locket. Her front teeth came down hard on her lip as she stared at the board.

"Ouija boards can summon spirits, right? Well, I dare Seraphina to sell her soul to one." Daphne grinned.

Morgan scoffed, but her voice wavered. "Yeah, right. Maybe if it was real..."

Aubrey reached for the board, but Daphne moved it away.

"Well, then what's the harm in testing it?" She looked at each of us in turn. "I'm sure *one* of you losers has something you want bad enough to find out..."

"Let's go downstairs and watch a movie." Aubrey reached for the board again.

Daphne slapped her hand. "Shut up, Aubrey." Daphne sat up straighter on the bed. "We're playing a new game now. The rules? Everyone has to sell their soul to a demon. Anyone too chicken to do it has to leave." Daphne craned her neck slightly to peek out the window. "And it's pretty dark outside."

Morgan rolled her eyes and slapped her hands on her pillow. "Daphne, this is stupid. We're not going to—"

"I'll do it."

Maddie.

I gaped at her. "What?"

Daphne's smile curled up her face, revealing far too many teeth. "Excellent."

Maddie's face had paled, but her face was set and determined.

Daphne's eyes glittered as they feasted upon Maddie. "Well, I think we all know what sweet little Maddison Rose wants..."

"Daphne!" Aubrey gasped at her cruelty.

Maddie's jaw tightened, but she remained impassive. "Let me see it."

"Okay, this isn't funny anymore..." I reached for Maddison's hand and tried to stand with her, but she didn't move. I looked at her sharply. "Maddie, this isn't right; to even pretend—"

"I want to do it, too..." Kaitlyn spoke up with a hint of a smile. "But shouldn't we do it at an *actual* crossroads?"

Cheryl gasped at Kaitlyn's suggestion. "No way! Not in the middle of the night at a crossroad!" Cheryl crisscrossed her legs, hugging the pillow in her lap. She shook her head.

Daphne scoffed. "We aren't. Chill out, Cheryl."

Cheryl's cheeks blushed a pretty pink underneath her dusting of freckles. "I guess it's okay then...because it isn't real."

Morgan hesitated. She looked at Aubrey, and then she looked at me. "If it's just for fun..."

"I don't think this is such a good idea..." Aubrey slid her locket back and forth along its chain.

"It's not," I said flatly.

Daphne giggled and bounced a bit on her bed. She looked down at the box, her eyes scanning the cover as she waved a hand at her stepsister. "Aubrey, go get some candles and a kitchen knife. A *big* one."

Aubrey hesitated. "Why do we need—"

Daphne rolled her eyes and groaned. "Please, Aubrey. For once in your life, stop being dead weight. You said so yourself: it's not real." She looked at me with another wolfish grin. "It's as fake as Seraphina."

Aubrey sighed. She shot me an apologetic wince as she left the room.

Daphne giggled. "Okay, Maddison's first, and then—"

"Maddie, this isn't right..." I whispered harshly in her ear. "To even *pretend* to give up your soul. It's—it's an abomination. Bad karma, at least..."

Daphne snorted and rolled her eyes. She leaned forward over the Ouija board. "You know, you've been playing *The Craft* all week, and it's getting freaking old. Either sell your soul or leave..." Daphne paused, savoring her words as she leaned back and sat up straight at the edge of her bed. "And you won't. I know you won't. And you want to know why?"

I jutted my chin out. "Why?"

"Because you know if you try to summon a demon—it won't work. And then everyone here, and soon the whole school, will know for a fact that Seraphina Grey is just an ordinary loser from Nile with no magic at all."

Her words cut so deep my eyes blurred.

I clenched my teeth.

Do. Not. Cry.

"Daphne—" Morgan warned.

"She's not a loser," Maddie snapped loyally.

"And Seraphina's never bragged about anything," Cheryl commented with a sweet smile at me.

"Whatever." Daphne shrugged with a satisfied smirk. "It's true. And now everyone knows it."

I looked from Morgan to Cheryl to Maddie.

"Why don't you just do it with us?" Kaitlyn asked impatiently. "It'll be fun. We can watch *The Craft* after..." She smiled eagerly at Cheryl.

Slowly, I shook my head.

No.

"Seriously?" Kaitlyn snapped, her voice sharp with annoyance. "Ugh—why not?"

I chewed on the inside of my cheek. It wasn't that I believed it might happen; it was the act itself. There may not be demons or whatever, but there *was* a soul. And to even pretend to give it up— to claim to *sell* it...the thought made my skin crawl. I'd heard of soul magic...I stumbled across the subject briefly mentioned in the library at Blackwell Manor. Messing with the soul in any way was a form of the darkest magic. Too evil and abhorrent to even think about.

Everyone stared at me.

Kaitlyn moaned angrily. "Can we just move on with the game? Watching Seraphina's internal moral struggle is boring."

Daphne snickered. "Boring as *Hell*?" She winked at Kaitlyn, who burst out laughing.

Kaitlyn's eyes watered as she grinned at me. "Come on, Seraphina. Just do it."

Daphne cleared her throat. "Anyone who walks out will not be let back in this house," Daphne said matter-of-factly.

"No." I shook my head again. My jaw tightened as I frowned. "No. I'm leaving. Is anyone else coming with me?"

Maddie didn't look at me. Her eyes were on the board.

I looked at Cheryl, who shrugged. "It's just pretend…"

I turned to Morgan. She studied my face. Silence buzzed loudly in our ears. Then she started to stand.

Kaitlyn grabbed her arm. "Morgan, you're our ride. You can't leave."

Morgan sighed heavily. "I'm sorry, Sera. I promised Kaitlyn I'd take her home."

I swallowed thickly and nodded. My chin held high and fighting back the tears that threatened to spill, I stood, grabbed my bag, and walked out.

I didn't stop at the doorstep or loiter in the driveway or on the sidewalk by the mailbox. I kept walking, putting as much distance between myself and that house as possible. Tears flowed freely from my eyes as I dug deep into my bag. My fingers found the old flip phone and without any hesitation, I dialed Cole's number.

He was half asleep but sobered up quickly when I told him I was wandering around town in the middle of the night.

"I'll be right there." He hung up almost as soon as I'd told him the street.

I leaned into the stop sign at the end of the block and gripped the cold, corrugated metal so tight my hands hurt. And I stood there, waiting underneath the yellow glow of the streetlamp across the road. I fought to keep my breathing steady, my tears under control. I rubbed my cheek into my hoodie in a weak attempt to dry my face. I raked a hand through my hair, untangling the knots tied by the breeze. I probably looked like a hag. What would Cole think when he saw me?

By the time Cole showed up, I was quiet and still. There was a soft, misty rain that showered like snow in the lamp light, leaving tiny droplets in my hair and on my hoodie. I got into the van and buckled up without a word. Nirvana crooned softly on the stereo, and I leaned back in the seat and soaked up the warmth. Cole waited, his hands on the wheel, as he glanced at me sideways, patiently giving me time to speak.

I cleared my throat. My voice was quiet and hoarse. "Do you think I can stay at Martin House tonight?"

"Of course, Phin." Cole shifted the van into gear, turned around in a driveway, and headed toward campus.

"Phin? What happened?" Rachel yawned as she leaned unsteadily against her open door. She rubbed the sleep from her eyes, squinting at me as I walked through the doorway of her dorm. "Are you okay?"

I dropped my backpack at the foot of her bed. "Do you mind if I sleep here for the night?"

"Sure, Phin...but what—"

My eyes burned, and I scrunched up my face as I shrugged. "Sleepovers aren't my thing."

Rachel's brow furrowed in confusion. She opened her mouth but closed it again. She wrapped an arm around me and gave me a squeeze. "I'll go grab some extra pillows and stuff...you okay to wait here?"

Wordlessly, I nodded and managed a grateful smile. Within a few minutes, Rachel came back into the room, her head hidden behind an arm full of blankets and pillows. She tossed them to me, and I spread them out on the floor beside her bed in a makeshift cot.

"Did Phoenix enjoy the game?" I asked softly. Something about Rachel's room, the black walls or the rock band posters, reminded me of Nix. I missed my sister. Badly.

"Nix?" Rachel tried to stifle a yawn. "She didn't come."

I inclined my head as I looked up at Rachel, sitting back on my heels. "Well, whatever. It doesn't matter." I sighed heavily.

Rachel yawned again, kneading her eyes with her palm. "Are you sure you don't want to talk about it?"

I stripped off my hoodie and snuggled underneath the downy covers. I nestled my head in the puffy pillow. I stared up at the ceiling, my hands folded over my stomach. "I'm fine, Rach..."

Rachel plopped onto her bed with a soft bounce and disappeared over the side. "Let me guess...truth or dare?" Rachel mumbled through a yawn.

I raised an eyebrow. "How'd you know?"

"Nile girls are pretty ruthless when it comes to truth or dare," Rachel murmured. "I've walked out on a sleepover before, too...it happens more often than you'd think."

"What did they want you to do?" I whispered.

"Let's just say there are some things I won't sell my soul for."

ALL SIGNS POINT TO CHURCH STREET

Still in her pajamas and me in yesterday's outfit, Rachel and I went down for breakfast in the dorm kitchen. When we made it down the stairs, I stumbled a bit on the last step. The common room wasn't empty as Rachel had promised it would be. Instead, Aubrey had curled up on a plush, cushy chair with her face hidden behind a book by the fire, which was snapping quietly. Maddison sat across from her, sipping from a mug with a book open on her lap, looking in a much better mood than I had ever seen her. Damien sat at a small side cafe table; he had one of those trick butterfly knives in his hand, which he spun around absentmindedly as he bent over a car magazine but stared at Aubrey instead.

Rachel hesitated. "Should we go to Hallowed Grounds for breakfast?"

Before I could answer, Aubrey looked up from her book with wide eyes. She stood in one fluid motion, tossed her book on the seat, and hurried over to us.

She wrapped her arms around me in a tight hug. "Sera, I'm so sorry! I had no idea that you'd left!"

"Don't worry about it...it's fine." I forced a smile.

"What are you doing this afternoon?" Aubrey pulled away, fingering her necklace as she looked up at me with hopeful eyes.

I glanced at Rachel, who stood awkwardly off to the side. "I actually have cheerleading tryouts today."

Aubrey's face fell a bit. "Oh..."

"And the Tracks..." Rachel added. "Nix is meeting us at 10:00, so we better—"

"Oh...okay," Aubrey murmured, crestfallen. "Well, I guess I'll see you later. And again, I'm sorry about last night, Sera. But yeah, I totally understand—"

She turned to head back to her chair, but I stopped her. "Wait, what do you mean?"

Aubrey sighed heavily. "It's all right. I get it. Daphne is good at driving my friends away. Just ask Rachel."

I scrunched up my face in an affectionate frown. "Aubrey, we're still friends..."

"Oh." Aubrey blinked. "I thought after last night—"

I gave her shoulder a squeeze. "It wasn't your fault. I don't blame you."

Aubrey smiled. Her whole face brightened, and she grabbed my arm as a thought came to her. "Hey, why don't we head to Church Street for brunch!"

I glanced at Rachel.

"Oh, duh." Aubrey touched her head and smiled awkwardly. "You have plans..."

I bit my lip. "Well, I haven't been to Church Street in a while —it could be fun..."

Rachel raised an eyebrow. "What about Phoenix?"

I gave Rachel a small nudge. "She won't miss me—trust me."

Rachel opened her mouth to argue, but before she could speak, Cole appeared at the bottom of the boys' staircase, looking half asleep. He shook his dark hair from his eyes and squinted at us. "Morning...I was heading to Hallowed Grounds for some salted maple pie. You guys want to come? We've got some time before we—"

Rachel tore her eyes away from me. "Yup."

Cole looked at me expectantly.

I glanced at Aubrey, who was looking uncomfortably around the room, anywhere but at Rachel and Cole. "Aubrey and I are going to Church Street...catch you guys later?"

Rachel gave me a small smile, coupled with a light nudge. "Tryouts are at three o'clock. Don't be late, okay? If you miss it, you might lose the spot. Amber said Daphne's been asking about it. And if I have to put up with her—"

I smiled reassuringly. "I'll be there, Rach. Don't worry."

Cole looked like he wanted to say something but thought better of it, and, with a little wave, headed out the door after Rachel.

My stomach churned guiltily.

Aubrey went over to her seat and tucked her book back into her bag. "I just have to put this in my room and grab my purse...I'll be right back!"

I took a seat in Aubrey's now vacant chair. "Did you want to come, too, Maddie?"

Maddie glanced up from her book. "My mom's picking me up soon."

I nodded with a sympathetic smile. The silence was loud and uncomfortable. I peeked at Damien, who was looking increasingly sullen as he flipped through his magazine. My leg jiggled anxiously as my eyes continued to move around the room.

Maddie cleared her throat with a small cough and then spoke in such a fast rush of words, I could barely understand her: "I was actually going to ask you if you wanted to come to my birthday party..."

Brow furrowed, it took me a second to process what she'd said. "Oh, yeah, sure—when is it?"

Maddie blushed scarlet as she ran a hand through her raven

hair. "Well, it's not a party exactly... It's next Saturday...after the Apple Fest. I'm helping Mom at our art stand, but afterward we can walk to my house?"

"Sure! Who else is coming?"

Maddie sat up a bit, beaming in the face of my enthusiasm. "Courtney said she'd come." She started ticking the names off on her fingers. "Morgan, too, and Lacey—she's from the public school...I haven't asked anyone else yet..." She shrugged shyly.

Maddie's phone vibrated loudly on the side table. She grabbed it quickly and checked the screen. "Oh, that's my mom." She unbuckled her duffel and tucked her book into her bag before tossing it over her shoulder. "Can I give you my number?"

I looked around for a pen. "I don't have a pen—" I slapped my pockets and felt the phone in my hoodie. I'd forgotten about it. Hesitantly, I pulled it out and turned it on. I handed it to her in an effort to hide the fact that I had no idea how to add a number to the contacts.

Maddie quickly tapped in her number. "There, and now..." There was a beep from the phone and then her phone vibrated again. "I have yours too. I'll see you later, Seraphina!" She passed back the phone with a sweet smile.

As soon as Maddie was gone, Damien sauntered over and sat on the arm of my chair, draping his arm around the back of it. "What's this about a party?"

I frowned as I eyed him critically, seriously considering moving to a different seat. "What do you want, Damien?"

His arm slid off the chair and wrapped around my shoulders as he gave me a squeeze. "Just being friendly."

I flinched at his touch. "Do you mind?"

He removed his arm and held up his hands in mock surrender. "Sorry. What I really wanted to ask you about was Aubrey..."

I looked up at him sharply, studying his face. All signs of his sleazy, jerky demeanor were gone, replaced by an almost sorrowful seriousness that made me hesitate. "What?"

Damien pushed off the chair and sat on the couch opposite me where Maddie had just sat seconds before. He pulled out the trick knife again and started to spin it. "Look, Aubrey and I used to date —for a long time. And I care about her—a lot. I just wanted to make sure she was okay…" He snapped the knife closed and looked at me with sad eyes. "Is she?"

"I'm fine, Damien."

The both of us jumped at the sudden sound of Aubrey's voice. I turned in my seat, grateful to see her and to be saved from an incredibly awkward conversation. Damien stood quickly at the sight of her.

"You really should get a fidget spinner or something. A lot less creepy." Aubrey wasn't smiling. Her face was cold. "Are you ready, Sera?"

I nodded and headed for the door, but Damien cut in front of Aubrey so she couldn't leave. "Aubrey, I—"

"Why don't you worry about Daphne and leave me alone?" Aubrey's voice was high and breathless as she pushed past him and hurried out the door, with me right behind her.

Aubrey didn't have a car, so we walked down the quiet black tar road that cut through the trees and down another road and across the train tracks toward the bus stop. It wasn't until we got on the nearly empty bus and into downtown that Aubrey spoke.

"They are dating…Damien and Daphne." She didn't look at me. "It hurts to think about…let alone talk about it."

I didn't know what to say. My heart hurt for her. I watched a single tear spill onto her hand as she slid her locket back and forth along the chain.

I put a hand on her knee and squeezed. "I'm sorry, Aubrey… but for what it's worth—Damien doesn't seem like a guy to get too torn up about."

Aubrey sniffed and rubbed her nose on the sleeve of her sweater as she laughed darkly. "Fair enough." She shrugged then and squinted up at me. "I guess I have a bad habit of burying bad things...avoiding them...pretending they aren't there. You know what I mean? Like, if I don't talk about them, they didn't happen?"

"Right. Makes sense..."

She took a shaky breath and looked up at me, her mouth slightly parted as though she might say more, but then she bit her lip and dropped her gaze with a sad shake of her head.

The bus shrieked to a stop, and we both headed out onto the sidewalk toward Church Street, the heart of downtown. What once had been an actual street was now paved over with cobblestone brick, cutting between two stretches of shops that ended in a high-steepled church. It was a huge marketplace where people walked from one length to the other, wasting time and shopping.

The buildings were all slapped against each other, shoulder to shoulder. Aubrey led me past shop after shop, until she stopped outside a bagel café with a sign that read "Plain Jane's Bagel." She opened the door and almost ran smack into Courtney.

"Oh, hey guys!" Courtney flipped her messy golden braid over her shoulder and grinned. "What are you two up to?"

Aubrey raised her eyebrows toward the cafe. "Bagels..."

Courtney laughed. "Right. How was the sleepover?"

Aubrey spoke up for me. "Daphne crashed it."

Courtney winced. "Ugh. Well, I'm off to meet Hannah—have you met her yet, Sera?"

I furrowed my brow and shook my head.

Courtney touched my arm and smiled. "Well, you will—everyone meets everyone eventually—well, in Nile anyways." She shrugged good-naturedly before nodding across the cobblestone street. "We're heading to Quills & Crow for some herbs and stuff for—"

"Seriously?" Aubrey chuckled nervously as she glanced at the black wooden door nestled between a bookstore and an empty pub. "I've only been inside once—and that was for a Halloween party..."

Courtney's eyes widened, and she grabbed my arm. "Oh, that's right! Sera, the night before Halloween—Cabbage Night—the Nile girls all spend the night at my family's lake house. You have to come—please?"

Aubrey smiled. "We don't usually get into too much mischief."

I blinked, amused by their eager expressions. "Halloween is like two weeks away—"

Courtney gave me a playful push. "Never too early for an invitation. What's your number?"

I hesitated and then pulled out the phone. "Uhm...it's new, so—"

Courtney cocked an eyebrow at the old flip phone, and I blushed. "I mean, new to me..."

Courtney grinned and took it from me. "Here, let me see." She tapped through the phone and like Maddie before her, she sent herself a text from my phone. "There. You have my number, and I have yours." She hurried across the cobblestones and then shouted over her shoulder, "Don't forget, Cabbage Night, my place! Blanchard Drive."

She gave us a quick wave and ran across the street.

Aubrey gave an indulgent sigh. "Gotta love Courtney...maybe she'll actually make it this time."

I laughed. Then Aubrey held out her hand. "Here, you should have my number, too."

I passed her the phone. She inputted her number, and her face fell. "Low battery; you should probably charge this."

I powered down the phone and pocketed it quickly. "If I had one."

Aubrey gave me a sympathetic smile. "Yeah, that thing's pretty old...I bet they don't even sell chargers like that anymore."

I rolled my eyes with a smile. "Whatever. It was a hand-me-down anyway."

Aubrey giggled. "I know how that is...come on, I'm starving."

I nodded in agreement as my stomach growled, and we headed inside for delicious designer bagels. Then, settled in the warmth of the cozy cafe, we discussed everything from the Apple Fest to homeschool, and I was really happy to be with Aubrey as opposed to skipping rocks off the Tracks back in Nile.

But then, as though she'd read my thoughts, Aubrey suddenly fell quiet, her face sad, and she murmured, "I'm sorry I took you from Rachel this morning."

I inclined my head as I took a sip of coffee. "What do you mean?"

Aubrey sighed and her eyes looked off to the side, refusing to meet my gaze as she tugged nervously on her locket. "I just—I didn't want to be alone today..."

"Why today?"

Aubrey slid the locket back and forth along its chain. "It's my mom's birthday today."

I frowned, my brow crinkled in confusion.

Aubrey inhaled deeply, her eyes downcast. "I haven't wanted to talk about it..." She forced a smile as she met my eye with tears in hers. "But I've been seeing this therapist, and she says talking is the best way to work through things...or something..."

I nodded sympathetically. "Sure. That makes sense."

Aubrey swallowed and asked in a voice breathless and low, "Has anyone told you about my mom?"

I shook my head as I studied her face.

"I didn't think so." Aubrey closed her eyes for a moment. When she opened them, they shined with tears. Her lower lip trembled as she looked to the ceiling and took a big gulp of air. "You know that couple on East Shore South?"

An uneasiness seeped through me, and my heart stalled in my chest. "Yes..."

Aubrey's eyelashes fluttered, spilling tears down her soft, pale cheeks. "Sorry." She looked off to the side with an embarrassed, watery smile. "It's just, you know how everyone's been going out of their way to be nice to me?" She looked back at me, her brow furrowed over an imploring wince. "Like Damien, and Cheryl trying to get me to come back to cheerleading, and then Courtney and Morgan with the sleepover idea?"

I nodded earnestly, not trusting myself to speak.

"The couple was my parents...well, my mom and my stepdad. Sarah and Kyle Rousseau. And it's her birthday today."

I stared wide-eyed, frozen and horrified. "Oh my God. Aubrey, I'm so sorry!" I reached my hand out over the table, snatched up her hand, and squeezed it hard. I shook my head, blindsided and bewildered. I didn't know what to say. How on Earth to begin to help her.

Aubrey forced a smile as she squeezed my hand back. Then she pulled away and dried her face with the back of her hand. "God. I didn't want to tell you, at all. It's just been so nice being with someone who didn't know... That's the denial stage, or whatever." Aubrey rolled her leaking eyes. "But it's her birthday...so, yeah." She sniffed with another weak smile. "Hard day."

"Do you want to talk about it?" I prompted gently.

Aubrey licked her lips and shook her head. "No. No. Not at all. First step is acceptance...or something. Saying it out loud." Then she let out a nervous chuckle. "I do want to ask you a favor..."

I held her eyes with mine. "Anything."

Aubrey looked at me then, her smile grateful and her sapphire eyes hopeful. "Really?"

I smiled, and I nodded encouragingly. "Go for it."

Aubrey looked up at the ceiling. "I was hoping you'd go with me to Bird Island today."

My heart dipped low in my chest. I stared at her. "Why?"

Aubrey bit her lip and gave her necklace another tug. "It's a long story...but it's basically homework from my therapist." Aubrey's ivory cheeks burned red as she dropped her eyes to her uneaten bagel. "I know it sounds stupid, but—"

I blinked and shook my head. "No, no...it's not that—I just... uhmmm..." How could I explain? Bird Island was the last place on the planet I'd want to go...Grey witches never made it off the island alive. It was tainted by the torture of my family.

Aubrey's eyes were glassy with fresh unshed tears as she tried to steady her trembling lip and forced a smile. "I'm sorry. I'm really embarrassed. Let's just pretend—"

I took a sharp breath and shook my head. "No, no, Aubrey... it's just that I'm not allowed to go there. My mom won't let us."

Aubrey sniffed and tilted her head. "Why not?"

I took a bite of bagel and chased it with a sip of coffee, buying time. "Well, historically, there were—"

Aubrey's eyes widened as her face paled. "Oh, my God, Sera! I'm so sorry; I didn't even think—" she cried, mortified at her mistake.

I forced a laugh. "Don't worry about it."

Aubrey smiled weakly and then asked hesitantly, "Then, maybe you should go there, too?"

I raised an eyebrow and shifted in my seat. I took a long sip of coffee.

Aubrey's face warmed at the thought. "I mean, if anything, you would benefit much more from a trip there—healing generational trauma? Nothing could compare...right?"

I scoffed with an awkward smile as I put down my bagel. "Right. But my mom doesn't want us going there...and—" I shrugged, feeling increasingly uncomfortable. "I don't know, I guess, I'd want to ask her first. Sorry."

Aubrey giggled. "Well, then ask her!"

"She's Unreachable." I stumbled awkwardly over my slip, "I mean, I can't because she's—at one of those no cell phone retreat things." I smiled broadly as I took a bite of bagel big enough for Phoenix.

Aubrey grinned and twirled her platinum hair around her finger with a careless shrug. "Maybe we could just take a boat to the shore? Not go on the beach...just see it from the shallows?"

My face fell, and I shook my head. "Sorry, Aubrey, not until I ask my mom."

Aubrey's brow furrowed, and she looked down at her hands almost shamefully.

Guilt churned in my stomach. Her mom was murdered, horrifically. The killer hadn't been caught. And all she wanted was for me to go with her to a dinky old island. How could I say no to her? I bit my lip on an awkward frown. Then I jutted my chin toward her food, changing the subject. "How's your sandwich?"

Aubrey forced a smile, and we settled back into polite conversation, but the afternoon was now stained with embarrassed, uncomfortable energy. We left quickly after that.

When we hopped off the bus at our stop, Aubrey gave me a tight hug and whispered a soft, "I'm so sorry, Sera," before she took off at a near run and cut left toward her dad's house.

I stared after her for a moment, shivering in the cold breeze and hoping we'd forget all about this come Monday. Shoving my hands into my jacket pockets to keep warm, I took a right toward the campus.

I was cold and rosy by the time I made it to Martin House. I buzzed the doorbell and waited, hands fisted in my pockets, huddled over and shivering. The door opened and my grateful smile vanished.

I didn't move.

Damien held the door open wide. "You'd rather freeze?"

I frowned. "Thanks," I muttered as I pushed past him.

"You're welcome."

I headed for the girls' staircase without another word.

"Rachel's not back yet…" Damien called from the doorway as he closed the door on the cold.

My shoulders slumped forward as I came to a stop just feet from the stairs. I turned back to face him.

"You can grab her spare, if you want." Damien leaned against the door, his arms crossed over his chest as he watched me. "They keep spares of every dorm key in the office down the hall. We aren't supposed to use them, but in case of emergencies…" He shrugged.

"I just need my bag. Not really an emergency." I dropped into the chair by the fire and tucked my hands into my hoodie pocket. I fiddled with the phone, debating whether or not I wanted to use it again.

Damien took a seat on the couch across from me. He leaned back with his arms spread wide along the back of the couch. "How was Church Street?"

I chewed the inside of my cheek as I stared at him. "I'm just waiting for Rachel, Damien. I'm not interested in conversation."

Damien scoffed and rolled his eyes. "Look, I told you before. I care about Aubrey and I'm worried—"

"If you care so much about her, why are you dating her stepsister?" I raised an eyebrow expectantly.

Damien scowled, his eyes hard. "We always break up and get back together. It's what we do. But this time she said she was done. She couldn't take a joke. If she's done, then she shouldn't care if I date her mother."

We both froze. He'd forgotten. For a split second, he'd forgotten about Aubrey's mom. His face paled at his horrific words, and he leaned forward on his knees, burying his face in his hands as he muttered to himself.

Ignoring him, I pulled out the phone and dialed Rachel's number. She didn't answer. I tried again. Nothing. "Great," I mumbled as I turned it back off.

Damien looked at me between his fingers, impatience burning

bright in his icy eyes. "I'll get the spare." He pushed off the couch and stomped down the hall, as I stared after him in startled surprise.

He reappeared a moment later and slapped the key into my hand. It was large in my palm, old and intricate, with a chain dangling from the end. I looked up at him, eyes narrowed, unable to determine whether I was grateful or just plain annoyed. I didn't want his help. But I'd rather not endure his company...and I needed my bag. And tryouts started in...I checked my watch. An hour.

"Thanks," I muttered just as coolly as before.

"Whatever." Damien shrugged. "Just put it back before the House parents see."

I gripped the key hard in my hand and headed upstairs. I got to Rachel's room and pushed the key into the lock, but the door was already ajar. The key just tapped it. And the door swung slowly open. I squinted into the dark of the room, my heart quickening slightly in my chest. We hadn't left the door open. Rachel always locked her door. Hadn't she said this?

I pushed the door all the way; sunlight from the hallway barely illuminated a few inches into the room. Reaching my hand around the doorframe, I slapped at the wall for a second, finally hitting the switch.

The lights flashed on.

And I screamed.

ALL THE STRANGE THINGS

It wasn't real.

An inflatable doll in a blonde wig and black witch hat, hung by a green and silver-striped tie, nailed to the ceiling, dripped in red paint. Its eyes were blacked out and scribbles covered its mouth like black stitches. It was horrible and gross and made my stomach twist as it set my nerves on ice.

Someone came up behind me and halted in the doorway. I whirled around. Kaitlyn stood just behind me, eyes wide as she stared at the doll. "Oh, my God!"

I turned back to the doll and yanked it down, ripping the tie in the process. "Did you see anyone come in here?"

Kaitlyn continued to stare at the doll now clutched in my hands. "What *is* that?"

"A prank." I ripped the black hat off the doll and tossed it to the floor.

"Who would do that?" Kaitlyn's wide nose wrinkled at the sight of the limp thing dangling in my hand.

"Did you see anyone come in here?" I repeated impatiently.

Kaitlyn scoffed. "No. I just got here." She paused and looked at me with her eyes narrowed. "What are *you* doing here? This is

Rachel's room. And you don't board..." She crossed her arms and leaned against the doorframe.

"I spent the night with Rachel." I looked down at the doll in my hands. "I thought you were going home today."

"I changed my mind..." Kaitlyn arched a perfectly shaped eyebrow. "Like I had something to do with this? Please." She rolled her eyes and stalked away.

A moment later, Rachel peeked her head inside the room. "Hey, what was—Phin, what is that?"

I met her dark eyes with tears hot in mine. I tried to speak, but the lump in my throat blocked all my words.

Rachel rushed over, tugged the doll from my hand, and wrapped an arm around me. "Come on. We're going to Father LaValley. Now."

I sat awkwardly in the secretary's lobby, trying to get the grisly image out of my mind. Cole and Rachel stared at the television as the news flashed across the screen.

"What is going on?" Cole muttered.

"If he takes any longer, we'll miss curfew," Rachel grumbled sarcastically.

"Maybe we should just leave a message?" I suggested lamely.

Cole shook his head, his black hair falling into his dark eyes. "What is going on around here?" He spoke in a harsh whisper.

Rachel nodded solemnly. "Mom says there was another one over the weekend."

My brow knitted, and my forehead crinkled. I glanced at the television to see what I'd missed. The newscaster was interviewing a Nile farmer. I recognized him. He owned one of the fields off Bell Hill. "What are you guys talking about?"

Before he could explain, the door to Father LaValley's office opened.

My mouth parted and my eyes grew in surprise. Father

LaValley was dressed in the normal priestly attire: black cassock, white collar. But if it hadn't been for that, I would've thought him some kind of military man, straight out of an army base...or an action film with how handsome his face was. He was young, too, maybe just a bit older than Mama, with dark hair, parted like the soldier in that World War II movie with the tanks. His face was defined, with a strong jaw and chiseled cheekbones. He had a warm smile that reached his brown eyes; they crinkled pleasantly in the corners, making me feel welcome and safe. He nodded to the three of us and waved us inside his office.

I was last in the room, nervous and awkwardly bumping into Cole as I took one of the seats facing his big desk. He murmured greetings to both Rachel and Cole as though he knew them well. He didn't sit behind his desk; rather, he sat on top of it and extended a hand to me. I hastily wiped the nerves from my palm onto my jeans before shaking his.

"You must be Ms. Grey." He smiled broadly and his words came quickly, with genuine enthusiasm. "It is so good to meet you. Finally. Your mother is...was...an old friend of mine. A great friend." His smile grew into a grin, as he looked down at me fondly. "I was pleasantly surprised to get a call from her. I'd hoped to assist you with enrollment myself, but I had a meeting I just couldn't get out of; I'm so sorry we couldn't meet earlier. At any rate, I trust your first week went all right without my assistance." He gestured to Cole and Rachel seated beside me, then added with a broad grin, "How is she?"

I blinked. "How is...who?"

I could've sworn Father LaValley's cheeks almost blushed. "Uh, your...uhh, never mind." He cleared his throat and turned to Cole. "What's the problem? I was told the three of you needed to speak urgently?"

Cole glanced at me with an eyebrow cocked and a smirk tugging at his mouth. I shifted awkwardly in my seat. Then, this time it was Rachel who cleared her throat. "Someone left a doll dressed like Seraphina, hanging in my dorm room."

"Hanging?" Father LaValley asked, patiently. "Can you elaborate a bit more?"

"It was strung up with a tie, made to look like a noose."

Father LaValley's eyes narrowed. He studied the three of us. "That is certainly very concerning...why do you think it was made to look like Seraphina?"

"They put a blonde wig and a witch's hat on it," Cole said flatly.

"Daphne Collins has had it out for her since she got here," Rachel piped up.

Cole scrunched up his face as he glanced at Rachel. "Eh, I don't know. That new kid Logan has been following her around...maybe—"

"Cole!" I smacked his shoulder.

"Thank you all for bringing this to my attention." LaValley's hard expression softened, and he slapped on his easygoing grin. This time, his smile didn't quite touch his eyes. "I suppose a few girls got carried away with the spirit of the holiday, hmm?" He moved to the door and opened it, clearly showing us out. "I'll alert Mr. Whayland and Sister Francis. Let them know the seriousness of the situation. They will conduct a thorough investigation into the matter, I assure you."

We didn't move.

"It was dripping with red paint." I stared at him with hard eyes. "Like blood."

Rachel smirked. "Which is pretty alarming considering the *murders* in Nile..."

"And the dog mutilations..." Cole added.

I looked at him sharply. He nodded grimly.

Father LaValley raised his eyebrows, but quickly smoothed an easy smile back into place. "I could see how you'd be on high alert, considering...but I don't think you need to be reaching in that direction, Mr. St. Claire."

All of us exchanged glances. Then Father LaValley opened the door wider. "The dorm parents will notify you when the pranksters are caught."

There was an awkward pause before we stood from our seats and walked out the door.

Cole offered to drive me home, and I accepted without argument. To Rachel's disappointment, I'd missed cheer tryouts, and Daphne claimed the spot. But honestly, I didn't mind. After seeing that thing dangling by the green and silver tie, all I wanted to do was go home.

In the van on the way to the ferry dock, Cole snickered, "Dude was hot for your mom, Phin."

I tried to smile. "Did you get the feeling that he was...I don't know—hiding something?"

Cole nodded as he glanced at me sideways. "Like what?"

I shook my head. "I don't know. It was like, he was taking it all seriously until Rachel mentioned Daphne and then he kind of... rushed us out of there."

Cole frowned thoughtfully as he turned down Grey Lane and began to expertly swerve the potholes. He could never avoid them all, and we steeled ourselves for the jarring bumps through the woods.

He parked the van in the gravel driveway. He switched off the engine, cutting off Eddie Vedder mid-croon. "What are you going to tell Phoenix?"

"I'm not."

"Phin—"

I groaned and snatched at my backpack. "Cole, despite what Phoenix may think—she's not my mother. She's not even older, okay? It's not her business." I glanced at Cole. "Please, don't tell her."

Cole winced and raked a hand through his thick, dark hair. He sighed. "Okay."

He shoved open the van door, and we headed into the cottage. Before I was through the door, Fawn grabbed me and squeezed me tightly around the waist.

"I'm so happy you're home," Fawn mumbled through gritted teeth as her hug crushed me with all her strength.

I laughed in surprised delight. "Finally! I've missed you...*so much*." I squeezed her back.

"Me too."

"Thank God." I heaved her up, and she hugged me like a monkey. "I was worried you'd forgotten all about me."

"Can you drop out now?" Fawn breathed into my hair.

I chuckled as I returned her to the ground and tousled her mop of golden curls. "Not yet."

"Jinx it," Fawn cursed as she pulled away from me. "Well, come on; you can help me with my potion..."

She led Cole and me into the kitchen and dropped into her seat at the table with a defeated sigh. Then she picked up her knife and continued cutting and measuring different herbs beside her mini black cauldron. The fat, frothy bubbles of brew popped like pus-filled pox. The fumes were putrid. Cole coughed and gagged on the stench. I pinched my nose as my eyes began to leak. "Memoria potion?"

"Yes," Fawn muttered dully.

"How's your grandmother's?" Cole choked out the words.

Fawn made a face. "Staying at Blackwell Manor is like living at a school."

"Aren't you used to that?" Cole cocked an eyebrow and squinted through teary eyes. "You know, being homeschooled and all?"

Fawn giggled. "Not like this. Grammy thinks I'm a 'rare talent.'"

Cole coughed again. "Clearly, not with potions."

Fawn gave a scandalized squeal and stuck her tongue out at him.

I gave her a one-arm hug, as I came around to study her work. I couldn't cast, conjure, or curse, but I knew my herbs and potions. I knew the science behind the magic better than anyone. "I'll coach you through this as soon as I grab a cup of cider."

"And crack the window?" Cole grunted, as he leaned over the sink and yanked up the window, letting out some of the stink.

"Don't you have homework, or something 'ordinary' and lame like that?" Phoenix asked, lazily, as she strolled into the kitchen and plopped down at the table like a bored cat.

I frowned at her. "I can do it later." I smiled back at Fawn and tweaked her nose. "Fawn needs my help."

"You'd have been able to help her before it went bad, if you'd have been here where you belong, instead of at that school..." Phoenix muttered under her breath.

I glared at her then. "It's not like I'm boarding all week like Cole and Rach do. You'd think—"

"Not yet...I bet you'll have the form handed in by Monday." Phoenix propped her elbow up on the table and dropped her chin into her hand. "You didn't come home last night. Where were you?"

Before I could finish my retort, Cole cut in and stopped the fight before it could start. "Guess what?" He took Phoenix by the shoulders, bent down close to her ear, and said in a loud, mock whisper, "The principal has a crush on your mom."

Fawn shrieked in disgust. Phoenix grinned, appropriately amused, and I smiled weakly, allowing the conversation to shift to whether or not Charlotte Grey had kissed the priest.

· · ·

That night, I sat with Phoenix and Cole, roasting marshmallows. Fawn had taken a passage candle back to Blackwell Manor. The silence was awkward and as heavy as the thick smoke that billowed from the fire toward the woods. Phoenix and I hadn't really spoken since our fight days ago and clearly neither of us had plans to start.

Cole, struggling to make conversation, blurted randomly, "So, did you tell Nix about your stalker?"

Phoenix frowned. Fight forgotten, she repeated sharply, "Stalker?"

Cole shifted on the log and tried to explain. "Well, not stalker... just some guy who's been showing up a lot around Phin...at the gas station and..." He blushed in the darkness.

"What guy?" Nix snapped, her voice hard with concern and sharp with impatience.

I glared at her through the glow of the firelight. My cheeks flushed with shame. Once again, here I was blaming my sister for something that had absolutely nothing to do with her. It wasn't Phoenix's fault I had been humiliated by the kids at school, hazed by Daphne Collins, and followed by some wannabe G. I. Joe. But I still couldn't stop the snap from splitting my words. "Leave it, Phoenix."

I could feel Cole's eyes on me from across the fire pit. I stabbed a marshmallow with my stick and jabbed it into the flames.

Phoenix shook her head as she twirled her wand, sending golden orange sparks shooting out of it like tiny falling stars in the shadows. A sliver of sun still burned across the lake, setting the tops of the mountains ablaze. The gentle hills of the island just barely allowed a view of the water from where we sat, the rippling black waves glittering with the dying sunshine in the distance.

"You won't tell me about school." Phoenix spun her wand between her fingers like Damien with his butterfly knife. "Anything I hear, I have to hear from Rachel or Cole." Phoenix flicked her wand toward Cole. Sparks sprayed into the fire. "Some guy messes with you at the gas station, and you don't tell me anything...you ditched Fawn and her potions practice all week, you skipped the Tracks, you're moving out Monday... What is your problem, Phin?"

"You, Phoenix," I hissed. "*You're* my problem. How do you not get that by now? Just leave me alone." I pushed off the log and stalked back inside, shivering from more than just the cold October air.

We couldn't sleep in the heat of the anger that simmered off us and buzzed between us like heat lightning. As soon as Cole had left, we'd both stomped to bed. But that had been hours ago, and both of us were still wide awake, each glaring at our own half of the ceiling.

Phoenix turned and looked at me. I turned and stared back at her. Wordlessly, and silent as shadows, we moved through the cottage and out the front door. We went to the edge of the porch railing and hoisted ourselves onto the roof of the cottage.

Since we were little, the roof of the cottage was our favorite place to go to be alone, just the two of us. When we were small, it was like we were sitting on top of the world. From the roof, we could see over the neighboring fields, the tops of the cars driving down West Shore Road along the edge of the water, and even out across the miles of lake to the strip of New York mountains in the distance. Everything that mattered in our small, simple world was stretched out before us.

We climbed over the top of the roof and made it to the back side, overlooking the hills and the lake and the mountains. We sat, hugged our knees to our chests, and stared across the fields and up into the sky. The stars sparkled and the moon glittered overhead, casting a blue-black glow over everything. Silently, we watched the sky, until finally Phoenix spoke.

"I'm not your enemy, you know."

I didn't say anything. Why did she have to spoil everything? Why couldn't we just sit in silence and be together, for once, without a fight?

Phoenix tried again. "You're building a wall, Phinny. I just wish you'd let me inside."

I wanted to say she was wrong. I wanted to deny it, but I couldn't. My heart hurt.

"You always think the worst of me. You always think I'm out to get you. But I'm not. And deep down you know that."

Silence loud in the dark, Phoenix shook her head. "You can board. I won't be a hag about it. I get it. But don't let it force us farther apart than we already are...I mean, with the way the world is right now? We need to stick together. As a team."

I looked over at her. That was an odd thing to say, considering. Had Cole told her about the murders?

Phoenix's eyes shone in the darkness. "Just trust me, Phinny. *Just believe in me.* That's all I'm asking. Please."

Before I could break through whatever tongue-tying jinx was on my tongue, before I could whisper a word, Phoenix slipped off the roof with a soft thud into the grass and headed back inside, leaving me to stare into the night and wonder how everything had gotten so screwed up.

Sunday morning came at a crawling pace. Phoenix was gone when I woke up. I wandered into the kitchen and saw a note on the table with her untidy scrawl.

> *Off to Blackwell.*
> *Good luck boarding. (And I mean that.)*
> *See you Saturday. Apple Fest at 8 am.*
> *Don't forget.*

Nix

PS: A letter came for you.

I pressed a fingertip to my eye, catching a stray tear before it fell. I folded Phoenix's note and tucked it inexplicably into my jeans pocket. Then I lifted the beau-blue scroll from the table, untied the thread, and read:

Seraphina,

You have my permission to board at Martin House. As a word of warning, watch out for Sister Francis, the dorm mother...she's not the most pleasant of women. But Father LaValley is an old friend. Don't hesitate to trust him. Please keep your head and maybe try to mend things with Phoenix? You need each other. Especially now that I'm gone. And remember, if you're ever in over your head, Icarus can always reach me.

Love,

Mama

PS: I'll feel a lot better if you stock up on your potions. You never know when something might come in handy.

Monday, with a backpack stuffed full of extra elixirs and potions, and even a couple of jars of everything from owl feathers to bat wool, I headed off to school filled with a nervous, excited energy that made my heart race in my chest and coaxed a small smile onto my face.

At lunch, it was a relief to talk to Aubrey. I hadn't seen her since our weird Church Street bagel brunch and hadn't had a chance to tell her about the creepy doll thing. But somehow, she already knew.

"Kaitlyn told me...well, she told everybody." Aubrey's brow furrowed as she gave me a sympathetic pout and squeezed my arm.

I shrugged as we moved through the lunch line. "It's whatever." I bit my lip, feeling the swell of excitement. "I've been looking for you all day because I have a surprise..."

Aubrey didn't smile or look at all interested, like I'd expected. "You aren't bothered about it? Kaitlyn said—"

I rolled my eyes. "So, Daphne's trying to mess with me. What else is new? I refuse to let her scare me off—which is why I...what?"

Aubrey bit her lip and didn't meet my gaze. "It's just—Sera, I don't think Daphne is the one who did it..."

"What do you mean?"

"Well, she doesn't board, remember? So that means she can't get in the building...you need a keycard. And she's—well, she's telling everyone *you* did it."

I shook my head. I couldn't have heard her correctly. "Why would I—"

Aubrey winced as she looked up at me. "She's saying you did it for attention. She's trying to make everyone think you're desperate for popularity and loving all the gossip. That you're trying to live up to the witch label."

I stared at her, mouth agape.

Aubrey nodded with a grimace. "And I think people are starting to believe her."

Embarrassment and shame flooded through me, setting my

nerves into a panic. I had done tarot readings several times at the Hallowed Grounds. And told Daphne...and a few other people... that I'd hex them. But that wasn't real. I was being sarcastic. Everyone knew that. Right? I frowned down at my tray as I grabbed a thing of fries from the counter.

"What did you want to tell me?" Aubrey prompted gently.

I shrugged, thoroughly discouraged and no longer at all excited. "I'm starting to board today."

Aubrey squealed and jumped on the spot. "That's awesome! Have you got your keys yet? We have to celebrate!"

"Hallowed Grounds after school?" I forced a smile.

Aubrey nodded as she pulled out her phone. "Oh, Sera, I'm sorry...I gotta go. I'm meeting Maddie. I'll see you later?"

I blinked. "Meeting Maddie? Isn't she having lunch with us?"

Aubrey's cheeks tinged pink, and she ran a hand through her hair. She wouldn't meet my eyes. "Uh, no. She had some stuff to do in the library." Aubrey got out of line and returned her tray. With a wave, she was gone.

I sat at our lunch table alone, staring at my fries without moving. I could feel the eyes and hear the undercurrent of whispers beneath the chatter of the cafeteria. I scanned the crowd. My eyes flickered from one turned face to the next; all of them looked away as my gaze passed over them.

It was like the first day of school, only worse. I felt like quitting. Just heading home and getting back to my old life. But how could I now? Things with Phoenix were weird. And dropping out would just prove her right in everything that she had said. I wasn't ready for that. And what would I do at home? Nothing. There was nothing for me back home. I was stuck. Plus, I truly was excited to board. Or at least, I had been...

The bell rang. I winced and grabbed my tray, heading for the garbage. I dumped my fries, returned my tray, and headed to my last class of the day, conscious of the hundreds of eyes following me.

.   .   .

After school, I headed straight for the guidance counselor's office to file the permission slip. To cap off a perfectly awful day, I managed to run into Logan. Literally. He burst out of the counselor's office and stomped toward the waiting room door. He slung his rucksack onto his shoulder, smacking me in the process.

"Sorry," he grunted as he wrenched the door open, not bothering to look at who it was he had hit.

"Don't be," I quipped dryly to his retreating back. He froze mid-stomp at the sound of my voice and turned his head just enough for our eyes to lock.

Ignoring the flutter in the pit of my stomach, I flicked my fingers at him. "Move along." Then I turned on my heel and headed to the school counselor's door. I didn't trust Logan any more than Daphne. For all I knew, *he'd* left that doll for me to find.

I left the form with the counselor, who merely nodded, slightly dazed, and mumbled a few "mhmm"s before she signed off on the paper. Then she handed over my keycard along with a big metal dorm key dangling from a chain and a slip of paper detailing my room number and roommate. I tucked the keycard in my pocket and slipped the chain around my neck so that the clunky dorm key rested with Daddy's pendant, and I headed for Hallowed Grounds on foot. I didn't want to wait for Cole or Rachel and have to see the pity in their eyes for poor Seraphina Grey, the freak of Nile.

I waited. For an hour. Neither Aubrey nor Maddie showed up. So I sat in the chair by the fire, facing the door, watching as kids trickled in, laughing and talking with their friends. I turned on the phone for a minute to check for messages. Nothing. Before I could turn it off, it buzzed in my hand. It was Cole.

"Hello?"

"Hey—where are you? Do you need a ride home?"

I sighed heavily and started to pack up my bag. "No. I'm boarding now, so—"

"Wow!" Cole said, clearly impressed. "I thought after this weekend you wouldn't—"

"Well, Daphne's not that scary." My voice came out sharper than I'd intended. "Sorry, Cole. It's just—"

"No, I get it. Meet us at Martin House?"

"Sure." I heaved my bag over my shoulder and headed out the door, a burst of cold blasting my face.

"You need a ride?" Cole asked. The concern in his voice set my teeth on edge. "It's getting cold out…"

"No. I'm fine, Cole. It's not a far walk." And it wasn't…but it *was* cold. And damp and gray. And by the time I made it to Martin House, my nose was red and runny, and my hair was drenched in the icy October mist.

Cole and Rachel sat in chairs by the fire, looking increasingly irritated, and on the other side, sitting on the couch, Kaitlyn and Damien were in deep conversation. I sat on the arm of Rachel's chair.

She looked up at me with a sympathetic smirk and tapped my knee. "How you doing?"

I leaned into her and rested my head on hers. "Fine."

"There's the witch of the hour." Damien grinned and winked at me.

I gave him a deadpan stare.

"He wouldn't leave," Rachel said flatly in apology.

"I figured you'd need cheering up after today." Damien shrugged with a smirk.

"You mean after your girlfriend made her look like a psycho?" Rachel countered.

Damien ignored her and continued, "And Rach may be a cheerleader, but her whole goth aesthetic is downright depressing."

Kaitlyn's eyes were on Rachel. "Well, if Sera didn't do it, who did? Because she was the only one I saw upstairs." Kaitlyn regarded me coolly.

"I don't know—maybe it was *you*, Kaitlyn," Rachel shot back.

The door swung open.

Cold air flooded the common room.

It was Logan.

He didn't bother to look in our direction. He went through the double doors, headed down the hallway, and disappeared.

"That guy is so weird," Rachel muttered.

"Maybe *he* did it..." Cole commented uncertainly.

"Now *that* I'd believe..." Damien lifted his arm off the back of the couch and sat up straight, his eyes on the double doors. "He stays at the By the Lake Motel. Off East Shore South? Sometimes I see him on the dock at night." He looked back at Cole. "It's weird, man. Especially with all the twisted crap going on."

"What do you mean?" My stomach gave another feeble flutter.

"The Rousseaus hacked up in their living room. Dead dogs popping up everywhere..." Damien shook his head and lowered his voice. "Mikey and I go joyriding on the weekends. The streetlight on South Street has started flashing every night at three in the morning—and not flashing like it's on a timer—flashing like it's going haywire."

I let out a little sigh of relief. "Well, that's hardly stranger than—"

This time, Cole spoke up. "It's not just the light."

"Our horses have been throwing riders," Rachel mumbled in a dull tone. She glanced around almost nervously, as though she wished she hadn't said anything. "Jack Martin—Maddison's cousin. The kid who lives next door to me? He said their sheep have been charging the dogs. Trying to stomp them. His favorite shepherd was crushed." She licked her lips as though they went dry.

I interrupted her then. "Rach, how haven't I heard about any of this?"

"Dog mutilations are one thing. But stuff like this doesn't get reported to the police or the news stations, Phin," Cole answered gently. "No farmer, or in Rachel's case, no riding instructor is going to want insane things like this to get out...makes them look—"

"Crazy," Damien finished with a smirk.

"And the cows..." Rachel added softly. "Cows have been running into the highway." Rachel looked at Cole before she went on. "Like they *want* to get hit. Waiting for a car to come, before rushing into the road."

Damien smiled and leaned toward us, his elbows on his knees. "My old man said this has happened before."

Cole scowled at Damien. "Your old man is a *drunk*, Day. I wouldn't trust him farther than I could throw him...and I can't."

Damien's eyes narrowed, but his sly smile stayed in place. "Drunk he may be, Cole, but I'll bet if you asked *your* daddy, he'd say the same. They went to school together, after all. Things started going crazy in Nile back then, too. And right before Halloween, same deal. My old man said some kids started messing with things they shouldn't have, started making Devil deals, and bad things started happening—"

I thought of the sleepover. Daphne's dare. My eyes met Kaitlyn's.

She looked away.

"Shut up, Damien," Rachel muttered, her voice faltering.

Kaitlyn stood abruptly from the couch. "I need to find Cheryl."

Damien didn't stop there, his eyes following Kaitlyn as she headed up the stairs to the girls' dorms. His smile dark, he whispered loudly, "*A girl died.*"

"Yeah, right." Rachel scoffed. "Sure, Nile is the 'most haunted place in America'...whatever. Rosecrest House. Old Grey Lane. Bell Hill Road. Bird Island. Cow Man. That's all just legends and stories. People don't up and *die* in Nile..."

We all got quiet for a moment. Everyone seemed to be thinking the same thing, because Rachel added awkwardly, "*Kids* don't."

"Did he tell you her name?" I asked. "The girl who died."

This time, Damien's smile slipped from his face, his eyes sober and almost solemn. "Alice...he wouldn't say anything after that."

MIDNIGHT IN THE AFTERNOON

"I hope I'm not interrupting anything..."

I flinched at the gritty voice at my ear. My head snapped to the side to see a little woman in a nun habit and black dress cut off at the calves. Her grizzled old face was sharp and birdlike as she studied me with a fiercely critical expression. She rapped my leg sharply with a wooden ruler.

"Kindly refrain from sitting on the armchairs...Miss—?"

I slipped off the seat, face burning, and stood there quite awkwardly, towering over the woman by nearly a foot. "Grey. Seraphina Grey."

The woman pursed her crinkly lips as she regarded me coolly. "Grey. I might have known. Well, now's as good a time as any... come along." She turned sharply on her heel and headed for the hallway. I glanced back at Rachel, who winced and nodded me on.

Reluctantly, I hurried after the woman just in time to see her disappear into the side office. I jogged past the tiny library and caught a glimpse of Logan bent over a table, his eyes poring over an old book. I slipped into the office after the woman. An old, balding man sat slumped over in an armchair with a book open on his lap and his mouth wide open, clearly in a deep sleep. There were two desks in addition to the armchair and a bulletin board full of spare dorm keys. The old woman stepped up to the old man and tapped him sharply on the knee. He jumped to life, like a snoozing bloodhound, complete with the snorting noises. He looked at her, his pale, watery eyes wide and blinking.

"You've got to stop sleeping on the job, Mr. Whayland. I can't be everywhere at once. You let these hoodlums run the place."

The old man ran a hand over his face, pulling at his jowls. "You are right, Sister Francis. But have pity on an old man."

The old woman, Sister Francis, snorted indignantly and shook her head as she made her way to her desk and took a seat. "You'll excuse us, Mr. Whayland. Miss Grey needs to be debriefed."

Mr. Whayland stood slowly from the chair, his body rickety and unsteady. "Ah, well, then I won't keep you…" His back bent slightly, he walked out of the room, giving me a sly wink as he went.

A small smile slipped onto my face as I watched him leave, but it disappeared just as quickly when I caught Sister Francis watching me from her perch at her desk.

She cleared her throat, frowning so grimly her mouth looked like it was melting down the sides of her face. "Well—I can't say I haven't heard of you, Miss Grey. Your name precedes you."

I opened my mouth but shut it again. I had no idea what to say to that.

"In fact, you and your family are quite infamous, are you not?"

I looked off to the side and back to her harsh stare. "Sister Francis, I think—"

"Let me tell you what I know," Sister Francis interrupted sharply. "I know that every Grey girl who has slept under this roof has been more trouble than she's worth."

I flinched as though she'd slapped me in the face with her ruler.

Her sharp eyes pierced into mine. "I also know that Nile children are easily wayward…easily misled and influenced…and unfortunately, Father LaValley limits my powers as Dorm Mother

Martin...but I can assure you, that if I hear of any misbehavior, any rules broken by your hands, I will ensure your boarding privileges are swiftly and permanently revoked. Do you understand?"

I nodded, not trusting myself to speak.

Sister Francis's mouth flattened to a thin, crinkled line. "Very good. I trust the guidance counselor provided you with a dorm packet?"

I nodded again.

"In that packet you will find all the Martin House rules and regulations...I won't waste my breath going over them now. Be sure you read them and adhere to them if you want to stay in this House. I will also tell you that if I hear of any satanic behavior, up to and including so-called 'tarot card readings,' you will be sorely punished."

My key was heavy around my neck as I hiked up the steps to the girls' dormitories. Sister Francis's words were still loud in my head. How many Grey girls had stayed here before me? Just Mama? Certainly not Grammy...

As I approached my assigned dorm, the placard that read "Maddison Rose" shined prettily above the door handle. I hadn't seen Maddie all day. Was she in her—*our*—room now? Did she believe the rumors Daphne was spreading? Was she truly avoiding me, or was I just being paranoid?

I gingerly pulled the chain over my head and took the key in my hand. Even after my miserable day, my stomach was light with a kaleidoscope of butterflies. Somehow, this key and this room made everything better. My own room...well, at least my own room away from Phoenix. I bit my lip and slid the key gently into the lock and turned. The little click made me smile as the door unlocked, and I pushed it open.

No one was inside.

I flicked on the light. The room was smaller than my bedroom at home but cozy all the same. Two twin beds were positioned in an L shape against the back and right walls, joined together by a large square nightstand in the corner. It was clear which bed was Maddie's. The first bed had plain green sheets, but the bed against the far wall had bright-red Spiderman sheets. Her dresser was at the foot of the bed, pushed against the same wall. My smile widened as I noticed a small collection of crystals on the top. Intrigued, I moved closer. There were several figures all cut from brilliant crystal that shined like diamonds. I tilted my head as I studied the crystal girl with a delicately chiseled crystal basket hanging off her arm beside a crystal wolf.

"Little Red Riding Hood..."

I jumped and turned to see Maddie in the doorway with a small smile.

"Sorry, I was just—"

Maddie shrugged. "It's okay. I know it's weird—"

My mouth parted, aghast. "No! They're beautiful!"

Maddie's eyebrows knitted together in an anxious sort of smile as she approached the dresser. "They are, aren't they?" She pointed to the girl and the wolf. "My uncle gave me this one because—well, it's a long story." Her olive skin burned burgundy.

"I love the doves."

Maddie blinked as her hazel eyes shimmered. "Yeah..."

"I have a collection of crystals myself, but not anything like these. They're amazing."

"Thanks..."

Silence fell awkwardly around us, and then we both tried to speak at once.

Laughing and face hot, I waved her on. "Sorry, you go."

Maddie blushed prettily beneath her curtain of long, dark hair. "No. You."

I shoved my hands through my belt loops. "I just was going to say, I missed you at Hallowed Grounds..."

Maddie inclined her head. "What do you mean?"

I bit my lip. "Aubrey said you guys would meet me after school..."

Maddie smiled ruefully. "I've had a really messed-up day; I don't think I've seen her all afternoon. Why didn't you call me?"

"I thought maybe you didn't want to see me," I admitted.

"Why wouldn't I?" Maddie laughed. She gestured around the room. "I tried to make space for you as fast as I could. I only found out after school that you'd changed your mind. I hurried over and tried to move my stuff out of the way." She gave some boxes underneath her bed a gentle kick with her sneaker.

"Oh, you didn't have to pack up all your things!" I cried, mortified that she'd gone to such trouble.

"No big deal. I'm just excited we're roommates!" Maddie dropped her bag beside her bed and sat on the mattress.

I smiled and tossed my own bag on the empty bed. As I did, I noticed a pack of cards spilled just underneath Maddie's bed. "Here, let me—"

"Oh, that's okay—"

I picked up a card, but they all came up with it. I stared at the cards, all seemingly attached and dangling together in one long train. I raised an eyebrow as Maddie hastily took the cards from me, stacked them, and shoved them back under her bed.

"Were those trick cards?"

Maddie tucked a dark tendril behind her ears that were red with her embarrassment. Her sleeve fell a bit, revealing a bunch of pen marks scribbled all over her wrist. She bent down and pulled a notebook and pen out of her bag. "Yeah..." she mumbled and shrugged, burying her face inside her notebook. She started to scribble as she added, "I do magic shows for the kids at the Nile library...just a dumb hobby of mine."

My face warmed at the thought. "That's right! I totally forgot. Can you show me a trick?"

Maddison looked up and studied me for a moment, as though trying to decide whether I was making fun of her. "Okay..."

So, as I unpacked my things and organized my part of the room, Maddie showed off some magic tricks. We had so much fun laughing at my genuine shock and confusion, and discussing illusion versus tricks, that we didn't hear the buzz of Maddie's phone on the nightstand.

The beep of the message made Maddie freeze like an animal sensing danger. She dropped her cards. She scooped up the phone, gripped it to her ear, and listened to the message. Instantly, she packed up her magic stuff, kicked it under the bed, and hurried to her dresser.

"Is everything all right?" I watched apprehensively as Maddie began to stuff clothes and notebooks into her bag.

"Yeah, I'm just...my mom is picking me up..." Maddie smiled, face flushed and breathless. "I'm probably going to be staying at home the rest of the week, but you're welcome to any of my stuff. I've got a stereo over there, a few DVDs you can bring down to the House library. They've got a TV in there."

"Okay...do you need—"

Before I could ask, Maddie threw her bag over her shoulder, pulled me into a tight hug, and headed out the door.

I didn't see her again.

On Thursday, the Blanchard siblings, the St. Claire cousins, and I met at the Hallowed Grounds after school. Peter went to grab all the coffees and sweets, while Rachel and Cole argued over whose house to sleep at on Friday night. They each had to be up early for the Apple Fest setup. Rachel was supposed to help her mom with the pony rides, and Cole had to help the Martins set up the hay bale maze. They weren't the only ones. As Phoenix had reminded me earlier that week, I was also expected to help. Especially with Mama still gone, it was up to me and Phoenix to run the family tent.

The Apple Fest was an annual Nile event held on the third

weekend of October. The islanders would shut down Martin Road, line up different craft stalls, food stands, and trading posts on both sides of the road, and people would spend all day walking the length of it. Some islanders would set up booths to sell things, some would set up stands to educate about things, and the street would be packed full of people from all over the state, and even some from New York and Canada. It stretched for a few miles, with the Martin Farm in the middle.

The Martin family was an important family on the island. One of the old originals who had driven out the natives, settled the island, and given it their name. They owned the farm, the orchards, and all the land that hosted the event. The Martins' storefront and snack bar along one side of Martin Road was the heart of the Apple Fest. There was even a petting zoo beside the apple orchard on the opposite side of the road. It was a pretty big deal—the only time anything actually happened in Nile—so the planning around the event was always an important topic for islanders.

"What do you think, Seraphina?"

My eyes fluttered as Courtney's voice pulled me from my thoughts. "Hmmm?"

Courtney's eyes glittered with amusement. "I said, do you want to come with me Saturday morning? We could spend the night at Martin House, grab some breakfast here, and then head up to Nile?"

I bit my lip as I considered what to say.

"Pleaseee." Courtney's eyes fluttered as she smiled innocently. "I could really use the company. Morgan's helping her mom with their used book table. Everybody's working the Fest except for me. Usually I go with my girlfriends, but they're all mainlanders, and with all the whispers about Nile—everybody's blowing it off this year."

"What about Peter?" My eyes moved to where he stood at the counter. The coffee girl giggled at something he said.

"He's helping Lacey McGregor with Catherine Martin's antiques stall. And by antique stall, I mean junk sale." Courtney smirked. "You should see the stuff that woman digs up. But seriously, what do you think? Keep me company?"

Cole cut in before I could answer. "You're out of luck, Court. The Apple Fest is big business for the Greys. Family thing."

I narrowed my eyes ever so slightly at Cole and shook my head. "No, it isn't. My sister can handle our tent. If she needs extra help, she'll get my grandma. I'd love to keep you company." I smiled brightly as Peter appeared and passed around our drinks. Cole and Rachel both stared at me, each with almost identical expressions of shocked confusion. And as I took my mug in my hands, my heart slowly sank into the pit of my stomach. Fawn was going to be so disappointed, and Phoenix—she'd never let me hear the end of it.

Courtney bounced up and down on the couch. "Awesome! And we can go to Maddie's birthday party afterward."

Peter's brow furrowed, and he looked at Courtney curiously. "How's she doing?"

"Maddie?" Courtney pursed her lips over her coffee.

Peter nodded slowly as he took a sip from his mug. "Yeah, I mean—now that I think about it, I haven't seen her all week."

We all exchanged uncomfortable glances.

No one had seen her since Monday.

But the next day, Friday morning before school, I finally did.

I ran into Maddie at the bottom of the girls' dormitory stairs. Literally. I'd just finished breakfast and was heading up to meet Aubrey so we could walk to school together when Maddie flew down the staircase, and we collided.

"Sorry, Maddie!" I grabbed her arms to steady her. "Where've you been?"

She wrenched herself free from me, rubbing her arms where my hands had been. Her heart-shaped face was pale and blotchy in places from what looked like a lot of crying. Her wide eyes blinked oddly as she averted her gaze to the ground.

"It's fine. It's fine," she whispered so softly the words came out in a hushed hiss I could barely understand. Maddison dropped down to the ground to hastily pick up her notebooks that had spilled out all over the floor. "I just need my things…"

I went to help her, but Maddie pulled roughly away. "*I need my things.*"

She picked up her final notebook, which had been coiled back to a page where she'd doodled all over it. I frowned at the scribbles. Some were etched so hard, the paper had torn.

"Maddison, are you okay?" I put a hand on her shoulder.

Maddie shrugged me off as she looked up at me with narrowed eyes.

I recoiled at the hateful glare.

"*I'm fine!*" She pushed past me, wrenched open the House door, and slammed it behind her.

Shaken and concerned, I hurried up the steep steps to Aubrey's dorm. I gave a light rap on the door before entering. Something I'd learned in my first week of boarding: Aubrey made a point never to lock her door because she had a habit of losing her key.

To my surprise, Daphne was lying back on Aubrey's bed, reading a magazine. Her eyes shifted to stare at me. "What are *you* doing here?"

"I could ask you the same question," I replied coolly. "Last I checked, I actually live here. You don't."

Daphne continued to stare at me like I was a bug in a jar, and she was the kid with a magnifying glass.

"Think about what I said, Bre…" With that, Daphne stood from the bed and walked by me, shoving me into the doorframe as she passed.

Aubrey looked up from where she sat cross-legged on her bed.

"Hey…did you run into Maddie?" Aubrey asked sadly.

I hesitated, gripping the strap of my bag. "Actually, yes…"

Aubrey nodded solemnly. "She was just here. Her sister's taken a turn for the worse…it's hard on her."

I had no idea. "Is that why she went home Monday? Is her sister going to be okay?" I couldn't imagine what it would feel like to have Fawn or Nix hurt, possibly dying, helpless to stop it. I didn't want to think about it.

Aubrey shrugged sadly and jumped up to grab her bag. "Are you ready to go?"

I nodded, still feeling incredibly sorry for Maddison. All day, I was trapped in a fog of sadness, trying to think of some way to help. Maybe a gaudium potion would help…I was hoping I'd see Maddison at lunch, or passing in the hall, but I didn't see her again all day. And I wasn't the only one looking for her.

After school, Aubrey and I sat outside the school on one of the stone benches discussing the Apple Fest, when Logan passed by us in a hurry.

I couldn't help but watch him as he weaved through the cliques of kids waiting for rides home. The way he bobbed in and out of them, it looked like he was trying to find someone. I shivered in the cool autumn sun and pulled my sweater tight around me.

Aubrey followed my gaze. "There's something off about that guy. Looks like he's found someone else to stalk, or is *trying* to find someone else."

We watched him peek around the jacket hoods of several girls and then shake his head in obvious frustration.

Aubrey glanced at me from the corners of her eyes. "Who do you think he's looking for?"

I continued to watch him, frowning thoughtfully. "No idea."

"Let's ask him!" Aubrey grabbed my arm and shook me excitedly.

I looked at her in alarm. "What?"

Aubrey giggled. "Come on. Let's find out what he's doing! It'll be funny."

Before I could argue, Aubrey pulled me off the bench and into the crowd. "Wait, Aubrey! No!"

Aubrey didn't listen. Instead, she tugged me along with surprising strength for such a wisp of a girl and stopped behind Logan. Aubrey tapped him on the shoulder, and he whirled around.

"Can we help you with something?" There was a light laugh in her voice as she tugged on her locket. "You look like you could use some help..."

Logan looked from Aubrey to me with an exasperated sigh. "I'm looking for a girl I have a class with..."

Aubrey gave me a sly side-eyed glance. "What's her name?"

Logan raked a hand through his hair. "No idea. She's a bit on the shorter side. Dark hair. She had...uhhh...some kind of black suit on..." He squinted, trying to remember. "Duffel bag and a Spiderman backpack?"

I spoke up despite myself. "Maddie?" I looked at Aubrey for confirmation. "Maddie said she was in his class?"

I studied Logan's face. Why did he want to see her?

Aubrey frowned thoughtfully. "She does have dark hair...but a lot of girls do." Aubrey looked at Logan then, a sudden suspicious sharpness in her stare. "What do you want with her?"

Logan rolled his eyes with obvious impatience and started to scan the crowd again. "It's important. Do you know where she is? A phone number maybe?"

Aubrey's hand encircled my wrist, and she started to back us away from him. "Come on, Seraphina," she whispered harshly.

All I could think about was Maddie's sister and how upset she'd been this morning. Maybe something had happened? "Maddie boards at Martin House, but she'll be at the Apple Fest tomorrow—"

"Her number is none of your business," Aubrey snapped.

Logan scowled. "This is important."

I glanced uncertainly at Aubrey, who made a face at Logan as she laced her arm through mine and led me away, with Logan cursing behind us.

Aubrey's voice lowered to a harsh whisper. "We should talk to Maddie before we start handing out her number to random guys."

My cheeks burned, and my shoulders curled instinctively inward. Maybe I shouldn't have told Logan anything. Wordlessly, I let Aubrey drag me away from Logan and back to our stone bench.

"That guy is so creepy. Where did he even come from? You know it's not Vermont. Poor Maddison." Aubrey pulled me down to the bench beside her, her arm firm around me in a hard sideways hug.

I was silent. Guilt still stinging, I couldn't help but think how ironic it sounded for the girl who had dated Damien to call a guy like Logan creepy.

Aubrey suddenly stood up. "I'm going to warn Maddie. You'll be okay waiting for Cole without me, right?" She didn't wait for an answer. "See you tomorrow at the Apple Fest!" she tossed over her shoulder as she disappeared into the thicket of teenagers.

I frowned, watching Logan weave around the kids. I pulled out the phone and punched in Maddie's number. The phone rang loudly in my ear. She didn't answer.

"Hey, witchy woman."

Damien.

My day was not ending on a high note. I didn't bother to offer a greeting. I looked past him, my eyes searching the crowd for Cole.

Damien stood over me, blocking my view of the other students and casting a cold shadow that made me shiver.

"Have you seen Aubrey around?" he asked in a lazy drawl.

"She just left." I squinted up at him. "Why do you keep bothering her?"

Damien ignored me and sat next to me. Too close. I shifted away ever so slightly.

"You need a ride to the Apple Fest?" He pulled out his knife and started to spin it.

"No."

He laughed. "I didn't think so." He slapped the knife closed. "But, here." He grabbed my hand and held it fast as I tried to wrench it from him. He scribbled his number on my open hand, the Sharpie tickling my palm as he wrote. "If you need anything, don't hesitate to call."

"I won't." I smiled sweetly. "And when I say that, I mean I won't call."

He nodded as though he expected as much and stood, once again towering over me. "Be careful, Witch Spawn. With all the weird stuff that's going on...wouldn't want anyone to think you're responsible for it. Or worse—" He reached out to touch my hair, but I slapped his hand. "Have something happen to you. If you need help, just give me a call. I keep a gun under my bed." He winked.

My eyes narrowed. "I'll be fine, don't you worry."

"Eh, I don't know." Damien smiled his slow, cruel smirk. "My old man says witches are the first to burn when demons come out at night."

He turned and disappeared into the thinning crowds, leaving me glaring after him, my blood boiling and my anger setting my skin buzzing.

1 6

A LITTLE LESS SIXTEEN CANDLES, A
LITTLE MORE TAKEN

The morning of the Apple Fest was a perfect October morning in Vermont. The sky was a brilliant cobalt blue and the sun was bright, its weak, warm ribbons of gold weaving through the burnt maple leaves and dark-green apple trees that lined the street behind all the various stalls.

The road was a simple two-lane back road that had gentle grassy slopes on each side of it, which flattened out to meet the different vendors and makeshift shops. The Apple Fest resembled a medieval fair or marketplace, which was probably half the appeal, bringing people from all across the state to the little island town of Martin Isle.

It was weird heading to the Apple Fest from town. It was weird not being there to set up our tent. And it was really weird not being with my family. But I had to admit I was having a good time already, and we had just barely pulled up to the car drop. Courtney wasn't just really sweet, but she was a lot of fun, too. In between the laughter and conversation, I was able to force thoughts of my sisters out of my head and ignore the guilt souring my stomach. Almost.

Courtney parked, and we got out. The car drop was filling up quickly. Families and couples and groups of friends all spilled out into the field and headed toward Martin Road. I noticed the cheerleading squad was gathered by a big SUV and tried to ignore their stares as we passed.

"They all think I was the one who hung the doll, don't they?" I muttered darkly.

Courtney nudged me. "Don't worry about them, okay? We're going to have fun. I promise."

I forced a smile but winced slightly at the sight of Daphne and Damien trudging up the grassy hill toward the street. My eyebrows raised in surprise as Morgan hurried to meet them.

"I thought she was busy?" I muttered more to myself than Courtney.

Courtney scoffed. "Well, how do you like that? Morgan told me she had to help her mom!"

I sighed. "She probably just didn't want to risk having to hang out with me."

"Pshh. Morgan's not like that." Courtney made a face as she laced her arm through mine. She squeezed me close as we hiked up the hill to the street. "I'm sure it's something else..." Then she laughed. "Something apocalyptic must be going on for Morgan to be seeking out Daphne Collins."

I grinned at that, and we pushed deep into the crowd gathering at the start of the street. The rope blocking off the road hadn't been dropped yet, so the street itself was still deserted. Only the vendors had been allowed through to set up ahead of time.

By the time we made it to the front, Sheriff Vantine was just lowering the rope and letting everyone pass. The crowd of people was followed closely by the tractor that taxied whoever wanted a lift back and forth to each end of the street. It was faster to walk, though, and the only people who took advantage of the tractor taxi were parents with little kids who begged for a ride, elderly folks who couldn't walk, and bored teenagers with nothing left to do.

"You know," I squinted ahead of us, scanning the stalls, "I was thinking we could try to find Maddie's stand? She said she has—"

"Oh yeah, the art gallery! I love that one." Courtney grinned. "And that way we can check on her...I've been a bit worried that I haven't seen her around—I mean, not that we have any classes together or anything, but...I don't know."

"She's just got a lot going on, I guess." I tried to shrug it off, but I couldn't shake the strange sinking feeling as I remembered the last time I saw her. Aubrey had said her sister wasn't doing well.

Courtney flipped her blonde braid over her shoulder. "But it's weird, isn't it? That no one's really seen her at all this week?"

I jutted my chin toward the left side of the road. "Is it over there with the—what is that? A...a custom dog accessories stand?" I cocked an eyebrow as I studied the young woman moving around her stand. Her dark hair was pulled back, and her pale face was ghostly white, with striking ice-blue eyes nearly as cold as Damien's. Maybe they were related.

Courtney laughed. "Yes...Victoria Shaw. She graduated last year. She makes cute collars—but she's pretty...intimidating—to put it politely. I've gotten a few things for Squirrel, just to be nice."

I laughed. "You have a dog named Squirrel."

Courtney shrugged with a sly smile. "He never comes for anything else..."

We headed down the embankment toward the Rose family's stand. The young woman selling dog collars, Victoria Shaw, watched me with a cool stare as we passed. Yes, intimating was putting it very nicely.

The Rose stand was set back a ways, in the middle of several easels displaying different landscapes. They were beautiful and happy, like Bob Ross had inspired them. Courtney and I separated as we moved among the paintings. My face fell a bit when I noticed an original. Underneath a dark, bleak sky was a gray lake with angry whitecaps churning violently against the rocky beach of a thin strip of island, with a big, crumbling, gray barn off to the left. But it wasn't really a barn. It was a church.

"Oh, my God." Courtney came up behind me as I stood frozen in place. "Is that—?"

"Bird Island." I turned away from the painting, not wanting to see anymore. "Let's go find Maddie."

We approached the stand, and a woman with a kind face and dark hair with eyes to match smiled warmly at us behind the cashbox. "Hello, ladies. See anything you like?"

"Hey, Mrs. Rose—we were actually looking for Maddie. Do you know where she might be?" Courtney asked brightly.

Mrs. Rose's face fell a bit. "You know, I wish I knew...she worked at the library last night, but when I went to pick her up, Portia Molley said she'd called out... She probably stayed over at Martin House, hmm?" Mrs. Rose forced a smile that didn't reach her eyes.

Courtney and I exchanged looks. Maddie definitely hadn't slept at Martin House last night.

"I'm not worried." Mrs. Rose waved a hand. "It's her birthday party this evening. She wouldn't miss that for anything."

Courtney and I smiled and said polite goodbyes before we turned and headed back up the slope to Martin Road. I pulled out the phone and turned it on.

I dialed Maddie's number as Courtney eyed me uneasily. A moment later, I shut the phone and shook my head. "Voicemail. And her inbox is full."

Courtney laced her arm through mine. "Maybe we'll run into her on the road?"

I shrugged as we merged into the herd of people walking down the road. "What should we do now?" I glanced at my watch. "It's almost lunch—we should head back to the picnic tables soon... didn't we plan to meet everybody there?"

"Psh. They can wait. I don't know about you, but I say we go hunting." Courtney's midnight-blue eyes narrowed with a sly smile.

I raised an eyebrow as I glanced down at her. "Hunting?"

"Yup." Courtney nodded seriously. "For good-looking guys."

"Courtney!" I snickered. "No thanks. I've got enough to worry about."

Courtney rolled her eyes and gave me a little shove, which only made us both laugh harder.

"Why don't we check out the library stand?" I nodded toward a row of tables piled with random, disorganized books. The woman, seated in the lawn chair overlooking them, with a cashbox clutched in her claw-like hands, scanned the crowd with beady eyes, magnified by thick glasses. With her hunched back and slow movements, she looked remarkably like a sloth.

"Maybe... Oh, look!" She tugged me to her and nodded nonchalantly toward the crowd. "There's Logan...my, my, does he look good in purple. But seriously, what is it with him and flannel? Did I tell you, I finally got to meet him?"

I stumbled a bit and looked around quickly as I regained my footing. I just barely saw the flash of purple flannel disappear in the throng of people. "You did?"

Courtney smiled warmly at me. "Yeah, he actually seemed pretty nice. He was looking for Maddie, so I gave him her number. And I asked him, *discreetly*, what he thought about you"—Courtney giggled as I gaped at her—"and he said you smile too much." Courtney laughed, rolling her eyes. "Honestly, I think you'd both look really good together. All tall and blonde and all." Courtney chuckled at my stricken face. "Or not?"

"Not." My voice was firm, but my mouth twitched with a slight smile; Courtney's amusement was infectious. "Let's keep going."

"Yes, let's. I've got my sights set on Cole, anyway— Ah! And there he is now..." She jutted her chin toward our left. I turned, and my heart dipped in my chest. Cole was down the hill a ways, helping out at a pink and purple tent with tons of scarves and lanterns and cushions all around it and a long line leading all the way up to the road.

"Who's that girl he's with?"

"Huh?" I stalled for time as my heart fluttered, panicked, in my chest.

"Whoever she is...she certainly has Cole's attention." Courtney giggled as she pulled me to a stop to watch Cole help Phoenix collect cash from a group of kids and hand out ticket stubs, pointing them toward the tent.

"No wonder he's always sidestepping me. He's had a secret girlfriend hidden in Nile all this time." Courtney crinkled her nose. "Wait, isn't that your tent, Sera? Do you know her?"

"I...no?" Shame sent my heart racing. "No, I don't. Uhh, clearly Cole's taken. Let's go meet everyone at the picnic tables. I'm sure Rachel's already there."

"Excellent idea. Maybe she knows who Cole's mystery girl is." Courtney giggled again as I pulled her around and led her away as fast as I could manage, as though I might run away from what I'd just done.

But of course—I couldn't.

I half ran, half dragged Courtney all the way to the picnic tables, my heart still hammering guiltily in my chest as we waited for everyone to show up. First, Peter found us. Then Rachel. And then Cheryl and Kaitlyn arrived with trays full of bowls of apple caramel and whipped cream. Aubrey took a seat beside me with a soft smile. Morgan and Daphne came right after, Morgan hopping onto the bench beside Courtney with Daphne lurking moodily off to the side as she surveyed the festivities with obvious disdain.

Then Rachel spied something behind me and leaned up in her seat. "Phoenix!"

My heart dropped.

Great.

I turned and, sure enough, Cole was escorting a beaming Phoenix to our picnic table.

Rachel jumped up from her seat and hugged her tightly. "Thank God you're here," she muttered in a loud whisper.

My gaze drifted to Courtney, who eyed Phoenix and Cole with amused interest. Aubrey watched curiously as Cole slid onto the bench across from us, with Phoenix and Rachel following soon after.

I fixed Phoenix with a wide-eyed warning stare, but she only smiled back in return. Completely oblivious as usual. I clenched my fists tightly beneath the table.

"Who's this, Cole?" Courtney smiled. Her eyes glittered. Something about Courtney and matchmaking...it was her favorite form of entertainment.

"I'm Phoenix. Phoenix Grey," she added brightly as she picked up Cole's fork and stabbed through the whipped cream in his bowl, pulling out an apple that dripped with caramel. She popped the apple into her mouth with a loud squish, unaware of the shocked looks that flickered on the faces all around the table as they stared from Phoenix to me and back again.

Aubrey looked over at me with a small, sympathetic smile.

My jaw tightened.

"Grey?" Morgan asked incredulously. "As in—?"

Rachel rolled her eyes as she grabbed her fork and joined Phoenix at Cole's bowl of apple caramel sundae. Cole let out a grunt of protest as the two girls picked apart his food.

"Yes." Rachel batted Cole away with the sticky, drippy end of her fork. She continued slowly, as though Morgan were slow in the head. "This is Phoenix, Seraphina's twin sister."

I could feel all the eyes roll over me and then Phoenix. It made my stomach lurch.

Courtney's brow furrowed as she looked at me. "Wait—I thought you said you didn't know her?"

Phoenix snorted into her bit of whipped cream.

Daphne's eyes met mine. "Of course she did." She smiled wickedly. "Haven't any of you learned yet? Seraphina *had* to keep her sister a secret. Otherwise, she'd have to share the attention."

"Shut up, Daph," Cole muttered.

She shrugged with a satisfied smirk.

"I was hoping we'd finally meet this mystery second sister." Peter smiled, setting his dimples deep in his cheeks, completely oblivious to the tension bubbling up around the table.

"You're *twins*?" Aubrey whispered, her voice low and hurt as she tugged on her locket.

Aubrey knew I had a sister, but I hadn't ever explained that we were twins. Apparently, that was something friends were supposed to share. I'd hurt her feelings.

Before I could whisper an apology, Damien sauntered up and spied Phoenix. He grinned as he sat beside Aubrey, directly across from Phoenix. "Well, if it isn't the mysterious Miss Grey. I'd know you anywhere. You remember me? The State Fair a couple of weeks ago? At the Sights and Seers tent?"

Phoenix stabbed another one of Cole's apples and pointed the sticky slice at him. "And I bet *you're* the captain of the football team."

I glared daggers at Phoenix as she dared to give me a roguish wink.

Rachel continued to fight Cole for his apple caramel. Courtney and Peter began to discuss whether or not we shared any resemblance. Aubrey had gone silent. Morgan and Cheryl couldn't stop staring back and forth between us. And Damien chastised Cole for not bringing Phoenix to a football game.

Phoenix watched all of this with mild interest as she munched on another bite of Cole's apple caramel. She smirked at the unfolding scene. "Well, now that introductions have been made...who wants to go grab Cole's four-wheeler and take it through the woods?"

And with that, Phoenix was an instant favorite of the whole

table. I watched, my heart sinking, as everyone began to talk excitedly—except Cole, who glared at Phoenix. "The four-wheeler is a mode of transportation, not a festival ride."

"Oh, hush, Cole." Phoenix ruffled his black hair as she pushed up from the table. "Don't be such a grump."

Cole groaned. I frowned. He would cave. He never could say no to Phoenix. But could anyone? My face hardened. I could.

"Phoenix, don't you need to help Grammy at the tent?"

At that, Cheryl's eyes lit up. "Oh my gosh." She got up from her seat and hung on to Phoenix like she was afraid she'd try to get away. "That's your tent. Your mom is doing fortune-telling!"

"Grandmother, actually," Phoenix corrected with a smile that barely hid her laughter as she watched Cheryl continue to yank on her arm.

"Oh, Kaitlyn!" Cheryl was absolutely beside herself. "Let's get our fortunes told! Puhleaseee. That will solve everything!"

Daphne frowned disapprovingly. "I think I'm going to go... anywhere else." She stood slowly from the table and left without another word.

Courtney jumped up, tugging Peter to his feet. "I'm game!"

I raised my eyebrows, eyes wide as I watched all my friends, and then some, flock around Phoenix. I opened my mouth to argue but shut it slowly when the words soured on my tongue.

Aubrey was the only one still beside me on the bench of the picnic table. She took my hand and squeezed it reassuringly, as even Damien hopped up and joined the growing group huddle.

"Sounds like a plan to me." He clapped Cole on the back and grinned a devilishly handsome smile. "Fortunes and four-wheelers. My kinda Apple Fest."

Cheryl and Kaitlyn sidled up next to Phoenix and chattered away about all the things they couldn't believe: how Seraphina had kept Phoenix a secret from them, how cool her outfit was, how awesome her hair was, how unique her hair accessory was, etc.

Morgan and even Courtney had eyes only for her. I glared at Phoenix as she positively glowed under all the attention.

Aubrey and I followed, hanging back a bit, as Phoenix led everyone to our family tent.

"Hey, are you all right?" Aubrey murmured as she wrapped an arm around me.

Tears burned in my eyes as I blinked them back. The whole thing was ridiculous. I was upset because my friends liked my sister. How petty was that? How disgustingly insecure. I shrugged and shook my head. Anger bubbled in the pit of my stomach and boiled in my veins. If Phoenix would've just stayed at the tent... But, as usual, she couldn't let me have anything to myself. At least I had Aubrey. I sighed then, relaxing just a bit. "I'm fine. Let's go before we lose them."

"No..." Aubrey stopped and pulled me to the side of the road, away from the foot traffic. "You're *not* fine." She looked deep into my eyes, reached up and smoothed a gentle thumb underneath them, brushing away the tears.

I gave a watery laugh. "Okay, maybe I'm not."

"But you will be..." Aubrey gave me a sweet smile as she squeezed my arm. "You'll see. I'm sure we'll have fun." She pulled me back onto the road, and we started after them. Aubrey gave a nervous chuckle. "I just hope Courtney doesn't invite her to Maddie's sleepover tonight."

There was quite a line outside our family tent. It led all the way up to the street, so we all huddled at the side of the road. Conversation flowed freely around the group, but Aubrey and I remained silent.

Then Courtney smacked Phoenix playfully on the arm. "What are you doing after Apple Fest?"

My heart sank slowly into the pit of my stomach.

I looked at Aubrey, who gave me a sympathetic wince.

Phoenix shrugged, frowning good-naturedly. "Nothing, why?"

Courtney grinned and jutted her thumb toward me. "Sera and I are going to a birthday party. Do you want to come with?"

Phoenix raised her eyebrows at me. "That sounds—"

No. No way. I elbowed past Morgan and grabbed Phoenix by the arm. "Excuse us...Phoenix and I need to check something. We'll be right back." I yanked Phoenix out of the line and marched her down the grassy hill, around the back of the tent, and toward the fields beyond, out of earshot of everyone.

Phoenix was laughing. "What is your deal?"

I released her arm with a push. "What is *your* deal?"

Phoenix stopped laughing but couldn't hide her smile. "You want to talk about it?"

I folded my arms across my chest. "You first: What do you think you're doing?"

Phoenix rolled her eyes. "I thought I was getting invited to a birthday party..."

I scoffed. "You can't seriously expect to say yes?"

Phoenix shrugged lazily and shoved her hands in the oversized pockets of her baggy black pants. "What's it to you?"

I gritted my teeth. "I just figured it wouldn't be your thing..."

"Right." Phoenix snickered. "Unlike you, who can't get enough."

"I like hanging out with my friends...so what?!"

Phoenix shook her head with a nasty smirk. "Just because people hang out with you doesn't make them your friends."

"You can't stand it, can you?" I snapped accusingly. "I finally have something that you don't have, and you're so jealous, you can't stand it. You just had to swoop in and steal all the attention. You don't get enough at home, so you need it from my friends, too?"

"No, Seraphina, that's you," Phoenix replied coolly. "You're the one who can't stand being left out, can't stand not being the center of attention. I mean, look at you: you're having a meltdown because your so-called 'friend' invited me to a birthday party."

I scoffed, the hurt muddling my words in my mouth.

Phoenix shook her head and looked away. Then her eyes slid back to meet mine as she smirked. "You know what, maybe I *will* go to that party. See what all the fuss is about..."

My eyes burned as my blood surged, sending my heart into a furious pace. "Phoenix, I swear to God—"

Phoenix laughed. "Right—I wouldn't want to hurt your feelings."

"My feelings? When have you *ever* cared about my feelings?"

"Seriously?" Phoenix's smile slid to one side as she stared at me, open-mouthed. "*All of us* have to tiptoe around you, have to make sure we don't upset you with our magic. God, Phin, Mama doesn't even do magic to wash the dishes!"

Her words hit like a smack in the face. I jutted my chin up in an effort to hold back the tears.

Phoenix didn't stop there. "You ever wonder why I don't put in any effort in my studies? Why I slack off and goof around all the time?"

I backed up a step.

I didn't want to hear it.

But Phoenix stepped forward. "Because I don't want to make you feel bad by actually succeeding when you can't. I'm constantly dumbing myself down, so I can spare your feelings...but the funny thing is?" Phoenix gave a mirthless laugh as her face hardened and her voice went cold. "You couldn't care less about mine. You say you have all these friends?" She waved her hand back toward the tent in the distance. "You don't even know what it means to be a friend, Seraphina. If you did, you wouldn't have abandoned Fawn. And you wouldn't have shut me out. And you wouldn't blame me for every single thing that goes wrong in your life." She thumped her fist against her heart with each word as tears spilled unexpectedly down her face.

Her hand fell to her side, and she took a shaky breath as she continued in a low, broken voice, "And you wouldn't have told that girl that you didn't even know me."

The words were like barbed wire, wrapping around my heart and shredding it with each beat. Shame fell over me like a shadow. I tried to speak, but nothing came out. I couldn't argue with any of it. But I tried. "I didn't abandon Fawn."

Phoenix wiped her nose on the sleeve of her leather jacket. A cold, hollow laugh burst out of her. "Oh no? What is she working on lately? What's her favorite book these days? How have her potions turned out? You were supposed to help her with her herb collection for her potions; did you get around to that? You've been so wrapped up in your new 'friends,' it's like we don't even matter to you anymore."

"*You* don't, Phoenix. You don't matter at all to me. And I don't need you," I shot back, venom in my words.

Phoenix blinked at me. Her face darkened. "I know you don't mean that, Phin...but you'll regret saying that someday."

"Why?" I demanded, my eyes hot with unshed tears. "Because you can conjure and I can't cast to save my life? Big deal. Get over yourself."

Phoenix looked away in disbelief with a roll of her eyes and a shake of her head. "It always comes back to that, doesn't it?" Then she turned, her amber eyes hard. "You get over yourself and grow up while you're at it." She pushed past me and stomped back toward the tent. But then she paused and turned back, her face wet and sad. "We used to be best friends, Phinny. What happened to us?" She hesitated. Then she opened her mouth and closed it again. She folded her lips together as though she was trying to hold something back. But she couldn't. "That school has messed you up. Changed you somehow. Your whole attitude blows more bitter than a bad potion."

I sputtered as my head spun in circles, trying to make sense of what Phoenix was saying. Yes, I was hard on Phoenix, but it's not like I set out to be that way. I just got so angry with her some-times...I hadn't *changed*, though. Had I?

Phoenix kept going, encouraged by my silence. "And it's not just me who's noticed it. Cole and Rachel have both said things. You ever stop to think that if the people you hang out with start to bring out the hag in you, it's probably time to stop associating with them?"

My lip curled at that, and my wits snapped back into focus as my defenses hardened. "Why? So I can be alone forever like you?"

Phoenix smiled. "Well, I guess I'm lucky I have a twin then, huh?"

I hit harder. "I wish I didn't."

Phoenix's head jutted back as though I had taken a swipe at her, and her nose crinkled in disgust. She sniffed through tears as she chuckled darkly. "You know what, Phin? I'm done. I'm leav-ing. Keep your friends to yourself. Stay at that hexed-up school. *And don't ever talk to me again.*"

I stayed there for a while, tears flowing unchecked, frozen in shock. It was Aubrey who finally peeked around the tent and hurried over to me. She took her sleeve and dabbed at my face. Then she gingerly took my hand. "Let's go for a walk through the orchard. That always makes me feel better...and then we can meet up with everyone later."

I nodded, unable to speak, and allowed her to lead me back to the road and down the street.

We didn't get far before we heard the scream.

It ripped through the low rumble of the crowd.

Distinct and separate, shrill and scared.

I grabbed Aubrey tight. The two of us slowed to a stop in the middle of the road as a strange silence fell over the Apple Fest, the only sound the branches of apple trees creaking as they swayed in the wind. People all around us had frozen in place, and then every face looked left and right, craning necks, extended on tiptoes, searching for the source of the scream.

Then the crowd parted as a couple burst out of the apple orchard and ran up the slope to the street, clinging tightly to each other. The guy's face was pale, and the girl flung an arm out, pointing back toward the apple orchard.

"It's Maddie!" she shrieked. Her whole body trembled with her panic. "*It's Maddison Rose!*" She burst into terrified sobs that sent shock waves through her whole body. The guy gripped her hard, and his mouth formed silent words. His eyes were blank as they blinked and bulged in his head.

"Maddie?" Aubrey whispered, as the crowd came alive again with noise and activity.

A group of men pulled away from the mass of people and shouted directions to one another. Two were tasked with finding Maddie's parents, and the rest of them, including the sheriff's two sons, who were deputies, charged into the apple orchard.

The world seemed to spin as I stared wide-eyed at the teens, who had sunk to their knees at the side of the road. "Aubrey... Aubrey, let's go find my grandma..."

"Your grandma?" Aubrey asked softly, her face dazed.

I nodded, unable to tear my eyes from the girl who continued to carry on in a combination of shudders and screaming cries as the guy held onto her and buried his head into her brown hair. I nodded again. Yes. I wanted Grammy. Now. "Come on."

I grabbed Aubrey's hand hard and pulled her through the crowd, which was becoming louder and more panicked by the second. Soon everyone was running, pushing and shoving in different directions.

Before we could make it back to the tent, Damien shoved his way through part of the crowd, closely followed by Morgan. He seized Aubrey by the arm. "Let's go."

"Wait, Day! Seraphina said—" Aubrey tried to hold him back,

but he tugged her along in the opposite direction toward the parking lot.

"No, Aubrey. We're going. Now."

"It's okay, Aubrey," I shouted after them. "I'll call you later!" I didn't waste any time. I pushed past people and elbowed my way through the masses, my only thought to find Grammy as fast as I could. I ran down the sloping grass as soon as I saw the tent. There was still a line. People hadn't heard. They didn't know. Something had happened to Maddison Rose.

Someone grabbed me into a hard hug from behind. Cole. I clung to him and squeezed.

"I heard the screaming. Then I heard about Maddie—I looked for you everywhere—" He crushed me to him. "Come on, we need to get to Phoenix—"

"You heard about Maddie?" I let him lead me down the slope to the tent, grateful for the strength of his arm around my shoulders, keeping me grounded. "Is she okay? What happened? Aubrey and I didn't hear—"

Cole pushed me back and held me at arm's length, his eyes shining and his full lips drawn in a pained line. "Phin, they're saying she's dead."

MISS MURDER

"I haven't been able to stop thinking about Maddie. It's like my mom all over again. I heard they found her ripped apart. Like an animal attack, but much worse than that."

"Ugh, Aubrey, please." I closed my eyes, but the image of Maddison, shredded all over the apple trees, was now burned into my brain.

"Sorry," Aubrey murmured sincerely. "And I'm so sorry for everything that you're dealing with…"

"What do you mean?" My voice thinned with lost patience as I leaned against her locker.

A group of kids passed by us, their eyes moving over me. I glared back, biting my tongue so I wouldn't stick it out. One girl held her fingers up like a cross in my direction. The others laughed and hurried away.

Aubrey gripped her books to her chest. She looked up at me warily. "You haven't heard?"

I sighed heavily and leaned my head against the cold metal locker door. "Heard what, Aubrey?"

Aubrey hesitated. "People are saying you had something to do with it…Maddie, I mean." Aubrey winced as she said the words.

I scoffed. "Figures." That explained a lot: the dirty looks, the whispers, the fear in freshman eyes. Ever since Monday. The whole school had made grieving over Maddie that much worse.

Although, I was lucky I even got to go back to school at all. After what happened at the Apple Fest, Grammy had argued that both Phoenix and I should stay with her at Blackwell Manor until Mama got back to Nile. But Icarus refused to allow her to remove us from the cottage against our will, and neither of us wanted to go, so it was only Fawn whom she dragged back to Blackwell Manor.

Grammy wasn't too thrilled that she was overruled by a cat. Honestly, I'd never seen her so furious. But Icarus, as a familiar, had his own magic that was beyond any witch's understanding, and as powerful a witch as she was, Grammy couldn't cross him. And Icarus had specific instructions from Mama that I be allowed to attend the school and that Phoenix be allowed to remain at Grey Cottage. Until he heard otherwise, which he wouldn't because Mama was Unreachable, I was permitted to go to school.

Grammy could have sent him to Mama with a message, but wherever Mama was, whatever Mama was doing for the High Council, Grammy didn't feel this emergency warranted disturbing her. That in and of itself freaked me out.

Now, I almost wished I had gone with Grammy to Blackwell Manor.

"I wonder who started *that* rumor." I rolled my eyes in disgust. "How low can you get?"

Aubrey nodded solemnly. I pushed off the locker, and we started to walk to the auditorium for the assembly. Aubrey leaned into me. "You need to be careful, Sera."

"Aubrey, no one in their right mind would think that I had anything to do with—"

"It's not just Maddie," Aubrey breathed as we moved through the hallway. "Michael and Brentley both have chicken pox."

"So?"

"They both have had it before...do you know the chances of getting chicken pox *twice*? Like zero." Aubrey winced and threaded her arm through mine. "And that's what you said would happen to Brentley, remember? If he didn't leave you alone?"

My walk slowed, and I glanced down at her. I'd forgotten all about that. "But I didn't say anything about *chicken pox*—" Although, I had thought it...the varicella hex was Phoenix's favorite, and it had been the first thing I thought of at the time...

"I'm just saying, you need to be careful." Aubrey gave me a weak smile as we came to a stop outside the auditorium and joined the crowd of kids waiting to get inside.

As kids started to notice me, their attention shifted, and their voices lowered. I shuffled from one foot to the other, uncomfortable underneath the weight of their stares. I scanned the crowd as though I might find a way out.

I saw Kaitlyn and Cheryl huddled together off to the side of the cheerleaders. They looked like they were consoling each other... or arguing. I studied them as they talked animatedly together. Something was off... Kaitlyn. She didn't look well. Her dark skin had lost its glow, looking ashen and dull beneath the bad fluorescent lights. Her eyes were too wide in her head.

I nudged Aubrey. "What's wrong with Kaitlyn?"

Aubrey followed my gaze. "Oh, yeah. She's taking Maddie's death really hard."

I scrunched up my face. "They weren't close, were they?"

Aubrey shrugged.

I watched her whisper with Cheryl, whose face was so blotchy and red I could barely make out her freckles.

I frowned. "Was Maddie friends with the squad?"

Aubrey tugged on her locket as she watched Cheryl cling to Kaitlyn for support. "You know, I think the idea of what happened to her has messed up everyone...whether they were close to her or not."

"Maybe—"

Daphne's voice came from behind me. "You were close to Maddison, though, weren't you, Seraphina?"

I rolled my shoulders and turned around to face her, steeling myself for the worst. "What do you want, Daphne?"

"I want you to *leave*." Daphne crossed her arms, her black eyes hard with malice. "Go back to that dumb rock on the lake and leave the rest of us alone."

In that moment, I considered it...for the dozenth time that day. But then I remembered Phoenix...and how she'd told me almost the same thing. "You know what, Daphne...why don't you just leave *me* alone. This is getting really old."

"I know you did it," she whispered.

I scoffed. "Right. Keep telling yourself that."

"Oh, I am. And anyone else who will listen." Daphne gave me a final scathing glare, before disappearing into the crowd of students.

Hot tears leaked out of the corners of my eyes, and I slapped them away.

Aubrey bit her lip. "Are you okay?"

I choked on a dark, watery laugh. "No."

Aubrey nodded sympathetically. After a moment of silence between us, the doors to the auditorium opened. Rachel and Cole appeared beside us, and we all herded inside with the crowd.

Father LaValley had called the assembly to talk about Maddie. He spoke about how great of a person she was—great sister and loving daughter—complete with a slideshow that flashed all different candid pictures of Maddie throughout her life. There were a few pictures of her with Rachel and Aubrey, some of her with Peter and Cole, but most of the pictures were of her with a girl with white-blonde hair whom I recognized from the purple bus. ("Lacey McGregor," Rachel whispered.)

Then, at the end of Father LaValley's presentation, he wanted to assure us all that it was an isolated incident. Nothing to be afraid of. That the Nile sheriff had concluded that it'd been an animal attack. A dog mauling. There were murmurs of dissent throughout the rows of students. Eyes found me. I sank a bit lower in my seat. Cole wrapped an arm around me and squeezed. At the end of it, the bell rang signaling the end of school. Almost as one, the entire student body stood and flooded out of the auditorium. I didn't move.

Cole and Rachel stood with the rest of them but noticed I was still seated, and hesitated. "Phin, you ready?" Rachel asked tentatively. "We can head to Hallowed Grounds?"

"You guys go. I want to walk." I forced a weak smile.

"I'll walk with you." Rachel nudged my sneaker with her black combat boot.

I shook my head as I looked up at her wearily. "I just want to be alone for a bit. But I'll meet you there?"

Cole and Rachel exchanged a glance and then agreed begrudgingly.

I watched them go, my heart aching.

Aubrey stayed in her seat beside me, watching as the place emptied. "You know what I haven't been able to get out of my head?"

I sniffed, wiping my nose on my hoodie. "What?"

Aubrey nibbled her lower lip. "Well, remember that guy? The creep who was following you everywhere? He was looking for Maddie after school, remember? What was his name?"

I'd forgotten about that.

After they'd found Maddison, Sheriff Vantine had shut the Apple Fest down, and then the weekend...and this whole week had gone by in a haze of mourning. I hadn't been able to think straight, much less go into my dorm room. Rachel had let me drop my stuff in her room for now. My head had been so muddled with everything, I hadn't remembered much of what had happened last week, much less guys with piercing stares and pickup trucks.

"Logan?" His name left my lips in a whisper.

"Exactly." Aubrey's blue eyes widened. "This random guy is looking for her, and then a day later she shows up dead? That's...weird."

"Wait, wait." I rubbed my temple as though massaging away a migraine. "You're suggesting...?"

"I'm suggesting..." Aubrey bit her lip as she tugged on her locket. "We learn more about this guy than just his name."

I made a face. "How are we going to do that, Aubrey? It's not like we can bust into his dorm and look for clues, or..." I groaned as Aubrey nodded enthusiastically. "You want to break into his dorm room and look for clues? *Like what*?!"

Aubrey wasn't about to let it go. "It'll be easy. We just need to grab his dorm key from the office...they keep spares there for every room."

I frowned. This didn't feel right.

"Well, Aubrey." The voice at our ears made us both jump. We twisted around. Daphne. She straightened in her seat and grinned. "I never thought I'd say: interesting idea."

I grabbed my bag off the floor and stood quickly, dragging Aubrey up with me. "We were just leaving."

Daphne's eyes glittered. "I think you should do it."

"Do what?" I snapped impatiently as I shifted the weight of my bag on my back.

"Don't play dumb, Seraphina." Daphne stood and crossed her arms over her chest. "You want to prove you're innocent? Then actually prove it."

"First, I'm a fake, now I'm a wicked witch?" I sneered, lip curled in disgust. "Get your story straight, Daphne. It'll be more believable." Then I nudged Aubrey. "Come on."

Aubrey hesitated, eyeing Daphne with anxious interest. "If we find something on this guy—will you leave Sera alone?"

"Sure..." Daphne grinned, a sly sparkle in her black eyes. "I'll meet you guys at Martin House at midnight." She snickered as she turned on her heel. Then she walked down the row of seats and out of the auditorium, leaving Aubrey and me staring after her.

I sighed and looked down at Aubrey as she nibbled on her lip and tugged on her locket. "We can't do this, Aubrey."

"You heard her..." Aubrey lightly touched my arm, her eyes earnest. "If we can find something to connect that guy to Maddie, then she'll leave you alone!"

I had to laugh. "You know she's not going to, no matter what we find. And honestly, I don't care if she—"

"And it's not just that." Aubrey's sapphire eyes fell to her feet. "Sera, we have to check him out. We were the ones who told him Maddie would be at the Apple Fest, remember?"

I felt sick. The guilt twisted inside my stomach, churning with bile, hot and sour. *I* was the one who told him.

Aubrey met my eyes with a solemn stare. "On the flip side, at the very least, maybe we can clear our conscience."

I took a deep breath. "How are we going to do it?"

Aubrey took my hand and gave it a squeeze. "Meet me in the front courtyard in twenty minutes."

She was late. An hour later, I was still waiting and shivering outside the school on a stone bench underneath the cold, dying sun. I couldn't help but continuously check my watch as student after student jumped in a car or took off down the sidewalk in one direction or another. Eventually, the courtyard emptied, and only I remained.

The scurry of fallen leaves scratched passed me on the sidewalk, carried carelessly by the chilly breeze as I watched the front doors to the lobby, willing Aubrey to appear. But when the double doors finally flew open, it was Daphne who marched out...headed straight for me.

"Hey, Witch Spawn." She smiled cruelly.

I squinted up at her as she stood over me. "Didn't I tell you to leave me alone?"

Ignoring me, Daphne dropped her backpack onto the bench beside me. "Aubrey wanted me to give this to you." Gingerly, she pulled out a manila file and handed it to me.

I glanced around the empty courtyard as I took it reluctantly in both hands. "What is it?"

Daphne smirked as she crossed her arms and nodded toward the folder. "Open it."

It was marked DeVarney, Logan.

Clearly, it was his student file.

A trickle of foreboding sent goose bumps up and down my arms and prickled the hairs on the nape of my neck as I opened it to find—nothing. There was nothing. It was almost completely blank, save for a class schedule, his dorm room, locker number and combination, and a phone number. An out-of-state phone number.

This wasn't right.

Student files held class records, histories, medical documents... at least, they should. It was as though Logan DeVarney hadn't existed prior to his enrollment in Mater Christi High School.

I took out a pen and copied down the information on the back of my hand and passed her back the folder. I massaged my temple as I tried to think straight. "Where's Aubrey?"

"She went to gather her little detective supplies from my house." Daphne snickered.

Ignoring her, I studied the phone number on my hand.

Daphne fingered the folder in her hands. "So, what's your big plan tonight, Witchy Drew?"

"No idea." I grabbed my backpack from the ground and walked away.

"*I'll see you tonight,*" Daphne called after me in a singsong voice.

I slowed and turned with slumped shoulders. Daphne's eyes

were cold and her mouth was curved in a wide, white grin. Then she closed the distance between us, the manila folder pinched between her fingers as she teetered it back and forth tauntingly.

I jutted my jaw to the side, impatience clipping my words sharp. "Listen, I honestly don't care what you think of me, or what rumors you spread about me. I'm not doing this for you, or for me. So, why don't you just stay out of it and leave me alone."

Daphne pouted mockingly. "Right, right, it's for Maddie."

"Yup."

The phone vibrated in my pocket. I checked it.

I'll meet you in the common room at midnight.

Without another word to Daphne, I turned back around and headed down the sidewalk, huddled in my hoodie against the cold, toward Hallowed Grounds, with her laughter cackling behind me.

I didn't leave Hallowed Grounds until late—well after everyone else had left. I just couldn't make myself head back to Martin House. I hadn't been back in my dorm room since last week. After Maddie—well, I just couldn't make myself open that door. So, I was sleeping on Rachel's floor for the moment. And as I walked to Martin House, in the dark and through the wind, I was grateful to have her room to go home to tonight.

When I came upon the House, the lights, which I used to find cozy, looked eerie and cold, like little ghosts lurking in each corner of the windows and peeking through the cracks in the curtains. Keeping my eyes down, I headed inside to find the common room full of kids, all of whom stopped to stare as I cut through the crowd and hurried down the hallway.

When I made it to the kitchen, Cole was sitting next to Rachel at the table with a bowl of cereal in front of him as he talked on the phone. Judging by the hint of a smile in the corner of his mouth, he was talking to Phoenix.

Rachel passed me a banana as I took a seat. I took the fruit but didn't peel it. Instead, I only stared at it, lost in thought. Aubrey and I were never going to be able to sneak into the office for Logan's dorm key with all these kids around. We'd have to wait until the whole house went to sleep. And how would we even be sure he wasn't in his dorm already?

Suddenly, Damien sauntered into the kitchen and plopped down into a chair across from me.

Rachel glared at him as she took a bite of her banana and said around her mouthful, "What do you want?"

Damien leaned back in his chair, his hands threaded behind his head. He looked at me, ignoring Rachel. "Daphne told me to tell you he's not here tonight."

Rachel looked from me back to Damien.

Cole moved the phone away from his ear. "What? Who?"

Damien smirked and closed his eyes lazily. "Don't shoot me. I'm just the messenger."

I swallowed thickly, my mouth suddenly incredibly dry and sticky.

Rachel scoffed and looked at me. I shook my head. Rachel glared at Damien. "Well...message received. Now you can go."

Damien pretended not to hear her.

Rachel didn't stop. "I don't know what Aubrey ever saw in you, but I am so glad she got rid of you."

Damien slowly tipped his chair back into an upright position. His eyes opened to give Rachel a cold, deadpan stare.

"Especially after what you did to her last month," Rachel nearly spat.

Damien shoved violently off the table to his feet. Cole stood up from the table with him, his phone forgotten on the table, his eyes on Damien.

Eyes wide, I looked between the three of them.

Rachel gripped the table and leaned forward, her voice low and cold. "We all know what you did, Damien. Elijah told everybody."

Damien's handsome face had darkened into an ugly,

murderous sneer. His fists were clenched and his arms taut. "It was a *joke*."

"Time to go, Day," Cole said quietly.

Damien scoffed. "Screw this." He knocked over his chair in Cole's direction. He waved Cole off, his voice breaking. "I don't need this." Then he stalked out of the room.

I blinked. "What...just...*what*?"

Cole started to explain, but Rachel shot him a warning look, and he shut his mouth. Turning to me, she sighed heavily. "Has Aubrey told you about Bird Island?"

"Not really..."

Rachel gave Cole a pointed expression and gestured to me. Then she looked at me with a grim wince. "Then you'll have to ask her."

I sat in the common room until late in the night. It wasn't until almost three in the morning that all the students, along with the ancient dorm dad, Mr. Whayland, finally made it upstairs to their rooms. I don't know when I fell asleep, but I was startled awake by the front door beeping Aubrey and Daphne inside.

"Aubrey?" I rubbed the sleep from my eyes as Aubrey pulled me out of the chair. "Where have you been? I thought we said midnight?"

Daphne wore a surly expression and gripped a bag tightly in her hands.

"We tried to break into his locker, but we couldn't get in...then I had to go to Cheryl's house, and she didn't want me to leave. She keeps saying someone is watching her." Aubrey shook her head sadly as we snuck our way to the office room. "The whole Maddison thing, she's really tore up about it..."

I flinched at her word choice and stared at Aubrey, aghast. She gave a pained expression as she waved her words away.

Daphne leaned over toward the keys. "Damien checked

Logan's room for me. And he checked the sign-in sheet—Logan didn't sign back in on Monday...which means—" She pointed to the key with a number 22 tag. "It's that one."

I raised an eyebrow as Daphne continued to point as though she didn't want to take the key herself. I rolled my eyes. Typical. I reached up and took the key, squeezing it tight in my hand, and Daphne finished, "Which means—we don't have to worry about him being in there when you go inside."

"No, we just have to make sure no one sees us hanging around the boys' dormitory," I quipped flatly as we made our way back to the common room.

"You mean, *you*," Daphne corrected.

I stopped. "What? *Me*?"

"You." Daphne smirked. "I'm not involved, and Aubrey's too chicken. So that leaves you to break in, Aubrey to keep watch, and me to watch the show. Be careful, though...pretty sure you can get suspended for breaking into someone else's dorm..." Daphne's smile curved wickedly as she watched me process everything.

I looked from one girl to the next, my stomach heavy. "Aubrey—"

"It'll be fine." Aubrey walked briskly up to stand beside the boys' staircase. She leaned against the wall, her arms crossed over her chest and a weak smile on her face. "I'll keep a lookout down here. And if I see Logan—or any guy, for that matter—come inside...I'll get you out of there."

I cocked an eyebrow. "There are so many flaws in this plan."

Aubrey's smile faltered as her brow crinkled in concern.

I sighed. "What's your excuse for hanging around the boys' dorm stairs?"

Aubrey hesitated, glancing at Daphne anxiously. "We're waiting for Damien...?"

My stomach twisted into a little knot at the mention of his name. What had he done to her?

"Okay," I murmured finally. "But Aubrey...what am I hoping to find in there? Like...what do I look for?"

Daphne pulled a walkie-talkie out of her designer backpack. "That's what these are for. You tell us what you see, and I'll tell you whether or not to stuff it in my bag." Daphne held out the bag and the walkie-talkie.

I frowned as I snatched the bag and the walkie-talkie from her hands. "I thought you weren't involved..."

Daphne snickered. "Not on record."

I looked at the stairs. They teetered up just as dramatically as the girls' stairs. I glanced back at Aubrey, who nodded encouragingly.

We had to do this.

For Maddie.

"Talk to you soon."

And I headed up the staircase, my hand tight on the railing. As I drew closer to the top of the stairs, I realized the boys' dorms were a mirror of the girls', with everything going the opposite way. At the landing, the second small steps led to the right toward Mr. Whayland's room, from which snores vibrated loudly, reminding me of the sleeping dragon in Fawn's favorite fairy tale. I turned left down the hall and moved past door after door. I flipped the key over in my hand as I approached the dorm at the end of the hall with a 22 on it, but no nameplate. I glanced down the deserted hallway. Then I slid the key into the lock. In one motion, I turned both the key and the doorknob, and pushed my way inside.

"*Hey!*"

I gasped and glared angrily at the walkie-talkie. I squeezed the button. "I'm in, Aubrey. Hang on!"

My feet slipped a bit on something like dirt on the ground. Moving my hand along the wall, I found the light switch. I flicked it on as I shut the door behind me. Heart hammering, I took in the room. The mess I'd walked all over appeared to be salt or something similar. Whatever it was, he'd spilled it in front of the door and hadn't even bothered to pick it up. His bed wasn't made, so he'd slept in it once, at least. There was a pile of old books all over the bed. The floor beside the wastebasket was littered with empty snack-sized chip bags. He either had bad aim or just didn't care.

"*Seraphina!*"

I squeezed the walkie-talkie again as I looked at the desk. "What am I looking for here? It's not like he has a serial killer wall of death or anything obviously insane."

"Do you see any clothes?" Daphne's voice crackled out of the speaker, cold and sharp as ice. "Like a hoodie or something?"

"What?" I asked incredulously as I leaned over the desk to peek at what looked like a journal. "Why would we want his clothes?"

"If he murdered Maddie, there could be blood or something..." Daphne's voice crackled sarcastically.

I moved away from the desk and turned toward a pile of dirty clothes on the floor. "I highly doubt he'd leave bloody clothes lying around..." I muttered without squeezing the talk button. I was beginning to feel increasingly stupid for having thought snooping through his room would help anything. I studied the pile of clothes and noticed a purple flannel shirt on top of the pile. He'd been wearing that when Courtney pointed him out at the Apple Fest. Heart leaping a bit in my chest, I grabbed it quickly and stuffed it in the bag.

"Anything with his DNA on it?" Aubrey's voice crackled in the speaker.

I turned back to the desk, squeezing the talk button. "There's a flask here...?"

"What's in it?"

I put the walkie-talkie down on the desk and picked up the bottle. It was transparent glass, not like the metal ones I'd seen on TV. The liquid was clear. I unscrewed the top and took a tentative sniff.

"Why would he keep water in a flask?" I murmured, twisting the cap back on and dropping it into the bag.

My gaze was drawn to the journal again. Boys didn't usually keep journals, did they? I opened it. It was a miniature binder with little pockets on the inside cover, packed with random ephemera. The pages were covered with notes in an untidy scrawl that was almost impossible to decipher without squinted effort. There were symbols and markings, most of which I didn't understand, scribbled into the margins and sometimes taking up full pages. Not only were the pages messy with words, but there were several coffee rings and a few more stains on the weathered pages that looked suspiciously like blood. It was like some perverse Book of Shadows, but instead of spellwork and potions, it had descriptions of what appeared to be creatures...like an evil *Fantastic Beasts and Where to Find Them*.

Maybe he was some kind of horror buff?

I turned to the last few pages.

My heart dropped into the pit of my stomach as I read the list scribbled on the page:

Sarah Rousseau, Kyle Rousseau, Maddison Rose

1 8

DIRTY LITTLE SECRET

I stepped back from the book. My rushing blood pounded in my ears. That could be bad. That could be really, really bad.

"Guys...guys, I think I found something...it's like a journal..."

"Grab it quick. I hear someone coming," Daphne snapped, her voice static in the speaker.

"But he'll know someone took it!"

"Do it! Time's up."

Thinking fast, I ripped out the last few pages and shoved them into the pocket of my jeans. I slapped the book shut and did one final glance around the room, noting a metal baseball bat propped up against the bed, along with what looked like a huge machete in a sheath. I squeezed the key so tight in my palm it hurt. That's it. I was done. Tapped out of creepy.

Fighting the urge to throw the door open and run, I eased it ajar and checked to make sure the hallway was empty before I slipped out and closed it behind me. I turned the key, locking the door just as it had been before, and hurried down the stairs as fast as I could manage without falling face-first.

Aubrey grabbed me just as I stumbled down the final steps and pulled me toward the girls' dormitory.

I clutched at my chest as I caught my breath. "Who was it?"

Daphne shrugged. "False alarm." Then her hand lashed out and snatched her bag from me. She yanked it open, tilting it from side to side to see the contents. "This is it?" Daphne scoffed, wrinkling her nose at the shirt and flask. "I thought you grabbed a journal?"

I tossed her the walkie-talkie and tucked my hand in my pocket, shoving the journal pages even deeper. I shrugged. "I didn't have time to grab it."

Daphne rolled her eyes. "Whatever. This will work."

My brow furrowed as I studied her. "What do you mean?"

A sly smirk slid onto her face. Daphne zipped up the bag and slipped it over her shoulder. "Breaking into an assigned dorm is a suspendable offense...and stealing personal property is just as bad as vandalizing it with red paint."

Aubrey's face fell.

I blinked stupidly.

"Sister Francis nearly expelled me for that dumb doll prank..." Daphne shook her head and sighed with a satisfied smile. "Payback's a witch, girls."

Aubrey and I exchanged an anxious glance. "Daphne—"

"You realize how much trouble I'm in because of you snitches? You should've laughed it off like a big girl, Seraphina, but you just had to go running to LaValley." Daphne snickered and gave her bag a soft pat. "Enjoy your last night in Martin House, Seraphina... because I doubt you'll be going to school here come tomorrow morning."

Aubrey and I stood, stunned motionless, as we watched her go, slamming the Martin House door behind her.

Great.

"I'm so sorry, Seraphina." Aubrey tucked her hair behind her ear. "I just thought maybe—I don't know. I was stupid. If they try to kick you out, I'll tell them it was my idea..."

"Her story's a stretch at best." I shrugged and gave her a gentle nudge. "Don't worry about it. I'm not." I had bigger problems... like why did Logan DeVarney have Maddie's name on a list, along with Aubrey's mom and stepdad?

"I don't know, Sera..." Aubrey shook her head and moved away from me. Cold filled the space she left at my side. "I'm going to head up to bed...you coming?"

"I'll be right there. I'm going to grab a snack first..." I gave her a small wave and watched her disappear up the steps. Then I turned and headed for the library.

The Martin House library was simply a small room with shelves lining all the walls, with a computer desk and cramped couch and tiny boxed television in the middle of the room, making it hard to maneuver around the space. I took a seat at the desk and pulled out the journal pages, smoothing them out onto the wooden surface.

His handwriting was awful. A messy, untidy scrawl of crude cursive. There were random equations in the margins like 44.72-73.29 and a list: cows, horses, dog mutilations. Sarah Rousseau, Kyle Rousseau, Maddison Rose. Then there was a phone number. This one was local. Vermont only had one area code. I pulled out the phone and powered it up. The low battery flashed a warning. I typed the number into the message box, keyed in a message, and pressed Send.

Who is this?

I closed the phone and placed it on the table and waited. This was ridiculous. I was not getting anywhere staring at a phone. I picked up the papers again. I went to the computer and flipped it on. I waited for it to load as I studied the pages. Then I pulled up the old internet browser. I typed 44.72-73.29 in the search engine.

Nothing.

I tried it without the dash between.

A map of Kazakhstan flashed onto the screen.

I frowned and studied the numbers. Then I added north and west to the search. A map of Nile flashed onto the screen.

My heart stopped. The phone buzzed angrily on the table behind me, and I jumped an inch off my seat. I breathed deeply as I pushed back in my chair and hurried to the table. I flipped open the phone.

> You first.

I licked my lips. My mouth had gone dry.

> Seraphina Grey.

> Do you want to know what happened to Maddison Rose?

I let out a shaky breath. My fingers stumbled a bit on the numbers as I keyed in the letters.

> Who is this?

> A friend of a friend. Meet me at the Honey Bean at noon. Don't be late.

> Who are you?

"Do you know this number?"

Rachel took the phone from me. It had bothered me all night...when I wasn't tossing and turning from nightmares.

Rachel scrunched up her face as she studied the number.

"It's local...but nobody I know." I shrugged. "Aubrey doesn't recognize it either," I added.

"No." She passed back the phone. "Why?"

I sighed as I leaned against my locker and watched Rachel organize her CD collection in the wire shelves in hers. "They messaged me."

Rachel scoffed. "Weird. Did you try to call it?"

"Yup. No answer. Straight to an automated voicemail."

"Creepy." Rachel passed me a CD. "Give that to Nix, for me?"

I tucked it in my bag without a word.

Rachel gave me a shove. "That reminds me, are you going to the Tracks with us this weekend—you've skipped twice now..."

Before I had time to think up an excuse, someone tapped my shoulder.

Cheryl stood awkwardly off to the side. She bit her lip. "Seraphina—can I talk to you for a minute...in private?" she added, eyeing Rachel apprehensively.

I hesitated before pushing off the locker. "Sure...see you later, Rach."

I followed Cheryl around the corner toward an empty classroom.

"I'm really sorry to bother you. I just—I feel like I'm going crazy," Cheryl whispered as she stroked her cherry hair. Her eyes darted toward the students as they passed by us.

"Okay...how so?" I studied her carefully.

Cheryl took a deep breath and then licked her pale lips. "You know that stupid dare Daphne had us do that night?"

My heart began to race, along with my head. "Yes."

"Do you—I mean..." Cheryl bit her lip, hard. I could see a small blossom of red blood where her teeth had torn. She scratched at her wrist. "Do you believe in demons?"

I stared at her mouth, slightly agape.

Cheryl tried to laugh, but it came out like a breathless gasp. "I mean, if anyone would *know*, you would know, right? I mean…right?"

I hesitated, before answering honestly, "No, I don't believe in demons…I…why are you asking me that?"

Her hazel eyes shined as tears spilled down her cheeks. "I've just been having really bad dreams…like really, really bad dreams… and Maddie—" Her voice trembled softly, and she licked her bruised lip. "Well, it's just been hitting me hard, I guess. Sorry. I'm being stupid." She sniffed and forced a shaky smile. "I'll see you later, Sera."

And with that, she was gone.

I need a ride. Will you skip third period with me? I wouldn't ask if it wasn't important.

Where we going?

Honey Bean

Honey Bean was a cute little cafe, nestled between other random shops along a quiet street one town over from Mater Christi High School. On the inside, it was…different from Hallowed Grounds. Unlike Hallowed Grounds, which seemed open only to the students on the Mater Christi campus, at Honey Bean there were several college-aged kids with laptops and textbooks scattered around, in addition to a few older people in expensive suits sipping coffee. But it wasn't just the clientele.

While Hallowed Grounds was vintage, Honey Bean was modern and sleek, although still maintaining that cozy, comforting vibe. The chairs were plush but instead of the bright paisley pattern, they were a dark brown, like mocha chocolate. The mini oak tables were high, with thin chairs on tall legs. The walls were painted a soft sugar cookie color in the places that weren't lined with shelves of books.

At the counter were two young women, not much older than me, if I had to guess. One had a mess of gold curls and a bright, happy face, and the other had a short, shaggy, brown bob and a glint of mischief in her eyes as she spied Cole.

"St. Claire." She leaned against the counter as we approached. Behind the glass, there were a variety of baked goods dripping in golden syrup and cute jars of local honey. "What brings you to Honey Bean? Don't you Green Knights have your own watering hole?"

Cole took the lead as I scanned the place, trying to see whether anyone would look at me, to see whether any of them could be the person I was supposed to meet here at noon.

"Aw, Gracie, you know I can't get enough of this place." Cole smiled and shook his dark hair out of his eyes.

The blonde came up behind Gracie with a warm smile. "What can we get you, Cole?"

I patted Cole lightly on the back. "I'm going to grab a seat." I headed over to a table by the front windows. I plopped my bag on the tabletop and pulled out a vial of pax for calming courage and dabbed it on my wrists, before tucking it back inside the pocket of my backpack. I switched on the phone. No new messages. I turned it off as the low battery sign flashed.

Cole headed my way, and I dangled my backpack off the back of my chair to make room for his goodies. "Okay—I've got crullers, one black honey coffee and one French Vanilla." He took his seat and took a deep sip. "You know, I'm loyal to Hallowed Grounds, but...God, this is good stuff. It's the honey. They put it in everything."

I smiled, and after taking a sip, I had to agree.

"So..." Cole studied me with an amused glint in his eyes. "Are you going to tell me why we just skipped class to cheat on our coffeehouse?"

I took a deep breath, but before I could explain, the cafe door opened. A tall girl about my height with long, dark hair walked inside, the October air blowing at her back. She had on a black leather jacket over her dark-purple shirt. Her jeans were dark and well-worn, to the point that they were shredded at the knees. Her face might have been beautiful, if not for the hard lines of her expression. Her deep-brown eyes moved slowly around the cafe until they met mine, and I looked away.

Cole had looked toward the door as it'd opened, and his face broke into an easy grin. He nodded toward the girl. "What's up, Hannah?"

"Hey, Cole…" She approached our table with a small smile that softened the harsh features of her face. I was wrong. She wasn't beautiful—she was gorgeous. She nodded at me. "I'm actually here for Seraphina."

Cole inclined his head curiously. "Phin, why didn't you say anything? How do you guys know each other?"

"We don't," I said slowly.

The girl, Hannah, ran a hand through her dark hair. "Cole, can I steal her for a minute? We'll just be outside." She jutted her head toward the door. "Let's go, Grey."

"Er, okay, but I can't promise there will be leftovers." Cole lifted a cruller up and took a bite as he pulled out his phone and started to tap away.

I slid off the seat and followed Hannah outside the shop, into the cold afternoon, to a bench just in front of the Honey Bean windows.

"Sit," she said simply.

Frowning, I sat slowly, and she followed suit. She didn't look at me. Instead, she squinted into the weak sunlight spilling into the street from in between the squat buildings along the sidewalk.

"What do you know about Maddie?" I asked, impatience sharpening my words.

"I won't be in town long. And I'm new to this myself, but I figured you of all people would be able to put it together…"

"Put what together?"

"But Courtney told me you were as clueless as anybody." Hannah shook her head, as though she were disappointed in me.

"What are you—"

"Maddison Rose was killed by a demon." Hannah's words pierced my ears as she looked at me with hard, dark eyes.

I tried to speak, but nothing came out. I cleared my throat. "I don't understand…"

Hannah's jaw tightened, her impatience clear on her face. "Maddie made a demon deal."

"A *demon* deal?" I whispered harshly. I thought of the dare. And Cheryl. This couldn't be real.

Hannah crinkled her forehead as she studied me incredulously. "You *are* Charlotte Grey's daughter, right?"

My cheeks burned, and I frowned. "Yes."

"Hmm." Hannah's mouth formed a grim line as she stared dubiously at me. "Right. Well, I don't know anything about demons…not my thing. And I'm working a job in the mountains, otherwise I'd stick around to help. But Courtney called me…when Maddie…" She tilted her chin up and sniffed, either from the cold or emotion, I couldn't be sure which. Her jaw tightened, and she cleared her throat. "I looked into it a bit. I tried to see Charlotte, but she's out of town—as I'm sure you know…"

"Unreachable," I muttered, rolling my eyes at the cruel irony.

"Then when you texted, I figured you could use a shove in the right direction." She inclined her head, her chocolate hair spilling to the side. "How did you get my number, anyway? Did Courtney give it to you?"

I massaged my temples in an effort to steady my spinning head. "Wait, I don't understand. You're telling me somehow Maddison *summoned a demon*?"

"No…I'm saying she made a deal with it," Hannah said flatly.

"With a Ouija board," I continued in dazed disbelief.

Hannah scrunched up her face. "I have no idea, honestly. Demons are not my area of expertise. I'm new."

I blinked at her.

Hannah furrowed her brow sympathetically. "What I *do* know about them is that they tend to prey on the depressed and desperate...with her little sister in the hospital..." Hannah trailed off, her face blanched and sad. She cleared her throat again and shook her head. "Well, she was an easy target."

"A *demon*?" I repeated. My lips grew numb. I nibbled my lower lip to bring back the feeling in it. "Where'd it come from? Is it still—like, *around*?"

Hannah sighed and gave me a grim ghost of a smile. "Look... witches aren't the only thing out there that goes bump in the night. Charlotte didn't teach you about any of this stuff?"

I shook my head. "I know there are dark witches...and other realms...I didn't know there were—"

"Monsters?" Hannah scoffed. "Yeah...it'll take some time to sink in. It was hard for me to believe, too...*really* hard," Hannah muttered under her breath. Then she glanced at me and shrugged. "But anyway...like I said, I'm heading out of town for a job, so I can't help."

"A job?" I cocked an eyebrow.

Hannah nodded solemnly. "A literal monster in the closet. Eating kids."

My stomach lurched at the thought. "*Eating* them?"

Hannah smiled grimly at my shock. She shrugged again. "Anyway, being Charlotte's daughter, I thought—well, I just thought you should know that there might be a demon in Nile. Now it's on you to look into it. And if it's still around, take care of it."

I gaped at her as she stood from the bench and made to leave.

Hannah studied my face as she towered over me. "But whatever you do, don't bring the Blanchards into it. Courtney's been through enough, and Peter—he just deserves to be happy, okay? I told them both I'm handling it and to stay out of it."

"But you're leaving—"

Hannah scowled. "I'm handling it by telling *you* about it."

I blinked up at her from where I sat, still processing. Why was she telling me this? Did she assume I could just magic it away? Ha. What a joke. "I don't...what can I do?"

Hannah smirked as she hooked her thumbs through her belt loops. "Haven't you seen *The Exorcist*?"

"No," I mumbled lamely.

Hannah snickered. Then she gave me a little salute. "Good luck, Grey." She started down the sidewalk at a fast pace, and then she turned back toward me and walked backward as she grinned, her brown eyes sparkling with amusement. "I know a guy. I'll text you his number."

Stunned into silence, I watched her jump into the passenger side of an old pickup truck just before it pulled out of a parking spot and sped off.

Mama. I needed Mama. Now. I returned to the Honey Bean in a kind of dazed shock. How could she have kept this from us? There was a whole hidden undercurrent to the world that she'd just neglected to mention...how could she do that? She always had a reason. There must be a reason she kept us in the dark...kept us ignorant and defenseless against *monsters*. I couldn't think of any. And for the first time in my life, trust in my mother wavered. My heart hurt.

Cole cocked an eyebrow as I slid up onto the tall chair.

"What was that all about?" Cole took a sip of coffee as he watched me carefully.

I took a deep breath. "I think I need to try to reach out to Mama."

Cole flinched, taken aback. "I thought she was 'unreachable'?"

I shook my head, picked up my coffee and put it back down. My heart thumped loudly in my ears. My pulse pumped painfully in my wrists. "I need Mama." Hand still gripping the coffee cup, I slid my thumb over the Honey Bean logo. "I have things—questions I need answered."

"But, Phin, how—"

"There's a way. But I'll have to go home." I inhaled deeply, nostrils flaring. I looked at Cole. "And that means I need your help again."

He nodded, his face serious. "Sure, I'll drive you..."

I stared down at my cup. "We're going at night. When Phoenix is sure to be asleep." I took a deep sip, the rich, warm smell filling my nose.

"Why?" Cole eyed me uneasily.

"Because I'm not dealing with Phoenix on top of everything else."

We got back to class in time for last period. But I wanted to talk to Aubrey first. I caught her in the hallway on her way to class. She didn't look happy to see me. If anything, at best she looked uncomfortable—at worst, she looked scared.

"Oh, hey..." She tucked her blonde hair behind her ears and hugged herself. Her eyes shifted everywhere except for me.

I hesitated. "What's wrong?"

"Where were you?" Aubrey's voice was low as she continued to eye the kids hurrying past us to class.

"Cole took me out for lunch—why?"

Aubrey looked up at me, her eyes sad. "Daphne told Sister Francis this morning about what we did...."

I rolled my eyes. "Aubrey, I need to—"

"And then I couldn't find you after lunch..." Aubrey winced. "What if she expels you?"

"I'm not worried about that." I waved away her words.

"Aubrey, I need to ask you about what happened at the sleepover after I left—"

Aubrey blinked, taken aback. "What are you talking about?"

"What happened with Daphne's dare—her game?"

Aubrey shrugged. "By the time I got back into the room, you were gone and Daphne had us all take the board in turns..." Aubrey tugged on her locket, twisting it around her finger. "Why are you asking this?"

The bell rang, and I flinched.

"Sorry, Sera, I gotta go. I can't be late."

I started to protest, but she cut me off. "But please—be careful, and don't do anything...suspicious, okay?"

She hurried down the hall without a backward glance.

I was late. I opened the door, my eyes falling on Maddie's empty seat next to mine. The whole class looked up to stare at me. Whispers hissed all around as hands covered mouths and heads bent toward neighbors. Daphne and Damien grinned as I approached the back of the room. I gripped the strap of my backpack, steeling myself. I swallowed thickly as I hurried to take my seat.

"Where've you been?" Daphne pulled her seat up next to me. "Making another human sacrifice to Satan?"

Damien snickered behind me.

Daphne leaned over to rest her elbows on my desk. "You know, Damien won't shut up about your sister. Why don't you switch places with her? Everybody liked her a lot more than you, didn't they?"

Damien laughed.

I pulled out my math problems.

Daphne tried again. "Now that you couldn't pin it on that DeVarney dude, what's your backup plan?" She poked me hard with her pencil.

I focused my eyes on problem number one. "You've been

running your mouth a lot, Daphne…and I think that's because you don't want people to remember what you did."

Daphne grinned as I took her bait. "What I did?"

I continued to stare at the problem in front of me until the black print blurred. "What happened at that sleepover?"

Daphne snickered. "Nice try. But a Ouija board never killed anybody."

"No," I mumbled, still staring down at the paper. "But a demon might."

Did they summon a demon that night? And if they did, were they all in danger? Ouija boards were used by psychically gifted witches to communicate with spirits…they were used to link between the Earthly realm and the Heavenly realm…but was a demon a spirit? I knew everything about magic…but nothing about this. And it irritated me. An itch I couldn't reach.

And Daphne was still talking. "So, you can't frame Logan, you can't blame it on me," Daphne kept going, ticking off her fingers. "You gave the boys a disease, you killed Maddie…who's next?"

I blinked; the world shifted back into focus. The problem cleared.

"You know who's next…" I turned my head and looked blankly at Daphne. "Don't you? That's why you're harassing me. You're scared. Just like the rest of them."

Daphne smiled wickedly. "Why would I be scared?"

I stared at her, my face stoic and calm. "Because I told you *you'd* be next. Didn't I?"

Her smile flickered.

I rolled my eyes. "I'm done here." I grabbed my math, shoved it back in my bag, and stalked toward the door, Damien's laughter echoing in my head.

The door opened before I could get to it. Sister Francis lurked in the doorway. Her eyes scanned the students and fell heavily on me, freezing me in place. "Mr. Blake, I need to see Miss Grey, if you please?" She didn't wait for him to answer. "Miss Grey. Follow me."

I gripped the strap of my backpack as I adjusted the weight on my shoulder. I gritted my teeth as Daphne snickered behind me. I nodded stiffly to Sister Francis and followed her out of the room. She led me to an empty classroom and shut the door behind us.

"Do you know why I'm here?" She raised a gray tangled eyebrow.

I took a deep breath. "Sister Francis, whatever Daphne—"

Sister Francis closed her eyes and held up her hand, and I fell silent. She opened her eyes, meeting mine with her piercing stare. "I have it on good authority that you were snooping around in the boys' dormitories last night, after hours."

She waited for me to argue, but I continued to meet her stare evenly.

Sister Francis regarded me coolly as she continued, "Father LaValley may feel that the proof provided isn't substantial enough to warrant expiration of privileges or suspension, but let me assure you—I will be watching you, very closely, Miss Grey."

Where are you?

In the library. Why?

Do you know where Cheryl is?

Art studio.

I caught her eye through the glass window beside the door. Cheryl slipped outside the classroom and quietly shut the door.

"What's up?" Cheryl bit her lip and twirled her hair around her finger as she watched me.

"Earlier today, when you asked me about demons?" I asked pointedly.

Cheryl's eyes widened, and she backed up a step. "Look, Sera, I was just having a bad morning—"

"What happened when I left Aubrey's house?"

Cheryl's face went white. Her freckles stood out like constellations across her nose. "Why don't you ask Kaitlyn..."

I touched her shoulder. "Please, Cheryl. Tell me what happened."

Cheryl winced. "Talk to Kaitlyn. I need to get back to class." She opened the door and shut it in my face.

Kaitlyn was harder to track down. I waited outside the school, shivering against the old October wind as it billowed through the half-naked trees that dotted the courtyard. I flinched as the bell screeched through the silence and echoed across the grounds. My eyes flew back and forth between each of the double entrances until I spied her. Kaitlyn hurried out of the school with her head down, her arms crossed, hugging herself against the cold.

"Kaitlyn! Kaitlyn, wait up!" I jogged across the courtyard to catch up with her, but she just kept walking down the sidewalk.

"Not now." She kept moving. Her black braids, adorned with silver and green beads, slapped against her backpack as she walked.

"Please." I grabbed her arm and tugged her to a stop. She whirled to face me, her dark eyes hard, framed by perfect black edges that swirled down her temples. I licked my lips as I searched for the words. "Listen, I know you don't like me. I get it. But I need to ask you about something. It's important. Please, Kaitlyn."

Kaitlyn's jaw tightened as her eyes shifted away from me. She sniffed against the icy wind. Then she looked up at me with cold eyes. "You have five seconds."

I exhaled sharply; my breath left me in a cloud. "What happened at Aubrey's house that night I left?"

She scoffed and shook her head, eyes darting away toward the street. "Seriously?"

"Yes."

Kaitlyn rolled her eyes as she gripped her sleeves tight to her palm with her fingertips as she crossed her arms to hug herself once more. "We all did it."

"Who?"

"Did you forget who was there?" she snapped, her nose crinkling in her disgust. "Me, Cheryl, Morgan, Aubrey..." She pursed her lips on the final name. "And Maddison..."

It was everyone. Everyone except Daphne. "What deal did Maddison make?"

Kaitlyn's lower lip trembled slightly as she looked away. "That her sister would get better."

My blood surged in the hollow of my throat. It was hard to catch my breath in the cold air. "What was your deal?"

Kaitlyn's dark eyes shined, and she shook her head, almost pleadingly. "I don't want to talk about this right now, okay?"

She tried to push past me, but I held her fast, my hands gentle on her shoulders. "Please, Kaitlyn...I think you know why I'm asking—"

Kaitlyn scoffed. Anger hardened her eyes as tears leaked down her brown skin. "It was a *dare*. Okay? Not real."

"Kaitlyn—"

"No!" Kaitlyn's voice lowered to a harsh, taunting whisper. "You're trying to find something else to blame. But you're wasting your time because everyone already thinks you did it. Witch Spawn." Kaitlyn sniffed in the cold as she lifted her chin. "Now *move*." She pushed me hard with both hands and continued down the sidewalk, leaving me alone in the cold October wind.

I didn't need to go inside the cottage. I only needed for Icarus to hear me. I had Cole park at the top of Grey Lane, pulled over on the side of the back road, and I headed down Grey Lane on foot as it cut through the woods, dodging potholes and puddles the entire ten-minute walk to the cottage. I kept my head down and hugged myself against the cold. The trees ached in the wind, scratching at each other with their mostly barren branches. Occasionally, I heard something scurry past in the underbrush of slick, fallen leaves. The moon barely made it through, little slivers of light reflecting in the puddles or casting the gravel road blue. It was beautiful, and yet for the first time in my life, I was scared of it. A lifetime of walking this road and slipping through the woods, but now all I could think about was what Hannah had said and wonder whether some supernatural beast lurked in the dark just beyond the trees.

As I approached the clearing, where the road spread out for the driveway, my heart ached at the sight of the darkened sleepy cottage. For the first time, I realized how hard it must be for Phoenix without Mama home. Alone in the cottage with no one but Icarus.

Speak of the Devil.

There he was, perched on the porch railing, as though he were expecting me. And knowing Icarus, he probably was. I stopped in the middle of the driveway, my boots digging into the gravel as I planted myself firmly in place. I shoved my hands in my pockets and shook the hair out of my face, letting it catch in the breeze. "I need to talk to Mama."

Icarus blinked. "She is Unreachable, Seraphina." His lamp-like eyes glowed fluorescently in the dark. "You must go to your grandmother. She can help you just as well as your mother."

I frowned. "We both know you can get a message to her…one of the perks of being a bonded familiar. So send her a message— tell her I need to talk to her. Now."

"You misunderstand me, Seraphina." Icarus flicked his tail. "I *can* get her a message…but I won't. Not tonight."

My whole body seemed to deflate as my voice broke. "Icarus, please. It's important."

Icarus inclined his head. "Her work for the High Council is important. Distracting her now…could prove a fatal mistake."

"What could she possibly be doing?" I asked impatiently. "Tell me, what's more important to Charlotte Grey than her kids?"

Icarus's tail twitched, his fur bristling. "Why else would she leave you, if not *for* you? Come now, Seraphina, you know your mother better than that."

"Whatever." I scoffed in disbelief and turned on my heel, marching back through the darkness. "I don't know anything anymore."

"You want to talk about it?" Cole glanced at me sideways as we drove along the deserted highway that cut through Nile.

It was dark in the van, our faces lit by the glow of the radio, with its staticky crackle of a broken Nirvana song punctuating the heavy silence between us. A truck passed by, the headlights casting thick beams across the cab of the van. I shook my head. "I feel like I've been chasing my tail the past few days."

Cole nodded with a sympathetic frown.

"Thanks for bringing me out here, Cole."

He smiled at that. "Anytime. You know I love a good road trip."

I watched the black trees pass by in a blur and couldn't help but wonder what monsters might be hiding in the dark. "Cole, how well do you know Hannah?"

He shrugged. "Not really at all. I know Peter had a thing for her, but it didn't work out. I know she's friends with Courtney and Lacey McGregor. She seems cool, a little serious, maybe —why?"

"She told me something…something that I'm having a hard time believing." I nibbled on my lower lip.

"What was it?" Cole glanced at me, concern lining his face.

I cleared my throat. For some reason, I could barely get the words out. "Cole, do you believe in demons?"

He looked at me sharply before looking back at the road. His hands gripped the steering wheel.

"What?" I asked, alarmed by his reaction.

Cole shook his head and shrugged. "Did Hannah say something about them?"

"What do you know about them?" I demanded, my fear rising in my chest.

Cole sighed heavily. "Remember when Damien told us about what his daddy said? About the kids in Nile? The lot of them got together and started messing with things they shouldn't?"

Honestly, after everything, I'd forgotten. I nodded slowly.

"Well, I asked my dad about it...he and old man Barrow used to run together back in the day..."

"What did he say?"

"He wouldn't. He shut me down hard. Which made me think, maybe old man Barrow was telling the truth. So, I started doing some digging. I found an article from the *Nile Islander*...twenty years ago, there was a girl from Nile who ended up dead. Just like Damien said. She was sixteen years old and suspected of being a victim of a satanic slaying. They found her burned body on Bird Island."

My head blurred with panicked thoughts. Somehow, everything was connected...but my mind still couldn't make sense of it. "Why didn't you tell me this? When did you—"

"Phin, I didn't tell you because...the girl who died..." Cole exhaled sharply and tried again. "Her name was Alice Grey."

19

THE MIDNIGHT KILLER

I didn't speak until we got to the Martin House library and fired up the old computer monitor bigger than the old box TV. "Show me the article."

Cole nodded grimly, pulled up a chair in front of the screen, and typed in the search engine. Cole had a way with computers (a closeted code geek) and managed to pull it up quickly. It was just as he said. Local Nile girl. Sixteen. Alice Grey. I checked the year. Mama had been sixteen that year. None of it made sense. Alice Grey. A memory flashed through my mind. The night of the forging. Aunt Cordelia had said Mama had to go help the High Council because of Alice. I stared at the screen as I massaged my temples.

"This doesn't make sense."

"Was she like—a cousin?"

I shook my head. She couldn't be a cousin. "I don't understand. This girl...Alice Grey died twenty years ago...killed by a demon, let's say. Fast-forward to today: my mom has to go on some secret mission *because of* Alice Grey...who's been dead twenty years. And now, another demon murdered Maddison Rose?"

Cole winced. "Seems a little random...and out there..."

I laughed mirthlessly. "My thoughts exactly. None of it makes sense."

"Well, what do we know about demons?"

I shrugged and crossed my arms. "Up until today, I didn't know there was any such thing."

Cole sighed heavily as he looked back at the screen. "Do you think...maybe we should ask Phoenix?"

I looked at him, my face contorted in a mixture of hurt and disgust. "No."

Cole nodded and rubbed his neck. "Okay...then what—"

"We need to talk to Damien. Now."

I didn't bother waiting. I led Cole up the boys' stairs and moved through the dark hallway toward the room Cole indicated. I pounded on the door as hard as I could.

"Whoa, Phin...not too loud. You don't want to wake up the dorm dad..." Cole glanced back toward the stairs as I continued to pound.

A dorm door opened. Logan stepped out of his room; the light from his dorm spilled into the hallway. He leaned against his door-frame with his arms folded over his chest as he watched me beat on Damien's door. "You forget to steal a key this time?"

I flinched and turned to glare at him. "You forget to mind your own business?" I snapped. My cheeks burned at my lame retort.

"You looking for more shirts, or are you going for underwear this time?" Logan snickered.

"What is he talking about?" Cole muttered in my ear.

I groaned and let my stinging hand fall to my side as I turned to Cole. "Can you call him?"

"Phin, it's like—almost three in the morning..."

I jammed my hand into my pocket. "Okay, then *I'll* call him."

Cole sighed and took my phone to tap in the number for me. He held the phone up to his ear as he eyed me with a small hint of a smile in the corner of his mouth. "You're almost as bad as your sister, you know that?"

I rolled my eyes, offended by his compliment. I glanced back at Logan as Cole listened to the phone ring. Logan watched us, a smirk setting off the dimple in his left cheek and crinkling the corner of his eye. I never wanted to smack somebody more.

"Can I help you?" I called coolly down the hall.

His smirk broadened to a grin. "I was gonna ask you the same thing."

"Nothing needed from you."

Logan, still grinning, shrugged lazily and disappeared into his room, shutting the door behind him.

Cole lowered the phone and turned it off before handing it back to me with a defeated shrug. "You're just going to have to wait until tomorrow, Phin. And your battery's almost dead." He laid a gentle hand on my shoulder. "We should get some sleep."

"I think that's a wise idea, Mr. St. Claire."

We whirled around to see Mr. Whayland at the top of his handful of stairs, looking grim. In a disappointed silence, he saw Cole to his room and escorted me downstairs and into the office. He shut the door and turned to squint at me. He was a tall man, despite his hunched posture, and easily met my eye.

"Listen here, lassie..." His voice was dry, cracked with age, and riddled with a thick woodchuck accent. "I'm much too old to be chasing off boys, let alone chasing off the girls chasing after them... And believe you me, Damien Barrow is the last boy on Earth a nice young lady like yourself should be after. Hopefully, Mr. St. Claire can talk some sense into you, because for the life of me, I know you won't listen to the likes of me."

I blinked rapidly, mouth agape in horror. "Oh, no, Mr. Whayland. No. *Ew.*" I made a face and shook my head. "It's not what you think. Definitely not. I just—"

Mr. Whayland raised his bushy eyebrows and jutted his head forward with his hands on his hips and waited as I stumbled over my words and fell silent. "Yes, Miss Grey?" he prompted. "What is it *just*?"

I took a deep breath. "I needed to ask Damien something."

He gave me an ironic smile as he shook out his wrist and squinted down at his watch. "At this hour?"

"It couldn't wait..." I mumbled lamely.

Mr. Whayland sighed and rubbed his neck as he shook his head. "You know, Miss Grey, I wasn't born yesterday. I've been around a turn or two...and if you are in some kind of trouble—or maybe in need of some wisdom...well, I knew your mama once upon a time, and I'd be happy to offer help."

At the mention of Mama, I hesitated and inclined my head. "My mother, Charlotte, lived in Martin House, didn't she?"

Mr. Whayland's eyes narrowed beneath his bushy brows. "She did...why?"

I licked my lips as I tasted each question carefully. "And you worked here back then?"

Mr. Whayland scrunched up his crinkled mouth in a suspicious pout. "I did."

I took a deep breath. "What can you tell me about Alice Grey?"

The old man's face softened with a strange, unsettling sadness. Before he could answer, the door opened, and Sister Francis appeared in the doorway. Mr. Whayland nearly jumped out of what little hair he had left as he turned around to face her, clutching at his heart. "Holy Mother—Sister, you need to warn a feller before you go popping up out of the dark."

She ignored him, her eyes on me. "You mind telling me, Mr. Whayland, why Miss Grey is out of bed at this hour?"

"I met her on the way to the kitchen, both hankering for a midnight snack, I suppose." Mr. Whayland chuckled, but at the sight of Sister Francis's stony face, he straightened his and covered his mouth as he cleared his throat. "Well, I forgot to give her something I had of her mother's."

"Her mother's, Mr. Whayland?" Sister Francis eyed him coolly. "Why would you—"

Mr. Whayland waved her words away as he hobbled to his desk and rummaged through the drawers in his desk, one after another, until finally he emerged with a yearbook. He passed it to me with a pointed, meaningful gaze, and I nodded my understanding and took it from his shaky, overstretched hand.

I hugged the book tightly to my chest as though the old woman might snatch it from me. Sister Francis's eyes narrowed as they pierced the book.

"I'm...uhh—going to get some sleep." I flashed a wide, innocent smile. "Thank you, Mr. Whayland. I—"

"*Wait just a minute.*" Sister Francis slapped out her ruler, barring me from the door. Her eyes slid to Mr. Whayland. "What in Heaven's name have you been doing with a young girl's yearbook all these years, hmmm?"

Mr. Whayland shrugged. "She left it behind...when she moved out o' the House."

"Did she?" Sister Francis raised a critical, grizzled eyebrow. "And so you thought you'd hold on to it, did you?"

Mr. Whayland smiled kindly at me, squinting through the sharp fluorescent light of the office. "Folks had right nice things to say about her in that there book, and I thought it'd be a blooming shame ter toss it."

"And now—?" Sister Francis scoffed skeptically.

"Now, I'm passing it down ter her blood, Sister...and if you ladies will excuse me, I could use a cup o' joe..." He smiled broadly, revealing a few missing teeth, and gave us a brief bob of his head as he held his hand out for me, innocently, or perhaps strategically, blocking Sister Francis from stopping me again.

Without waiting for Sister Francis to reply, I slipped past Mr. Whayland and out the door.

Heart racing, I didn't dare look at the book. I stopped at the top of the stairs, staring uncertainly down the hall. I couldn't wake

Rachel. It was too late. The last time I'd barged in past midnight, she'd overslept the next morning. Plus, I'd need the light on. There was something in this book about Alice Grey. Mr. Whayland had made that clear as he could manage with that hag looking on. I took a deep breath and made my way down to the middle of the hall.

I paused outside our dorm, lurking in the dark of the hallway like a ghost. I pulled the key out from underneath my shirt and slipped it off my head. Taking a deep breath, I slid the key into the lock and turned. My hand moved through the dark and found the switch. I said a silent prayer for strength and flicked it on.

It was as though she hadn't ever been there. Maddie's mark on the room was gone. Someone had stripped the bed of Maddie's Spiderman sheets, leaving the mattress bare. They had also collected all the knickknacks off the top of Maddie's dresser and the stuff she'd arranged underneath and around her bed to make room for my things when I'd first moved in. Even her posters had been taken down.

I stood back and surveyed Maddie's side of the room. There was nothing left of her. I moved to the dresser and lightly touched the top where only last week I'd marveled at the crystals Maddie had collected. I swallowed thickly, blinking back tears. I backed away from the dresser, tossed my bag in the corner, and I walked slowly to the bed and sank into it, staring down at the yearbook.

It was definitely from the year Mama was in school. Was it really hers? Or was he just trying to cover for me? But if it was hers, why would Mr. Whayland have it? I opened it slowly, the binding cracking a bit. The front pages were graffitied with all different colors of ink. Signatures. Notes. But not to Mama. It wasn't Mama's yearbook.

I smoothed my finger over the words and read, "Alice, see you around at Hallowed Grounds."; "Alice, love ya, stud bud." I glanced at the year, did the math in my head, and turned quickly through the junior class pictures.

Adam Graham, Joseph Green, Alice Grey, Charlotte Grey.

It was impossible. *How could Mama not have said—* My memories blurred together in my mind as I tried to remember whether Mama had ever mentioned anything to suggest...then I remembered. Right before she'd left, she mentioned Alice...a young witch...like me. I stared down at the pictures, the two of them side by side. No. Not like me. A young witch like *her.*

Hot, angry tears clouded my vision. I blinked, and they spilled down my cheeks. Not cousins. Not even close. I gritted my teeth and went to shut the book, only to find more signatures and more notes on the back pages. One in particular caught my eye; it was written in bright-purple ink. "Alice, I wouldn't have survived this year without you. Thank Her for the hyde out. Hyde and Seek Forever. Calliope."

Two other notes in black beside it read, "What happens in the hyde out, stays in the hyde out, St. Claire" and "Hyde Our Secrets, Bear."

I paused for a moment, double-checking all the other notes, front and back, for anything similar. Nothing. I flipped through the juniors again and found Cole's dad easily. Plus, he'd signed his name below his picture. He looked just like Cole, except for the thin, feathered Han Solo hair and the cocky, lopsided grin. The girl, Calliope, was also easy. She'd left her name, too, scribbled in the same purple ink beneath her photo. Though I had no idea who she was, she seemed familiar in a weird sense. She was beautiful, in that model kind of way, where they look so odd, they're gorgeous. Her hair was dark and styled in that wispy, Farrah Fawcett kind of way.

I went to the Bs. My eyes rested on Michael Barrow. Underneath his picture was an untidy scrawl: Bear. He had a long face and wide smile and dark eyes that sat a bit too far apart, giving him a strange, shark-like kind of appearance. He looked like an awkward, goofy, overgrown little boy with his disproportionate face and mullet. Nothing at all like his son, Damien, who, for all his nastiness, was undeniably cool and handsome and disarmingly charming. My stomach turned a bit as I looked at him. I flipped through the pages searching for another clue. There was nothing else. I turned back to Calliope's note.

I rubbed my forehead as I tried to process. Damien's dad had told him a group of Nile kids started messing with things they shouldn't have...and Alice Grey died. This was the group. It had to be them. Alice, Matthew St. Claire, Michael Barrow, and Calliope Giannis. But what did it mean? Hyde. A "hyde out." The spelling was so specific. There was a Hyde Road in Nile. Could they be referencing the street? There was only one way to find out.

I met Cole in the morning before first period. I slapped the yearbook into his chest. "*They were twins.*"

"What?" Cole squinted groggily at me as he took the yearbook and flipped through it. "Hey, look—Pops." He chuckled and shook his head. "Look at that hair. This must've been right before he enlisted—what year is this?"

"Alice Grey and my mom. They were *twins*. Look." I jutted my chin toward the book as Cole stared at me, dumbfounded.

He opened his mouth and shut it again, his fingers fumbling through the pages until he found them. He scrunched up his face and angled the book to the side. "So, they look kind of alike—that doesn't mean—"

I groaned and pulled the book from his hands. "Never mind. That's not what's important." I turned to the back binding.

"It's not?"

"No. Look." I tapped Calliope's note in the swirly purple ink.

Cole inhaled sharply and took the book back. He ran his thumb across Calliope's signature.

"Do you know what they're talking about?"

Cole looked up at me, startled. "No. What?"

I frowned impatiently and tapped his dad's note and then

Michael Barrow's note. "The three of them are all referencing the same thing. Hyde. Do you know what they're talking about?"

Cole's brow furrowed as he studied the notes. "Damien's grandparents owned a bunch of land off Hyde Road. Maybe that's it?" Cole flipped through the pages, clearly distracted by the class pictures.

"I have to ask him." I shook my head as my thoughts clouded. "I have to go there. There's got to be something there."

Without looking up from the book, Cole mumbled, "What do you mean?"

"I think these are the kids, Cole...the first kids who brought a demon to Nile. Alice Grey, your dad, Calliope, and Michael Barrow. It started with them...and Hyde Road? I just know this has to mean something. I mean, right?"

Cole wasn't listening. He continued to stare at the yearbook photos.

"Cole!"

"Hmm?"

I groaned and yanked the book from his hands. "You are *so* not a morning person."

Cole winced sheepishly. "Sorry, Phin—wait, where are you going?"

I turned back to look at him as I hurried down the hall. "I need to find Damien. I'll text you."

I tucked the book under my arm and headed off to search for Damien.

I didn't have a class with him, so I waited outside his locker. Damien sauntered down the hall in his dress shirt and tie. Clearly they had a game tonight.

"I need to talk to you."

Damien leaned against the locker as he tossed his head to shake his dark hair from his icy eyes, and he grinned at me. "Just can't stay away, can you?"

I pushed the open yearbook into his stomach. He scowled and snatched the book out of my hands. I tapped the notes. "Do you know what they're talking about?"

Damien raised his eyebrows as he read, and then his bright-blue eyes narrowed. He looked up at me from the page. "I think I might."

"And?" I prompted, struggling to rein in my impatience.

He gave a lackadaisical, one-shouldered shrug and passed the book back to me. "And...what do you care?"

I took a deep, cleansing breath, praying for patience. I smiled politely and met his eyes. "Listen, Damien, it's *really* important. I need to know what they are talking about and—"

Damien studied me, his mouth in a bored frown. "Why?"

I pursed my lips, holding back a snarky retort. Instead, I admitted calmly, "Because I think you were right. I think your dad, and Cole's dad, and these girls—they are the ones who started this thing. I think whatever happened then is happening now. And I need *your* help to understand it. I need to know what they're talking about."

Damien's demeanor changed. His cool-guy, careless facade fell like a mask from his face. He pushed off the locker and looked at me, his eyes serious. "There's an old shed on the property. My dad built it when he was a kid. It's locked. No one can get in. It's impossible. I've tried."

I opened my mouth to argue.

Damien cut me off. "But I'll take you there anyway."

I blinked rapidly. Had I heard him correctly?

He shrugged again. "It's a bit of a hike to get to it...but I'll show you. Meet me at Hyde Road at midnight, by the speed limit sign—"

"Why so late? Why not—"

"I've got a game in Rutland, and I don't get home till late..."

I nodded gratefully. "Thank you, Damien."

"Yeah, it's whatever." Damien wrenched open his locker and switched out his books, before closing it with a loud slam. "Just make sure you tell Aubrey I'm being helpful."

We got there early. Hyde Road was a backroad stretch of pothole-riddled gravel, running a good mile or so along, parallel to West Shore Road, cutting through a dense wood. It wasn't far from Grey Lane, and as we sat, parked in the quiet of the van, as the rain dripped through the overhanging branches and bled down the windows, I studied the trees, wondering whether they connected to the Blackwell Woods that surrounded Grey Cottage. They could. Easily.

I shivered and turned up the heat as the rain tapped harder against the van. The trees, like black skeletons, their bones stretched out from the woods, knocked against the top of the van as the wind rushed past, pelting the sides with more rain. The road was a mess of slick black leaves and muddy grit as I stared up the road, waiting for the flash of headlights to appear.

Cole shrugged. "Maybe he's not coming."

My eyes fell on the radio clock. "He's got five minutes, and then we'll go in without him."

Cole winced. "How would we ever find the shed without him?"

I looked back at the road. The trees bowed over it like a long, dark tunnel. "He'll be here."

"Great. Can't wait." Cole scrunched down in his thick leather jacket lined with wool as he turned up the heat one more notch. "And what are we hoping to find?"

I pulled my jacket tighter around me. "You really need to fix the heat on this thing."

Cole's brow crinkled in offense. "Give the old girl a break— she's doing her best."

I scoffed and couldn't help but smile. "You got any cards back there?"

Cole waved his hand. "Nah, just Jean. You want to play Guess That Tune?"

"Can you tell me again, why you named your guitar?" I asked with a smirk.

"It's a guy thing..." Cole mumbled defensively.

"But why 'Jean'...isn't that a bit—" My grin faded as headlights flashed. A car turned onto Hyde Road. I sat up straighter. "That's got to be him." I twisted my hair back into two low pigtails and yanked my beanie over my head. The truck pulled up and parked in front of the van so that we were nose to nose. "You ready?"

Cole yanked his hat over his head with a sour grimace. He looked at me with his hand on the door handle. "You never answered my question."

"I'll know what we're looking for once we find it." I threw the door open and jumped out into the rain...and didn't realize until we were halfway through the forest that I'd forgotten my backpack in the back seat.

He'd brought Aubrey. She smiled weakly up at me from beneath the faux fur hood of her fitted parka. Her lily-blonde hair spilled out around her shoulders like flower petals, and her nose was pink in the glare of the flashlight Damien flickered between us.

"Everybody ready?" Damien shined the light in each of our faces. Cole scowled as he squinted through the rain and the light and gave a curt nod. "Stay close. You don't want to get lost in here."

"And if we do?" Aubrey whispered in the darkness as we followed Damien's lead off the road, down the embankment, and into the woods, the flashlight swaying back and forth as he walked between the trees. He didn't answer.

Huddled together, flinching as the rain dripped through the

barren trees, tapping overhead on the needles of the scattered ever-greens, our boots slipping on and coated with wet, fallen leaves, we weaved our way through the tangle of branches, stumbling over stray roots, following along what might have once been an overgrown path, but was now just another part of the woods.

I couldn't say for sure how far we walked, but within thirty minutes the sound of the rain tapping as it hit the cedars and the tops of our heads began to get loud and hollow. Then Damien's flashlight rested on an old shed; its weathered wood shined black in the dark of the rain that blew from the trees and ran steadily from its tin roof. It was creepy, emitting an ominous energy that made me hesitate. The air around the shed hummed like static, traces of magic left behind like a stain on the aura of the place.

Aubrey moved close to me, hunched over and leaning into me for warmth. "That thing's freaking spooky. What are we doing here, again?"

I didn't answer, only wrapped an arm around her small, shivering frame and gave her a squeeze, as I eyed a stack of firewood off the side covered with a slick, wet tarp. It looked like a figure lurking in the dark.

Damien, hanging back a few feet from the shed, pointed the flashlight at the door. "It's locked from the inside somehow. No matter what I tried, I never could get it open."

Cole, shoulders rolled forward against the cold of the rain, inspected the door. "There's no keyhole. How could it be locked?" He grabbed the handle and pulled. Hard. It didn't move.

"Fine. Stuck, then," Damien snapped as the three of us watched Cole struggle against the door. "Whatever. Point is, you can't get in. I even tried to smash a window. Doesn't work." Damien shrugged in the darkness, bobbing the flashlight up and down.

Cole gave up with a small shake of his head as he massaged his palms and stepped back from the door.

I gritted my teeth and stepped forward toward the shed. It had to open. I would make it open. I stepped forward and grabbed hold of the handle with both hands. It was old and rusted underneath my fingers. I yanked as hard as I could, putting all my weight into it.

"Sera, I'm telling you," Damien called from behind me as I strained against the door. "It's a waste of—"

Unbelievably, the door separated from the frame with a jarring creak that sounded like a scream in the dark. Everyone jumped back. I released the door, flinching away from the noise, allowing it to swing wide open.

The four of us stared in a stunned silence at the shed, a gaping black hole in the blue-black woods.

"I thought you said you tried everything, Damien," Aubrey muttered.

"I did." He shook his head, his expression hidden in the dark. "That door was sealed shut..." He shined the light in my face. "How did you do that?"

I winced away from the light and took the flashlight from his hands. Then I walked toward the shed. No one followed me. I stood in the doorway, shining the light along the sides of the door, and then over the interior.

There were shelves along each length of the shed, each one loaded with indiscernible items covered with blankets of cobwebs that draped over everything like white sheets. There was a small bookshelf at the back wall, beside which sat an oversized cushy chair coated in more cobwebs. There was an old, dusty lantern on a side table by the door and another on a side table beside the chair. I checked the lantern closest to the door. It was old, but there was a battery. I switched it on and blinked in startled surprise as it flickered on. I placed it back on the table, propped the flashlight up beside it so it shined like a spotlight on the ceiling, and I searched the room.

"What is this place?" Aubrey murmured as she followed behind me almost cautiously.

"No idea," Damien muttered from the shelf opposite us. "My dad built it when he was a kid. He didn't like to talk about it. Told me never to mess with it."

"Looks like his hangout spot." Cole walked over toward the chair, switched on the second lantern, and picked up a fashion magazine that'd been left on the armrest. He shook the dust off.

"And I hope he had some girlfriends—" Cole smirked as he tossed the magazine to Damien, who chucked it back onto the chair. Cole snickered.

"Oh, hey—" Cole leaned over the side of the chair. "I think this is my dad's!" he called out as he rummaged through the clutter. "We got a bat, a mitt—no ball."

I was only half paying attention. My focus was on the shelf. There were stoppered bottles with different liquids in them. There were herb bundles and different spices and various items all strewn about. In the middle of the shelf was a leather-bound binder sitting open to a specific page. There was a bottle of ink and a pretty fountain pen all coated in gray dust.

Aubrey came up behind me as I smoothed away the dirt and grime from the page. "What is it?"

I stared down at the book. It was a Book of Shadows. A witch's journal. Her spellbook. But the runes...it was all written in symbols I couldn't read. Symbols I'd never seen before. Like a different magical language I'd never learned.

"Oh, wow," Cole murmured from the opposite shelf. "A record player? Check out this vinyl...it's gotta be—"

"Let me see." Damien hurried over but stumbled over something that clanged and clattered across the floor.

I turned sharply at the noise, allowing the weathered page to fall back into place with a small crinkle. Aubrey gasped and clung onto my arm.

Damien cursed under his breath as he tried to regain his footing. "Dude, what the heck?"

Damien bent down to pick up the thing he'd tripped over. It was a large bowl. Its contents had spilled a bit onto the floor.

Cole crouched down to inspect the mess. "Wait, is that—what is that?"

We all squinted through the glare and shadow of the lantern lights.

Damien shook his head and held out the bowl. "What is *this*?"

I hurried over to the bowl and took it in both hands. I angled it toward the lantern light. I recoiled in disgust and hurried to drop the bowl onto the nearest shelf. It was a spell bowl filled with what looked suspiciously like congealed blood and bits of bones and hair.

"A page fell," Aubrey whispered.

"Where?" I scanned the floor, but Damien saw it first. He picked it up and held it up to the light.

Cole walked past me to inspect the bowl. "Are these—Phin, are these *bones*?"

I didn't bother to answer or turn around. My eyes were on the paper in Damien's hand.

"What's it say?" Aubrey squeezed my arm harder, pulling me to her.

Damien inclined his head. "I think it's Latin..."

My heart dipped into my stomach, and I stepped forward. "Damien, let me see it!"

He ignored me. "Hang on. Aubrey and I took Latin last year... it says...Invoco te de profundis tenebrarum. In profundis animae meae cognovi te. Cognoscis me ex intimis infirmitatis meae. Abominabile malum... venite ad me."

I flinched at the cadence of the incantation. The translation of the words. I tried to grab the paper from his hands, but he held it out of reach and tucked it neatly into his pocket. The stench of rotting decay and brimstone singed my nostrils.

"Damien..." My voice wavered as I tried to keep calm. "I need to see that." I held out my hand.

Damien inclined his head as though he couldn't understand what I was asking.

Aubrey made a little gasp and rushed forward. She tried to pull it out of his pocket, but he grabbed her hand and bent her fingers back. Aubrey cried out. Then time seemed to stall, and I watched as Damien smacked his forehead into hers. His skull cracked against Aubrey's, and she dropped like a doll. Her body crumpled to the ground, and she didn't move.

I gasped, eyes wide, as I stared down at Aubrey in a small heap at my feet.

Cole shouted and shoved past me. He dropped down beside Aubrey and pulled her into his lap, checking her over.

I looked from Aubrey back to Damien and stammered in shock, "Damien, what? *What did you do*? Why did you-"

Damien grinned wildly and laughed—

No...

He giggled.

Something was wrong.

He licked his lips as a sly smirk slid in place on his face.

His blue eyes burned gold in the lantern light.

"Maddie says 'hi.'"

FACE DOWN

Before I could react, before I could think, Damien grabbed my arm with strength that wasn't his and yanked me toward the door of the shed. Eyes wide with disbelieving fear, I looked back at Cole, whose face paled in the yellow lantern light as he jumped to his feet. Aubrey's head hit the floor with a dull thud. Damien held a hand out and sent Cole flying into the back wall. Cole's head knocked against the bookshelf as he crashed to the floor in a pile of books. I screamed his name. He didn't get up. Damien's eyes burned gold as he giggled manically. Then he held his hand out at the door and blasted off its hinges.

This didn't make sense. I struggled against him, kicking and thrashing, but there was no point. His hand was clamped onto my arm, his fingers digging in like the teeth of a bear trap. And as I tired, he clearly didn't. He continued at a steady, unwavering pace as he stomped through the woods and the rain, dragging me with him, the low branches slapping and scratching at my face.

"Stop! Where are you taking me?!" With my free arm, I reached out and snatched the trunk of a sapling tree, holding fast. But he only yanked me with a bit more effort and my fingers slipped, nails breaking in the bark. "No! Stop!"

Damien giggled again and shook his head. Then he pulled me into him with both hands, crushing my shoulders. He turned and slammed my back against a tree trunk. I flinched away from him, turning my head against the tree, flattening myself as best as I could manage. The rain clouds moved overhead, revealing the moon. Its soft light pooled around us, casting shadow upon his face. His eyes burned gold, glowing in the dark, as he looked up at me. Then his eyes cooled quickly back to normal icy blue. His hands released my shoulders. It was his power now—his magic?—cementing me against the tree. He ran his hands through his hair as his eyes moved over me in a way that made my stomach lurch.

His smile was almost sweet and tender, white in the darkness. He reached out a finger to trace through the strands of blonde hair fallen loose from my pigtails. His finger moved along the curve of my forehead and tucked the hair behind my ear. My skin itched. I flinched away from his touch. His hot, rancid breath was in my ear. "I've been waiting so long to meet you, Seraphina Grey."

I tried to stay strong, tried not to show fear, but my defenses weakened and the tears streamed down my cheeks. The stink of him. The evil radiated off him like a vibration. And all I could think about was Aubrey and Cole, crumpled in broken piles on the dirty shed floor. "You're not Damien," I said quietly, more to myself than to him.

The creature chuckled but didn't speak. He nodded indulgently, eagerly urging me to go on.

"That spell…" I sniffed and shivered in a mixture of the cold and fear. "You're a demon, aren't you?"

"Oh, little witch, you know the answer to that already."

"You killed Maddison Rose." My voice broke despite myself.

A crazed smile cracked on its face, revealing all its teeth. Damien's teeth. I tried to look away, but he snatched my chin and forced me to look at him. "Oh, Maddie was fun. But that wasn't my fault. She *asked* for it." The thing hissed through its smile. "And they all did, didn't they? So once I'm done with you, maybe

I'll go after the rest of them...one...by...one. You'd like that, wouldn't you? Morgan, Kaitlyn—"

"I won't let you," I snapped lamely.

"Aw, don't worry, Seraphina, you're first." The demon giggled. "I've got something special planned for you."

Eyes narrowed, I spoke through gritted teeth. "What do you want with me?"

A deep growl vibrated within Damien's chest. Then he sneered as he grabbed my face, crushing my lips together. He shoved my head into the tree. Dark spots burst in my vision as I struggled to remain conscious.

"I'd like to ask you the same question, Seraphina. What do you want with *me*?" He chuckled as he released my face and waved his hand around the woods. "I mean, it's not like I'm not grateful for the invitation, but I'm extremely curious to know—" He paused and licked his lips, leaning in close to breathe hot into my ear. "Why you let Damien Barrow recite Auntie Alice's spell in the first place..."

I flinched from the heat and the stench of his words as I struggled to free my arms from the invisible bonds that tethered me in place. "I didn't think it'd work. Damien isn't a witch."

The demon giggled. "You didn't think it would work? Now that I find hard to believe..." He moved around me, circling the tree as he leered at me from the other side of the trunk and bopped my nose. "And you didn't lift a wittle witchy finger to stop him. Not a single spell. Nope. I think you *wanted* him to summon me here..." The demon lunged at me. Its eyes burned as it pulled me into it, crushing me against its chest. Its face was inches from mine, its hands and fingers digging into my arms as it held me in place.

My nose crinkled in disgust as I turned my head away from it. "I didn't think it'd work!"

"DON'T LIE!"

I winced underneath the power of his rage. "I'm not!"

"I think..." he continued softly, ignoring my words and

breathing on my face. "You wanted to bind me to you. *Enslave me just like Alice Grey.*"

"No. No. I didn't know." Tears streaked silently down my cheeks. "I didn't know about any of this...she never told me."

The demon chuckled darkly and stuck out his tongue. I shrieked and struggled against him as he licked the tears from my cheek.

"Oh, come now." His tongue—Damien's tongue—was like rough, slimy sandpaper as it lapped at my cheek. "You wanted me here. Which is why you haven't even bothered to use your magic against me now."

"No!" I tried to shove him off me. My face burned with shame at my obvious impotence, and my eyes blurred at the violation of my body. "Let me go!"

"Nope." He slammed me backward, his power slapping me hard against the tree once more. Then he stepped back to study me. He crossed his arms with a shrug. "Can't do that. We're going to take a little trip to Bird Island. Just you and me." He closed the distance between us, his eyes burning gold as they moved over me.

Filled with a feral fear, I struggled against his power and fought even harder. He would not take me to Bird Island. Ever.

The demon watched me as I strained against the tree, like a little kid watches a bug as it drowns. Then he smiled. "Wait..." He giggled and bounced from one foot to the other. "Is it true? Tell me it's true..." He flicked one of my pigtails and gave it a hard tug. Then he slipped his hand into Damien's pocket and pulled out his butterfly knife. I flinched as it glittered in the moonlight, and he laughed, a deep throaty chuckle. "You don't like knives, do you, Seraphina? Needles either, I'll bet. Well, that's good to know." His voice bubbled deeper, like a burp, as he smiled. "That's *really* good to know."

He spun the knife around and around and then caught it in his hand. He held it up to my cheek. I winced. "Tell me, Seraphina— why aren't you trying to defend yourself right now?"

I flinched away from the blade, but his power held me fast. He flicked the knife up and took off my hat.

"Tell me *why*—or I start slicing..." He hissed in my ear as he slid the blade gingerly along my face. It burned sharp, like a paper cut. He traced the knife point along the hollow of my throat. I flinched away from him. He pressed harder.

I groaned and spat, "I can't cast."

I started to sob then, overcome by the fear of the knife and humiliation of my pride.

He moved the knife away from me and held it back like an artist with a paintbrush studying a canvas. His eyes glowed molten gold in the dark, and Damien's face curled into a nasty, mocking smile in the light of the moon. "A witch without magic? Now, isn't that interesting...where have I heard this story before?" He giggled, again, tongue sliding over his teeth. "My, my, history does *repeat* itself, doesn't it? And what does Mommy think about that?"

I continued to struggle against his hold. I had to do something. How could I fight back? What did I have?

"How disappointing for the great Charlotte Grey..." he waved his arms wide as though proclaiming the news to the entire forest, "to have a daughter as depressingly disappointing as her sister." He looked back at me with a cruel smirk. "Apparently, I grabbed the wrong witch..." He fluttered the butterfly knife and bit his lip, as though holding back a secret. He held the knife to his lips and tapped it against his mouth as his excitement seemed to grow.

"Is that why you went snooping through her little hideout? To steal power from a demon? Just like Auntie Alice before you?" He spun the knife and slipped it through my hair. "It must be hard being powerless—useless," he murmured softly as he traced the knife down my throat again. "I could show you what it's like to be powerful...I could slip inside that skull of yours and make you do things you can't even imagine...walk you home and slice up your little sister..."

I looked at him, horrified, which sent him into another fit of deep-throated giggles. I had to fight back. *What did I have?* I had a phone. But I couldn't move to reach it. And who would I call?

The demon's power held me fast against the tree as he began to pace around me again, swinging the knife. "You know, I can hear Day Boy rattling about in this thick skull of his. He's a *nasty* little boy. The kind of things he thinks about would make you sick. And the things he wants to do to you? *Messed up.*" He shook his head as though disappointed, and then he smiled. "You know...demonic possession...it changes people sometimes. Leaves a mark on the soul that you just can't wash away. And for people like little Damien Barrow..." the demon gestured down the length of him, "who are already a little deviant? They *rot.*" The demon giggled. "And I'll be honest with you...Damien's already rotting away inside...he's going *bad*. You better watch out for him. But then, he was already pretty bad to begin with. Did Aubrey tell you what he did to her?" The demon raised his eyebrows and shook his head. Then he moved closer to me, leaning into the tree.

Did I have a pen? Anything sharp? I didn't have anything.

"Like you, Damien has a thing for knives. But he *loves* them. And he's hoping I'll use his right now. He'd be happy if I took his knife and..." The demon slipped the knife along my throat.

The blade scratched against the chains around my neck. My dorm key. Was that sharp?

The demon inclined his head as the knife caught on my necklace. He lifted the chain with the point of the knife, holding my amulet up to study it in the blue-black light.

His eyes burned gold. "But first I want to know...where you got your hands on this charming little trinket you have hidden underneath your shirt..."

I would've been surprised at the question, if not for the mortal terror of my situation. "My dad gave it to me..." I mumbled distractedly. I had my dorm key.

The demon ripped me off the tree and shook me as it bellowed in a voice that rang in my ears. "*Don't lie!*"

"I'm not lying!" I tugged away from him, mind racing. The key was all I had.

"And who *is* the mysterious Mr. Charlotte Grey, hmmm? It's certainly not the priest..." The demon's words erupted from deep within Damien's chest like a burp as he dissolved into another fit of giggles. The way the demon flickered between emotions so violently made him seem all the more dangerous.

"Why do you care?" My eyes scanned the trees. What could I do? How could I escape him? Where would I run?

The demon licked Damien's lips and hissed through his teeth. "Listen, you little—"

It happened out of nowhere: a baseball bat whistling through the air as Cole swung hard at Damien's head. But the demon was fast. He caught the bat in one hand, wrenched it from Cole's grasp, and tossed it into the trees. Then his hand lashed out, snatching a fist full of Cole's hair as he yanked back his head, so he could leer into his face. "Cole St. Claire...how nice to officially meet you. I met your daddy once. Your mommy, too." He bit his lip, stifling his giggles. *"I've heard so much about you."*

His hands latched onto the scruff of Cole's wool jacket, and he lifted him up onto his feet. Damien's eyes swirled like molten gold as he held Cole up to his face. "What shall we do with you..." He took Cole's arm and snapped it backward.

Cole's scream echoed through the forest. There was a crunch, and Cole bellowed in pain as he bent over, clutching at his leg.

The demon waved his hand.

SMACK.

Cole hit the tree beside me.

Rain fell from the tree as it vibrated with the impact.

The demon pulled me into him and spun me around to face Cole, who was crushed against the tree. Cole's teeth gritted together as though wired shut. His nose was bleeding black in the darkness. The demon held me from behind with one arm hugging me to him, the other fluttering the knife toward Cole's face.

"Where should I cut first, Seraphina? Pick quick, or I will..." The demon's laugh bubbled up from the depths of Damien's chest.

Cole jutted out his chin ever so slightly, his nostrils flaring as he stared unflinchingly at the demon.

This only made the demon giggle. "How long until he starts crying, Seraphina, hmm?"

My mind went into overdrive. I had to stop him. I had to save Cole. The demon's hold on me was just loose enough as it taunted Cole. Relief flooded me as I realized—the demon's power worked like ours: concentration required. The demon was focused on Cole. Me? Not so much.

This was my chance. Moving fast and desperate, in one fluid motion, I yanked the chain at my throat, freeing the key. I gripped it like a dagger and stabbed it backward into the demon's eye.

The demon screamed, a horrible sound that ripped through Damien's throat and vibrated in my bones. I felt the invisible magic bonds on me vanish completely. Cole fell to the ground at my feet. I turned to face the demon, the key gripped in my hand, ready to stab again. But I hesitated, horrified, at the state of Damien's eye, which appeared to have been *burned* by the key. His eyelid was blackened and singed like a crispy marshmallow. Whatever hold the demon had over us had disappeared as he clutched at his face, howling in pain.

I gripped the key and stabbed again at his head. But the demon was faster. His remaining eye burned gold, fluorescent and feral, and he splayed his hand in my direction. I was yanked violently to the right, my body sent through the air. My head cracked against a tree and everything went dark.

21

MAKEDAMNSURE

My eyes flew open.

I blinked around, trying to process what I was seeing in the fog of my brain.

The key was still in my hand. I was in a tangle of pine branches hidden against the base of the tree. I laid motionless, cold and wet, as I squinted through the damp needles, searching for movement.

It was still dark. The blue light of the moon flooded through the gaps in the trees, illuminating the forest floor with a navy tint. As far as I could tell, there was no one out there. I was alone.

The demon was gone.

And where was Cole?

I pocketed my dorm key, wincing as I strained to zip up the pocket. My head ached terribly. It turned my stomach and made it hard to focus. I struggled to my hands and knees and crawled out from the shelter of the pine tree. Then I forced myself to my feet. The world spun slightly, and I closed my eyes for a moment to allow it to steady.

Then I scanned the woods, trying to get my bearings. I had to find Cole. And Aubrey. I staggered to a nearby naked maple tree and gripped onto the trunk for support. I fumbled around my pocket for the phone. I turned it on. The low battery message flashed. Then a voicemail popped onto the screen. I blinked at the message box, willing my eyes to focus, the spinning of my head starting to slow, as the dull throb on the back of my skull intensified.

It was from Aubrey.

I held it up to my ear and listened: "Sera! *Seraphina, please answer*! I'm taking Damien home, he's—he's not well..." Her voice dropped dramatically, muffled static on the phone. "He told me you both drove home—but the van was still on the side of the road...I'm scared that—*I think he's lying.* Please tell me you're okay! Call me back!"

I deleted the message. My stomach heaved. She was driving around with the demon in the passenger seat. But I couldn't worry about Aubrey. Not now. Now I needed to find Cole. I called his phone. He didn't answer. I held the phone away from my ear and dialed again, hoping to hear his ringtone.

I strained my ears. Nothing. I looked back at the tree I'd woken up in and then back toward the direction I'd come from. I'd start there. I pocketed the phone and stumbled my way through the forest, teetering between the roots and branches like a newborn deer.

The bat. There was the baseball bat. I picked it up from the ground and gripped it one-handed over my shoulder like a ballplayer, as I scanned the woods, half expecting the demon to pop out with its glowing eyes. If the bat was here, Cole should be here somewhere. I leaned against the tree we'd been forced against and dialed again. Nothing.

I gritted my teeth and headed back in the direction of the shed, eyes alert for movement in the shadows, praying Cole'd be there.

My nostrils flared as an acrid stench wafted toward my nose. I coughed as the gritty stink filled my lungs. My first thought was the demon. It was the same stink. But wincing into the darkness, I realized a huge mass of smoke was drifting slowly into the treetops, and I started to run.

My heart dropped as my pace slowed. The shed. It was gone. A bit of the structural bones still stood, blackened by a now-extinguished fire, as the innards had crumbled to a pile of ashy rubble still smoking lightly in the dark.

I flipped the phone open and tried Cole again, still holding the bat at my shoulder as I stared numbly at the shed. I flinched as I heard it. His ringtone.

I lowered the bat and ran toward the sound. It was coming from a darkened underbrush just feet from the shed.

He was still—crumpled, face down on the ground with his soot-caked cheek pressed into the mud and leaves. I dropped to my knees, my hands moving over him, searching him for a pulse.

There.

It was there.

My fingers moved to his nose. He was breathing. He needed help. I needed to get him to the hospital. I looked around for something...anything to roll him onto. I managed to find the tarp, but it'd been mostly charred by the flames. I rolled Cole onto what little was left of it and laid the bat gingerly beside him in the crook of his lifeless arm. As I worked, I couldn't help but glance over my shoulder every few seconds, terrified the demon would be back, its glowing cyes burning from the depths of Damien's skull.

I gripped the end of the makeshift stretcher and had to bend over to yank it as I walked backward and hauled Cole out of the woods.

It took forever.

But by the time we made it to the road, Cole was slowly starting to regain consciousness. I pulled him up to the bottom of the little grassy hill that sloped up to the road and bent down beside him as he let out a dry, raspy cough. My aching fingers moved over his blackened face, smoothing back his ashy hair. "Cole?"

His thick lashes fluttered. "Phin?"

I moved a hand over his forehead. He was burning up. "I'm going to move you to the van and take you to the hospital, okay?"

He blinked rapidly as his eyes tried to find me, to focus on my face. "Where are we?"

"Just outside the woods." I threw open the van door. Then I moved to sit behind his head and slipped my hands under his armpits. I was tired, and sore, and weak, but I had to get him in the van. Then I could rest. "You ready?"

He shook his head. "No, wait...wait."

Gingerly, he pushed himself into a sitting position, cradling his left arm. He groaned and his face contorted in pain as he leaned back against me. "All right," he grunted through gritted teeth. "Arm and leg: officially broken."

"Yeah, I figured." I leaned over his shoulder to look into his eyes. "I'm going to lift you, okay?"

He shook his head slowly, and his hand came up to my cheek. He blinked, clearly dazed, as he studied my face. "Are you okay? Did he hurt you?"

I took his hand off my face and squeezed it gently. "I'm fine."

"Phin." He winced, as though it hurt to talk. "*What was that?*"

My heart dropped into my stomach as I took a deep breath. "You don't have to worry. I'm going to take care of it."

Cole gave a sort of pained smile that I could barely return. My mind raced, trying to process the fact that Damien was possessed by a demon and Aubrey was potentially in danger.

"But first, I need to take care of you."

"I can get up—"

"Cole, don't—"

He staggered to his good leg as I scrambled up with him to help support his weight. Together, we helped him hop and hobble up the embankment and into the van. I shut the door and made my way around the front to the driver's side. As I switched on the car lights, they flooded the empty road ahead. Damien's car was gone. The demon was on its way home with Aubrey right beside him, and I couldn't do anything to help her.

They wouldn't let me stay with him. I brought Cole in, and they took him away. I could barely even call goodbye before they wheeled him through the double doors on a stretcher. Because I was under eighteen, they made me leave him there. Told me to come back during visiting hours. So I headed for the van. I tried to call Aubrey again. Still no answer. I checked the time. Five in the morning.

I tried to drive to Martin House, but I could barely keep my eyes open. Reluctantly, I pulled over in a church parking lot and fell asleep with the key clutched in my hand.

I awoke with a start a few hours later from a nightmare of molten fire eyes.

The church parking lot was empty. The sun had barely begun to rise. I checked my watch. Half past seven.

I pulled out the phone and switched it on. The low battery message flashed. The text message counter jumped up in number before my eyes.

> Where are you?

> I need you now!

> Call me Sera please!

> WHY AREN'T YOU ANSWERING?

> WHERE ARE YOU?

All from Damien. I didn't understand. Was the demon gone? I flinched as another Damien text message popped up on the screen.

Call me please

With shaking fingers, I dialed Aubrey's number.

"Sera?" Aubrey's voice was low and hoarse, like she'd been crying. A lot.

My heart leaped into my throat. "Are you okay?"

Aubrey sniffed. "I-I don't know what happened. The last thing I remembered was trying to get—but then I woke up and the whole shed was on fire. Damien...He...His eye was all b-burned and bl-bloody. I took him to the-the hospital."

I sat up straighter in the seat and got ready to crank the engine to life. "Are you still there? Where are—"

"But then he wouldn't stay—and I told him he *needed* to stay, they hadn't discharged him yet...then Daphne called him and—and he left me on the side of the road—"

"He *what*?" I gripped the phone, pressing it hard into my head. "So, he's not at the hospital."

"There was...something *wrong* with his eye." Aubrey gasped.

"He had an accident—"

"No!" Aubrey exclaimed almost pleadingly. Her voice was low as her breath blew into the phone. "The *other* one...it, it wasn't the right color!"

My heart raced, and the phone slipped a bit in my slick palm. "His eye?"

"I tried to call Daphne—I couldn't call my dad—and she didn't answer."

"Are you okay? Do you need a ride?" I fired off questions quickly as my panic rose.

"No, I walked home...I'm home. But I can't find Daphne. She's missing. Gone. Seraphina, what *happened* last night?"

I blinked, head racing too fast to think. "Listen to me, Aubrey—you need to stay away from Damien, do you understand? He's not—he's not right...okay, can you promise you won't—"

"Hang on—" Aubrey's voice lowered, and her words blew against the phone. "I gotta go...my dad—"

The call ended.

I shut the phone and ran a hand through my hair. His eye wasn't the right color. Daphne was missing. I closed my eyes and shook my head as my fingers gripped the dorm key. My heart slammed against my chest as I struggled to catch my breath. My head was foggy with too many thoughts. I needed to start at the beginning.

I took a deep, calming breath.

Everyone did the dare at Aubrey's sleepover. Sold their souls. The demon killed Maddie. Were the other girls next? Damien's dad said this happened before.

Alice Grey.

Alice Grey, a witch without magic, summoned the demon for power all those years ago. And ended up dead on Bird Island.

Mama's doing secret High Council work because of something to do with Alice Grey. So maybe that meant demons, too?

Damien found the spell—presumably Alice Grey's spell. He recited it. Summoned the demon. But he wasn't a witch...it shouldn't have worked. Though Alice didn't have magic either, and it must've worked for her...how did that make any sense? Only witches had magic. And Damien wasn't a witch. This much I knew. So how had the spell worked? I swallowed, my tongue thick in my mouth. Up until a few days ago, I hadn't known demons or monsters—the supernatural part of our world—existed...maybe there were different kinds of magic that existed...magic that I didn't know or understand? My stomach churned. It was too much. My world, and the laws that ruled it, were falling apart all around me.

I shook my head as I gripped the steering wheel hard in my hands, the key crushed in my palm. I had to focus. Follow the trail. The demon possessed Damien. I had to get it out of him. But how could I fight a demon?

The key.

I turned it over in my fingers. It was rusted in places. It could be iron...and iron had purification properties. That could explain the effect it had had on the demon...whatever the reasoning behind it, the key was my only proven defense.

So, the key hurt it...

And now Daphne was missing? Why? Was the demon now hunting the others who had done the dare? Hadn't it said as much? But Daphne hadn't done the dare herself—it'd been her dare. So she couldn't be dead...it wouldn't come for her. Would it? I glanced down at the phone, packed full of frantic texts from Damien...or the demon? Wanting to see me. Is it after me now? And why did the demon want to take me to Bird Island?

My head hurt. I needed help. I needed help *now*. I took out the phone again and tapped through my contacts. Aubrey. Cole. Hannah. I tapped open our text messages. She'd given me a number to help. I swallowed thickly as I stared down at the number. It was an out-of-state area code, but it looked familiar. I repeated the number in my head over and over as I began to tap it in.

I pushed Send.

The phone went black.

I moaned softly as I shut the phone. Dead. It died. I chucked the phone to the floor of the passenger side with an exasperated shriek.

What did I need to do? Next right action. I bit my lip. I needed to exorcise a demon. That's what I needed to do.

I looked up at the church.

And who better to help me exorcise a demon than a Catholic priest?

I got onto campus within twenty minutes and parked the van in front of a giant brick building with dozens and dozens of windows. The rectory. I pushed the buzzer and demanded to see Father LaValley. The secretary—or whoever she was—was not pleased.

"Father LaValley is preparing for the morning Mass...you children need to stop bothering him at his home. This is the second time I've—"

"I need to talk to him now. *Please*," I added hastily.

There was silence. I winced as a gust of icy wind pressed into me, huddled at the door. I bounced up and down in frustration and cold. Then the buzzer beeped. I threw open the door and made my way inside. The room was warm and cozy. I flexed my frostbitten fingers as I hurried to the desk, unbothered by the angry woman's withering stare. "Where is he?"

The woman was old, with a thin, pointed face and an even thinner mouth. She pointed to his office door. I didn't bother to ask for permission. Instead, I walked straight past the woman and up to Father LaValley's door and banged as hard as I could, despite the protests of the woman at the desk.

Father LaValley opened the door.

"I need your help. Can I come in?" I didn't bother to wait for an answer. I barged right into his office and dropped into a seat, my back straight and my hand gripping the key like a blade.

Father LaValley shut the door, eyeing me curiously as he slowly lowered himself into his chair behind his desk. He didn't say another word. He sat perfectly still, studying me, evidently waiting for me to gather my thoughts and compile my words.

I took a deep breath and blurted, "How do you exorcise a demon?"

Father LaValley was quiet for a moment. His face was unreadable. "Have you spoken with your mother about this?"

My heart still pounded uncontrollably fast, so fast I felt like I might be dying. I kneaded my fist into my chest as I tried to take deep, steadying breaths. It wasn't working. I grabbed for my bag and pulled out my herb satchel and a lighter. Quickly, I pulled out a bundle of sage and lit it, fanning the smoke all around me. "I'm sorry, what?" I snapped, impatiently.

Father LaValley frowned as he stood up to fetch me a bottle of water from a mini fridge. "Drink," he ordered. Then he leaned against the edge of his desk as he looked down at me. "I said: before I begin to discuss something as serious as this with you, I'd like to speak with your mother first..."

I put out the sage bundle and gulped the water down. "My mother is gone. She's Unreachable. That means—"

"I know what it means," Father LaValley interrupted softly. He stroked his chin, silent and staring.

I would've been surprised, but not anymore. "I need to know how to exorcise a demon. Can you help me or not?"

Father LaValley's eyes narrowed and his frown deepened. He opened his mouth and then shut it tight so his mouth was a thin, pained line. "I can't, I'm sorry..."

I sat still for a moment. I blinked my burning eyes and stared up at the ceiling, refusing to let any more tears fall. I looked back down and shrugged. I guess that was it.

Father LaValley glanced at the door before he pushed off his desk. "But I know someone who can help you."

I stared at him, relief flooding me with renewed hope. "You do?"

He scrawled a note on a pad of paper. He looked up, his eyebrow cocked. "I expect you to tell your mother all about this when she gets back."

"Fine."

He ripped off the paper and handed it to me.

I took the paper out of his hand and hurried out of his office, back out into the lobby. I slapped at my jacket for the phone and then remembered it was dead on the floor of the van. I stalked up to the cranky crow of a woman. "May I use your phone?"

Lips pursed and eyes narrowed, the woman handed me the phone, its curly cord tangled and taut. I uncrumpled the note and without bothering with the name, I punched in the numbers. The phone began to ring. My heart fluttered with nerves.

"Who's this?" demanded a gruff voice.

"Hello, is this..." I glanced down to read the name on the note. I sucked in sharply as though I'd been kicked in the gut. "Logan DeVarney?"

2 2

HEY THERE, DEVARNEY

"Who wants to know?" Logan asked again.

I squeezed the phone and rolled my eyes. This had to be a joke.

"Hello?"

I bit down on the inside of my cheek as I tried to think fast. Was Logan like Hannah—some kind of...evil creature killer? If he was, it would explain *a lot*. Like why he hated me so much. Being a witch, I wasn't exactly a normal human, was I? I took a deep breath that rattled in my chest as I studied the paper again. I could hang up. But my phone was dead, and he came Catholic priest recommended. Logan was my surest shot at getting rid of the demon before it killed anyone else.

"Okay, then," Logan quipped, sharp with annoyance. "Hanging up now."

"Wait!" I gritted my teeth, groaning inwardly. "Father LaValley gave me your number and told me you could help me. Is that true?"

I couldn't help but roll my eyes as his tone immediately changed to one of concern. "I got time. Where did you want to meet?"

• • •

It was nearly empty in Hallowed Grounds. There were only a few kids—kids I didn't know—scattered around the place. The only person I recognized was the guy behind the counter with the brown shaggy bangs and dopey grin, who'd flirted with Courtney that day. I took a seat at a little table in the corner so I could watch the door with my back to the wall.

And I waited. And all I could do was stare at the door, my mind blurred with panicked thoughts of problems I couldn't do anything about.

Logan said he'd meet me as soon as he could...apparently, for him, that meant hours.

I flinched as the door swung open fast, blowing a gust of cold October air into the coffeehouse, and Logan walked through the doorway. Finally.

When he saw me, his face clouded. He cursed under his breath as he shut the door behind him. My eyes narrowed. He stood in the doorway, his hands shoved into his pockets, staring back at me as though debating whether to turn around.

His scowling face set my temper on fire. This was ridiculous. I held up a hand, gesturing to the empty seat at the table.

He didn't move. Instead, he took a deep breath and sighed. Then he headed for the coffee counter to place an order. He came back to the table carrying two coffees in a drink carrier and two slices of pie.

Logan passed me a to-go cup. "Witch's Brew?"

I blinked stupidly up at him as he snickered and took the seat across the table. "Half coffee, half hot chocolate? It's called a Witch's Brew."

I scoffed. "Well, that's the stupidest thing I've ever heard."

Logan took his cup out of the carrier and shrugged as he sipped. "It's your drink, not mine. Have you tried their salted maple pie? It's the best pie I've tasted—ever. And that's saying something."

I frowned as I watched him. "Father LaValley said you could

help me…but I think this might have been a mistake…"

Logan snorted as he put down his coffee and grabbed his plastic fork. He shrugged again as he took a bite.

I pursed my lips together as we stared at each other. There was a hint of a smile in the corner of his mouth as he chewed. His dimple gave him away. He wasn't going to make this easy on me…at all. I tried again. "Why did Father LaValley tell me to call you?"

Logan smiled then and shook his head, rolling his eyes as he took another sip of his coffee. "It's killing you to ask for my help, isn't it, Sam?"

I frowned. "It's Seraphina."

"Bless you."

I scoffed. "Fine." I rolled my eyes over my coffee cup as I took a sip. "I have a few questions for you…"

Logan smiled, then took a bite of his pie and mumbled around the crust, "First one's free, then you'll have to PayPal me."

I hesitated, my mouth slack in shock. Logan chuckled as he sipped more coffee. A joke. Funny. I glared at him coolly. "First question: Why have you been watching me?"

He didn't miss a beat. "You've got a nice smile."

My face burned as I tucked my hair behind my ears and frowned. "*Honest* answers, or I'll walk out right now."

Logan studied me for a moment over the top of his coffee. He took a sip and then lowered it slowly. "I was making sure you didn't go dark."

My forehead crinkled. I'd had a feeling, and I appreciated his honesty, but it was still jarring to hear. I held my chin up higher and asked another. "Why were you looking for Maddison Rose that day?"

Logan's face fell. He took a deep drink from his cup. Then his eyes held mine. "I was trying to help her. Like I'm trying to help you now, if you'd ever get to the point."

I frowned at his comment but took comfort in his answer. I

took a deep breath and exhaled slowly. "Is it possible to be possessed, but not know you're possessed?"

Logan cocked an eyebrow as he lowered his coffee cup, the laughter gone from his face. His eyes were hard as emeralds as they studied me. "Yes. Explain."

I rubbed my forehead. "None of it really makes any sense…"

Logan continued to watch me as he took another bite of pie.

"This guy got his hands on a summoning spell. He—not a witch, mind you—recited the spell and managed to summon a demon. Now the demon is in this guy…and he doesn't seem to know it. And it's the same demon that killed Maddison Rose."

Logan cocked an eyebrow over his coffee. "Why do you say that?"

I massaged my forehead as I tried to explain it in a way that made sense…even though it didn't make any at all to me. "Look, some friends of mine—Maddison Rose included—were playing truth or dare. One girl decided to pull out a Ouija board. She dared everyone to 'sell their souls' to a demon. They thought it was pretend, obviously. I did, too. But then—"

"Maddison Rose." Logan nodded grimly.

I took a deep breath. "Right." My brow furrowed. "But I'm still confused as to how that even happened?"

Logan scoffed darkly. "Well, one thing's for sure—it wasn't the Ouija board. You use them to contact spirits, sure…but you can't make deals with the things. Not how it works."

I pursed my lips, unimpressed and slightly unconvinced. "Right. Well, as I was saying, I didn't realize that everyone who did the dare might actually be in danger until this girl told me—"

"Hannah Green." Logan nodded with his eyes closed and a smug smile in the corner of his mouth.

I recoiled, taken aback. "How did you—?"

Logan opened his eyes, smirking. "She asked me before she gave you my number. It's just good manners."

I shoved a hand through my hair. "Wait, how—" I shook my

head as I struggled to process. I held up a hand. "You know what? Never mind."

He jutted his chin toward me. "By the way, how's that phone treating you?"

"*Anyways...*" I continued pointedly, not about to let him know I'd irresponsibly let it die with no way to charge it. "This demon? It's been here before."

Logan gave me a skeptical frown as he went for another bite of pie. "And you know that how?"

"It told me."

Logan smirked. "Demons lie."

"My friends and I found the old shed of the witch Alice Grey. Damien Barrow found her spell and read it aloud and summoned the demon."

"Alice Grey?"

"Yes. She was a witch without magic. My mother's —relative."

Logan glanced up from his coffee, his eyebrow raised and a smirk on his face. "Did you say a witch without *magic*?"

My face burned but I continued evenly, as though I hadn't heard his question. "My next question is: How could a person without magic perform a spell?"

Logan bit his lip on his smile, his eyes glittering with mischief. "You witches and magic—it's not all for you, you know..." He paused and took another sip of his coffee. "Most demon-summoning spells are nihil spells...of course, I'd have to see it to confirm it, but—"

"Damien stuffed the spell in his pocket..." My nose crinkled as I tried to understand. "Nihil—nothing—a *nothing* spell?"

"If you say so. It's all Greek to me." Logan fought a smirk. "Either way, you don't need magic to power a nihil spell."

"Don't need magic for a spell?" I scoffed. This time it was my turn to raise an eyebrow. "That's an oxymoron."

Logan shrugged lazily. "I didn't say it was smart."

I blinked. "What?"

Logan stifled a laugh as he took another bite of his pie. "Okay, simple layman's terms: that spell is powered by the demon itself. So anyone can cast it. No user magic required. Dangerous in the wrong hands. Obviously."

I frowned thoughtfully as I studied him. It went against everything I knew to be true about magic. I'd never heard of a nihil spell. It was yet another thing I'd been ignorant of, another thing Mama had neglected to tell me. I'd thought I knew everything about magic. Clearly, I didn't.

"Well, the spell was cast last night and summoned a demon. The same demon who killed Maddie."

Logan shook his head. "I highly doubt that."

I frowned. "Why?"

Logan leaned forward over the table, both of his hands cradling the to-go cup. "Because Maddison Rose made a crossroads deal. The chances of your boyfriend—"

"He's not my boyfriend," I snapped.

"Randomly summoning that same exact demon? A million to one." He sat back in his seat. "If that."

I shook my head. "I'm sure it's the same one..."

Logan gave me a sympathetic smirk that set my teeth on edge. "Like I said—demons lie."

My anger heated my face. "Look, Maddie didn't make a crossroads deal—she wouldn't do that. She wouldn't even know *how* to do that."

Logan shrugged indulgently. "Then what do you think happened?"

I exhaled sharply, ignoring the impertinent question. "This demon possessed Damien Barrow, and he's been blowing up my phone ever since, asking for help. Like he doesn't realize he's possessed. Also, the girl who brought out the Ouija board is potentially missing...and I think this demon may be targeting the rest of the girls at the sleepover."

"Because of a Ouija board?"

I shrugged as I gave an exasperated sigh. "Because he told me as much, okay!"

"And?" Logan sipped his coffee, unable to hide his dimples.

I frowned. "*And* I need your help to stop it."

Logan raised his cup to me. "Took you long enough, Sam."

I stared at him, unimpressed. "How are we going to go about this? I thought I'd scared it off—" My words faded on my lips and my eyes narrowed as Logan burst out laughing over the top of his cup. He was laughing at me.

He shook his head, still smiling. "Sorry. Sorry. It's just—" He tried to stifle his laughter, but only managed to soften it to a snicker. "How could you—*especially* you—scare off a demon?"

My lip curled, and I scrunched up my nose. "How is that funny?"

Logan took a deep breath and smiled. "Don't you know *anything* about demons?"

This was getting ridiculous. I did not have time for this. "No! Obviously not! If I did, I wouldn't bother with *you*, would I?"

His brow furrowed and he studied me, a smile still tugging at the corner of his lips. "You're an odd witch, Sam."

My eyes flashed. "Forget it. I'll figure it out myself." I tossed my backpack over my shoulder, snatched my untouched coffee from the table, and marched toward the door, slamming it behind me. The cold wind pressed against me, pushing me back toward the coffeehouse.

I heard the door creak open as I hurried down the steps. I didn't stop.

"How are you going to do that without my help?" Logan called after me, a laugh lingering in his voice.

My shoulders tightened along with my hands as I headed toward the van. "Don't worry about it."

"Oh, come on. You forgot your pie." Logan came up from behind, falling in step with me, and passed me the to-go box.

"Hannah Green gave you my number because she knows I can help. Father LaValley told you to call me because he knows you need me."

I scoffed and stopped short to glare at him. He was so close to me, my hand, still holding the coffee, brushed his flannel shirt.

"Whoa." Logan held up his hands in mock surrender. "Don't drop the coffee..." A smile teased the corner of his mouth.

Suddenly, my temper cooled in the brisk October air as I looked into his eyes. Green speckled with gold. My expression softened. I opened my mouth to argue, but I couldn't find any words. His eyes were like the forest in summertime.

He lowered his hands and took a step closer. I moved my coffee off to the side.

"This is what I do," he said softly. The amusement was gone from Logan's face, replaced with the stony, hard mask he always wore. "My brother and me? We hunt things like this demon. We hunt them down and kill them. And then we move on to the next town and hunt down the next thing."

I sucked in sharply. I studied his face, searching for truth I was unable to fathom. The woods around the back of Hallowed Grounds blocked out most of the sinking sunlight and in the thick of the trees, in the strange, yellowy shade from the burnt, dying leaves, his words were unsettling rather than reassuring.

"What kinds of things?"

"Evil things."

"So what Hannah Green said, about things in the dark... Demons aren't the only evil things?" I studied his face, looking for a lie and finding none.

"No."

I shivered in the cold, pulling my jacket tighter around me. "Closet monsters that eat kids?"

"Every dark thing you can think of and then some...I hunt them and kill them. But don't worry—" He clapped me on the shoulder, knocking me off-balance. "I'm making an exception for you. Now, come on."

I stood in the gravel drive, coffee in one hand and pie in the other, stunned at the insult.

Without another word, he headed for the line of parked cars.

And I didn't stop to think or question. I didn't have the luxury of time. I hurried after the witch hunter, the wet, fallen leaves sticking to my boots.

THIS AIN'T A SPELL, IT'S AN EXORCISM

"Which one is your car?"

I stared at him blankly.

"You *do* have a car, right?" Logan added when I didn't answer. "I really don't want to take a cab back to the island..."

"It's the—" I hesitated. "Wait...what happened to your truck?"

"Left it at the By the Lake Motel."

"How did you get here then?" I demanded suspiciously.

Logan shrugged and a boyish grin broke across his face. "Courtney gave me a ride."

His smile was infectious. Like a virus. Sickening. My eyes narrowed, feet planted firmly in the gravel drive. "Courtney? Courtney Blanchard? Courtney Blanchard just happened to give you a ride?"

Logan chuckled, pleased with himself. "She saw me walking down Route 2 and offered me a ride."

I stood there, torn between indignance and shock.

"Don't worry, Sam." Logan nudged me. "It was just a ride."

I scoffed and nodded toward the van. "Just get in."

Logan laughed and pulled open the driver's side door. For a

minute, I thought he was holding the door open for me, but he hopped inside himself and held out his hand. "Keys."

"Wait a minute! You can't—"

"Keys." He jutted his head toward the inside of the van. "Hurry up and get in, will you?"

Eyes wide and temper buzzing, I stalked around to the passenger side, wrenched the door open, jumped in, and threw the pie box onto the dashboard and tossed the keys at him, half hoping to hit him in the head. But, of course, he caught them with a chuckle and cranked them in the ignition. I chucked my backpack in the back seat, just narrowly missing his face as he pulled out of the parking space.

"You need to work on your aim, Sam."

I clenched my jaw so hard it hurt and cranked the stereo.

Logan winced and switched off the dial. "Grunge? Really?" Logan glanced around the van. "And I definitely didn't peg you for a hippie..."

I ran a hand through my hair. "Yes, *really*. And it's not my van." I took a sip of my coffee, my eyes closing slightly as the rich, earthy warmth hit me like a hug. "And it's not a hippie van."

Logan glanced at me sideways as he drove over the train tracks and off campus onto the main road. He glanced in the back as the guitar case slid back and forth along the floor and clanged with the baseball bat as he drove. "Guitar Boy?"

I nodded, taking another greedy sip. "Cole."

"Where's he at?"

Cole slamming into the tree flashed in my mind. Blood oozing from his nose.

I lowered my coffee and massaged my temple. "He's at the hospital."

Logan looked at me. "He okay?"

Squinting, I nodded, again. I didn't trust myself to speak.

"What's the deal with him, anyway?" Logan glanced at me

sideways, an amused glint in his gold-speckled green eyes. "Seems a bit broody..."

"Well, I know he doesn't keep a diary," I said dryly.

Logan chuckled and nodded appreciatively.

I pursed my lips into a pout to keep from smiling back. "What's the deal with *that* thing?"

Logan cocked an eyebrow at me. "Are you telling me witch dudes don't keep Books of Shadows?"

"So all that is—what?" I shrugged as I took a sip from the to-go cup. "Notes? On real things?"

"Yes. Real things." Logan nodded with a smirk. "It's a field journal, really." He tilted his head toward me. "And don't think I didn't notice you snatched some pages. But no need to feel guilty about your petty larceny. You only managed to grab the initial case notes."

I rolled my eyes. "A flask of liquor, a shirt, and scraps of paper hardly qualify as—"

"Holy water."

I looked at him. "What?"

Logan smiled at me, amusement crinkling in the corners of his eyes. "It wasn't liquor, you nerd. It was holy water."

My cheeks burned. "Oh."

"How old do you think I am?"

I shrugged. "You don't seem like the kind of guy who worries about breaking the law..."

He scoffed and rolled his eyes. "Thanks."

"So." I cleared my throat, keeping my eyes on the road ahead as the lake appeared between the trees. "You were looking for Maddie to help her...how did you know she needed help?"

"I saw the marks on her arm." With one hand gripping the wheel, he twisted the radio knob, scanning the channels, but only found garbled stations and static. He cursed under his breath and switched it off again. "But there's a lot about this case that doesn't add up—it's been a head scratcher, for sure."

Logan pulled into the ferry docks and parked in the line of cars waiting to board. The boat wasn't due to arrive for another few minutes. I looked across the horizon and spied it slowly making its way back across the lake, the sunset at its back, casting it in shadow.

"How so?"

Logan's brow furrowed as he stared out at the lake. "Well, for one thing...the demonic signs...they haven't been consistent."

"Signs?" I prompted. "Like the animals behaving strangely and the streetlights flickering?"

"Right. There are different kinds of demons...some are low level and weak, some are extremely powerful and frigging frightening. But each has a specific set of signs that follow it around—kind of like a disease. When they infect a town, it displays certain symptoms...like when Maddison made that crossroads deal? The ground surrounding the road is scorched, and I found nightshade growing underneath the street sign. The psychotic animals, the dog mutilations, crazy electrical episodes...all say lower-level demon. But I've looked into it—there's no sign of demonic possession anywhere in Nile. It's like Nile is suffering from the presence of a demon that isn't there."

"How can you be sure?"

Logan grimaced as his hands gripped the steering wheel. "You can't. Ever. But when a demon possesses a human, you can expect —to put it lightly—abnormally bad behavior. I've talked to Sheriff Vantine, and a few church leaders, and store clerks...nobody's seen anybody acting out of the ordinary."

"But you *know* Maddie made a deal. So there was a demon somewhere. And if you knew Maddie made a deal—why didn't you hunt the thing down?"

"A crossroads deal is one and done. An incorporeal demon makes a deal and then gets sucked back down to Hell...they don't get to hang around. They've got no body tying them to the ground. Thank God."

"So, how did it—you know...come back for her?"

Logan's jaw tightened. "A grim tracked her down."

"A grim? Like the grim reaper?" I scoffed.

Logan snorted. "No. Reapers are creatures that take souls to Heaven. Grims are something else. Beasts from Hell that hunt down the marked souls and tear them out of people. Drag the souls down to the pit."

I winced at the image, refusing to think of Maddie. "Why, though? Why do they want our souls?"

"Souls are power. Energy. The more souls a demon can corrupt and absorb, the stronger that demon can become...move up the food chain, you know?"

"So demons have...a hierarchy?" I raised an eyebrow.

"A lot of evil things do. Don't witches? You're not all equally powerful...it doesn't work like that."

I didn't answer. No one understood a power hierarchy better than me. I cleared my throat as though I might clear my thoughts. "What *is* a demon? Like a spirit, or—?"

Logan glanced at me from the corner of his eye as he pulled the van up the ramp and parked on the ferry deck among the rest of the cars. "You really don't know anything about anything, do you?"

I looked out the window at the lake. The fiery sunset highlighting the waves turned the water brassy orange and gray. "Forget it."

"No, it's just...weird. What'd you do all your life? Keep your nose buried in your spellbooks, not bothering to look up?"

I gnawed on my cheek. What would he think if he found out I couldn't cast to save my life?

"All right, well, I'll start with the basics since we have a long boat ride and the signal in the middle of the lake blows."

I snorted and jabbed the CD button. A sharp blast of gritty grunge met our ears, and he winced.

"What?" I asked dryly. "Too good for Nirvana?"

He ignored me and continued, "I'm a hunter—"

"Like your father before you?" I quipped over the top of my to-go cup.

Logan grinned at the reference. "Hell yeah."

He turned a bit in his seat to face me better, an arm draped over the steering wheel as the van bobbed gently with the boat. "My brother and I travel all over the country looking for weird deaths, mysterious disappearances, and strange murders that could use our expertise. You being case in point...most people don't realize there are things lurking in the shadows, ready to rip them to pieces. We try to keep these people in blissful ignorance, all while saving their necks in the process."

He wore his arrogance like a decorated warrior wore his medals. I studied him as he spoke. The pride he felt for his...profession...was evident. My mouth twitched in a slight smile, despite myself.

Logan thought for a moment. "Civilians are all like cows. Docile things that don't like being spooked."

"I see. Wonderful. You're a real-life Superman. And demons?" I snapped impatiently, hiding the fact that I was honestly impressed and a bit envious of him. Logan couldn't be more than a year, if that, older than me, and yet here he was, an ordinary, powerless human, making a difference in the world. He was so sure of his place. If only it was like that for me.

"A demon is a damaged human soul."

"So...people become demons when they die?" I asked dubiously. I bit my lip on my childish retort that that wasn't what my mother said.

"Only really *evil* people...you're telling me you don't understand the concept of a human soul?" Logan asked skeptically. "Come on, Sam, I'm surprised at you."

"I understand what I've been told." I frowned. "Apparently, my education was biased in favor of ignorance."

The ferry docked and the cars began to unload.

Logan gave me a sympathetic smile. "Don't blame her too harshly. If I had a kid, I'd keep it as stupid as possible, too."

I shot him a nasty look.

Logan shrugged matter-of-factly, and then he put the van in gear and drove off the dock.

"A human soul is the purest form of life. It's our God energy," I recited stiffly.

Logan nodded. "Right. It's our..." He screwed up his face as he tried to think of a way to explain. He turned the car onto the highway that cut through Nile. "It's the God particle...the spark of life infused into us by our Creator."

I cocked an eyebrow. "Poetic."

Logan grinned. "You like that? Pretty good, huh?"

I had to smile. No...it wasn't.

"So, evil acts damage a soul. The more bad things you do, the more messed up your soul gets. By the time a reaper harvests your soul, and it's your soul's time to make the journey to Heaven...it can't. It gets stuck down here on Earth. Over time, it gets even more warped and twisted, absorbing all the negative energy around it like a magnet. Then it gets rounded up and dragged down to Hell. Now, they are supposed to stay down there, but sometimes there are cracks in the Gates, and they get out." Logan rolled his eyes. "Or idiots mess with magic and summon them here."

"So..." I pursed my lips as I tried to absorb all the information. "A demon is a ghost?"

Logan took a big breath. "No. A demon isn't a ghost. A ghost is a soul who *could've* gone to Heaven but was too afraid or too angry or too guilty to move on. They get stuck on Earth because they refuse to let go."

I nodded slowly. "And magic isn't needed to work demon spells. Because they are nihil spells...which don't need magic." I glanced at him with an eyebrow raised.

Logan looked at me out of the corner of his eye. "Right. Demon-summoning spells don't need magic from the caster to work...they tap into the power of the demon. A lot of dark magic is like that...dark magic is easy."

"So, everything is real?" I threw up my hands in exasperation. "Vampires?"

Logan nodded.

"Werewolves?"

Logan nodded again.

"Zombies?"

Logan held up a hand. "Not since the last outbreak in 1920. It's a dark magic virus that pops up every few centuries."

"Mermaids?"

Logan cocked an eyebrow. "Lake Champlain is full of them."

I laughed in surprise, genuinely delighted by the thought. "So, Champ is real then?" I challenged.

Logan nodded, a satisfied smirk on his face. "You're telling me you don't know what these Nile dudes do?"

I cocked a dubious eyebrow.

Logan winced as though he didn't want to tell me. "These sick idiots take a girl out in the middle of the lake and leave her there. 'Sweetheart Sacrifice,' they call it. The Nile historian, Zan? Apparently, her grandson rescued a girl about a month ago. Nearly blue from hypothermia, half drowned." Logan's lip curled in disgust. "People...sometimes they're worse than the monsters."

I hugged myself, sick at the thought, and quickly turned the topic around. "When did you talk to the historian?"

"Aw, have you met her?" Logan grinned. "Awesome woman. She was telling me about it a few weeks ago when I saw her about Bell Hill..." He glanced quickly, almost awkwardly, at the road.

I shook my head with a bemused smile, still feeling like it was all a little hard to believe.

Logan seemed to read my expression because he jutted his thumb at me. "You yourself are a witch. Why is it hard for you to believe there could be other monsters out there?"

I raised my eyebrows at his choice of words. Logan shrugged

sheepishly, but he didn't bother to apologize. My fingers found their way to my amulet, and I began to fiddle with it as unease flooded my veins and sped up my heart. I'd forgotten. He hunted witches, too.

Then I remembered. "And what does quicksilver do to witches?"

Logan looked at me sharply and then rubbed his neck uncomfortably. "For *dark* witches. A lot of times, they use dark magic to —well...it's the only thing that'll put them down for good."

My jaw tightened, and I regarded him coolly. "And I'm sure you make sure they've gone dark *before* you chop off their heads?"

Logan winced at my tone. "Yes."

I scoffed and stared pointedly out the window at the farms as they passed.

"Listen..." Logan shrugged. "I'm sorry about what I said before. When the demon signs started, and there wasn't any demon to be found...well, I wasn't sure if—"

I kept my eyes on the trees as they passed in a blur of gray and brown and green. "I'd 'gone rogue.' Right."

An uncomfortable, almost animus silence hummed between us as he continued to drive through Nile, heading steadily east.

"So, where are we going?" I asked, finally breaking the silence.

"My brother and I are staying at the island motel."

"Do you always take your clients back to your motel room? Standard DeVarney business practice?" I glanced at him. My attitude toward him had soured. It was guys like him who had strung up our ancestors, burned us alive, and tried to force us from Nile.

"No." He chuckled. "Honestly, he probably wouldn't be happy that I'm doing this either, but he's not here, and I gotta do what I gotta do. We're going to need a game plan before we confront this thing. And I can't just let you loose in the school with a demon running around. So, I'm stuck with you."

"Explain the demon thing again...why do they possess people?"

Logan shrugged. "Because they can? I mean, without a body,

they're just another nasty spirit. But thankfully, demonic possessions are pretty rare. You're more likely to be possessed by a ghost than a demon." Logan held up a finger. "Now, ghost possessions are easier to deal with because at least you can kill a ghost. You can't kill a demon."

My stomach tightened uncomfortably. "You can't?"

Logan's smile crinkled the creases and dimples in his face. "That's why we exorcise them and kick their demented souls back to Hell, where they belong."

I nibbled on the inside of my cheek while I fought to contain the question that'd been bothering me for a while. "Why did you call my house?"

Logan cleared his throat and switched his hands on the steering wheel. "I didn't."

I raised a dubious eyebrow, but I didn't bother arguing for the truth.

Logan cleared his throat again, changing the subject. "We're almost there. Why don't you give me some more background on what we're dealing with...not the Ouija stuff—the actual, concrete case we are dealing with."

I nodded slowly, unconvinced by his obvious avoidance, but happy to be doing something productive. I explained the spell, and all that had happened from the moment the demon was summoned to the moment I left the woods.

By the end of the story, Logan nodded toward the road. "We're here."

I looked up as we turned down yet another dirt road and drove down a hill. With the lake to my right and the By the Lake Motel across the street, we pulled into the deserted parking lot. We hopped out of the van, and Logan led the way to room three. He fumbled in his jeans pocket for the room key and jammed it into the lock.

"Watch the salt line, please." Logan nodded toward the floor as he held the door open for me.

I looked down at my feet. A thick line of salt lay in front of the door. I stepped over it, muttering, "And I thought you were just a slob…"

"First line of defense is a mineral one." He shrugged as he twisted the lock and slid the lock chain in place. "Salt keeps out most evil things…but it doesn't hurt to double lock the door."

"Where's your brother?" I eyed the room. My nose crinkled against the stink of smelly feet mixed with sage. They'd clearly cleansed the room, but it wasn't enough to drive away the stench of the place. I stood awkwardly near the door, not wanting to sit on the chair that had a suspicious stain on it, nor on the bed that, from the look of the rest of the place, was probably crawling with bugs. I pointed to the bed. "You sleep on that thing?"

"Uhhh…he's on a hunt," Logan muttered distractedly, not turning around. He was busy studying the left wall, which was covered in news clippings and handwritten notes and maps.

I walked over to stand beside him, surveying the wall myself. It was like those serial killer walls in the horror movies Phoenix watched with Rachel. What I'd half expected to find in his dorm the other night: the stalker wall of death. My eyes slid sideways to glance at him. "Everybody said you were a stalker…"

Logan looked at me in surprise. A slow smirk twitched in the corner of his mouth, and he chuckled darkly. "Sure. If you want to put it that way. Go ahead."

"Monster stalker?" I raised an eyebrow in amusement.

Logan grinned as he shoved his hands in his pockets, shrugging sheepishly. "A monster stalker. I'll own that."

I couldn't help but smile.

Logan's eyes held mine for a moment.

Then he looked away quickly as he cleared his throat. "The wall helps to make connections that I might miss otherwise. I'm a visual kinda guy." He stepped closer to the wall, waving a casual hand at the clippings. "I started gathering all the signs and possible leads I could after the first signs started…the day after you started school. I tried to connect the Rousseau murders, the double homicide down the road on—"

"East Shore South."

"Right, but no signs of demonic presence in the house or around it—"

I regarded him sharply. "You broke into their house?"

Logan snorted with an easy smirk. "Of course. How do you think we get the job done? Breaking and entering is standard procedure. I learned to pick my first lock when I was four. But, anyways—signs started after your first day. But they weren't consistent; nothing was making sense. As you can see, not much there..."

I studied the wall. "Wait—what about all these then?"

"Just a case I dug up. The deaths on Bell Hill Road? Just a ghost thing. No big deal. They don't call Nile the most haunted place in America for nothing." Logan turned to flash a lazy grin, meeting my gaze with his own. "Have you heard about that haunted house off..."

I bit my lip as I watched him scrunch up his face to think.

"God, what was the street...anyways..." He inclined his head with a small twitch of a smile.

I was staring. Hastily, I looked back at the wall and said the first thing that popped into my head. "How long have you and your brother been doing this?"

Logan chuckled. "Since my mom left...I was...what? Maybe three?"

Embarrassment forgotten, I turned to him, eyes wide with alarm. "Your *mother* left?"

This time, it was Logan's turn to look embarrassed. A soft pink warmed his tan cheeks and he shrugged, turning back to the wall.

I curled my fingers into my palm to keep from touching him. Cole's mom left him when he was a baby. I knew how much it haunted him. Instantly, I felt for Logan.

"It's not a big deal. I don't even know why I brought it up...she wasn't the greatest person..." He chuckled darkly. "Although, if you asked my brother, he'd say Mother Dearest was an angel."

"So," I spoke slowly as I tried to understand, "you've been on the road with your brother...hunting *monsters*...since you were three..."

Logan laughed. "When you say it like that, it sounds bad, but—"

"It's heartbreaking!" I cried.

Logan's easy smile returned, and he looked at me with such a warmth I felt I could melt underneath it. "Don't approve of five-year-olds setting vamp traps?"

At the horror in my face, he clapped a hand on my shoulder and shrugged. "I was with my brother. I wouldn't want to be anywhere else. Especially now...this one demon we've been tracking? Super bad...like boss level bad. We've been hunting it for nearly a decade."

"Is that why you showed up here in Nile? For the boss demon, I mean?"

"Nah. The trail had gone cold down in Louisiana. This demon...it's unlike any other demon we've come across."

"How so?"

"She has a body."

"What do you mean?"

"She's a corporeal creature. A demon with a body of her own. She's not possessing anyone. And she can disappear and reappear wherever she wants, so she's impossible to track."

"Are you sure she's a demon?"

Logan glanced at me, his head tilted to the side with a smile crinkling the corner of his eye. "You know, I've honestly never questioned it..." Logan snickered. "That is a good question... maybe she isn't? But she claims to be, she hangs out with demons, and her eyes glow molten gold like a demon—"

"But she doesn't behave like one?"

Logan gave me a downturned smile and shook his head

slightly. "And she's working with a witch—a wicked—you all call her the Dark One…"

I scoffed, nose crinkled with disdain. "The Dark One?"

Logan nodded with a smirk. "Right? Anyway, decades ago, there was a war against the Dark One and some kind of demonic army. She was trying to let the Devil out of Hell. Unleash him on humanity. But she lost—obviously."

I stared at him, mouth parted and unable to speak. What could I say to all that? Mama told us the Devil wasn't real.

"Anyway, I felt like we should've headed to the Carolinas, you know, head after the demon; we call her Carmen…" Logan shrugged sheepishly, as though he'd admitted something embarrassing.

I stared at him blankly.

He raised his eyebrows, his brow crinkled expectantly. "You know…where in the world is…no?"

I blinked. "Uhh—"

Logan waved a hand. "Never mind. Anyways, Hannah Green called us for help with a closet critter…and then, LaValley needed help with a gargoyle…and then Trav had to deal with—well, something else, so he called up LaValley to stick me in that dumba—dorm," Logan finished, eyeing me as he struggled to keep his speech clean. "LaValley and my dad were buddies back in the day, so—"

My eyes widened and a smirk played at the corner of my lips. "I knew there was something off about him…"

Logan chuckled. "His spellwork tattoos give it away?"

"I was talking about his muscles, and his crew cut. He has tattoos?" I giggled.

"Hey, don't judge. Protection is life-or-death in this business. I've debated getting some ink myself, but I don't do needles." He made a face.

I quietly agreed. Nothing sharp. And no blood in places it

shouldn't be. Bleh. "So, do you always make it a point to keep up with your education on your monster hunts?"

"My—oh...no." Logan made a face. "Part of the job."

I smiled a bit. "You went undercover as a high schooler? How'd you like it?"

Logan's smile crinkled the dimples in his cheeks. "It was nice to see Courtney today, I'll say that."

I gave him a shove and rolled my eyes.

Logan laughed. "No, seriously, though? I hate it. I hate sitting around when I can be doing stuff that actually matters. Helping people, you know?"

I frowned thoughtfully.

"And I get to work with my brother. I mean...you've got a sister, right? Wouldn't you rather go on a road trip with her, than sit in a math class or go to some lame party?"

I didn't answer. How could I? If things were different... But they weren't. "You haven't met my sister," I quipped drily.

Logan snickered, and his green eyes glittered. He opened his mouth, but I blurted my next question, desperate to change the subject away from Phoenix.

"Why'd he leave you behind?"

"Traven? Oh, he got pulled into a job by a friend of his...there's no telling how long he'll be gone."

"He wouldn't let you come along?" I inclined my head as Logan rubbed his neck and looked away.

"I didn't ask...plus, I had that ghost case. It was a time-sensitive kind of haunt. And then Maddie...I felt like I should stay."

Quiet, uneasy and uncomfortable, settled around us.

Logan ran a hand through his sandy hair as he studied his notes on the wall. "All right. Enough small talk. Let's talk game plan."

I frowned. "There's something you're not saying..."

Logan met my stare with one of equal strength, his eyes hard as emeralds and his jaw set.

The silence in the room rang in my ears.

"Fine, don't tell me." I threw up my hands, and then crossed my arms impatiently. "The demon, does it need a person to...I don't know—walk the earth?"

"They sometimes behave like spirits, floating around like stinky smog, but usually they like to possess people."

"So it could be inside anybody?"

"Well...technically, but demons have a sentimental streak. They tend toward the familiar...and they don't usually leave the person they've possessed, voluntarily. I mean, it's really hard for them to gain possession over a person unless there's a spell involved. The body, the soul—it fights back against possession. That's why demonic possessions are rare—not many demons can escape Hell, and not many demons can easily possess a person."

"Unless you use a spell?"

"Right." Logan smirked. "If you use a summoning spell, you're basically inviting the demon inside you...not my idea of a good time. And as I said, they will dig their claws into you and never let go, if they can help it."

"So, it'd still be in Damien? Even though he's acting like it isn't?"

"It would make the most sense. Like I said, I've never heard of any demon voluntarily leaving a body unless it's under threat of exorcism." Logan snickered. "They *do not* like going back to Hell. And you didn't exorcise it, so—" He shook his head, frowning.

"I stabbed it," I pointed out.

Logan tried to hide a smile. "I'll admit that was pretty quick thinking. Although I'm sure a spell would've come more naturally, the iron stab was the best thing to do." Logan clapped me on the back again.

I stumbled forward a bit. "Yeah, not really. I just grabbed the first thing I could think of...I didn't make the iron connection until after."

Logan burst out laughing. "You just figured you'd poke a demon in the eye and see what happened?"

My face burned. I turned pointedly back to the board. "What does a demon do after it possesses someone? I mean, like...what do they want? What's the point?"

Logan moved to the coffee machine and fired it up. "Most want to bring pain and suffering, mischief and evil, you know? And all of them like it better topside. I mean—life here is tough, but it sure beats burning in Hell, right?"

"So, it's probably still possessing Damien?"

"Well, yes and no..."

I frowned; annoyance narrowed my eyes. "That's a helpful answer."

Logan chuckled. "As I said, possession isn't easy. The more depressed and damaged a person is, the easier they are to possess. Honestly, they're just a magnet for demons." Logan gave a little shiver and made a face. "Ever heard the phrase, battling your demons? Well, it's a lot more literal than you might think."

His back was to me as he shuffled around with the mugs. The rich smell of the roast wafted through the stuffy, stinky room, and I couldn't decide whether that was a good or bad thing.

He lifted the pot to me. "Coffee?"

I shook my head. "And that's what happened to Maddie?"

Logan frowned and replaced the pot without pouring a cup. "No. I told you. She made a deal with one."

I drew a sharp breath and shook my head. I crossed my arms in a protective hug around my body. "So what happened to her?"

Logan sighed wearily. "She made a deal. People out running demon deals start seeing things...horrible, messed up, evil things when their time starts to expire...visions of Hell. Then they start compulsively drawing these visions, desperately trying to get it out of their heads." Logan paused and ran a hand through his hair again. His voice was heavy. "Maddison had drawn all over her left arm. So hard she was bleeding."

I remembered the last time I'd seen her. Maddison had drawn all over her notebook. So hard it ripped the pages.

"You couldn't help her?" I breathed, overcome by the darkness of it all. My eyes scanned the newspaper clippings and images stuck to the wall.

"No. I couldn't help her." Logan turned toward me, frowning. "I couldn't find her, remember?"

I flinched at his words, guilt lighting my nerves on fire. "Right." I met Logan's heavy gaze then, silver fusing with emerald. "What's the plan?"

Logan smiled and nodded appreciatively. "We need to draw a sealing circle and lure the demon into it. That way it can't use its magic against us as we exorcise it. I don't know if you'd noticed, but demons have powers of their own..."

"Yeah, I noticed." I winced as I saw Cole's body slam against the tree. The blood oozing from his nose. I had to think of something else. "What if it tries to possess me?"

Logan cocked an eyebrow at me, his forehead furrowing. He reached over and tugged my amulet. "Did you think I hadn't noticed?"

I swatted at his hand and closed my fingers around the necklace. "Do you mind? My dad gave me this."

"Well, hate to break it to you, but Daddy gave his little girl an anti-possession pendant." Logan smirked at my stunned expression.

I recoiled, taken completely aback. "Why would he do that?" I breathed, squeezing the amulet hard in my palm. "That doesn't make any sense."

Logan shrugged. "They're pretty rare." He held up a key strung on a chain around his own neck. It wasn't a dorm key. "My old man gave me his skeleton key."

My eyes widened, and I had to resist the urge to reach for it. Skeleton keys were ancient magical artifacts able to open any lock no matter what enchantments were placed upon them. I'd never seen one before, only read about them.

"Dads do things like that." He shrugged and cleared his throat, clearly uncomfortable. "Now then. Let's get this over with."

I held up my hands, deferring to him.

"You said Damien's been trying to see you, yes?"

"Mmhmm."

"Okay. We use that to our advantage. If you invite 'Damien' somewhere, the demon won't be able to resist coming to you."

I looked up at the ceiling, trying to think. I frowned at a series of more questionable stains. "I should try to bring him here, right? I mean, isn't it better to have home court advantage, as they say?"

Logan raised his eyebrows. "How would you do that?"

I smiled. "That part's easy. Damien has had it out for you since you showed up at school. The demon will know this, right, so it'll make sense if I make it seem like I'm trying to snoop through your stuff—"

"Again?" Logan crossed his arms with a smirk.

I ignored him and kept going. "I'll tell him...*it*...that I think you are responsible for bringing the demon here in the first place, and I stole your motel key...sound believable? Maybe?"

Logan ran a hand through the short crop of hair on the top of his head. "It's possible...but you have to sound really convincing. We don't want a tipped-off, ticked-off demon."

"Right." I stood and walked over to him. I held out my hand expectantly. Logan stared at me, clearly confused. I smiled. "May I steal your key, please?"

He laughed and dug into his pocket. "Truth to every lie, huh? Here." He passed me the key. Then he went over to his rucksack and dug through it. "Before it gets here, we draw the sealing circle using various sigils and spellwork, and then once it's inside, we perform the exorcism."

I nodded, glancing out the smudgy window. "What happens to the demon then?"

"The exorcism is just a simple prayer that sends the demon back through the nearest Gate and back into Hell."

"And when you say 'Gate'...you mean like a Veil? Or a—"

"Exactly. The Gates are just portals to Hell. It, again, doesn't require the caster to have magic, so you don't even have to be here if...you know, you want to go home, or something..."

I grimaced at the severity of it all. "I'm helping."

Logan raised an eyebrow, giving me an appreciative grin. "Okay...last lesson on demons. Iron burns them pretty bad. But nothing they can't recover from. Holy water is the same. Although, the stronger they are, the less effective those things are. But, yeah, unfortunately nothing will kill them." He paused and gave me a nudge. "Besides, even if you could kill a demon, you couldn't kill it without killing the host. And I think you'd want to avoid that, however unpleasant the person may be." Logan flashed me a boyish grin that sent a fluttering in my stomach. "Now, about that spellwork."

I put my hands on my hips, resisting the urge to hug my stomach. I blinked as I tried to process what he'd just said.

"You being a witch...you probably want to take the lead on this, but I'd prefer it if we—"

I took a step back from him. "No, you definitely should take the lead."

His eyes glittered with mischievous amusement at my obvious discomfort. Logan took a step toward me, a sly smile on his face. "Why do you say that?"

I bit my lip. "I just..." I couldn't tell him the truth.

"Yes?" He grinned and crossed his arms.

"It's just that I don't have any experience with demons. Or any of it. I mean, I just learned about all this today. My...my mind is kind of blown," I finished lamely.

Logan frowned thoughtfully, shoving his hands into his pockets.

"What?" My voice came out high and strained. My face burned. Had he caught my lie?

Logan shrugged and waved a hand in my direction. "I just assumed you'd be chomping at the bit to help. You must have a ton of spells stocked up by now. I don't know, you seemed the type."

"What type?" My eyes narrowed, searching for the insult.

"You know, the 'has to be good at everything' type. Meticulously curated, perfectly cataloged spellbook." Logan shrugged.

I opened my mouth to argue that my spellbook was in fact meticulously curated and perfectly cataloged.

He cut me off. "But that's good." Logan clapped me on the back. "Too many cooks, you know? I don't like to work with... extra help...if I can help it, no offense..." He forced a smile that didn't deepen a single dimple.

"Extra help? Like witchcraft?" I raised an eyebrow and gave him a critical study. My silver eyes flashed. "You really don't like witches, do you?"

Logan had the decency to look slightly abashed. "Honestly, I haven't ever met any worth liking."

The truth hurt, but at least he wasn't a liar.

I bit my lip. Having me do it would not help in any way...but maybe if the caster had magic, it *would* work better, at least easier. Phoenix would probably be able to send the demon out with a snap of her fingers. I nibbled on my lower lip, feeling sick with inadequacy. "I'll follow your lead. No extra magic from me. But I'd really like to help, if you'll have me."

He nodded slowly, thinking it over. He moved to the kitchenette and poured himself a cup of coffee. "Would your mom be okay with this?"

I took a deep breath. No, she wouldn't. But she wouldn't have wanted me to mess with demons in the first place. However, she'd expect me to correct my mistakes. I felt the weight of Logan's stare and remembered he was waiting for an answer. I moved toward the table and unzipped my backpack. "She's Unreachable."

Logan stared blankly at me, and I smiled. "In layman's terms: she's not home, and without cell service. I mean, you *are* a professional, right? Nothing could go wrong..." I trailed off and looked at him expectantly.

He smiled, mug in his hand, leaning against the kitchenette. "You ready to set a demon trap?"

24

GRAND THEFT EXORCISM/WHERE'S YOUR DEMON

I pulled the phone out of my pocket and flipped it open. My heart sank. "Jinx it."

"What was that?" Logan fought to keep a straight face.

My eyebrows knitted together, and I frowned as my face warmed. "What?"

"I gotta say...you cuss like a fairy princess." Logan's face split into a grin that made my heart flutter.

I scowled at myself as much as his comments and held up the phone. "It's dead," I admitted, slightly embarrassed to be holding us up over something so trivial. "I don't have a charger...and this thing is so old, they probably don't sell any that fit it."

Logan smirked. "Why don't you just—" He wiggled his fingers.

I jammed my fist into my hip. "Seriously?"

Logan snickered and put down his mug on the kitchenette counter. Then he grabbed a bag off the floor, dropped it on the bed, and rummaged through it. He emerged with a black cord and tossed it to me. "Hook her up."

"Thanks." I unraveled the cord and plugged it in, along with the phone. Logan, meanwhile, slapped an open rucksack across the tiny table and pulled out several cans of salt, a jug of water, an old bandana, and a large machete. I stood over the spread with my arms crossed. Then I pointed to the machete. "And that's for...what?"

Logan glanced at me with his eyebrow raised and an amused glint in his eye. He slipped the machete into its holster and hitched it to his pants. "Insurance...things go sour—demons have a hard time possessing a body without a head on it..."

I gasped despite myself. The thought of hacking Damien's head off was...disturbing, to say the least.

I tilted my head as he pulled out a mason jar of thick, red liquid that smeared the insides of the glass as it sloshed in his hand. He placed it on the table with a thunk. My stomach heaved, and I closed my eyes as the room spun.

I squinted at him, refusing to look down at the table. "Please don't tell me that's—"

Logan regarded me quizzically, then his eyes glittered. "Don't worry." He struggled to hide the knowing smile that pressed into his dimples. "I won't."

I crinkled my nose. "That's disgusting."

Logan laughed.

My face burned, and I crossed my arms as I shrugged defensively. "So, I may have a thing about knives and needles and blood in containers...it's whatever."

Logan grinned wickedly. "Well, now I know I don't have to worry about you going darkside."

I winced as I tried to get used to the jar. Of blood. On a table. "What do you mean?"

"Dark witches love bottling up bodily fluids."

I put a hand on my stomach as it churned. "No, thanks." I made a face. "So, why do we need it? And do I want to know where you got it?"

Logan chuckled as he continued to rifle through the rucksack. "It's for the sealing circle...to trap the demon. It seals their powers inside, keeps them within the circle, and gives us time to exorcise it without it fighting back. A circle of salt will hold them for a few minutes, maybe longer if the demon is weak, but the only *sure* way of containing them is to paint a circle with the right sigils in human blood."

I eyed him warily. He gave me a hearty smack on the back. "Don't worry, Sam. It's donated."

I scoffed as a smile slid onto my face. "Right."

"Seriously!"

I swallowed thickly as I stared down at the blood. In a jar. "Show me how to paint the circle."

Logan cocked an eyebrow at me, clearly surprised, if not impressed. "You sure?"

I nodded, jaw clenched.

He grinned and shrugged. "Okay...don't pass out on me, or anything." He passed me an extra bandana and we got to work, our fingers wrapped in cloth coated in blood, painting a large circle on the underside of the motel rug, and then waited for it to dry.

Once we'd cleaned off our fingers, Logan grabbed his mug, snatched up my box of pie he'd snuck in from the van, and dropped onto one of the beds with the remote in his hand. He slid the pie onto the nightstand beside him.

He turned on the TV. "What's your pleasure?"

I shrugged and sank down onto the bed opposite him. "Doesn't matter. I don't watch much television."

Logan snorted as he clicked through the channels. He bit his lip on a smile but didn't make a comment.

He stopped on a channel. "Here. You might get a kick out of this."

The show was just starting. It was clearly an old show. The credits flashed over a cartoon...of a witch flying on a broomstick.

I turned slowly to glare at Logan, who laid back against the headboard with his head resting in his threaded hands and a sly, half-hidden smirk on his feigned innocent face. "What?"

I opened my mouth, but before I could spit a snarky remark, the phone buzzed loudly as it finally turned on.

He sat up and turned off the TV. Logan nodded toward the nightstand. "You ready?"

I jumped up quickly and picked up the phone. The message counter continued to climb again. All from Damien. Here we go.

> Hey, Damien. I need your help. Where are you?

> West Shore Ferry. I need to see you.

> I think you were right about that Logan guy.

> I need to see you.

> Meet me at the By the Lake Motel. Room 3.

I glanced at the clock. If he was at the West Shore ferry, we had fifteen minutes at the most. "Run through the plan one more time..."

Logan put his mug on the nightstand and repeated patiently, "You open the door and lead him to the rug. Remember not to panic. I'll be in the bathroom, so he doesn't get spooked. But if you run into trouble, remember it's not your boyfriend. It's a demon. So feel free to hex, jinx, whatever you think is necessary at the moment—"

"You don't need my magic," I cut in quickly as my heart fluttered helplessly in my chest.

Logan gave me a funny look. "No, but if you feel you need to use it, be my guest."

"But we don't need magic," I insisted again.

"Right..." Logan went around the room, making sure that everything was in order and didn't look out of place. "Anyways— oh, I forgot this." Logan reached into his pocket and pulled out a vial of clear liquid and shook it in front of me. "Holy water. If it gets too close, splash it in its face. Burns like acid."

I took the vial in my hand and smoothed my thumb across the glass.

Logan gave me a small nudge with his shoulder. "And if all else fails, you can always stab it with your dorm key." He winked roguishly.

I rolled my eyes and pocketed the holy water.

"As soon as it finds itself trapped in the circle," he gestured to the rug positioned beneath the wall of news clippings, "give me a shout, and I'll jump out and start the exorcism." Logan eyed me uncertainly. "Are you sure you want to hang around for this? Exorcisms aren't fun. It'll get pretty nasty before it's over."

I nodded. "I want to help. I can handle it."

Logan gave me a soft smile that warmed his eyes. "I know you can." He gave me a small wave and disappeared into the bathroom.

My heart started to pump harder as soon as he left my sight, my blood surging fast through my veins. "Logan?" My voice was thin and frail, barely carrying across the carpet.

He stuck his head out of the bathroom. "Yeah?"

I bit my lip. Everything remotely related to magic I messed up...nothing ever worked. I winced as I raked a shaky hand through my hair. "If...if it goes wrong...if I screw it up somehow... you'll come out right away?"

His brow crinkled, and he walked over to me and rested his hands on my shoulders. "You don't have to do this...you lured it here, that's huge. Why don't you go wait in—"

I shook my head. "No." I struggled to swallow the lump lodged in my throat. "No, I want to do this." But *could* I do this?

Logan gave my shoulders a reassuring squeeze. "You'll be fine. You have nothing to be afraid of. I'm here. It's just a demon, Sam."

I took a deep, trembling breath and tried to remember why I was doing this as Logan headed back to the bathroom. The demon would go after the girls. I had to stop it.

"You *are* a witch, remember?" Logan tossed over his shoulder with a grin that sent my stomach fluttering, and he headed into the bathroom, cracking the door behind him.

I nodded to the empty room, feeling worse than before. I moved to sit at the table. I jumped up quickly as a knock tapped at the door, startling a few tears from my eyes.

Hastily, I wiped them away with the back of my hand and slapped at the curtains to make sure it was the demon. I rolled my eyes. As opposed to what? Somebody *really* dangerous?

I shook my head at my nerves and willed myself to be strong. I took a final deep breath to steady myself and sent a prayer up for courage. Prayers were the way normal people made magic happen...and right now, it was all I had. I could do this. All I had to do was let it in and get it to walk onto the rug. I reached up to slide back the lock chain and then paused at the doorknob, my palm slick with sweat. Then I twisted the lock, turned the knob, and I let it in.

I gasped at the sight of him—the pallor of his skin, his sunken, bloodshot icy eye paired with a bandaged one. He looked ghoulish and sick. He staggered into the doorway.

I gritted my teeth, recovering quickly from the shocking state of him, and remembered the plan. "Get in. Quick. Before he comes back." I grabbed his arm, thankful he was still wearing his jacket so I didn't have to touch him, and pulled him inside.

I shut the door behind us and leaned against it, to steady myself. My legs trembled.

Damien—the demon—stumbled to a chair and dropped into it, his eyes flickering anxiously around the room, flitting toward me every so often.

I needed to get him onto the rug. I hurried over to stand on top of it and pointed vaguely at the clippings on the wall. "I found this. It—It's completely creepy. It must have something to do with what happened to Maddison, and the whole demon thing...right?"

Damien licked his pale, bloodless lips and didn't answer. His hands fumbled into his pocket for his butterfly knife and began to fiddle with it.

"Sera—I really need to talk to you...about what happened last night." Damien's voice cracked a bit, as though he hadn't spoken in days.

I crossed over the rug completely, so it was now between the two of us, my boots planted firmly on the wood floor. I leaned my back against the wall. "Okay...but first, I want you to read this—" I reached up behind my head and pulled down a random piece of paper and glanced down at it. "This article about the car crash on Bell Hill Road...I want to know what you think of it." I held it out for him.

He didn't get up. He didn't move except to finger the knife. "There's something...wrong with me, Sera."

I nodded quickly. "Sure—sure, Damien, you've been through a traumatic...traumatic experience."

Damien looked at me, his eye finding mine. "I need your help."

"Of course," I breathed as the paper shook in my outstretched hand.

"I keep having these...these thoughts. These really *bad* thoughts, Sera." Damien's low voice cracked. "Have you?"

Cole slammed against the tree. Blood leaking from his nose. Damien's tongue, slimy and scratchy on my cheek.

It took every bit of self-control I had to remain rooted to the floor and not run for the bathroom. "Yes."

"I remember every moment it was inside me." As it spoke, Damien's eye glazed over ever so slightly. "It was like hearing a second person's thoughts in your head. It was weird...when it... grabbed you and..." His eye slid back to my face. He licked his pale lips. "I can't stop thinking about it."

My skin itched as his eye moved over me. I couldn't take much more. I needed to get him onto the rug. I let the article fall from my hand, and I crossed the carpet and walked over to him.

His eye widened as I neared him. He inhaled sharply as I took him by the hand and started to pull him to his feet. "Damien, I know it's—it's hard, but I feel like once we figure all this out, you'll start to feel better. I want to know what you can make of all this." His palm was cold and clammy, slick with sweat. I squeezed his hand to hold mine in place, fighting the urge to wipe it on my jeans. I kept my eyes locked on his and moved backward slowly, my free hand ready to grab the holy water.

He followed me. Slowly. Inch by inch.

"Do you remember that sound?"

I backed up a step. We were just a foot from the rug. If I could just get him across it...

"When Cole's head cracked against the tree?" His hand tightened on mine.

My breath caught in my throat as the black of his eye spread over the icy blue, dilating like a shark.

"I can't stop thinking about it."

I backed up one more step, taking him with me.

"I liked it, the sound," he whispered, his hot breath on me. I fought the urge to turn away from the stink of curdled cheese and pickles. He reached a hand up and brushed my hair back from my face. "And I couldn't help but think, what sound your head would make..."

He grinned almost shyly and stepped toward me. I took a quick step back from him, my boots moving across the thick, dirty rug. He followed. I looked down at our feet. He was in the circle. I jumped back from him off the carpet toward the wall. But I didn't yell for Logan. I didn't even make a noise. Something wasn't right. Damien was still coming for me. He walked across the rug...across the circle...over it...and out of it.

He was out of the circle, a breath away from me, pinning me against the wall.

My mind raced, keeping pace with my heart. My eyes narrowed, and I studied him. Something was wrong.

"Sera...I've been thinking about this since last night." He

gripped the butterfly knife and fluttered it around. Then he gripped it tightly, snatched my arm and yanked me into him. He held the blade up to my face.

I flinched away, but he held me fast. I glanced at him sideways with an ironic smile. "You aren't possessed anymore, are you?"

Damien leaned in closer. His eye widened with a desperate hunger as he pressed the cold blade against the hollow of my throat. "Nope."

"LOGAN!" In one fluid motion, I brought my knee up into his groin, and Damien staggered backward with a groan.

The bathroom door burst open.

Damien turned, still doubled over in pain, the knife raised.

With my back against the wall, my eyes met Logan's, and I shouted, "Not the demon!"

Logan moved so fast I almost missed it. He closed the distance between us, smacked Damien's knife hand out of the way, and punched Damien in the face, knocking him unconscious in one blow. Damien crumpled to the ground.

The two of us stared down at him in silence, processing what had just happened.

"Not a good week for him," I muttered lamely, my chest still heaving and my back still flat against the wall.

Logan looked at me. "You said he was possessed."

I blinked at Logan. That's all he had to say? My hand went to my throat and came back with a small tinge of blood. Damien had nicked me when I'd kneed him. "We *both* assumed he was possessed," I corrected coolly. "Who else would be?"

Logan frowned. He shook his head and sighed heavily. He bent down to make sure Damien was still breathing. Then he grabbed his cup of cold coffee off the nightstand. "I don't know, Sam...maybe—maybe he was faking. Just a psycho kid trying to get your attention. Maybe the thing he read wasn't really a spell at all."

"Logan...that thing was sending me flying into trees last night.

It was a demon. I saw his eyes! They glowed. And it said it killed Maddison."

"Well, then where is it? I told you before, demons don't give up possession if they can help it..."

"I don't know, okay? We'll just have to find it! Because the only thing I do know is that it's the same one that killed Maddie, and it's probably going after the other girls next."

Logan sighed as he rubbed the back of his shoulder. "Listen, I know you wanted to believe that it was the same demon that killed your friend...but like I said, the chances of you summoning the *same* demon—"

"I know it was the same demon. You said so yourself—they're sentimental."

Logan scoffed over the top of his mug as he drank deeply, shaking his head.

My jaw tightened. "This demon was summoned by Alice Grey twenty years ago, and it was summoned back again by the girls at the sleepover, during which they may or may not have sold their souls, and then it was summoned again by Damien at Alice Grey's shed."

Logan regarded me with a sympathetic impatience that set my teeth on edge.

I stood there, struggling between embarrassment and hurt. "Whatever, that doesn't matter...what matters is there is still a demon out there, and we need to—"

"I need to," Logan corrected.

I cocked an eyebrow. "Excuse me?"

"*I* need to look into it. And I will...but honestly, Sam, you probably blacked out and exorcised it yourself." Logan gave me a half amused, half impressed smirk.

"What?" I snapped incredulously. "That doesn't even—"

Logan shrugged. "It's been known to happen. Real powerful witches can exorcise a low-level demon with a finger snap...but in your case, you probably blacked out and your powers took over.

It's a defensive thing. I've *seen* it happen. A dark witch'll be down, and her powers overtake her, and—"

I scoffed. "I didn't block anything out."

Logan pointed a finger at me as he gripped his coffee mug. "Like the old lady who lifts the car off the kid."

"Logan, that demon is still out there somewhere." My voice wavered. "Daphne Collins is missing, and my friends are in danger."

Logan crossed the room to give me an impatient pat on the shoulder. "Like I said, I'll look into it."

My eyes widened as he dropped down on the bed and flicked on the TV. He grabbed the pie box and flipped it open.

I followed him, standing at the foot of the bed, in front of the TV with my arms crossed. "So, you don't believe me?"

Logan sighed again. "I don't know, Sam...a lot of what you told me just doesn't fit. Like the Ouija board thing. Maybe that would make sense if the demon had been there at the sleepover thing. There are demons that roam around making deals...but Maddison made a *crossroads* deal. One and done. I know this for a fact because the crossroad where she did it is scorched and covered in nightshade."

"But—"

"And now you're saying that after this thing had you unconscious and Guitar Boy up a tree, it decided, 'Oh, that's enough evil for one night' and ghosted out of that idiot?" Logan made a face. "Why would it do that, Sam?"

I glared at him. I had no answer.

Logan nodded sympathetically. He knew I had no answer. "Think about it. There's no reason for it to give up his possession. No reason to leave you and Guitar Boy alive. None at all that I can think of. The only logical thing, if there was a demon summoned at all, is that you managed to exorcise it with your magic. Which is an awesome thing, and you should be proud of it. Otherwise, you and Guitar Boy would be dead, and that moron," he jutted his chin toward the corner of the room where Damien lay crumpled, "would still be riding shotgun with a demon at the wheel."

I opened my mouth but nothing came out. I tried again. "I don't know why it would leave. But I know I didn't exorcise it, Logan."

Logan rubbed the back of his neck. He squinted up at me but didn't bother to respond. He picked up the plastic fork and took a bite of pie.

I rolled my eyes to the ceiling. Unbelievable. I scoffed angrily as I shook my head. Fine. I stalked over to Damien and bent down to heave him onto his back. I dug through his pockets and found Alice Grey's spell. I tucked it gingerly into my jacket before I began to lift Damien up. He was heavy. "Help much?" I snapped over my shoulder.

Logan raised an eyebrow, leaning up on the bed to see better as I wrestled with Damien's weight. "Why don't you just..." He waved his fork like a wand.

I grunted as I stuck my hands underneath Damien's sweaty armpits and pulled him toward the nearest wall to prop him up. "Forget it."

Logan watched me, a smirk on his stupid face. "Just use your magic."

Hot, angry tears spilled from my eyes as I continued to struggle against the weight of the full-grown teenage psycho.

Logan chuckled. "Fine." He tossed his pie box onto the bed and marched over to me. He hoisted Damien over his shoulder easily. Logan turned to me. "Where do you want him?"

I sniffed, my nostrils flaring. I pointed to the second bed. "Sit him up there."

Logan dropped him on the bed. Damien's head knocked hard against the headboard and slumped onto his shoulder. "Oops." Logan smiled almost cheerfully as he stood back. He glanced at me. "Now what?"

I heaved his rucksack off the table and moved it to the chair.

Then I grabbed my backpack and dumped out all the bottles I had snagged from the house onto the tabletop. I turned them over in my hand, smoothing my thumb over the labels.

Logan stood over my shoulder.

Truth. Memory. Suggestion. I took the veritas and unstoppered the vial, tipped Damien's head, and counted three drops on his tongue.

Damien's eye fluttered open. He had a blank, vacant stare.

"What is your name?" I asked gently.

"Damien Michael Barrow."

"Were you possessed by a demon last night?"

"Yes."

Logan leaned against the wall with his arms crossed, an impressed smirk playing at his lips. I scowled up at him. I didn't need his approval. Especially when he didn't believe me.

"Did the demon leave your body?"

"Yes."

"Is it in Hell?" I bit my lip, sending a silent prayer for a useful answer.

"No."

I looked back pointedly at Logan before turning back to Damien. "Do you know where it is now?"

"No."

I gritted my teeth. This wasn't helping at all. "Do you know what it wants?"

"Revenge."

Then Damien's eye closed, and his head lolled back onto his shoulder.

I waved a hand at Damien. "I told you."

Logan cocked an eyebrow, a doubtful expression on his face. "You should ask him what the demon's name is...that would be helpful..."

I blinked. "They have names? Do they remember who they were? Like, is there a demon Hitler out there?"

"Now that's a demon I'd like to kick back to Hell." Logan smiled indulgently. "But, honestly, I have no idea. That's a great question for a mage, though."

"A mage?" I repeated.

Logan shook his head and gave me a nudge. "You gotta get out more, Sam. A mage—egghead, scholar type—"

"I know what a mage is," I snapped defensively. "I just didn't realize *you* did."

Logan snorted. "Yeah, unfortunately. They tend to be the Watson to our Sherlock, you know? An annoying, occasional necessity...at least for us—"

"Why do you want to know the demon's name?" I asked with an uneasy feeling.

"You need the name before you can exorcise it. Ask him. He might know it."

My heart sank. "I can't ask him anything else."

Logan made a face. "Why not?"

I sighed and picked up the bottle of memoria, as I explained, "Veritas is toxic. One drop gets you two questions...one or two—sometimes three—word answers, but yes or no questions work best. I wouldn't dare give him more than three drops."

Logan made a pfff sound. "What help is that?"

I shot him a reproachful frown before I grabbed Damien's chin and counted five drops onto his tongue. I forced his jaw closed and hoped he bit his tongue. I placed the bottle on the bed beside me and took the last vial, mendacium, pulled open his mouth and dripped five drops onto his tongue, clamping his mouth shut one final time.

His eye fluttered open once more, and he looked at me expectantly.

"You've been walking around the island all day looking for your phone. You dropped it last night on the way to a party. You will keep walking until you get too tired to go on. Then you can stop."

Damien moved off the bed and walked toward the door. He swung it open and left the motel room without bothering to shut it.

"Seriously?" Logan pushed off the wall and looked out the door into the parking lot. "He's just going to walk around all night? What about his car?"

"He'll find it eventually." I watched Damien as he left the parking lot and started to walk along the side of the road, a little unsteady, as though he were sleepwalking.

I shook my head. The weight of crushing defeat slumped my shoulders. "I'm leaving."

I grabbed the potion bottles and dropped them into my backpack. Then with one quick swipe, I dumped all the other bottles, herbs, and random things back into my bag, threw it over my shoulder, and stalked out of the room and into the parking lot.

Logan hurried after me, his boots crunching the gravel.

"Call me when you get home safe...or do you not want to lift a magical finger to do that either?" Logan bit his lip on his smile, his eyes sparkling with mischief in the moonlight.

"Nope." I wrenched open the van door and tossed my bag into the passenger seat, and got in. Logan caught the door before I could slam it.

"Hey...listen...I'm going to look into this for you. I promise you, I will look into it. But like I said, you probably cast it out with your magic in the heat of the moment...it's not unheard of. Witches are stronger than most demons—"

"No, Logan." I jerked the door out of his hand. "I didn't cast it out."

He just looked at me with a small smile, which only made me madder.

"Did you not hear what Damien said? The demon's not gone."

Logan scoffed. "That creep wouldn't know his butt from his belly button." Logan smiled at me with a warmth that made my breath catch. "I'm telling you, as soon as it knocked you out, your magic took over and—"

"Logan—"

Logan opened his mouth to argue, but I cut him off sharply.

"I can't cast. Okay?" I shrugged, eyes burning, with a down-turned smirk. "I can't cast. I can't conjure. I can't do magic." I slammed the door in his face and cranked the van to life, the tires spitting gravel as I drove away.

Only to drive back there a few minutes later.

I had just pulled into the ferry dock when I realized I'd forgotten the phone. It was still plugged in at the motel. I had to turn around.

When I finally made it back to the motel, I parked quickly and stomped my way up to the room. I banged on the door, eyeing Damien's car still parked off to the side in the shadows. I glanced at Logan's truck. A trick of the yellow streetlight combined with my heightened paranoia, I could've sworn I saw something move in the darkness behind the tailgate. I stared at the truck bed, eyes narrowed for a moment, but I turned back toward the room as the curtains fluttered in the corner of my eye. Then the door was yanked open.

Logan pulled me inside and locked the door back up. "Couldn't stay away?" He smirked, plopping back down on the bed. "You didn't need to knock. You still have my key, you know."

My nose crinkled at the sight of him as I shoved my hand into my pocket to retrieve the key.

Logan laced his hands behind his head, eyes back on the black-and-white TV screen. I frowned and tossed the key at him without bothering to explain nor wait for an answer, half aiming for his face.

He caught it easily. "You know, you should really work on your aim, Sam."

I snatched up the phone and ripped out the charging cord.

"Wait. You want to order a pizza, watch TV, or something?" Logan slid off the bed.

"Not even a little bit." I slammed the door behind me and stalked to the van, rolling my eyes as I heard the motel room door creak open and the crunch of his boots on the gravel as he followed me.

"Hey." He came up behind me and gently grabbed my arm, pulling me around and into him. "I'm sorry if I made you feel... bad about...you know..."

I stared at him, eyes blazing. "I don't care about that!" I snapped, my voice watery with emotion and unshed tears. And for once, it was true. "You say the demon's gone. Well, I *know* it's not."

Logan shook his head and gave my arm a little squeeze. "Forget about the demon. I'm going to take care of it, okay? I just, I'm sorry if I made you feel...I had no idea you couldn't...I mean..." He rubbed the back of his neck, awkwardly shifting his feet.

I looked up at him as he struggled uncomfortably.

I inhaled deeply and said calmly, "Goodbye, Logan."

And with that, I left him in a dust cloud underneath the blue light of the moon, and I never looked back.

25

EVERYTHING'S FINE

It was all on me. A witch without magic. A walking punchline. I would find the demon and send it back to Hell myself. Alone.

Somehow.

But first, I needed to research. I drove through the night and pulled into Martin House. The parking lot was empty, which was unusual, but considering it was the Saturday night before Halloween, maybe everyone was at a party or something. I beeped my key fob and felt my way through the dark common room to the hallway and into the library.

I tossed my bag onto the table and went over to the computer. Once it finally powered on and loaded up, I pulled up the search engine. I dug through the trenches of the internet, searching for anything that might look legitimate. Some sites were blocked by the proxy server, but all the major religious ones I could access. There was a lot. But how much of it was true? There were loads of information about witches on the internet, but none of it was fact. What would make demon knowledge more trustworthy?

But I had to start somewhere. I scowled and pressed Print. And I kept searching and printing. Anything that looked even remotely reliable, I printed until my eyes began to blur and my eyelids began to droop, and I couldn't search anymore.

Then I gathered up all the papers, sat at the table, and spread everything out in front of me, and I read and annotated all the information. It was tedious and aggravating. Every article seemed to contradict the other and nothing was concrete enough to build my plan upon. I sighed heavily as I tossed my pen aside and covered my face with my hands. I moaned softly and massaged my temples.

I checked my watch. Three in the morning. I needed caffeine. I went to the kitchen and fired up the coffee machine. As I waited for it to brew, I raided the cabinets for several cans of salt, stuffing them unceremoniously into my backpack. Then I returned to the library with an oversized mug of coffee. I set the cup down on the table as I dropped into the seat.

Okay. Back up to the basics. I took a sip of coffee, wincing at the harsh, dark roast. It was like drinking hot mud. I made a face, sticking out my tongue as I put the mug back down. I shook myself.

What did I need to do?

I needed to find the demon, trap it, and exorcise it.

What did I know?

I knew how to draw the circle. The markings were basic. Easy.

What did I have?

I slapped at my jacket pockets. A dorm key. A charged phone. Alice Grey's spell.

I frowned thoughtfully as I slipped my hand inside my pocket and retrieved the spell. I smoothed it out on the table in the center of all the printed chaos. I ran my finger over the weathered page and the old, faded ink. Thankfully, it was in Latin...not the strange runes from the shed I couldn't understand. Any learned witch was well-versed in Latin. It was the language of God—and of magic. And I, Seraphina Grey, knew magic.

So, I read through the spell.

Over and over, I read her spell. Until the words began to run together on the page. I brought the paper closer to my face. The wording she used...this wasn't just a demonic summoning spell —*it was demon specific*. There was no name, but the phrasing was clear and with intention. A summoning spell for a specific demon.

My heart dipped a bit in my chest, and I barely resisted the urge to call Logan. This was the answer. This was why the spell had summoned the same demon from twenty years ago—I frowned and squinted hard at the page. But it didn't explain how Maddie found the demon at a crossroads... I lowered the paper slightly. And I couldn't use this spell to summon it because, as Logan had said, the spell essentially invited the demon *into* the caster. Not what I needed right now.

I studied Alice Grey's writing, her verbiage, and the deep scratches of ink that marred the errors she made, and the scribbles in the margins, noting her changes. She was a witch...a learned witch, judging by her drafting. I bit my lip, suddenly overcome with empathy for her. I knew her struggle. How desperately she wanted it to go right. How she *needed* it to go right. How many times had I worked on a spell? Researched it and adjusted it and edited it, over and over, until it was perfect. Only to have *nothing* happen.

My hands flew to my forehead, and my fingers rubbed over my face. I was losing my mind. Alice Grey was a dark witch...this was a dark spell. We were not the same. There was no excuse for going dark. The end did not justify the means.

I took a deep gulp of coffee and blinked rapidly as I forced down the roast. Blech. I flinched and returned the mug to the table. I went over the spell again. I picked up my pen. There was something here. There had to be something here.

Then I saw it.

I grabbed a printout from the mess of papers scattered around the table and flipped it over to the back. I hesitated. My pen hovered over the blank, white page. I studied Alice Grey's spell for a moment, my heart in my throat. I put my pen to the blank printer paper.

And I drafted a new spell.

By the time I'd finished, the light of dawn spilled into the hall just outside the doorway. I returned the mug to the kitchen, then collected all the papers I'd printed and shoved them into my backpack. I tucked my spell, along with Alice Grey's original, into my jacket pocket, and headed upstairs to bed. As much as I wanted to keep going, I hadn't slept much in days. And if I was going to do this thing right, I needed to rest.

When I woke up, I immediately checked my watch. It was late in the afternoon. Really late. Jinx it. I'd slept through my alarm. I called Cole.

Rachel answered. "Hey, Phin—it's me."

"Oh, hey—" I stammered, completely caught off guard. I rubbed my forehead. Rachel. What did Rachel know?

"Listen." Rachel cut me off quickly. "Cole was in an accident. He's in the hospital, but he's going to be okay...just really busted up. He's resting right now. Nana's with him. He said something about Damien driving?" She scoffed, her breath blowing loudly in my ear. "Why would he be driving around with Damien? I think he's lying to me...he wouldn't let me tell Nix anything—and you know that means he's hiding something..."

"Oh, my God," I mumbled, stalling for time. I gripped the phone as I tried to process what she was telling me.

"Yeah, he should be out by the end of the week...maybe. Make sure you don't tell Nix. He was pretty adamant about—Oh, Phin —sorry, I gotta go, my nana..."

"Sure, Rach, tell him—"

"I'll see you tomorrow!" She hung up.

See her tomorrow at school.

At least Cole was going to be okay. Good. Because I still had work to do. I grabbed my bag and headed out, locking the door behind me and pocketing my key. I left Martin House, got in the van, and drove the minute-long drive to Hallowed Grounds. I parked in the nearly empty parking lot and hurried inside. I ordered a large coffee ("Witch's Brew?" the barista smiled kindly. Same girl who'd flirted with Logan that one day. What day was that? Time was blurring together.) and a bag of cookies and headed upstairs. I took a small table against the back wall by the fire escape and sat down. Then I pulled out the printed papers and my pen and got to work.

I annotated and cross-referenced and inferred in between sips of Witch's Brew and bites of maple cookies.

Then I drafted a second spell.

A spell to exorcise the demon.

I didn't finish until well after closing. The barista girl came upstairs to give me a polite push to pack up my things, and I headed back to Martin House with a second coffee and another bag of cookies on the house.

The dorm parking lot was no longer empty, filled with the cars of Nile kids who didn't want to wake up early for the Monday morning commute. Steeling myself for more whispers and stares, I slung my bag over my shoulder, gripped the paper bag of cookies in my teeth, and held my coffee in one hand and the House key fob in the other. I beeped in the door, praying the common room would be empty.

Of course, it wasn't.

I kept my eyes down as I headed for the dorms. The whispers slithered after me up the stairs: "She thinks she's a witch."; "I'll bet she's the one who butchered those dogs."; "Maybe she killed Maddie."; "Who does she think she's kidding?"

I unlocked my dorm door and slammed it behind me. I stalked across the small space and sank to the floor, leaning against the bed, and laid out my work in an arch on the floor around my crossed legs. I pulled my old CD player out of my bag, slipped my headphones over my ears, and pressed play. The gritty groans of Kurt Cobain's voice blocked out everyone else, and I drafted my plan.

First thing—I had to warn the girls. The demon had already gotten Maddie, possibly Daphne, and it could easily be after any one of them next. I recited their names in my head: Aubrey, Morgan, Kaitlyn, Cheryl. Tomorrow morning, I'd pull everyone aside and...what? Tell them to watch their back? Hold onto their dorm keys? Pass out holy water instead of soda at Courtney's annual Cabbage Night sleepover?

Whatever I said, hopefully it wouldn't matter if they believed me or not after tomorrow. Tomorrow *was* Cabbage Night...but it was so much more than that. It was the beginning of the Thinning of the Veil. As soon as the sun set, all the hours in between then and Halloween night existed outside of time, blurring the space between worlds. And if I had any chance of these spells working, I wanted to give myself the best conditions possible...which meant tomorrow night on hallowed ground, I would summon the demon and send it back to Hell.

BANG.
BANG.
BANG.

I awoke with a start, the kind of leap-in-your-heart panic that sends you flying out of bed, half conscious. I stumbled for the door, instinctively grabbing my key, and tossing my bag over my shoulder. My hand on the doorknob, I flinched as the pounds against the door sounded in my face.

"Who is it?"

"Sera! *Sera, it's me.* Open—"

I threw open the door, heart hammering, bracing myself for terror. Aubrey backed up a step as the door opened. I recoiled at the state of her. Aubrey did not look well. Her light hair was limp. Her face was drawn and lined, with a sadness that was so unlike her, it made my skin crawl. Her eyes were bloodshot, rimmed with dark-purple circles. Aubrey obviously had not been sleeping. She grabbed at my arms, tugged at my clothes.

"Aubrey, what's wrong?"

Aubrey burst into fresh tears and clung to me, as I held her firmly and stroked her hair. My heart slammed against my chest as my head flashed images of gold-burning eyes and blood dripping.

"I need to talk to you..." Aubrey gulped through fresh tears as she pulled me down the hall toward her room. *"And not out here."*

I kept my arm wrapped around Aubrey as I led her down the hall to her dorm room. I opened the door and guided her inside. I dropped my bag and led Aubrey to the bed and sat her down.

I smoothed back Aubrey's hair from her wild, terrorized eyes. I tried to remain calm, but all I could think was the demon had come, and I was not at all prepared to fight it.

"Aubrey—"

"You've got to tell me what happened in the shed..." Aubrey pleaded, pulling at my clothes.

I tried to steady my breathing. "Aubrey..."

"What did he do? Damien? In the shed?" Aubrey's eyes were unnaturally wide, and her lips were pale as she bit down hard. She clutched at her locket, pulling it so hard it left red marks on her thin, white neck. "I need to know everything, *please*, Seraphina."

I took a deep breath and shook my head. "I think it's best if—"

"I've been having nightmares," Aubrey added desperately. "The past two nights. You know..." She licked her dry, bloodless lips and swallowed. "Since it happened, I mean. Since, you know, Damien..." Aubrey stumbled over her words, as though trying to get them into an order that made sense. "I...I try to stay awake like those kids in that Elm Street movie, but whenever I close my eyes and nod off for even a minute, I have dreams...nightmares of horrible things..." Her sapphire eyes bulged wide in her small,

sharp face. Her words began to jumble together as they bubbled forth from her mouth. "Gold like molten fire. Fire eyes. And blood. So much blood. And screaming. My mom! My stepdad... Maddie... *Oh, my God, Seraphina, what am I going to do*? I feel so helpless. I can't stand it." Aubrey's body shook with her sobs, and her breath rattled, raspy from the depths of her chest.

"Oh, Aubrey..." Fear seeped into me like a poison. Was Aubrey having the visions Maddie had? Was she next? How could I know for sure?

"Damien wouldn't tell me anything...Daphne's missing..." Aubrey added, panic stalling her tears.

"No one's found her yet?" I asked stupidly.

"Where's Cole? *I need to find Cole*. Have you talked to Cole?" Aubrey clung to me desperately, hopefully, as though Cole would answer all her problems.

I nodded. "He's still in the hospital. But they might release him by the end of the week," I added hastily at the sight of Aubrey's stricken face.

Aubrey hugged her hoodie to her, her shoulders hunched inward. She looked so small and lost, so frightened. I pulled her into a tight hug. Aubrey yanked at me, as though desperate for warmth. Like she was drowning and only I could save her.

She turned and breathed into my hair. "*How do I make the nightmares stop, Seraphina?*"

I squeezed her tighter, and stroked her hair like I would Fawn.

I slipped off the bed and went for my bag. I pulled out a vial of somnum. I pressed the bottle into Aubrey's clammy hand. "Three drops in your tea before bed and you should have a dreamless sleep. But make sure you only take three drops...otherwise you'll sleep way too long." I forced a smile as Aubrey's hand closed around the bottle.

"Thank you, Seraphina," Aubrey mumbled, wiping her nose with her sleeve.

I forced another smile as I rubbed Aubrey's arm reassuringly, as though I might bring some warmth back into her. "I'm going to figure this out, okay?"

Aubrey nodded, but she didn't smile.

"Figure out what?"

We both flinched and turned toward the door.

Daphne stood in the doorway, blocking out all the light from the hallway so that she was drenched in shadow.

"Daphne?" Aubrey gasped and ran to her just as she had to me.

"What is the matter with you?" Daphne's voice snapped with irritation as she gripped Aubrey roughly by the arms and held her at arm's length to look at her.

I stared incredulously at Daphne. "Where have you been?"

Daphne stepped into the room and dropped her pink designer bag onto Aubrey's bed. "Damien ditched me after the game Friday night, so I went to Michael's for the weekend."

I frowned as I watched her closely. "But Aubrey said she tried to call you…"

Daphne looked at me, her nose crinkled with disdain. "Michael has a cabin up at Smuggs…that's a ski resort in the mountains," she added in a slow voice, her eyes wide, as though I lacked basic comprehension skills.

She snickered cruelly and shook her head as she kicked off her designer heels and dropped onto the bed. She crinkled her nose and shooed me away. "Do you mind? I'm crashing here until lunch."

I scoffed and stood up from the bed to allow her to stretch out.

Aubrey, meanwhile, had moved to the corner by the door. Hugging herself, she rocked back and forth.

Daphne glanced at Aubrey. "Aubs, what's the matter with you?"

I stared at Daphne. "We thought…everyone thought something bad had happened to you."

Daphne arched one perfectly shaped eyebrow. "Aside from getting ditched after the football game?"

"So...you haven't been seeing things or feeling...off?"

Daphne propped herself up on her elbows and regarded me coolly. "No." She rolled her eyes and laid back on the bed, her hands threaded behind her head. "Seriously, Michael's cabin was lame, too. I hope Courtney's sleepover is worth the trip. It's tonight, right? I'm totally crashing."

I didn't answer. I was looking at Aubrey.

She glanced at her, too. "What is your *deal*, Aubs?"

Aubrey shook her head. Tears flooded down her face as she tugged at her necklace. Aubrey looked at me almost fearfully with wide, watery eyes.

Daphne's eyes darted from me, back to Aubrey and back again. "What did you do to her, Witch Spawn?" Scowling, Daphne slipped her shoes back on and jumped up from the bed. She grabbed her bag and threaded her arm through Aubrey's. "Let's get you a coffee. Hallowed Grounds is gross...but I don't have any cash for Starbucks. Come on..."

Aubrey yanked herself away from Daphne. She shook her head wildly and then started pulling at her hair.

I stared at her in shock, horrified as Aubrey continued to claw at her hair. "Aubrey, Aubrey!" I hurried to grab her wrists as her fingers began to tear her beautiful blonde hair out of her head.

Daphne backed away from her with her hands up. "What is wrong with her? *What did you do to her!*"

Aubrey shrieked and scratched at her head, ripping at her face, cutting deep red tracks down her cheeks. Chunks of skin packed underneath her fingernails. I tried to grab her, hug her to me, but she moved away from me, stumbling backward out the door into the hallway.

"Aubrey, stop! *Aubrey!*" I reached for her, desperate to hold her still.

Aubrey shook herself, her hair flying every which way, as she thrashed away from me. She was too close to the window. My heart nearly stopped at the thought of her falling. I lunged for her, but she slipped from my hands. Then she ran down the hallway.

I tore after her. Aubrey's shrieks pierced my ears, my heart dropping into the pit of my stomach, as she continued at break-neck speed toward the stairs.

"Aubrey! STOP!"

I reached for her, platinum hair slipping through my fingers as she disappeared around the corner. I grabbed the railing and watched in horror as she lost her footing...

And fell.

Face-first into the dark stairwell below. Her small frame slammed against the stairs, crumpling her body in impossibly crude angles.

There was a cascade of thuds and a final smack.

Then a scream, long and tortured, came from the bowels of Martin House. And another. Thundering footsteps in the hall behind me. Shouts echoing up from underneath my feet. There was a crowd of people at the bottom of the stairs, all shouting and crying as I hurried down the steps.

"Peter, call 911!"

"I knew those stairs were going to kill somebody!"

"Her head—it's, oh my God, it's bleeding—"

"Well, put pressure on it!"

I had to step over her. She was motionless and broken at the bottom of the stairs. My stomach lurched at the sight of the blood pooling beneath Rachel's fingers as she tried to stanch the wound, buried beneath her lily-blonde hair.

Damien looked up with his one good eye and met my gaze. "What'd you do, witch? Push her?"

"Shut up, Damien," Rachel snapped as she smoothed back Aubrey's hair.

I bent down to check her pulse. Heart still beating.

"The ambulance is here! Everybody move!" Peter called from the front door as he beeped the paramedics inside.

Thinking fast, I grabbed Aubrey's sleeve and rolled it up.

Nothing.

No pen scratches tearing up her skin.

My head spun as we all backed away from Aubrey, and the paramedics took over. They lifted her onto a stretcher and wheeled her away. As I watched the door close behind them, I met Daphne's dark stare.

I tried to get Morgan, Cheryl, or even Kaitlyn alone, but they were constantly with Daphne. The three of them seemed to be in much better shape than last week. But they all seemed to be purposefully avoiding eye contact with me. The only thing that kept me from losing my head completely was the knowledge that tonight I would take care of it. I would summon the demon, send it back to Hell, and everything would be okay.

Just before lunch, I followed Morgan and Cheryl to their next class.

"Hey, I need to talk to you—"

Morgan held up a hand and glanced at Cheryl, who looked down at her sheepskin boots. "Listen, Seraphina...we don't want to talk about...anything weird. Daphne explained everything to us...and we just want to forget about the whole thing, okay?"

I frowned. "Daphne explained...?"

Morgan gave me a sympathetic smile, her dark eyes warm but sad. "She said the popularity has gotten to your head...what with everything they say about you...and what happened to Maddie... and we all somehow got wrapped up in your hysteria, too...it happens."

I opened my mouth, but no sound came out. I had no words. I scoffed. "Listen, I don't know what she's been telling you, but you both need to—"

"Sera." Morgan rested a gentle hand on my arm. "Don't worry. We're still friends. We're not mad. We just don't want to hear it anymore, okay? I mean, look what happened to Aubrey..."

My eyes burned as my vision blurred. I looked at Cheryl, who continued to look down at the ground, almost guiltily, twirling her cherry-red hair around her fingers.

"We'll see you at Courtney's sleepover tonight?" Morgan gave a final awkward smile with an equally awkward wave, before grabbing Cheryl and hurrying away.

By lunch, the whole school heard about Aubrey cracking her head open at the bottom of Martin House staircase, and I was sure Daphne played a big part in spreading the news. The whispers followed me as I moved through the halls: "Aubrey was looking for that island girl."; "The Grey girl pushed her."; "She probably killed Maddie, too."

I met Rachel and Courtney at a round table near the back of the lunchroom. Kaitlyn and Cheryl walked by us, making a point to ignore me as they took seats at a table off to our left. It was so obvious, Rachel brought it up. "What's with them?"

I shrugged as I watched the two of them bent together, whispering, occasionally shooting glances in my direction.

"Daphne told them I'm nuts," I muttered, rolling my eyes. "It doesn't matter." And it didn't. After tonight, I would handle it. I just kept that mantra going, over and over in my head: summon the demon, trap the demon, exorcise the demon.

"What do you mean?" Rachel made a face. "Why would...okay, seriously—*what is your problem*?" Rachel snapped at the girls from across the room. All the other kids within earshot at nearby tables cast uneasy glances our way. The cafeteria quieted in an eerie, unnatural silence.

Cheryl bit her lip and looked at Kaitlyn, who had the decency to look abashed. She smoothed back her silky dark hair and called across the room, "We just heard a few things...about Aubrey."

"We heard you tried to push her out the window," Cheryl blurted.

"And you attacked Damien...and put Cole in the hospital," Kaitlyn added haughtily.

"*What?*" Rachel demanded, thumping her water bottle on the table so hard it sloshed over the sides.

Cheryl looked close to tears. "Daphne said—"

Courtney rolled her eyes. "And since when does anyone care what Daphne says about anything?"

Kaitlyn frowned, ignoring Courtney and staring straight at me. "What happened to Maddie...you shouldn't twist it, Sera...it's not funny."

Cheryl's eyes shone with tears as she looked back and forth between us.

I sat there, stunned into silence, as though Kaitlyn had slapped me.

"What are you talking about?" Rachel snapped.

"Ask Seraphina what she's been telling people about what happened to Maddie." Kaitlyn jutted her chin out to me as she sat back straighter in her seat. "It's sick."

My heart pounded loudly in my ears as seemingly everyone in the lunchroom turned to stare at me. I blinked back tears. "I didn't...I..." I broke underneath the weight of their scrutiny, and I ran from the cafeteria.

Rachel caught me at my locker.

"Hey..." She gave me a weak smile.

I could only muster a grimace. My head spun with too many thoughts to focus clearly. No one was going to listen to me. Especially if I started talking about iron and salt rings. And what about tonight? If the demon really was gone, and I summoned it back—

well, that'd just be creating unnecessary danger for everyone. But if it wasn't gone, everyone was already in danger...and I couldn't convince them to protect themselves.

And then there were the spells.

The idea of attempting magic again made my lungs collapse and my heart stall in my chest. I couldn't handle messing up again. Failing—again. And this was life-or-death. Actual life-or-death.

But it was Aubrey that troubled me the most.

I couldn't even begin to think about what happened to her. And what *had* happened to her? I was so sure she'd been suffering from hallucinations like Maddie...but her arm was clean. Logan said the marks were proof. Again, I had no proof.

Rachel cleared her throat. I'd forgotten where I was, and I looked at Rachel, surprised to find her still standing there. "Courtney's mom called from the hospital. She's a doctor at Ethan Allen? She said Aubrey's probably going to be okay...just has to stay there for a bit..." Rachel offered.

"That's good." I spun the lock on my locker as my heart stuttered uncomfortably in my chest at the thought of her lying lifeless on a hospital bed all alone.

"You know..." Rachel shifted her feet awkwardly. "I was thinking we could stop by the hospital to visit Cole, skip fourth period?"

I forced a smile. "Sounds good."

I had plenty of time to kill before sunset.

LIVE WITHOUT THE V

"Cole St. Claire? I'm sorry, hun. You just missed him. He was checked out early this morning..."

Rachel stared at the nurse. "Are you sure? Can you check again, please?"

"Sure...give me just a sec...yup. Cole St. Claire, checked out by a Ms. Agatha St. Claire." The nurse smiled warmly. "I remembered him the moment you asked. He's a southpaw like me. He had the hardest time signing his papers...I had to help him. Such a sweet boy."

"Southpaw?" Rachel raised an eyebrow and glanced at me.

I shrugged.

The nurse laughed. "Left-handed, dear. Gosh, get along now, I'm starting to feel my age."

We thanked the nurse and started back through the hospital.

"Sorry, Phin. You'd think they'd have told me if they planned on bringing him home early..." Rachel sighed as we turned down a hallway. "Oh, well...maybe tomorrow we can stop by Nile for a quick visit after school? I'd go tonight, but Amber would kill me if I missed another cheer practice...as it is, she's making me skip

Courtney's party tonight..." Rachel rolled her eyes. "But at least we can call Cole at home now—"

I wasn't listening. We were approaching the entrance to the emergency room. I came to a stop and pulled Rachel into me. "Hold on."

Rachel stared. "Phin, what are you—*Seraphina*!" Rachel hissed as I slapped the button on the wall, and the ER doors opened. "We can't go in there! Wait!"

But I had already slipped in through the automatic doors. I cut through the flurry of doctors and nurses and moved past each bed, peering between closed curtains until I found her. Aubrey was still in her school uniform, lying listless on the bed, her beautiful elven hair spread out around her head like her crowning glory. Cautiously, I moved to her right side.

"Seraphina...we can't be here..." Rachel whispered from the foot of Aubrey's bed. She glanced back uneasily as numerous nurses passed by the curtains from every which way.

I tried to steady my heart as it began to pound against my ribs. Then I pulled back Aubrey's right sleeve.

Rachel gasped.

I flinched and looked over at Rachel. "Aubrey's left-handed."

His dad's truck wasn't in the driveway when I parked. Neither was his nana's. I hurried up to the door, and I knocked sharply. I leaned in toward the door. I could hear scuffling sounds and movement inside the house. Then the dead bolt scraped back, and Cole appeared in the door, leaning on crutches.

I inhaled a sharp hiss at the sight of him. I blinked, unable to process what I was seeing. His face looked gaunt and sick, as though he'd been fighting a really bad case of the flu. His big, dark eyes with their beautiful black lashes looked wild and bulging. He smiled at me but it looked more like a scowl than anything.

"Come on in." He hobbled to the side, and I hurried through the door.

Cole's family was one of the older families of Nile. Old family meant you were either filthy rich or dirt poor. There was no in between. And the St. Claires, living in a trailer with a tarp on the patched-up roof held down with old tires, were poor. Of course, unlike some poor families (like the Barrows), they weren't poor due to any fault of their own. The St. Claire men had all been hard workers, responsible and capable, but for some reason, in Nile people rarely changed their station, no matter how hard they tried. There were rumors of curses and bad luck enough to go around. But whatever it was, the St. Claires proved to be no exception. No matter how hard Cole's daddy worked hauling stone, he never could make more than enough to get by.

Inside the trailer, the furniture was worn and outdated, like you'd find in someone's grandparents' house. The television was a big box with knobs to turn the channel and control the volume. The bunny ears were wrapped in tinfoil and regularly needed adjustments to get in a halfway decent picture. The place stunk of cigarettes, and the smoke that permeated the air clung to hair and clothes. Phoenix and I barely ever visited Cole at home (his daddy didn't like us Greys), but whenever we did, Mama was sure to make us shower afterward because we often brought the smell home with us.

I helped Cole to the couch, which was a crisscrossed stitching of different colored threads that scratched mercilessly at the skin. I hated that couch, but it was the only place to sit in the living room. We sat down. Silence settled around us, uncomfortable and itchy like the threaded couch on our skin.

Cole was the first to break it. His voice was low and scratchy, as if he hadn't spoken much in the past couple of days. "It was a demon, wasn't it?"

I bit my lip, nervous I might say the wrong thing. "You don't look like you've been sleeping...did you want one of my tonics?"

Cole shook his head.

I pursed my lips, trying to hold in the words I was so close to letting go.

Cole eyed me warily. "I can handle it, Phin. Just talk to me...please."

I sighed. It was pointless to keep anything from him. "Cole... you have to promise me that you won't freak out, and you won't tell my sister."

Cole's abnormally large eyes studied me.

I bit down on both of my lips, as though that might keep the words held back. But I took in the sorry state of him and sighed heavily. "It was a demon...but I checked it out, and it's not possessing Damien anymore."

Cole's face blanched a bit more as he swallowed slowly and nodded. "Okay...so what now?"

"He's going to be...fine," I finished quickly, curling my fingers into my palms to keep myself from reaching out to touch him. I tried not to think about Damien, and his new sadistic fantasies. "He's back to—to normal...his eye has a pirate patch from where I stabbed him. He looks like an idiot...but he'll live."

Cole ignored all that and asked in that croaky, rusty voice, "So, it's gone? The demon?"

"No...I think it's still out there somewhere." I eyed him anxiously as he processed this information. "And it's targeting Nile girls..."

Cole's jaw tightened. "It killed Maddie?"

I nodded. "But I've got a plan."

Cole winced and glanced nervously back at the front door.

"I'm going to summon it, trap it, and exorcise it, before it can hurt anyone else." I forced a smile. "I just have to round up a few ingredients and pick a place that's holy—and deserted."

Cole's brow furrowed as he cocked a dubious eyebrow. "Because summoning it worked out so well the last time?"

"Cole..."

He raked a hand through his hair. "Listen, Phin…I think you need to talk to Phoenix about this…"

My heart dipped a bit at his doubt. "No, Cole. I don't need her. All I need is a good, secluded plot of holy ground."

"There's Bird Island…" Cole hesitated at the look on my face. "I know you hate it—but it has a church…even if it *is* falling apart. It's still consecrated ground. We could grab my old man's boat?"

I scrunched up my face into a thoughtful pout as I considered this. "Better than Nile Cemetery, I guess…too many people might see me and stop to see what I'm doing." I made a face.

"What *we're* doing," Cole corrected with a wince.

"Cole—"

"You won't let Phoenix help you. You'll have to let me." He shook his head. "Because I can't let you do this alone…"

I pursed my lips on a smile. "Fine…just don't expect me to carry you."

Cole's face remained impassive. "Are you sure we shouldn't wait until—"

"We can't wait, Cole. It's already gotten Maddie…" I gritted my teeth. I couldn't tell him about Aubrey.

Cole flinched.

I nodded grimly. "I told you. The demon found them at the sleepover. I think it's going after each girl. Aubrey's—struggling… Cheryl is…well, and Morgan…" I stumbled over the half-truths, not wanting to freak him out. I ran a hand through my hair. "This is serious, Cole. I can't just sit on this when I might be able to actually do something about it." My silver eyes pleaded with Cole to understand.

He sighed heavily. "What about Phoenix? Maybe she could…"

"No," I said firmly. "I told you. I don't need Phoenix. And honestly, it's better if she doesn't know any of this."

"But with her magic…"

I frowned as my heart dipped again. "Magic from the caster isn't needed for any of this stuff. I can do this, Cole."

I scooped up my backpack. I bent down and gave Cole a tight hug. "I'll be back here to pick you up as soon as I gather everything." I pulled away from him and headed toward the door. "That way we can get to Bird Island, summon it, and exorcise it, all before morning. It'll be over once and for all."

Cole stared at me from his spot on the couch, his face almost anxious. "You really think we can do this without Phoenix?"

"I'm summoning the demon, Cole. Tonight."

And as I shut the front door, I whispered, "And I'm not going to screw it up."

We made it to the island just before midnight. The entire time, as the boat sailed across the lake, I kept my eyes fused to the long, thin, black shadow of Bird Island, steeling myself for how it would feel to land. It was...wrong. The atmosphere that hung around it, vibrated off the rocks, hummed in the air around the island...it made my skin crawl and my stomach sick. There was something— wicked about the island. It reminded me of the way it'd felt in Alice Grey's shed...but worse. So much worse. But I couldn't think about that. I had a job to do.

It took a bit of time to help Cole hobble his way across the rocky beach and across the dry, dead grass to the weather-beaten church. He was so focused on making it to the church, I don't think he had time to notice how unnatural the island felt...but then, maybe he couldn't feel it. Maybe only witches could feel it.

I pulled open one of the doors, and it opened with a low groan. Inside, as on the outside, the church was decrepit and decayed. The moonlight dropped down from the gaps in the ceiling beams, glowing in thick pools on the dusty floor. The windows were shuttered, boarded up against the elements in a last-ditch effort to protect the place before it was abandoned and left to die. The pews were still intact, and the altar and other random bits of furniture looked virtually untouched, as though any trespassers on the island avoided the church entirely. There was no graffiti or vandalism, just a thick layer of dust. And dust was everywhere. It coated the floorboards like a blanket of snow and floated through the air, visible in the moonlight like grimy bits of dirty clouds. The smell inside was strange and unpleasant. I couldn't help but scrunch up my nose as the stench crept up my nostrils.

I didn't speak. I was too uneasy to speak, as though the ghost of the hangman might hear me. They hanged Greys on Bird Island. They burned us here, too. I passed the flashlight to Cole, who held it underneath his armpit as he carefully lowered himself into the front pew. I slipped the hair tie off my wrist and pulled my hair up into a quick ponytail. I approached the altar, eyeing a lone back door off to the left as though someone might jump out and grab us. I swallowed thickly and blinked furiously, trying to maintain my focus on the task at hand. I placed my backpack gently onto the ground at my feet and felt my way around the bag. My fingers closed around the jar. My stomach heaved slightly.

Don't think about it.

Don't think about it.

I lifted it out, the jar heavy in my hands, and got to work.

"Wait—Phin, is...Seraphina, is that *blood*?"

I winced at his question and gagged as I dipped my fingers into the thick, cold red. Not trusting myself to open my mouth, I nodded with gritted teeth as I started to paint the circle onto the dirty, dusty floor.

Don't think about it.

"Phin—where did you get a jar full of blood?" Cole demanded, his voice cracking.

Don't think about it.

I gagged again, struggling not to vomit. Cold sweat dampened my neck. I needed to do this right. I needed this to work. I needed to focus and paint the sigils. I narrowed my eyes as I continued to dip my grimy fingers and coat the floor in just the right pattern.

When I finally finished, I sat on my heels to survey my work and wiped my forehead with the back of my hand, brushing away wispy strands of stray hair. I tried to clean my hands on my jeans, but the blood had dried on my fingers into a crusty dust.

"Are you sure we shouldn't get Phoenix involved?" Cole asked bluntly, eyeing the circle uneasily, casting the thin beam of flashlight across the floor. "I know you said you were protecting her, but honestly, Seraphina, don't you think we might have a better chance of this working if she helps?"

I frowned and looked back at Cole, squinting through the yellow light. "I told you, Logan DeVarney works this kind of stuff all the time, Cole. He said stuff like this channels the demon's power. It doesn't require anyone else's...it's a nihil spell," I added, as though that explained everything.

Cole lowered the flashlight and gave me a dubious look in the darkness. "But don't you think her magic...having her power boosting this would help? Your spells don't tend to...well..."

I couldn't believe he was going there. Now. I stared at him incredulously. "It *will* work, Cole. It's all right here." I gave the papers a little frustrated shake. "The spell will summon the demon, along with whoever it's possessing, and the circle will trap him inside. Then this," I shuffled the pages and shook the second sheet, "will exorcise the demon from whoever it's possessing and send it straight back to Hell. I'm sure of it. I know this will work, Cole. We just need to get it to say its name first. Simple." I reorganized the papers and muttered, "I don't need Phoenix."

"If you say so..."

Ignoring him, I cleared my throat. "Okay, now I light the candles..." I bent down with my lighter and began to light the candles. The candles weren't necessary...but I wanted to give myself the best possible conditions to do the spell right. I had to get it right.

"And then drop an object touched by the demon into the middle..." I yanked the key out of my pocket. I held it out over the middle of the circle—

"Phin, the candles—"

I glanced down. Several candles had gone out. I cursed silently and fumbled for my lighter, somehow dropping the key in the process. My face burned with embarrassment as I bent down to relight the candle. It took a few tries. Then I fumbled in the dust for the key and snatched it from the ground and straightened, mumbling a mortified apology without meeting Cole's eye. I took a deep breath and held out the key over the circle. Then, almost reluctantly, I dropped it into position in the center of the circle. "Okay, object touched by the demon. Now—I read the summoning spell..."

I stood back and cleared my throat again. I had to swallow a few times before I could manage to utter a word. It was my first time performing a spell since the Forging Ceremony. I tried to force the memory from my mind. To focus. My eyes stared wide into the middle of the circle. I took a deep breath and said in a voice clear and strong, *"Ex oculus eius te cognovi. Novi te interfectorem amici mei. Novi te de foetore inferi. Horrendum malum...Hic appello."*

I shuffled the papers so that the exorcism spell was in front of me. I was ready for it. My nostrils flared, awaiting the stench of it to fill the crypt. My stomach twisted anxiously, my skin tingling with nerves. I continued to stare at the center of the circle, my eyes wide and unblinking.

Nothing happened.

There was an eerie quiet and stillness that settled around the two of us as the truth became obvious.

Cole glanced at me. "Phin..."

My heart began to quicken. I shook my head as my eyes flew over the pages again; my fingers rifled through them, making sure I didn't miss anything.

"Phin..."

"I did everything right," I whispered, breathlessly. My grip crushed the edges of the paper into my palms. *"I did everything right*," I repeated, overcome with the familiar feeling of impotent failure.

Cole shifted on his crutch. "We need Phoenix, Phin."

I shot him a pained look of disbelief. I opened my mouth, but nothing came out.

Cole leaned into his crutch again and dug his phone out of his pocket. "Here, let's call her and—"

"She's at home with Fawn," I lied, knowing full well Fawn was now with Grammy. "Mama's gone."

Cole's expression flickered. "Right, you said that. Well, you could stay with Fawn, and Phoenix and I could—"

I began to busy myself with putting out the candles. "Yeah, maybe." Irritation sharpened my words like razor blades. "Listen, Cole, I'll drive you back home...and I should probably..."

Cole shook his head. "Phin, we have to deal with this demon. You said so yourself. People are going to get hurt!"

I couldn't help but glance at his leg, and shame flooded me, leaving me breathless. "You're right."

Cole gave me a sad smile and nodded sympathetically. He knew how much this failure stung.

I bit my lip. "I'll talk to Phoenix and let you know in the morning..."

Cole opened his mouth as though he might argue, but closed it again and nodded. "I know it's hard, Phin. But having Phoenix help us through this will be the best thing. Pick me up tomorrow. We can come back here, and we can finish this together."

I was silent the whole ride back to the island. I didn't want to talk. I didn't want to think. I definitely didn't want to ask Phoenix to bail me out of this mess. But why hadn't it worked? It was all I could think about. *Why hadn't it worked?*

I wasn't going home.

Home was the last place I wanted to be. But I didn't tell that to

Cole. After I dropped him off with a promise to call him tomorrow, I found myself driving down several back roads toward East Shore South and down the hill and past the By the Lake Motel. I slowed down as I drove by the motel. Despite the hour, the light in Logan's motel room was still on. And without pausing to think, I turned sharply into the driveway, just before I missed the turn, and whipped the van around and parked next to Logan's old pickup truck.

I turned off the van, pulled down the visor to check my reflection, running a quick hand through my hair, and then hopped out. I hurried through the dark toward his room. I glanced behind me, squinting through the darkness. The single streetlight cast a weak, waxy yellow light over the road beyond. I looked back at the door, took a deep breath, and knocked.

There was no answer.

My face burned in the cold October air. I knocked harder, my eyes on the curtain, watching for movement in the window. Still no answer.

"Logan?" My heart started to race. Something wasn't right.

I tried the door. It wasn't locked. I pushed it open, but the door bumped against something solid. I shoved it, but the door slammed against the lock chain.

And all I could see through the crack in the door was Logan's pale, bloody face looking up at me from the floor.

JUST THE GIRL

is eyes wide, his mouth gasped for air he couldn't seem to breathe. He seized on the floor, convulsing violently. I shoved against the door, slammed my body against it with all my strength, but it wouldn't budge.

I ran to the van and snatched the baseball bat out of the back. I charged at the window, winding up for a swing, and smashed the glass. I slid the bat along the frame, knocking out the bigger shards, then tossed it inside. I chucked my backpack through the window after it, and then hoisted myself through the frame, glass tearing into my palms. I climbed over and fell hard to the floor. I scrambled to Logan, dragging my bag with me, and pulled his head up into my lap.

"Logan! Logan, what is it?" I shrieked. My mind raced in a hysterical panic as I fumbled in my bag for a potion that could help.

Logan's eyes focused on mine. Blood continued to bubble up from his mouth as he struggled.

I looked around the room, praying for some clue as to what to do. The room was completely torn apart, as if he'd been looking for something. Logan's body continued to twitch in my lap. His throat gurgled like he was drowning in his own blood. I looked down at him, tears leaking from my eyes. "I don't know what to do! *Tell me what to do!*"

Logan's mouth started to move, like he was trying to speak. Then I had an idea. I fumbled through the potions for veritas. I dropped three drops into his mouth.

"What is wrong with you?"

"Curse."

My heart slammed against my chest. Not good.

"Where haven't you looked?"

"Truck."

"Where are the keys?"

"Pocket."

I slid his head off my lap as I patted down his pockets, tears flowing in frustration as he coughed up more blood. A lot more blood.

I slapped at his leather jacket. He had too many pockets! I smacked at his jeans. There. I dug my hand deep into his pants pocket and wrenched the keys out of his jeans. I snatched my lighter and white rose oil from my bag and scrambled to my feet, leaving Logan lying alone on the motel floor. I shoved the door shut, ripped off the chain lock, wrenched it back open, and ran out the door into the night.

I fumbled with the keys, but I stopped before I hopped in. Logan had his keys. The doors were locked. Maybe it wasn't hidden inside the cab. Gasping for breath that I couldn't catch, I ran around the truck. I pulled down the tailgate and jumped in the truck bed. I slapped around in the dark. There was nothing in the back except a toolbox...with a lock. I scrambled out, off the truck bed, and went for the gas tank. I yanked it open, flinching as it creaked loudly, echoing in the night. I shoved my hand inside. There. My fingers closed around something soft.

I tugged it out of the tank and turned it over in my hands. I fumbled and winced, recoiling at the feel of it. The hum of the curse inside. I unstoppered the bottle of white rose oil and drenched the entire contents onto the bundle. Bag soaked, I held it out in front of me and flicked the lighter underneath it. The flame licked the bottom of the damp, purple flannel and sparked. It caught fire, and I dropped it on the ground as white smoke billowed from inside the bundle, streaming up into the night sky. Then it burst into a ball of fire, engulfed in flames at my feet. And as quickly as it had come, the fire vanished as though snuffed by a big breath. And the small purple bundle was gone.

I tore back to the motel room. As soon as I made it back, Logan was already struggling to sit up in the doorway. Forgetting any sense of boundary or restraint, I dropped down beside him. My hands moved over his bloody face, pushed back his hair, and ran over his neck and chest, searching for a steady pulse. I was crying, hyperventilating, overcome by the pressure and the state of him.

"It's okay..." Logan winced, coughing and clearing his throat, as he took hold of my hands in his and held them in between us. "It's okay. Hey, hey, look at me—"

He forced me to meet his eyes. I blinked furiously and nodded as I gasped for breath, tears continuing to streak down my face.

"You did good, Sam." He gave my hands a squeeze and a small shake. "You did good. And you were right."

"What?" I stammered, still dazed from the adrenaline.

He started to stand, and I quickly moved to help him up.

"You were right." He shut the door, twisted the lock, and slid the lock chain in place. Then he walked to the bathroom, leaving me standing in the room staring stupidly after him.

"You were right about this not being over," Logan called from the bathroom as he turned on the water.

I stared around the gutted room and ran a hand through my hair. I shivered in the cold as a breeze blew in through the broken window. I moved to pull the curtain back, blocking out the night. I blinked about the room and started to straighten up the mess. By the time Logan had cleaned himself up and left the bathroom, I'd started to make the beds. He went around the other side to help me. I tossed him a corner.

"Clearly," Logan smirked, "someone doesn't want me around to help you, which means you're onto something."

I glanced at him as I fitted the sheet. "If that's an apology, you stink at it."

Logan rolled his eyes. A smile twitched in the corner of his mouth.

Before he could shoot back, I asked, "When did your symptoms start?"

"When you left. The second time." Logan scoffed. "I'm sure glad I'm so good-looking…"

"What?" I snapped as I threw the sheet across the bed.

"That's why you came back tonight, right?" He flashed a cocky grin and gave me a roguish wink that made my heart stumble.

I shook my head incredulously as my face burned hot. "What? No! That's not—"

Logan snickered as he threw over the comforter. "Okay, what's your excuse for coming back a third time?"

I gritted my teeth as I tucked in the blanket. "Now, I wish I hadn't."

Logan burst out laughing, and I struggled not to smile at the sound. I snatched a ripped pillow from the ground and then reached for another.

"Where'd you find it?"

"Gas tank," I mumbled. As I tossed him a pillow to restuff, feathers floated all around us. I rubbed my forehead as I remembered. "It was your shirt."

Logan inclined his head as he shoved feathers back into the pillow.

I swallowed as my heart started to sink and my thoughts started to clear. The purple flannel...it was cut from his shirt...the same shirt I had taken from his dorm. The shirt I'd stuffed into Daphne's bag. My heart dropped into my stomach, which twisted painfully. I looked at him. "It's Daphne. The demon's in Daphne Collins."

Logan cocked an eyebrow as he shoved the torn pillow back into the case and tossed it onto the bed. "Hold on. Are you sure? You jumped to conclusions with that last guy...what makes you think it's her?"

My eyes itched. I massaged my temples as my head began to pound, and I started to pace the room. "I don't get it myself, but that cloth came from the shirt I took from your dorm." I sniffed and wiped my cheeks with my sleeve. "Daphne had the shirt...and I threatened her with a fake curse bag a few weeks ago."

Logan frowned. "A shirt is a little weak..."

"True. But out of everyone, she's the only one who had that shirt," I said softly. I shook my head and stared up at the news clippings and notes up on the wall as I tried to piece it together.

"Oh, and there's this..." I closed the distance between us and pulled Alice Grey's spell out of my pocket. "Check this out." We leaned in together, bent over the paper. I could feel the warmth of him and the smell of leather and sandalwood. I quickly sidestepped just far enough that I could still see the paper. He didn't notice.

Logan studied it for a moment. "This isn't any random summoning spell...this is—it isn't like anything I've seen before... look at the wording. It's written to summon a specific demon."

My eyes moved over the paper as I nodded. He was very astute. I was impressed, despite myself.

Logan glanced at me over the paper and smiled as he folded it and handed it back. Amusement glittered in the gold of his eyes. "Good catch, Sam."

"The demon is the same one from twenty years ago—but that still doesn't explain Maddie, does it?"

Logan shoved his hands in his pockets as he thought this over. "It does if this Daphne person was possessed from the start. Was she at the sleepover?"

I looked up at him as he shrugged. "You thought Maddie made her deal during truth or dare, right?"

"And all the other girls...my best friend Aubrey has all those pen scratches on her arm...she's in the hospital—"

Logan nodded grimly. "Well, the nonsense you told me about a Ouija board doesn't track...but if the demon was *there* and actually making the deal, a spell wouldn't have been needed, at all. Just a verbal contract."

I rolled my eyes and nibbled on my lower lip. "How did she get possessed in the first place? And not just possessed—possessed by a demon that was stalking Nile twenty years ago?"

Logan opened his mouth and shut it again.

"What?" I eyed him suspiciously. "You're not telling me something."

Logan rolled his eyes and shoved his hands back into his pockets.

"That's the second time you've avoided a question."

"Oh, yeah?" Logan grinned. "What's the first?"

I pursed my lips into a thoughtful pout. "Why you called my house..." I said softly as I touched my forehead. My head hurt as I tried to think. He was avoiding a question about the past. And my house. How were they connected? My heart skipped and I inclined my head as I studied him with narrowed eyes. "Do you know my mother?" I demanded, my voice high.

Logan met my eyes with a hard stare.

I didn't flinch. Silver clashed with emerald.

Logan inhaled deeply as he rubbed the back of his neck. His nostrils flared as his dimples creased his frown. "Pain in my ass, Sam."

I held my chin out.

Logan leaned against the wall, his arms folded across his

broad chest as he faced me. "All I can say is what I told you before: demons are sentimental. If the demon was here decades ago and then exorcised...if it managed to crawl back out of Hell, it stands to reason, it'd come back here. And it stands to reason, if Butterfly Boy summoned it out of Daphne Collins—it'd want to go back to her. So, that would explain your random ghosting...and didn't Idiot Scissorhands say the demon was after revenge?"

I crossed the room to stand in front of him. I put my hands on my hips and stared up at him. "That answer's not good enough."

Logan shrugged, a hint of a smile in the corner of his mouth that set off his dimple. "It's gonna have to be."

I groaned and rolled my eyes. I turned away from him as I began to pace again, hands flying in exasperation as I spoke. "So, a demon with a Nile obsession possessed Daphne, murdered her stepsister's parents, and then started targeting her friends. Is that what we are going with?"

Logan shrugged as he watched me stalk around the room. "What matters is that you think the demon is possessing Daphne now. The past or whatever happened before isn't a factor. Do you think the demon is in Daphne?"

"Yes." I stopped mid-step and scoffed at my stupidity. "I was with her so many times, and I wasn't even smart enough to see it."

Logan shifted awkwardly where he stood. "Well...now you know. What are you going to do about it?"

My mind turned over and over. There was something I was missing...something that didn't fit...didn't seem right.

Daphne was the obvious choice. Nasty. Cruel. But something scratched at the back of my brain...something I hadn't put together yet.

I tried to imagine where Daphne was now. What was the demon's plan? Pick the Nile girls off one by one? *Or all at once...*

My heart stopped. "We have to go now." I choked out each word.

As I hurried to scoop up all the scattered potions into my backpack, Logan came up behind me.

"What? Why?"

"Every single girl who sold her soul is at Courtney's lake house right now. And Daphne said she'd crash the party."

Logan grabbed his rucksack off the table. "We'll take my truck."

"No. We might need the extra room."

"Keys?"

I scoffed. "Nope. I'm driving this time."

Logan cursed under his breath but didn't argue.

"So, Daphne is the demon. The demon wants souls..." I shook my head as I squeezed the steering wheel. "I don't understand...I thought you needed to make the deal at a crossroads?"

Logan had his elbow propped up on the windowpane. "You can. And the signs say Maddison did...but if the demon was already possessing a body, it can make whatever kind of deals it wants. Wherever it wants. As many times as it wants."

I shivered despite the heat blowing steadily out of the van's heater.

Logan shook his head. "There's still something strange about this whole thing..."

"What do you mean?"

"Well, if the demon was making the deals at the sleepover—"

"Why did Maddie make her way down to the crossroads for hers?"

Logan nodded. "Yup. The whole thing feels...off. Like we're missing something. And there weren't any of the usual demonic omens until after your first day at school. Like your presence triggered something—but even afterward, the signs weren't what I'd expect to see from an actual demonic possession. Something still doesn't fit..."

Silence fell as I turned down another back road toward the heart of Nile. The weight of what we were about to do crushed me from all sides, squeezed the air out of my lungs and made me breathe in little panicked puffs.

Logan noticed. He pushed the CD button and barely flinched as Nirvana whined about heart-shaped boxes.

"What is this even about?" Logan muttered.

"Don't ask." I managed a smile, touched at the thoughtful gesture.

Logan scoffed.

I glanced at him. "Okay, then. Who do you like to listen to while heading into battle?"

Logan grinned and flipped open a pocket of his rucksack. "Well...since you asked..." He pulled out a CD case and stuck it in the player.

"Is this—" I looked at him sideways. "Frank Sinatra?"

Logan shrugged, a little pink coloring his cheeks. "I have Led Zeppelin or Lynyrd Skynyrd if you'd prefer...Nick Cave and the Bad Seeds?"

I shook my head with a slight smile. "This is good." I felt Logan's eyes on me as I drove. I took a deep breath. "The Cabbage Night party started hours ago...who's to say anyone will be left alive?"

Logan nodded grimly. That was the reality of it. But there was also the possibility that I'd screw it all up...just like with Cole...and before that with Damien.

"And if we *do* find them alive...how are we going to deal with the demon? This feels like Damien all over again. That didn't work at all," I muttered dully.

"Only because Damien wasn't possessed," Logan pointed out.

I thought of my failed attempt with Cole. All the good I had done. My heart ached.

"You're not telling me something..." Logan cocked an eyebrow. "What's up?"

I took a deep breath and told him everything about my Bird Island attempt. "It's like—even spells in which no magic is required...I still manage to mess everything up."

Logan studied me, his face scrunched up pensively. "Let me see the spell."

Gripping the wheel in one hand, I fished out the slips of paper and passed them over.

Logan studied the papers. He glanced at me. "This is good—like *really* good...I mean—I don't know anything about this Alice Grey knockoff, but the exorcism?" He gave me a lopsided grin. "This would definitely work. I mean, I'd still prefer my own...I'm old school like that...but seriously, I'm impressed. How did you come up with it?"

I nodded slowly as I chewed on my lower lip. "See? The spells are good. I know they are... It's just me." I tugged the papers out of his hands and tucked them into my jacket pocket.

Logan sighed. "Listen, the Alice Grey knockoff—it's probably a good thing it didn't work because the original is a flat-out possession invitation...by the way—" He glanced at me sideways with a mischievous glint in his eye and a smirk piercing his dimple.

I rolled my eyes and tugged Daddy's pendant out from under my shirt. "Not possessed."

Logan grinned.

I didn't.

"Come on, Sam. You shouldn't be so hard on yourself. I mean, sure, I've never heard of a witch without magic. But, honestly, like I said: it's a good thing it didn't work. I mean, how the heck were you going to trap it? A salt ring doesn't hold up very well against—"

I frowned, my hands squeezing the wheel. "I memorized the sigils of the sealing circle."

Logan chuckled. "They don't work if you write them in chalk."

My jaw tightened, and I turned down another back road. "I didn't."

Before he could comment, I asked pointedly, "Should we talk game plan?"

Logan cleared his throat. "Once we find the demon, we trap it—with the blood in my ruck—" he said sharply, giving me a sidelong glance. "Then we have to get it to say its name. To do that, you chant 'dic nomen tuum,' over and over, until finally it spits it out. Then once we have the name, you can do the honors with your exorcism spell, or—"

"I'm not doing any spells," I muttered coolly.

Logan cleared his throat. "That casts it out and kicks it right back to Hell." Logan glanced at me as I took another side road deeper into Nile. He cleared his throat again. "And you can do it just as easily as anyone else. You just have to remember: it's like a prayer. Not a spell. And God listens to everyone...not just witches."

"I'm not a witch," I snapped.

"Of course you're a witch." Logan gave me a funny stare.

"I don't want to talk about it." I waved a hand through the air. "We have more important things to worry about."

"You're like a redhead..." Logan shrugged with a smirk. "It's rare, kinda hot, skips some generations, but it happens."

"Logan!"

"All right, all right..." Logan held his hands up in surrender. He looked out the window at the rundown houses and distant farms. "I thought you said lake house?"

"We need to stop somewhere first."

By the time we bumped our way down Grey Lane and parked in front of the cottage, my heart was back to panicked pumps. I gripped the steering wheel and took a few deep breaths.

"I'll be right back."

I walked up the steps of the cottage and paused at the door. For some reason, I couldn't bring myself to walk inside. I'd done everything I could to leave this place behind...and now, here I was —crawling back with my tail between my legs.

I banged loudly on the door.

It took her awhile, but after a few minutes, Phoenix threw open the door. Her hair was twisted up in a messy bun with the orange tips going every which way, her wand sticking out of the top. She was in her pajamas—black flannel pants and an oversized, white AC/DC T-shirt. Her amber eyes widened in surprise and then narrowed. She crossed her arms over her chest and leaned against the doorframe. "What do you want?"

I took a final shaky breath. "I want to say I'm sorry."

Phoenix's face was impassive. Stony and cold.

I gritted my teeth and tried again. "I'm sorry, Phoenix. I'm sorry, and I need your help."

Phoenix considered this a moment, then she straightened off the doorframe and snapped her fingers. Her Converse appeared on her feet in a burst of orange glitter. Her black jacket with too many pockets fluttered off a nearby hook, and she slipped it on. Her backpack shining with band pins, cracking with keychains, and accented with patches flew from somewhere inside and hooked on her outstretched hand. She tossed it over her shoulder. "Let's go."

I hurried after her as she headed straight for the van. "Wait, Phoenix, there's something—"

Phoenix had already opened the back door and tossed in her backpack. When she saw Logan in the passenger seat, she whipped out her wand from her hair. The wand sizzled like an orange sparkler.

But before she could cast, I grabbed her around the waist and swung her around, her legs kicking in protest. "Phoenix! What—"

"*Geoffmephin!*" she grunted as she thrashed. Her elbow got me in the gut. I shoved her away from me and the van. Phoenix stumbled a bit, her Converse skidding in the gravel drive.

"*What's the matter with you?*" I snapped breathlessly.

Phoenix scoffed in disgust. She stabbed her wand through her hair, marched over to the van, slammed the door so loud it echoed like a gunshot in the dark, and she whirled around to stare openmouthed at me. Phoenix jutted her thumb back at Logan, her eyes narrowed and face furious. "What are you doing with the hunter?"

I stopped short in the driveway and looked from the grumpylooking Logan to the hexed-off Phoenix and demanded, "You *know* him?"

Phoenix sputtered something about not wanting to be in the same car as him as I groaned, wrenched open the door, and shoved her inside. My boots crunched on the gravel as I stomped around to the driver seat. Logan was silent and brooding. Phoenix was still sputtering like an overfilled teapot. I shoved the van in gear and tore out of the driveway. I managed to slam into every pothole on the road before ripping the wheel left onto the back road toward West Shore.

"Why is he here?" Phoenix repeated nastily.

I glanced at Phoenix in the rearview mirror and asked wryly, "Do either of you want to tell me how in the hex you know each other?"

Logan snorted and stared pointedly out the window.

Phoenix rolled her eyes. "This bigot and his idiot brother—"

"Oi!" Logan twisted back to glare at her.

"Showed up looking for Mama. I told them she was Unreachable. Then his brother ran after Mama, as though he knew all about her High Council work. He said he had to warn her about some wickeds in Louisiana. Like it was some kind of secret spy mission," Phoenix mocked, complete with air quotes. She crossed her arms and kicked her feet up against Logan's seat.

"OI!"

"Is that why you called the house?" I asked sharply.

"My brother, Traven, called. It's Traven's burner phone…" Logan's voice was raised as Phoenix struggled to talk over him.

"If you ask me…his brother's got a crush on Mama, and he's got her on a wild-goose chase," Phoenix snapped scathingly. "I'm surprised Junior, here, can stand sitting next to you, Phinny. He thinks we're all hags. Don't you, DeVarney?"

I glanced at Logan sideways, fighting back a smirk at the sight of clear annoyance on Logan's face.

"Are you sure we need her?" Logan said loudly. "I feel like we'll do fine on our own…"

Phoenix kicked the seat again, sending Logan grunting in protest.

"Phoenix!" I snapped. "This is serious. I need both of you to start acting like it."

Phoenix waved her hands wide. "Care to fill me in?"

So, as I turned down West Shore Road, I told her every embarrassing, shameful detail, but Phoenix didn't seem too surprised—and I realized somehow, she'd had the monster talk already.

But before I could call her out on it, Logan dug into his bag and passed a glass vial to me. "Holy water."

Phoenix leaned up toward the front seat expectantly, but Logan just shrugged.

Nix scoffed. "That's okay…I don't need any protection, thanks." Phoenix rolled her eyes.

"I didn't realize we'd have company," Logan muttered, digging through his bag again.

"You operate like your big brother, huh? Get the girl alone and—"

"Phoenix!" I gasped, face burning.

"Here." Logan tossed a second vial back to Phoenix, who caught it just before it knocked into her nose. "Keep those tucked out of sight."

My stomach twisted anxiously as we turned down the driveway. My voice was low as I whispered, "How are we going to do this?"

"We're going to just make it up as we go...okay?" Logan gave me a reassuring smile that I could barely return.

The lake house came into view. The lawn and deck and stone path leading to the beach were all drenched in black night. The trees surrounding the property blocked out the stars. The only light, a blue flickering glow, came from one of the windows at the very top. The television maybe.

"What if you're wrong, Phin, and they are all just...sleeping?" Phoenix whispered from the back seat.

I parked the van beside Courtney's car and switched the engine off. "Honestly, I could be wrong..."

Logan studied me. "You don't think you are, do you?"

I met his gaze. "No."

Phoenix shrugged. "Good enough for me."

"Here's the plan." I turned in my seat to face both of them in turn. "The demon doesn't know that I know who it is...I think it's our best bet to have me go in first and distract it. You and Phoenix can sneak inside and set the trap."

"So, you're just going to knock on the demon's front door and play pretend?" Phoenix scoffed.

Logan was quiet as he looked at me, his face grim.

"It's the best plan we've got. The best card we could possibly play." I shrugged easily. "I'm just a girl trying to crash a sleepover."

I bit my lip as I looked from Logan to Phoenix.

Logan's jaw tightened. "I don't like it...it puts you at too much risk..."

Phoenix sniffed approvingly.

I closed my eyes briefly as I pleaded my case. "I've been around Daphne so many times. As long as the demon thinks I don't know, I'm safe. And it's the only way we can get inside without drawing its attention. You know I'm right, Logan."

Logan gritted his teeth. I could see his jaw clenching as the lines of his face hardened. "Fine." He fixed his narrow eyes on mine and pointed a finger at me. "But if you get in over your head—"

Phoenix sputtered more protests, but I interrupted. "I can do this, Phoenix...and if I can't, you'll be right there to help me."

Phoenix's scowl eased into a smile. She held out her hand.

I grasped it and squeezed.

28

I WRITE SINS NOT TRAGEDIES

We all left the van, closing the doors as quietly as we could manage. The plan was simple: Logan and Phoenix would wait in the shadows around the side of the house while I went inside. Then after a few minutes, Phoenix would open the door, with magic if necessary, and they would draw the sealing circle in the living room.

The sliver of moon reflected in the black water as the waves hissed against the rocks in the distance. The wind was picking up, blowing cold lake air between the trees. I pulled my jacket tight, blocking out the chill. My boots crinkled through the dusting of dead leaves littering the ground. The trees were thin and skeletal as they stretched up to the sky like hands scratching at the stars. My eyes, watery in the wind, were on the door as I mounted the steps. I paused, steadying my breathing. My fingers gripped the strap of my bag slung over my shoulder.

I could do this.

I knocked on the door.

I waited, my ears straining for any sound. Hearing nothing, I tried the door. It was unlocked. I pushed it open and blinked into the darkness. Moving through the rooms, I took the stairs, following the blue glow of the television as it moved along the walls like water. I tried to steady my heart, but it pounded relentlessly in my ears with every step. I could feel my pulse in my palms. In my neck.

Cautiously, I peered around the corner and moved down the darkened hallway toward the back room. The door was open and the room was tinted in the blue-black glow of the television. There were two sleeping bags at the foot of the bed. The huge TV flashed silently on the wall. I peeked at each girl in turn. Cheryl. Kaitlyn. Not dead. Just asleep. I hoped.

"Seraphina?"

I flinched, my hand flying to the pocket of my jacket and resting on the flask.

Aubrey. She sat up in the bed, the TV remote laying limply in her hand.

"Aubrey?" I breathed in disbelief. "Are you okay? What are you doing here? How could they let you leave the hospital? Your head was..." I weaved my way through the bodies to get to her. I grabbed her hand in mine and squeezed. "Where's Daphne?"

Aubrey twisted the chain of her locket around her fingers. "She's not here."

"Courtney and Morgan?" I stammered, still trying to understand what she was doing here.

"They're down the hall. Everyone's fast asleep. Three drops, you said. Right?"

I blinked. "Three drops—oh, yeah..."

Something wasn't right. There's no way they would've let her out of the hospital...there's no way she should even be conscious...

I dropped her hand. I took a step back.

Aubrey slid off the bed.

My eyes went to the TV.

"Just some home movies...my friends made."

It was like an old home video...but silent. Of everyone on a boat, laughing and smiling. The sound was off. They had just docked at Bird Island. Damien carried a grinning Aubrey out of the boat like a princess. He pretended to toss her in the water, and she laughed. The way they looked at each other, it was clear they were happy—in love. Daphne pulled her sunglasses down, and Brentley helped her onto the dock. She was watching Damien. Kaitlyn and Cheryl ran off the dock onto the beach, lugging the cooler onto the shore.

"I wanted to watch it..." Aubrey murmured from beside my ear. "It's important to start at the beginning before you get to the end."

I flinched and stepped to the side. My pulse pounded in the hollow of my throat. This was wrong. "Aubrey...where's Daphne?"

Aubrey nodded toward the TV.

The scene had changed. Daphne had her arms wrapped around Aubrey as they both hugged and smiled for the camera.

"Do you know what they did to me on that boat that night?" Aubrey's eyes were wide as she stared at the screen. Bathed in the blue light, she inclined her head as she watched. On the screen, Damien grabbed a squealing Aubrey by the waist and carried her out to the lake, tossing the pair of them into the water. They played and splashed in the waves as the camera panned to Daphne, whose smile had slipped as she sat alone on the rocky shore.

"Aubrey—I don't know what's going on...but I need to find Daphne, right now."

"She had everything. But it wasn't enough." Aubrey nodded toward the screen.

The scene changed. It was dark. Night. And the only light came from their cell phone flashlights as they boarded the motorboat. Damien was no longer the laughing boy from the beach. He looked as I knew him, cold and calculating. Brentley kept flipping his shaggy hair back, looking anxious but eager. The camera was unsteady as it panned to Aubrey and Daphne seated together, holding hands.

They bumped along, over the waves for a while, then the boat slowed to a quick stop. The boys must have said something off-screen. Aubrey's eyes widened with fear as she glanced around the darkness surrounding the boat. She shook her head furiously, her hands gripping the sides of her seat. She looked to Daphne, her eyes begging for help.

Daphne laughed. Aubrey snatched her phone and held it up to her ear. She screamed into the phone as tears streamed down her face.

Then Damien moved into the frame. He grabbed Aubrey around her waist just like he'd done at the beach. But this time, there was no joyful love brightening her face. Instead, Aubrey's face was white in the harsh spotlight of the boat, terror shining in her eyes as she screamed and kicked and fought against Damien.

But he was too strong.

He tossed her overboard into the darkness. Daphne continued to laugh as all of them, including the camera, peeked over the side of the boat.

Aubrey's face was white in the water, wet with tears as much as the lake. She was begging, pleading with them, as she treaded the waves and eyed the black water swirling around her with a face taut with fear.

Then the boat started to move. Aubrey's face contorted in a scream I couldn't hear as she disappeared in the darkness as the boat drove away. The camera zoomed in on Daphne as she bit her lip on a cruel smile, her dark eyes black in the spotlight. A little bit off-screen, Damien sat down in Aubrey's seat, his jaw set and his eyes cold.

Like a narrator at the end of a movie as the film cut to black, Aubrey spoke. "They left me there." Aubrey's voice was soft and almost confused.

I looked at her, sickened by what I'd just witnessed.

Aubrey inclined her head as she stared at me, blinking as though dazed. "My boyfriend and my sister left me in the middle of the lake, in the middle of the night. Alone."

I put a hand on her shoulder, completely forgetting why I was there. What I was supposed to be doing. "Aubrey—"

"They had planned it...Nile guy rite of passage...sacrifice your girl to Champ..." She paused, her voice soft and dull. "It was my fear...and he knew it. They both did. Dark, open water..."

"Aubrey, I'm so sorry."

Aubrey blinked up at me in the black glow of the TV and gave me a watery smile. "Not as sorry as they're going to be."

Something hard pressed against my hip. I froze.

"It's a good thing you're here," Aubrey murmured patiently, digging the barrel of her pistol into my side as she tugged on her locket with her other hand. "We were hoping you'd come sooner or later."

My heart sank, heavy with disappointment. *What had she done?* "Where's the demon, Aubrey?"

Aubrey stared at me, the gun lowered but still clutched in her hand. "What makes you think I'm not the demon?"

"Demons don't need guns, do they?"

Aubrey nodded, conceding the obvious point. She shrugged. "It's Damien's. He doesn't need it anymore." Aubrey's voice faded to a whisper as she pushed the gun harder into my hip.

I winced.

"Aubrey, put down the gun, please," I breathed softly so as not to spook her. I'd never been around a gun before...the hard metal, finality and unforgiving nature of the thing frightened me to my core. "I can't think when you do that."

Aubrey stepped back out of my reach and tapped it against her forehead as though she were trying to recall a memory.

Tears prickled my eyes. As I blinked, they fell down my cheeks. "Aubrey..." I could taste my salty tears as I spoke, words hushed and stumbling. "Aubrey, listen to me..." I held out my hands, palms out, willing her to stop. "I understand you're hurting...but that gun isn't going to help anything." I shook my head as my lower lip trembled. "That gun isn't going to stop the demon. I need you to tell me where it is so I can—"

Aubrey laughed, but it was hollow and forced. She lowered the gun to her side. "You still don't get it, do you?"

I tried to take a step toward her, but she backed up, gun raised, freezing me in place. I lifted my chin and closed my eyes briefly as I tried to calm my panicked thoughts. "Why don't—Aubrey, why don't you just put down the gun and explain it to me?"

Aubrey nodded, frowning thoughtfully. "Okay." She lowered the gun. "We have a little time."

"Time? Time until what, Aubrey?"

Aubrey stared silently at me. She paused only briefly to check her watch. "The grim should be here soon...it won't be long now."

I let out a small gasp. "What do you mean?"

Aubrey smiled, almost sadly.

My mind began to race. Panic seeped into my blood, pushing my heart far too fast. I had to keep her talking. I couldn't do anything about Logan or Phoenix. I had to help Kaitlyn and Cheryl.

"Aubrey, I don't understand...help me understand."

Aubrey looked at me, her eyes brimming with tears and her lips in a quivering pout. "No one can understand."

"Help me. Help *me* understand," I repeated, encouraged by Aubrey's sudden emotion.

"No one helped me," she murmured in a bemused, dreamy whisper. "Not my mother. Not my stepdad. Not my so-called friends." Aubrey sniffed, taking her free hand and rubbing away her tears. "Maddie wasn't my fault, though. Maddie was your fault, Seraphina." Aubrey's voice thickened, watery with her grief.

"No." I shook my head. "I didn't know...I had no idea what would happen..."

"Her death is on *your* hands." Aubrey gave a rueful smile through her tears. "It doesn't feel very good, does it?"

"Tell me what happened." I blinked through blurring vision.

"Aubrey, what happened? Did it possess you? It's not your fault—"

Aubrey tried to scoff, but she only managed a sniff. "Yes, it is. It *is* my fault. I've known that since the shed..." She shook her head. "But that's okay, because it's coming for me."

"The demon?"

Aubrey rolled her eyes. Tears leaked down her face, shining in the light.

"Aubrey, tell me what's going on, and I can help you!"

She stared at me, tears running like tiny rivers down her cheeks.

"Aubrey, you're my best friend..." I cried lamely. "I want to help you."

Aubrey blinked and sniffed. She wiped her nose with her free hand.

"Whatever you've done, it wasn't your fault." I took a deep breath and slid a bit closer to her.

Aubrey didn't notice. She stared at me, unblinking, and spoke in a soft, lost voice as though she couldn't understand it herself. "They left me there. Alone, in the middle of the lake. As a *joke*. I'm terrified of open water. They all knew it." She shook her head, eyes wide and staring. "It's twelve miles across Lake Champlain. Did you know that, Seraphina? And there aren't any lights on either shore. Except that little line of lights from the prison off in the mountains. It was like I was lost in the ocean."

Her lip trembled, and her haunted eyes continued to stare at me. "I was so scared. I got tired. I couldn't keep my head up anymore. I went under... It's a miracle I didn't drown. I still don't know how I survived. He says it's because I was sent to save him." She smiled slightly, licking her lips. "When I woke up, all I could see was stars. It was beautiful. My head hurt from laying on the rocky shore. I was on Bird Island. And freezing. The lake is only sixty degrees in September. I took shelter in the old church. *But I was still so cold.* I searched the place for a lighter or matches. Anything to make a fire. That's when I found it."

Aubrey held open her palm, revealing her locket. She smiled slightly.

"The locket? You found a locket?" I prompted, moving another inch closer.

Aubrey didn't notice. She looked down as her hand closed over the locket again. "I was drawn to it. Called to it. I put it on. And that's when he first spoke to me. He told me everything. How he was trapped inside the locket by the witch Alice Grey. Cursed. Bound to the locket. He told me he needed my help to free himself of the curse. And if I helped him, he would help me..."

"Help you?" I shook my head as I inched closer. "Help you what?"

Aubrey licked her lips. She flinched and looked toward the window as though she'd been startled by a noise only she could hear. "It's almost time. It's coming for me."

I rushed at her, but she aimed the gun at me, and I backed up again. "Nice try, Seraphina. But I'm not done just yet."

"What about Cheryl?" I pointed toward the girls in sleeping bags. "And Kaitlyn? We need to help them before—"

"No." Aubrey's eyes narrowed. "They both had a hand in it."

Aubrey, gun still in hand, crossed the room and slapped the girls awake.

"Let's go, girls. It's time to make your payment."

Cheryl let out a low wail at the sight of Aubrey and the gun.

Kaitlyn stammered, "Aubrey? Aubrey, what's going on?"

I tried to stand between Aubrey and the girls, but Aubrey pointed the gun at my stomach, and I backed off. "Don't play dumb, Kaitlyn. You sold your souls, remember? Time's up."

Cheryl started to cry and pull at Kaitlyn. Kaitlyn shook her head. "It was a game. We thought it was a game."

"Aubrey..." I tried to keep my voice even and calm. "They don't have anything to do with—"

Aubrey shook her head with an ironic smile. "Ask them. They'll tell you what they did...or maybe they won't because they are too ashamed to admit it..." Silent tears streamed down Aubrey's cheeks despite her furious face.

"We didn't know, okay? We didn't know!" Cheryl shrieked, her voice high and panicked.

"*It's all your fault*!" Aubrey screamed, shaking the gun in her face.

Cheryl shook her head again, her eyes wide as though she couldn't believe what she was seeing. "We made a mistake, but we didn't do anything!"

"That's the point. You didn't do anything! You didn't do *anything* to help me!" Aubrey's screams were tortured and pained as she looked from one girl to the next. Suddenly, she grabbed Cheryl by her beautiful cherry-red hair, yanking her to her feet and pushing the gun into her temple. "Do you know what he did to me?" she screamed into her ear. "*Do you know what he did*?" Aubrey shrieked.

Cheryl shook her head, sobbing loudly and near collapse.

I held up my hands and moved toward Aubrey. "Hey! Hey! Aubrey...Aubrey, talk to me...just talk to me." The silver met the sapphire, and Aubrey's lip quivered as she shoved Cheryl back to the floor in disgust. Kaitlyn grabbed Cheryl and pulled her into her arms. "Tell me what they did!"

"I called them," Aubrey whispered to me, her eyes leaking and face pained. "I called them screaming, begging for help." Aubrey shook her head, her eyes and face shining in the blue glow of the TV. Aubrey spoke in her soft, gentle voice. "They didn't come. They didn't even try to send help." Her face contorted again and her voice began to rise, louder and louder. "And later...what did you say? You said it was my own fault. *It was my own fault*!" Aubrey was shrieking again.

"We didn't mean it like that...we didn't say it like that, Aubrey," Kaitlyn whispered.

"You left me for dead"—Aubrey, eyes wide and face tortured,

scoffed and shook the gun at Kaitlyn—"and now I'm going to do the same."

"You *wanted* us to sell our souls," Cheryl murmured. "It was you the whole time."

Aubrey smiled but it looked more like a wince, for there was no happiness behind it, only hurt. She nodded. "He needed souls. And now I get the honor of harvesting them." She counted the girls, pointing the gun at each in turn. "One of Damien's hollow points for each of you..."

Cheryl cried harder. Kaitlyn recoiled. My eyes burned. "Oh, Aubrey..."

Aubrey flinched away from me. "By the time his plan is finished, and we free him from Alice Grey's curse, Daphne will rot at the bottom of the lake...Damien will rot in prison. And you all will rot in Hell..." Aubrey murmured, "with me." Aubrey toyed with the locket as she stared at the black screen.

My mind raced. I had to stop her. Before she started shooting.

"So is the demon in the locket now?" I asked breathlessly.

Aubrey scoffed. "You don't know anything about magic, do you, Sera?"

"Teach me," I whispered, struggling to hide the desperation in my voice, emboldened by the fact that Aubrey seemed to be distracted from the girls.

She frowned thoughtfully. "He *was* in the locket. Bound inside by Alice Grey. For a witch without magic, she certainly knew how to use it once she got it. The strength it took to bind him with a curse...he said it was unheard of. But after a while, he wasn't just entering my thoughts...he was controlling my actions...I could feel him in my head; he whispered things...put suggestions in my mind." Aubrey blinked. "But he didn't fully take over until we saw you."

"Me?"

Aubrey inclined her head as she regarded me curiously. "The sight of you..." She pointed the gun at me, and my heart jumped into my throat. "Awakened him in a way he'd never been before, and after that—he possessed me completely."

"Wait—" I winced in horror as I began to understand.

Aubrey laughed, low and hollow. "I wasn't ever *me*, Sera. You don't know me. We aren't even friends." Aubrey smiled sadly. "You were best friends with a demon, and you didn't even know it."

My eyes burned.

Aubrey kept going. "I will say one thing—it felt so good to give in to him." Aubrey sighed. "But he was restless. He was trapped, bound to the locket. He wanted to free himself. He said we needed to start at the beginning. So we went out to Bird Island and started looking through the wreckage. There was a book that he wanted. Alice Grey's spellbook."

"The book from the shed?"

Aubrey stared at the TV as though she hadn't heard me. "But we couldn't find it. So he needed a new plan..."

"That's why you kept your door unlocked. He couldn't use the key. And why you—*he*—had me sneak into Logan's room...the key and the salt line..."

"The hunter was getting in the way. We needed him taken care of and what better way than a curse?"

"But Damien cast Alice Grey's spell..." I said.

Aubrey frowned. "Yes. That wasn't supposed to happen." She spoke with words heavy with heartache. "The locket still had power over him, but that spell allowed him to move between bodies. And he left me."

"Damien?"

She looked up at me, startled, as though she'd forgotten I was there. "My demon."

The room swayed as I tried to process everything. "But at Martin House—I saw you, Aubrey—you were so upset...traumatized by what the demon had made you do—"

"No." Aubrey blinked rapidly and swallowed. "I couldn't bear to be without him. He'd promised to be with me. Keep me safe. Keep me strong. I was nothing without him."

"No, Aubrey." I took a small step toward her. "That's not true. You were horrified. Horrified by what you'd done. Weren't you? You still are!"

Aubrey inhaled sharply, her brow furrowed as she considered this.

I inched closer. "You *are* my best friend, Aubrey, and I know you. Your heart is hurt, but it's still so good."

Aubrey blinked her leaking eyes.

I slid my boot one more step. "Demons twist the souls they get close to...damage them, warp them. This isn't you. I mean—you saw what it did to Damien! It isn't your fault what happened. The demon is like a virus. He infected your mind, distorted your pain, and *used* you. As soon as it was away from you, you broke down because of your guilt, your remorse! I saw it! About Maddie, and about your parents—"

Aubrey's lip trembled, and she shook her head furiously. "No. No, no, no. My mom and my stepdad were a necessary sacrifice..." Aubrey breathed, her eyes lost for a moment in her pain. "When I couldn't find the spell fast enough...he needed to reach out to another demon—a much more powerful demon, but she wouldn't help. It didn't matter...because once I gave Daphne the idea for her dare and all of you..." she spun the gun slowly around the room, "were stupid enough to sell your souls—he just needed one."

"But, what about Daphne? It's Daphne who—" Cheryl sniffed.

"Daphne has been dealt with..." Aubrey whispered softly, her eyes dilating in the dark. "And now I want both of you to know what it feels like to be scared...to be truly terrified and know that *no one* is coming to help you. Like you made me feel."

"Aubrey, please." Kaitlyn's voice broke as she stood with Cheryl still clinging to her for support.

Suddenly, Aubrey flinched. Her eyes darted toward the

window. Aubrey sniffed back a few more tears and rolled her shoulders. "We're running out of time. The grim is coming."

"*What's a grim?*" Cheryl cried. Kaitlyn's eyes darted to the doorway. Aubrey walked slowly toward Cheryl.

I took my chance. I lunged at Aubrey, grabbing her wrist and aiming the gun toward the TV. I squeezed the trigger as many times as I could before it emptied, a big gaping hole in the TV. The sound was deafening. Each bang shook my bones and clapped against my eardrums.

I wrenched the gun away from Aubrey, tossed it to the floor, and held her tight to my chest as she shrieked protests. Behind me, Cheryl and Kaitlyn ran from the room.

"Wait!" I shouted after them, but they didn't listen. The front door slammed, and I knew I'd never reach them in time. The grims were coming...they would hunt them down just like Maddie and tear them apart to get to their souls. My stomach twisted as I struggled to hold Aubrey.

Aubrey writhed and raged against me as fresh tears fell, smashing her small fists into my chest. I held her to me, and Aubrey dissolved into pathetic sobs. "I want them to pay. *I want them to pay!*"

"Enough. Enough! It's over." I held her at arm's length and looked hard into her eyes. "Now you have to make this right, Aubrey. Tell me how we help them."

Aubrey, sapphire eyes still streaming and her lip curled into a nasty frown, shook her head. "No one helped me."

I hissed in frustration as I shoved her away from me and ran from the room after the girls.

Aubrey's shrieks echoed behind me. "What are you going to do, Seraphina? *What are you going to do!*"

I ran down the stairs. "Logan! Phoenix!" They weren't in the living room. I didn't have time to find them. Or time to worry why they hadn't come running at the sound of the gunshots. I tore from the house, shouting after the girls.

They were gone.

I squinted into the darkness. The light from the moon poured into the grassy clearing from above the lake. The surrounding woods were obscured in the night. Did they head up the long driveway on foot? Into the trees to hide in the shadows?

Aubrey came up behind me on the porch.

I whirled around to face her. "Aubrey, we have to help them! Tell me how we help them!"

She blinked rapidly, spilling tears that shined in the moonlight. She nodded toward the left. "It's too late. You're out of time, Seraphina."

I turned toward the shore.

A massive creature, dark as shadow, stood at the edge of the grassy bank, outlined in the rolling black waves of the lake beyond. Its eyes burned gold like a demon. I grabbed Aubrey, pulling her into me.

Aubrey made a little moan.

There was a moment, a silent stillness, as though time had paused to take a breath.

Then the creature charged, bobbing back and forth as it ran at us. I threw open the door and shoved Aubrey back inside, slamming the door just as claws scraped the wooden deck.

I slapped on the lights, dropped my bag off my shoulder, and pulled out a can of salt. I flipped the top and poured a thick line along the door.

"We need to help them!" I grabbed Aubrey's shoulders and pulled her toward my face. "Aubrey, you need to call them off. How do we call them off?"

Aubrey's sapphire eyes still leaked. She didn't speak. She simply stared at me.

The creature's frenzied claws ripped away at the door.

I flinched at the sound. "Aubrey...you need to stop this. *Please, help me stop this.*"

Aubrey looked away.

I bit my lip, struggling to find the right thing to say to convince her. "Please, Aubrey..." The words caught in my throat as I realized: there was only one.

There was only one grim. And it wasn't hunting Cheryl. And it wasn't hunting Kaitlyn.

"It's not here for them, is it, Aubrey?" Fresh tears blurred my vision as I looked at her, so small and tortured, like an elven princess in a dark fairy tale. "It's here for you."

"I wanted to scare them." Aubrey slowly turned. Sapphire met silver. Her lip trembled with the weight of her regret. "I didn't want to kill them..."

We winced as the grim's claws hacked at the door, splintering wood.

"And Maddie...she wasn't your fault, Seraphina." Aubrey bit her lip as it quivered. "But I didn't—it wasn't *me*. You have to know I wouldn't have—it was him."

My eyes searched her pale face.

She reached for my hand and gave it a squeeze. "You need to leave...there's nothing you can do now. I made the deal." She stiffened her lip and looked deep into my eyes. "*What happens next is not your fault.*"

I moaned as the creature slammed itself against the door, over and over, shaking the house with each impact. "Aubrey, why? Why did you do it?"

"Maddie didn't work." She shrugged, as if it made perfect sense. "He needed a soul to help break the curse." Aubrey blinked more tears and tried to smile. She put her delicate hands up to my cheeks and smoothed away my tears. "It's okay. It's okay. I'm not afraid."

I shook my head, squeezing her shoulders. "I won't let it take you."

"You can't stay here, Seraphina. You have to go." She blinked through the tears. "He has your sister."

I couldn't catch my breath. I choked out a sob. "What?"

Aubrey licked her lips and nodded. She flinched as the creature hit against the door. "He took your sister to Bird Island." Aubrey lifted the locket off her neck and dropped it over mine. "Go help her."

I gritted my teeth as hot tears blurred my vision, snot and saline dripping into my mouth. "I'm not leaving here without you."

There was silence.

We turned slowly toward the door.

Then there was an explosion of glass to our right.

And the grim smashed through the window.

KNOW YOUR ENEMY

It was unlike anything I'd ever seen. Its eyes burned gold in the black of its furry, reptilian face. Its ears were pointed like horns. It stood on its back legs. Its long arms curved inward at its sides and ended with long fingers capped with thick claws. It bobbed slightly, shifting from clawed foot to clawed foot, crunching broken glass underneath its weight in the pools of moonlight spilling onto the wood floor. A long, thick tail flicked slowly back and forth behind it. The grim slowly lowered its head and arched its back, its thick black fur standing up in spikes like an angry cat. Its burning eyes on Aubrey, the grim opened its mouth, revealing sharp fangs and teeth like pointed razor blades. The grim's tongue uncurled as it let out a hiss that chilled my blood.

I grabbed Aubrey and forced her back as I grabbed the salt can and frantically spilled a crude circle around our feet. The grim hissed angrily, its tongue flicking along with its tail. It pawed at the ground as it gnashed its teeth.

Behind me, Aubrey gripped my shoulders and whimpered softly. I shoved my hand in my jacket and pulled out the flask and popped the top. I tried to catch my breath. This tiny bottle against this giant beast would barely buy us a moment of distraction...I'd seen it run. It would be on us in seconds.

The grim's lips curved in a smile, its fangs protruding and teeth shining. It moved closer in the same bobbing motion.

I held up the flask as it approached the salt circle. The grim lowered its head to the floor and sniffed at the circle. Its breath blew the salt bit by bit until the circle was broken. Now it could cross.

My heart thundered in my chest. I still couldn't catch a breath. The grim raised its head, so it was almost eye level with me. Its fanged smile parted, allowing its tongue to flick at me. I was hyperventilating. It inclined its head, bobbing back and forth on its feet. I was going to pass out. I swallowed and gritted my teeth.

It was going to lunge.

This was my moment. In one quick motion, I splashed the holy water into its face. The grim shook its head, water dripping from its dark fur.

It didn't work.

I stepped backward, pulling Aubrey with me. Not daring to turn our backs to it, we scrambled away from it as fast as we could manage, shuffling backward into the kitchen. I stepped in front of her, shielding her from the grim. But the grim only grinned. Then it bent low, arching its back. And then, claws outstretched like hands ready to rip us apart, it charged.

"NO!" I flinched away from it, eyes slammed shut. I covered my face with my arms, bracing for teeth and claws.

Nothing came.

I opened my eyes and peeked between my arms. I was face-to-face with it. The grim had stopped inches from me. Its eyes, glowing bright, stared at me as it inclined its head—like it couldn't understand how I'd made a sound.

"GO AWAY!" I screamed.

The grim hesitated, as if it didn't know what to do.

Hope fluttered inside me like a caged bird, beating hard against my ribs. "LEAVE!"

Its eyes narrowed.

Then it hissed in my face, blowing my hair back and showering me with spit. And then I blinked, and it vanished in a misty black cloud of shadow. It was gone.

Aubrey's nails dug into the flesh of my arms, and she clung to me in a backward hug. Her small body shuddered against me as she gasped for air. "How—how did you do that?"

I fell back a step, eyes wide and unblinking at the spot where the grim had been. The only signs that it'd ever been there: the deep scratches in the wood floor, the splintered gaps in the door, and the broken window. The flask was limp in my hand as I stumbled backward a bit into Aubrey. Keeping a hold on me, she moved around to face me. She put a shaky hand on my cheek. "We're okay. Sera—Seraphina, you're in shock." She patted my face and pulled at my ears. "Hey, we're okay. You did it, Sera. You saved us... you saved me."

I looked down at her, blinking stupidly. Saved her. Save her. Phoenix. I stoppered the flask, saving what was left of it, and tucked it into the back pocket of my jeans. It didn't work on grims, but I knew it would work on a demon. Then I shoved the can of salt into my bag and slung it over my shoulder. I grabbed Aubrey by the arm. "Tell me the Blanchards have a boat."

We ran outside into the night and around the back of the house.

I stopped as I spied the bags, Nix's keychains shining in the blue moonlight. *This is where they were taken.* I had a split second to decide. I dropped down beside them in the cold grass and unzipped Logan's ruck first, then my backpack. As fast as I could manage, I dumped the contents of my backpack inside the ruck. The potion bottles clinked loudly as they clattered against one another and tumbled inside. I winced as the sound disturbed the quiet of the night. I glanced over at Phoenix's backpack. I didn't have time or room to empty hers. The moonlight glittered off her pins, and then something else caught my eye. I reached for it in the grass. Phoenix's wand. The smooth, hard metal felt cool in my hand as I gripped it. I hesitated for a moment, in awe at the intricate, delicate forge of it—of the feel of it as I palmed it. I shook myself. I didn't have time for this.

I pulled a hair tie off my wrist and tied my hair in a top knot and stabbed Phoenix's wand through my hair. Then I grabbed Logan's ruck and heaved it over my back, my shoulders hunched forward as I bent under the crushing weight of it.

"Come on!" Aubrey hissed in the darkness. She was only a shadow in the distance.

I hurried after her, leaving my empty bag behind, and she led me across the grass to a stone staircase that connected to a dock. In the water below, the little tin can motorboat bobbed in the black water. I tossed the ruck into the boat, which dipped and swayed like my stomach as I climbed in after the bag.

Aubrey hung back on the dock. "Do you know how to start it?"

I stared at the motor and back up at Aubrey. "Do you?"

Aubrey nodded, her face hidden in the darkness. She hesitated. "Move over." She hopped into the boat beside me and fired up the engine.

I flinched as the motor rumbled to life like a monster in the dark.

It was a cold and wet ride to Bird Island, but I didn't feel it. All I could feel was the ramming of my heart against my rib cage as I prayed with each pound that my sister was okay.

Aubrey steered the boat to the rocky shore, and we both hopped out to guide it up onto the beach. Aubrey glanced at me through the wind and the lake spray, the moonlight shining in her eyes. "What are you going to do?"

My jaw tightened, and I swallowed, but I didn't flinch. Fallen tendrils of hair whipped around me in the wind, as I peered down at Aubrey. "I'm getting my sister. You stay here."

Aubrey nodded, shivering in the cold. "Be careful."

I ran up the beach. My wet boots stumbled on the rocks until I managed to make it to the mound of sand and dirt in the middle. The island was nothing but rocks and dirt with the lonely, beaten remains of a wooden church falling apart in the center. Underneath the moon overhead, it looked like a creepy shack from a slasher film. My stomach lurched at the thought of what I might find inside. My hand went to my pocket, feeling the hard outline of my dorm key.

I approached the double doors of the church as quietly and as quickly as I could manage. The door was nothing but rotting wooden planks nailed together. It was light and easy to yank open. I winced as it creaked, but I didn't hesitate. I stepped inside.

I squinted through the darkness, scanning the benches. A dark shadow sat motionless in the left front pew. I hurried down the aisle, hand in my pocket, ready to grab the holy water. I came to the front. My heart dropped. Logan and Phoenix were slumped together on the bench.

"Don't be dead. Please, don't be dead." I ran to them, hands moving over their necks and faces. A pulse. Another.

I slapped at their cheeks. Nothing.

I tossed the ruck onto the bench and dug through it. My fingers snatched potion after potion, holding them up to the weak moonlight that slipped through the cracks in the walls to read the labels. "Excitoserum," I whispered as I found the right one. I forced Logan's head back and poured half the bottle into his mouth. It leaked out the sides as I shoved his mouth shut. It only took a few seconds. His eyes flew open as he gasped for breath like a dying man. He grabbed my wrist and forced my hand away from his mouth as he coughed and sputtered against the foul potion.

"It's me, Logan! It's me!" I hissed, gritting myself against his crushing grip.

He released me, rubbed his head as he groaned. Then he slapped at his jacket and pants. He cursed as I moved to help Phoenix. Cradling her face, I dumped the rest of the potion down her throat and closed her mouth. It leaked and spilled out of the corners of her mouth, running over my fingers.

"We gotta go." Logan's voice was hoarse as he stood up. "Get your bag."

I looked up from Phoenix as I held her head. I jutted my chin toward the bench. "Get yours."

He followed my gaze and quickly dug through it.

"Do you remember anything?" I murmured to Logan as I kept my eyes on Phoenix, watching her closely for signs of life. I glanced at my watch. It shouldn't be taking this long. I pulled her wand out from my bun and tucked it gingerly back into hers.

"Nothing." Logan dug a handgun out of his bag and checked it. He tucked it in the back of his waistband and then dug into his bag for another. He checked that one too and then held it low at his side. "Where are we?"

"Bird Island." I bit my lip as I watched her.

"We gotta go, Sam."

"Right." I stuck my arms underneath Phoenix's armpits like I did with Cole in the woods, my stomach sick and aching that I'd put her in this situation. It was all my fault.

"No, no." Logan tapped my shoulder, and I released her as I looked up at him.

"What?"

Logan shook his head and tossed his ruck on his back. He passed me the second gun, and then lifted Phoenix in one swoop, cradling her like a knight saving a princess. "You're going to have to carry it."

I stared wide-eyed at the cold, hard metal in my hands. Such a different kind of power than the wand. I didn't like it. I looked up at Logan and shook my head.

Phoenix gasped in his arms, her eyes fluttering.

Logan forced a pained smile. "Just don't point it at anything you don't want to kill. And when you do point it, switch off the safety, and pull the trigger. But remember, you need to work on your aim…"

"Logan, I—"

"You can do it." He nodded encouragingly. "Let's get off this rock."

I shook my head, my mind racing. "Bird Island. We're on Bird Island." My head started to clear. Bird Island. I understood. Finally, I understood. *I was the wrong witch.* "It's Phoenix. It was always Phoenix. We have to get her out of here now!"

The stink of brimstone and rotting decay seeped into the church, and a giggle came from the shadows to the left of the altar. Logan slid Phoenix to her feet, and she staggered into me. In one swift motion, Logan snatched the gun from his waistband and pointed it at the darkness. I held onto Phoenix as she struggled to find her footing, coughing and sputtering, gun limp and useless in my hand, as Logan moved to stand in front of both of us.

"You're finally putting it together, Seraphina Grey."

From the darkness, the demon stepped into the light.

And it wasn't Daphne.

HIT OR MISS

It was Cole.

Hot tears flooded my vision. The haunted, gaunt look was gone from his face. He was as dark and handsome as ever as he crossed the creaking wood floor. But his dark-brown eyes burned molten gold. "Oh, come now, DeVarney. You don't bring a gun to a demon fight."

Phoenix moaned in protest, finally finding her strength, as Logan shot at Cole's feet.

The demon only held up a hand. The bullet froze in midair. A smirk curled across Cole's face. "Iron?" As he spoke, the bullet dropped to the ground with a small clink. "Well, that's interesting."

Logan fired again and again. The demon stopped every one. Then he waved his hand, and Logan flew backward across the room. Wood burst to pieces into the air as Logan slammed through every pew until he hit the wall. "Please, sit back and enjoy the show. I think you'll get a kick out of it."

The demon turned toward us then...a cruel, twisted smile marring Cole's kind face. I stepped in front of Phoenix, but before I could lift the gun, the demon waved his hand and the gun was ripped from my fingers and tossed across the room. Phoenix reached around me and pointed her wand at Cole. But she didn't cast. Her hand shook, the wand wavering up and down beside my face.

"Aw, what is it, Pheeny?" The demon pouted, clasping his hands together. "Too scared to hex your boyfriend?" The demon giggled.

Phoenix inhaled sharply.

"What a shame...all that magic and no place to put it." The demon giggled even harder as he bounced on the balls of his feet. "It's okay. I can show you where."

My mind flashed over and over: Get him distracted from Phoenix. Keep talking. Buy time. Keep Phoenix safe. "It wasn't me." My voice came out in a croak as I struggled to catch my breath. I reached my hand to my back pocket and popped the top of the flask with my thumb in barely another movement.

The demon giggled devilishly, shaking his head. "Of course it wasn't you, Seraphina. It never is, is it?"

"This was all a trap for Phoenix," I whispered. My grip on the bottle tightened. If he got too close, I was ready. "When you were possessing Aubrey...you wanted to take me here...but then at the shed you realized I didn't have magic—so you needed Phoenix."

The demon nodded, threading his fingers together, as though he could barely contain his excitement.

"And when I went to visit Cole, when we came here—you really wanted Phoenix...you kept telling me we should get Phoenix —" I shook my head as though I cared to understand. "Why?"

The demon held out a finger and wagged it from side to side. "No spoilers."

Footfalls creaking on the wooden planks of the floor made us all turn to the door. Aubrey. Her eyes bloodshot and face blotchy, she rushed past me and threw herself at the demon. At first, I thought she was trying to fight him, but she was clinging to him.

The demon looked at her and smiled a smile too wide for Cole's face. Aubrey fell onto him, clutching at him, desperate for him.

The demon stood rigid, and his eyes danced in amusement. "You can't outrun it forever, Aubrey. The grim will find you."

Aubrey let out a soft wail. "It's gone. It didn't work. Maddie all over again. I tried. I'm sorry, I'm so sorry."

The demon's head snapped in my direction, his eyes wide. For the first time, he looked unnerved. His voice was a low rumbling growl as he hissed, "Impossible."

"Please, come back to me," Aubrey gasped, still pawing at Cole's leather jacket. "I can't stand it without you."

The demon shoved Aubrey off him. "Enough. Don't lie. I know you were having second thoughts. I smelled the stink of your doubt and betrayal from across the lake...you disgust me. You—"

"*ABSCONDITUS!*"

Everything went black, instantly submerged in darkness.

Phoenix's hand found mine, and she dragged me from the pew.

"I DON'T THINK SO!" the demon bellowed from behind us.

We tore down the aisle, but suddenly a power so much stronger than gravity knocked into the back of our knees and forced both of us to the ground. It felt like the air weighed as much as an ocean. It bore down on the backs of my calves, keeping me there. My leg muscle pressed down hard, nearly separating from the bone with an impossible pain. I tried to breathe, but despite my gasps and gulps for air, I couldn't manage to inhale. Something pressed down on my lungs, squeezing the breath out of them, refusing to allow them to expand. Phoenix was beside me, mouth agape as though she were a fish out of water. The two of us grabbed at our throats and pressed against our chests, desperate to find the source of failure.

Slow steps came from behind, as the demon walked around to

face us, Cole's hand clenched in a fist. The hand that crushed our lungs. Aubrey followed him, silent as a shadow at his side.

The demon twisted Cole's fist in front of our faces. The pain was like fire. My lungs burned to breathe. My vision began to cloud, and my head began to fog. I was suffocating, still forced down on my knees by the demon's power.

"Take the wand, Aubrey." The demon giggled as it watched us begin to die, crushing his fist harder still. He couldn't touch it. It was forged of magical iron.

Obediently, Aubrey picked up the wand from the ground by Phoenix's knee and quickly moved behind the demon again. Aubrey placed a hand on his arm. "You said you don't need Seraphina anymore..." Aubrey reminded him softly. "I heard you say that—"

The demon sneered. His hand dropped to his side as he turned to glare at Aubrey, who seemed to shrink beneath his stare.

Phoenix and I both coughed, gasping for breath as our lungs began to work again.

"You want me to let your new little BFF *go*? Is that it, Aubrey? After everything you've done, you can't bear to see any more? IS THAT IT!" the demon bellowed in her face.

Aubrey's lip quivered as she flinched against the tears that had begun to wash over her face.

The demon grabbed her by a fistful of lily-blonde hair and yanked her down to her knees beside us. Aubrey whimpered and sobbed as the demon screamed in her face, "WHY DON'T I JUST—"

This was my chance. I grabbed the flask from my pocket and splashed the demon. The demon howled in pain. Instantly, we were released completely from his power. I scrambled to my feet and dumped the remainder of the bottle onto Cole's head. The demon screamed. His hands flew to his face, which was smoking and steaming and red. I tried not to look as Cole's face bubbled and boiled. I grabbed Aubrey by the arm, tugging her to her feet and wrenching the wand from her limp hand. I passed the wand to Phoenix.

Wasting no time, Phoenix pointed the wand at the demon and cried, "*STUPEFACIUNT*!"

The demon reached out a hand, deflecting the spell. He wiped Cole's still steaming, red face with the back of a hand and shook Cole's hair from his eyes.

He waved a hand. Aubrey and I slammed into the left wall. The demon's power held us firmly in place against the broken and splintered wood. I groaned as lights sprang into my eyes. Dizzy from the impact, the single thought I had was to get to Phoenix, but I couldn't move. I was stuck to the wall. All I could do was watch as he grabbed Phoenix by the throat and pulled her into him.

"LEAVE HER ALONE!" I struggled to pry myself from the wood. I had to get to her. *I had to get to her.*

The demon ignored me as he smoothed a hand through Phoenix's hair and twisted her wrist back so that she dropped her wand. It fell with a soft clang. "Tsk, tsk, tsk. Oh, my little Phoenix Grey, I'm surprised at you. All that magic bubbling beneath the surface, and you can't think of a single spell, can you?" He giggled and sniffed at Phoenix's hair like a dog and growled into her ear. "You stink of fear...and you *should* be afraid...because once I've bled you just enough, I'm going to rip the skin off Seraphina and make your boyfriend here a nice new jacket from her hide. Then I'm going to grab little Fawnie from the forest and eat her up while you watch."

My eyes widened as Phoenix crumbled.

"Don't listen to him, Nix! Think, Phoenix, think! You can save us! Think!"

The demon smiled too wide for Cole's face and a deep, booming chuckle rumbled from the depths of his chest. "She can't...because I'm wearing whittle Coley's face! It's too much for her little brain to take."

Phoenix let out a tortured sob as the demon licked her cheek, grabbed her by the hair, and dragged her into the back room beside the altar. The door slammed, shaking the bones of the church.

There was silence. Then Phoenix's screams sent tremors through my body. Not seeing, only hearing her was unbearable. "PHOENIX!"

The hold of the demon loosened on my limbs, and I continued to struggle against it. He was weak. He was a weak demon. He couldn't split his focus. I fought harder.

Aubrey spoke softly from beside me. "He wants her blood. She won't survive...he'll cut her, bit by bit, until she's nothing but slits of skin."

I looked over at Aubrey in horror. "Why? Why does he want her blood?"

Aubrey just stared at me, the tears still silently flowing down her cheeks like rain down a window.

Suddenly, we slid a foot down the wall; splinters cut into my head and into my ankles where my jeans rode up my calves. The demon was putting all his focus into hurting Phoenix. His hold on us was failing. This was my chance.

"Aubrey, please!" My voice broke as my whispered words were drowned out by another tortured scream.

Aubrey winced. "He needs her blood to undo the curse put on him by Alice Grey." Aubrey bit her lip, her blue eyes glassy in the moonlight streaming through the beams.

Nothing made sense. It didn't make sense. My heart hammered as I willed myself not to panic.

Aubrey swallowed and took a shaky breath. "That's why he messed up your spell—he swapped your key with a fake when you weren't looking...he wanted you to fail and run to Phoenix for help. He needed to get her here—to Bird Island. The other demon told him it was the only way. She said if he fails again, she's coming to Nile."

I wasn't listening.

He messed up my spell.

That was it.

"I'm sorry, Seraphina." Aubrey hung her head as tears dropped from her eyes. "You should've let the grim take me."

I fought the urge to roll my eyes.

Phoenix screamed again, long and drawn-out and punctured by sobs.

Then Aubrey and I dropped to our feet as the demon's hold on us vanished completely. At the same moment, Phoenix screamed, "WHAT DO YOU WANT FROM ME?!"

I wasted no time. I grabbed Phoenix's wand off the ground and hurried back to the altar. I dug into my jacket for my spells.

"What are you going to do, Seraphina?" Aubrey mumbled from behind me.

I didn't answer. I looked down at the floor. My blood circle had been broken. I couldn't use it anymore. I'd have to improvise.

I took the salt from my bag and poured out a large circle. I ripped Aubrey's locket over my head and dropped it in the center.

I stepped out of the salt circle. I gripped the exorcism in one hand and the summoning spell in the other, and I spoke without hesitation. *"Ex oculus eius te cognovi. Novi te interfectorem amici mei. Novi te de foetore inferi. Horrendum malum...Hic appello."*

The stink of rot and brimstone penetrated my nostrils. My eyes widened and gasped as Cole, eyes glowing menacingly, materialized in a cloud of rancid black smoke. He made a movement to charge at me, but stopped short of the salt, as though an invisible wall were positioned in between us.

The demon let out a feral growl that rumbled and clicked in the base of his throat. "Ssseraphiiiinaaa..."

I held out the paper in a shaky hand, my mind racing as fast as my heart. I shouted the words, *"DIC NOMEN TUUM."*

He bared his teeth and snapped his jaws like a rabid animal. His head thrashed side to side. "You can't do it. You can't do anything." The demon hissed, its eyes glowing gold. "The salt line won't hold forever...and as soon as it fails, I'm going to make you watch as I rip your innards from your belly!"

I repeated the words again. "*DIC NOMEN TUUM!*"

The demon's eyes bulged in Cole's head, and he dropped to his knees.

"*DIC NOMEN TUUM!*"

He let out a furious roar and charged against the salt line, only to be thrown back as though he'd run into a barrier.

"*DIC NOMEN TUUM!*"

The demon started to twitch and twist. Cole's body contorted in movements that resembled a spider. He charged against the salt line again.

"*DIC NOMEN TUUM!*"

"Sera! The line! It's failing!" Aubrey shrieked as she grabbed my arm.

The demon panted heavily, Cole's nostrils flaring, as a cruel smile slid onto his face. "I think it's time we invited Mr. St. Claire to join the party..." The gold went out in his eyes like a candle flame. Then Cole's head fell forward, bowing down into his chest.

And then he looked up, his dark eyes wide and fearful. "Phinny? Please...Phin, let me out of here...I don't want to be here anymore. *Please*, Phin. *Please, help me.*"

Then Cole's arms were thrown backward at crooked angles. His foot snapped in the wrong direction, and he screamed in pain. "Help me, Phin!"

My stomach lurched. I couldn't catch my breath. I flinched at the sight of his twisted foot. I made a move to go to him.

A heavy hand squeezed my shoulder. "Don't."

I turned my head, startled, tears leaking from my eyes. Logan.

I looked back at Cole. He was sobbing, his arms still stretched impossibly far behind him. His arms would soon break off.

Logan's voice cracked in my ear. "Don't cross the line, Sam."

My grip on the paper tightened, but I hesitated.

"Keep going."

Cole moaned, "Please, Phin. It hurts. It hurts so bad."

My eyes darted toward Logan. He shook his head. "He's tricking you, Seraphina. That thing is not Cole."

I looked back at Cole. My fingers crushed the edge of the paper into my sweaty palm. The gold burned in his eyes, and he sneered. His voice bubbled up like a low frog croak. "That's right... It's not Cole...but I'm curious, Phinny...what makes you think Cole is still alive in here, hmm?" He inclined his head with a taunting smirk. "Maybe he's dead..." The demon shrugged. "Did you ever think of that? I mean...maybe you do manage to send me back...but then Cole drops down dead. Jussst like Maddieee..." He hissed, licking his lips.

"*DIC NOMEN TUUM*!" I yelled.

"Shouldn't you go help your sister right now?" the demon spat. "She's dying in a pool of her own blood...and you don't even care!"

My eyes burned.

Logan shook his head. "You can't stop now. Where is she?"

I pointed the paper toward the door by the altar, my eyes on the demon who grinned like the Devil.

My confidence shattered in the face of evil.

"Wait! Logan!" I screamed.

But he was gone.

The demon chuckled in a deep rumble that vibrated from his chest. "You don't think you can do it...*do you*?"

Cole's jaw was stretched inhumanly wide as he bellowed in a strange voice, low and slow. "You want to know *whyyyy* your sister's so important? You want to know *whyyyy*?"

I bit my lip. My eyes flickered from the spell to the burning gold of the demon.

The demon twisted Cole's head to the side like a doll. All the veins in his face and neck seemed to darken, black against his pale skin. "I can tell you..."

"*DIC NOMEN TUUM*!" I shouted as curiosity nagged at me.

"Why haven't you asked about Alice?" The demon sneered.

I gritted my teeth, desperate to focus. "*DIC NOMEN TUUM*!"

"Dear Auntie Alice," the demon belched. "Your mommy's little twin, Alice Grey...a twin who was just like *youuu*...WEAK. POWERLESS. USELESS."

My jaw clenched, not daring to speak.

Cole's head thrashed back and forth. Then his neck swayed like a snake as he stared at me with gold-burning eyes. "Alice haaaated being a twin. Just like little Seraphina haaaatttesss it."

"*DIC NOMEN TUUM*!"

"So, Auntie Alice made a deal...sold her dirty soul for magic... but she was a nasty little wench. A liar and a cheat." Cole's body started to seize, and black foam bubbled up out of his mouth. His body dropped to the floor.

I moaned at the sight of him motionless on the ground. He looked dead. What if he was dead?

Then Cole's head popped up, eyes burning gold. "I can make a deal with you, too, Phinny...I can give you magic stronger and greater than anything Phoenix could ever do...just *imagineeee* what you could do with magic."

My eyes burned with hot tears. Would it be so bad to make a deal? I could beat him at his own game. Use the magic against him. Logan said witches can defeat demons with a finger snap. If I had magic, I could rip him from Cole right then and there...

"You know, Phinny, Auntie Alice had a theory..." The demon's voice hissed through the air and echoed in my head. Hypnotic. "She thought...the reason why she didn't have any magic—was because her *twin* soaked it all up...starved her of all the magic and left her with none..."

The church seemed to spin and blur all around me as his words seeped through my thoughts. Like a trance.

"She thought...maybe that's why Charlotte Grey was such a 'rare talent'...because Charlotte Grey had stolen magic that was meant for two...do you think that's what happened to *youuuu*?" Cole crawled on all fours and looked up at me sideways, like a dog with a broken neck. His tongue dangled from his twisted smile. "You want the magic, Phinny. You deserve the magic, Phinny. It was yours all along. She took it from you. Just say the word, and I can give it back. Just say—yes."

I inhaled a shaky breath.

I wanted it.

I'd always wanted it.

And in that moment, I wanted magic more than anything...

But I didn't need it.

"*DIC NOMEN TUUM!*"

The demon roared again, smashing his teeth.

"*DIC NOMEN TUUM!*"

"Sera!" Aubrey's scream pierced my ears. "Sera! THE SALT!"

My eyes darted to the ground. The salt had blown away. The line had broken. My eyes, wide with panic, watched in horror as the demon jumped up to its feet, shook off his jacket, and walked out of the broken circle.

"*DIC NOMEN TUUM!*"

The demon winced. He struggled to continue toward me. But he managed to close the distance. He grabbed me by the throat and pulled me into him. The stink of him turned my stomach. Bile bubbled up to my throat, and I couldn't swallow. Vomit spilled out of my mouth. He crushed my throat. I ripped at his hands with my fingernails. My lungs screamed for air. I choked on bile.

"You should've made the deal..." he hissed in my ear, as I struggled and gagged. "Poor, pathetic, little Phinny." He squeezed harder with every word. "And this is the end of Seraphina Grey. The annoying...pathetic...WORTHLESS...failure of a witch!"

His nails dug deep, burning my skin.

"Cole..." I coughed. My fingers pried desperately at his hands as they crushed my throat. I looked into his eyes. "Cole... Don't let him kill me, Cole."

The gold burned and then went out. Dark eyes blinked as the hands at my neck loosened. I gasped. A fresh breath flooded my burning lungs. My fingers massaged my throat as I coughed up more bile. Cole shoved me away from him. I stumbled backward into a pew.

"Quick!" Cole groaned. "Quick, Phin, do it! I can't hold him—"

The gold flared brightly in his eyes as Cole was taken over once more.

I scrambled to my feet, fists clenched and bracing myself. I sucked in a deep breath and bellowed, "*DIC NOMEN TUUM*!"

The demon lunged for me, but as my words rang out all around us, vibrating violently against the walls of the church, he fell to the ground a few feet from where I stood. Cole's face looked up at me, tortured and pained. His skin darkened to an ashy gray before my eyes. Then the skin of his face started to crack, like it was burning from the inside out. He looked as if he had been carved from a blackened burning log, a human charcoal, ready to crumble to pieces. His whole body was smoking, and his shirt had started to char.

"Aubrey..." the demon hissed, his words soft and snakelike. "You'll never be able to live with yourself without me...you need me...you killed your mommy...and Maddie...and drowned Daphne at the bottom of the lake—"

"*DIC NOMEN TUUM*!" I shouted over his words, drowning them out. "*DIC NOMEN TUUM*!"

"DEBIL!" The demon's deep roar shook the ground.

I blinked rapidly, shocked and confused. I'd forgotten I'd needed his name. Panting, heart racing, stunned that I'd actually done it, I rushed at him and took his face in my hands. "*Debil, ego eiciam vos in nomine dei. In nomine domini, Debil, mando tibi, dimitte animam hanc. Debil, dimitte hanc animam et revertere ad infernum—*"

I saw movement in the corner of my eye.

I looked up. Aubrey stepped forward with Logan's gun in her shaking hand. She flicked the safety and pointed it at me, her eyes streaming once more. "S-s-stop, Sera. Sera, stop, *please*. Take your sister and leave. I won't let him hurt you. You...you can go. But—y-y-you can't send him back. *I need him.*"

I looked down at the demon, eyes vacant, his head heavy in my hands. I looked back at Aubrey, and for a moment, I saw myself.

"I understand, Aubrey." I smiled ironically. "I know what it's like to feel desperate for power and control. They took your power back on that boat...this demon gave it back. But you're so much stronger than you think. That's how you found it in you to help me."

Aubrey lowered the gun, sniffing back tears.

I gave her a rueful smile. "You don't need a demon, Aubrey."

Aubrey flinched. She shook the gun wildly, still aiming at me. "No." Her lip trembled as she spoke in a thick, watery voice. "I need him. The things I've done...I can't...I can't live with myself without him."

My heart dipped.

"I'll do it, Sera." Aubrey's lower lip trembled again. "Don't think I won't." She shook her head. "Let him go." She gritted her teeth and growled through her tears, "Or I shoot."

I closed my eyes and prayed with all my heart.

Then I whispered, "*Vadat.*"

"NO!"

The gun fired.

THINGS I'LL NEVER SAY

There was light. Blinding and white. All I could see was light. I was dead. This was Heaven. Aubrey had shot me. Point-blank. No coming back from that. But Cole...Cole had to be okay. I was sure the demon was cast out. I had done what I was supposed to do. A cold tear slid down my face. But I hadn't gotten to tell Phoenix I was glad we were twins.

I was on my back, staring up at the light. I didn't feel pain, just the cold of the tear as it dripped down my neck. And the hard ground. That didn't seem right.

"Phinny. PHINNY!"

I blinked and tried to move. This wasn't Heaven. I tried to call out, but I couldn't make my mouth move. All I managed to do was move my tongue around my teeth.

"*Libero!*"

The light vanished. I blinked, seeing spots.

"Cole? Logan, is he—? *Cole!*"

I felt soft, gentle hands pull me up. Phoenix held me, cradling me in her lap. Her hand smoothed back my hair. I blinked up at her, trying to focus on her face. Her big brown eyes were wide and staring somewhere off to the side.

Then Phoenix screamed, "LOGAN!"

"*He's fine!*" Logan snapped from somewhere off in the distance. "He'll be fine. Can you focus on your sister, please?"

I tried to speak, tried to turn to see what was happening, but I still seemed to be frozen. All I could do was stare up into Phoenix's face, which was paler than usual; her amber eyes were bloodshot and leaking a quiet stream of tears.

Phoenix looked down at me as she stroked my cheek. "Hey, Witch." Her face warmed with a ghost of a smile. "You'll be able to move more in a second. I kind of overdid it with the stunning spell."

My heart swelled with a sisterly pride I hadn't felt for Phoenix in a long time. She'd stopped a bullet with a stunning spell. That had to be some kind of record, right? My body loosened, and I opened my mouth, taking a deep, gasping breath. I moved my hand to cover Phoenix's hand, still cupped at my cheek. "I'm lucky..."

Phoenix scoffed with an incredulous smirk. "I'd say so—"

I shook my head. "I'm lucky to have you for a sister. And I'm so grateful to be your twin."

Phoenix blinked back fresh tears and gave me a rueful smile, but before she could speak, a scream made us both flinch.

I pulled myself up, and Phoenix yanked me to my feet. I swayed as the room spun. Had I screwed up the exorcism *again*? Phoenix stood with me, holding me to her. But it wasn't a demon. It was just Aubrey.

Aubrey, still lying on the ground where the spell had blasted her, screamed and howled in pain. She banged her fists against the wooden floorboards, and she writhed and twitched as though she were being tortured.

I made to move toward her, but Phoenix grabbed my arm. "She tried to shoot you, Phin."

Logan was crouched beside Cole, holding him down as he fought to sit up.

"Gedoff me!" Cole grunted from the ground. "PHOENIX!"

Logan grimaced as his hand clamped down on Cole's shoulder, forcing him back down on his knees. "You're going to hold on a minute while I make sure you are who you say you are," Logan snapped as he pulled out a flask of holy water and dumped it onto Cole, who sputtered and coughed. Logan smirked and pushed off Cole, dusting off his jeans.

Cole struggled to his feet, his dark hair wet and dripping into his eyes. He crossed the floor and grabbed Phoenix roughly into a hard hug. I edged away from them, feeling instantly uncomfortable, like I was intruding on a private moment. I slowly approached Logan as I struggled to ignore the sounds of their bickering.

"What are we going to do about Aubrey?" I asked softly.

He turned to stare down at the girl as she sobbed and thrashed on the floor.

Logan frowned. "I'll call LaValley...they're probably going to have to commit her...it happens." Logan's eyes were on Cole. "Demonic possession messes up the best of people."

I was quiet as I watched Aubrey. I couldn't let her suffer like that. I bent down carefully beside Aubrey and pulled her into me. Instantly, she grew still, her sobs stifled to whimpers. I checked her pockets and found the somnum. It was almost empty, but I didn't need much. I took her head in my lap and gently guided her mouth open. Aubrey closed her leaking eyes, and I pressed three drops onto her tongue, and she was still.

Logan got hold of LaValley, and we loaded Aubrey, still sleeping, into the belly of the boat. Logan started the engine and steered us toward Nile. The sun was rising over the trees, setting the sky ablaze with gentle yellow light, softening the blue and chasing away the dark. It warmed my heart and gave me courage. I tried to soak it in, but each crash of the boat against the waves was violent and jarring, so much so that I was knocked off my seat. Logan grabbed me just before I landed in the hollow of the boat and shoved me back into place.

Phoenix, on the other hand, didn't seem to notice the sun or the waves. Her attention was focused entirely on Cole, who made a point to sit in the front of the boat, away from all of us.

When we made it back to the rectory, Cole pulled around the back and parked beside a large white van with *Maple Leaf House* printed on the side. LaValley stood at the back of it with a few women in scrubs. Logan nodded at them through the window as we got out, and instinctively, I followed him. The two of us approached them, with me hanging back a bit, letting Logan take the lead.

He shook LaValley's hand. LaValley placed a gentle hand on my shoulder. Then he gestured to the women. "Mages from the Viridi Order in Rutland. They work undercover at Maple Leaf House, assisting on the paranormal cases."

I blinked in surprise at the women as they pulled a stretcher out of the Maple Leaf House van. The three of them regarded me quietly with kind faces and matching knowing expressions. Mages. *They were mages.*

"I've also contacted the mages in place at the Burlington Police Department. They've found the girls at the Blanchard lake house —safe and, aside from any psychological trauma, unharmed. Two of them were under a pretty potent sleeping potion, but the mages were able to rouse them. Unfortunately, they've yet to find Daphne Collins or Damien Barrow...but based on evidence, will sadly turn their attention to the lake." LaValley nodded grimly at my shocked face. He cleared his throat. "And where is Miss LaMothe?"

I stared at him, lost in grisly images of Daphne floating face down in Lake Champlain, her inky hair splayed out about her like black seaweed.

Logan nudged me gently, and I recovered quickly. "Oh, yes. Sorry. Aubrey...she's this way..." I led the ladies to the back of Cole's van and opened both doors wide. We'd laid Aubrey out among the blankets and pillows Cole had stashed for when he took overnight snowboarding trips in the mountains, and I'd held her the whole drive into the mainland. But sometime in between when I'd jumped out of the van and opened the back, Aubrey had curled up in a ball beneath the covers, hugging a pillow to her chest.

The women went right to work. Together, they lifted Aubrey out of her nest of blankets and laid her gingerly onto the stretcher. Then one of the women turned to me as her companions secured Aubrey's wrists and ankles with padded straps. "Was she given any medications, elixirs, potions, tonics..."

I blinked again. "Uhh...yes, three drops of somnum..." I bit my lip as I hesitated. These women were like magical doctors. I should tell them everything. "She's been possessed for a few weeks," I blurted. I licked my lips and bit them closed. Father LaValley probably had explained it already. I was making a fool of myself. But for some reason, these women made me nervous. Uneasy.

The woman tilted her head with a sad smile. "Was the possession of a demonic or spectral nature?"

I took a deep breath. "Demonic...from contact with a cursed necklace," I added anxiously.

The woman searched my face with narrowed eyes. "Do you have the necklace?"

Phoenix appeared at my side, bumping into me as she came to a stop. "Nope."

I looked down at Phoenix with an eyebrow raised. She glanced up at me sideways, a glint of warning in her amber eyes. I closed my mouth and looked back at the woman with a sheepish shrug.

The woman smiled slowly. Then she reached a hand out to touch my shoulder. "Thank you, Witch Grey." Then she stepped back and nodded to Phoenix, her smile cooled. "Phoenix the Red." She turned to her companions and inclined her head toward their white van. The two women slowly wheeled Aubrey away and loaded her into the back of their van. The woman made to follow them but glanced back at us over her shoulder. "Maybe we'll meet again someday…"

Phoenix scoffed before muttering under her breath.

I forced a smile and gave her a polite wave. Then all three women got into the Maple Leaf House vehicle and drove away.

Phoenix stomped to Cole's van and slammed both back doors shut. She slipped her arm through mine and quipped, "She better hope we don't see her again."

I looked down at Phoenix, eyes wide. "Right? Weird vibe, huh?"

"Creepy vibe. Come on." She tugged me around the back of the van to the driver's side.

Father LaValley was…it looked like he was giving Cole a physical…like a checkup. He had a kit that resembled an old fishing tackle box, open at his feet. He listened to Cole's heart with a stethoscope. Logan held the driver door open, his arm draped over the top, leaning in to watch LaValley work. The lines and angles of Logan's face were sharp and defined, his forehead crinkled as his golden-green eyes searched Cole's face. Cole, meanwhile, simply stared blankly, eyes downcast toward the ground. He blinked in an uneven rhythm, as though he were struggling to stay awake. His face was sallow and pale. His lips were dry and cracked. He looked sick.

Phoenix and I joined the huddle around Cole. He flinched as we approached.

Then he shivered and tugged Logan's jacket tighter around him. He'd left his leather one back in the church. He hadn't wanted to touch it. His eyes flicked up at LaValley and then shifted away. "Almost done?" Cole mumbled hoarsely. "You haven't checked Phoenix yet. She needs…" His voice cracked and tears spilled down his cheeks. He cleared his throat. "You need to help Phoenix."

My heart dipped at the state of him.

Beside me, Nix scoffed. "I can wait."

I glanced at Phoenix with eyes narrowed. "Yeah, right..."

LaValley straightened and turned to Phoenix. "No need. Mr. St. Claire seems to have sustained no permanent damage to his soul."

"Can I quote you on that, Father?" Logan eyed LaValley warily.

LaValley scooped up his tackle box of magical first aid and clapped Logan on the back. "Absolutely. His soul is still intact. Healthy. No damage." LaValley placed a gentle hand on Cole's shoulder. "Now, Cole, you need to rest. Sleep is the only thing that will cure your symptoms. And I expect with a full twenty-four hours of sleep—give or take—you should feel like yourself again."

Cole forced a smile, but it came out a grimace.

"And I must say," LaValley gave Cole's shoulder a small shake, "you put up one hell of a fight."

Cole cocked an eyebrow as he peered up at LaValley.

LaValley smiled warmly as he held his gaze. "Not many men could hold off demonic possession for hours, let alone two and a half days. It shows an incredible strength of character, heart, and soul. That's something to be proud of...I hope you remember that."

Cole's eyes fell back down to the gravel drive.

LaValley gave his shoulder a final squeeze before he turned to Phoenix.

Cole took that opportunity to swing his legs back into the van. Without a word, as though instinctively understanding his need for privacy, Logan shut the door for him. And shut inside the van, Cole folded his arms over the steering wheel and bent his head down.

LaValley smiled kindly at Phoenix. "Well, Miss Grey...what is it now?"

Phoenix grinned a cheesy, aw-shucks smirk and gave LaValley a playful punch. "Aw, you know...just a bit of demonic torture, no biggie."

My eyes moved between the two of them. They knew each other. The familiar tug of jealousy twisted in my stomach. *How did they know each other?*

"Come on, Grey," Logan muttered. "We're not leaving until you get checked out."

Phoenix blew her bangs out of her face and rolled her eyes to the sky. "Fine. But just LaValley."

LaValley held a hand out toward the back of the van. Phoenix groaned and, still grumbling, she marched around to the bumper. LaValley followed Phoenix to the privacy of the tailgate with an indulgent shake of his head.

Logan and I were left standing outside Cole's window. Logan shoved his hands in his pockets and leaned against the van door. I shuffled my boots in the dirt drive as I snuck a glance toward the back.

"Don't worry, Sam. She's tough."

I looked back at Logan. "Yeah..." I bit my lip on my question: How does Phoenix know Father LaValley? And how did Logan know she was tough? I leaned against the van, keeping a few feet between us. I crossed my arms over my chest, shivering slightly in the early morning cold of dying October.

Logan cleared his throat. "You did good, Sam."

I scoffed with a lopsided smirk as I glanced up at him. "You say that a lot. I like it."

Logan peered at me sideways. He didn't say anything, but I grinned at the twitch of a smile hidden in the hard lines of his face.

I raked a hand through my hair, blonde strands catching in the breeze and blowing around my face. I pushed off the van and turned to face the wind, my hair streaming behind me and out of my face. I closed my eyes, held my arms out at my sides, and let the air wash over me as though it might clear my head. I inhaled deeply, drinking in the cold.

"I'm sorry, Sam."

My eyes opened, and I looked at Logan in surprise. "What do you mean?"

Logan's jaw pulsed, his eyes staring hard off into the woods that surrounded the rectory parking lot. Then he met my gaze, emerald to silver. "You shouldn't have had to do all that alone." He shrugged and scowled down at his boots. He licked his lips and shook his head in disgust. "It was a demon. A bottom feeder, at that. I should've been able to track it down weeks ago. Before Maddie made the deal...before you had to—"

I scoffed with an incredulous smirk. "It wasn't your fault—"

"I've hunted demons a hundred times stronger than that thing within days." Logan shook his head again, his face marred with self-deprecation. "I should've been able to—"

I had to smile. "But, Logan, he wasn't possessing Aubrey! Not really."

Logan made a face, his forehead crinkled. "What do you mean?"

I reached into my jean pocket and pulled out the locket. I passed it to him. "He was bound inside the locket the entire time... well, at least until Damien cast the spell in the shed, and then he spent the weekend trying to take possession of Cole." I gave him a soft smile. "You were coughing up blood on a dirty motel room floor the whole time."

Logan turned it over in his hands. He glanced over at me, his eyebrow cocked. "He was bound inside...like a Frodo thing?"

My smile crinkled my eyes. "If that helps you..."

Logan scrunched up his nose and continued to study the locket. "How?"

"Alice Grey summoned the demon—Debil—and made a deal for magic..." I paused and shook my head, torn between disgust and admiration at her skill. I looked up at Logan as he squinted down at the necklace. "But she tricked him."

Logan looked at me, his eyebrows raised in surprise. "She trapped him in this thing?"

I nodded. I ran a hand through my wind-swept hair and stepped closer to get a better look at it. "She cursed him. He couldn't leave the locket. Much less take her soul."

Logan inclined his head. "I've never heard of anything like that."

"See?" I had to smile. "That's why you couldn't find him. He wasn't technically possessing anyone." My smile faded, and I shivered, hugging my jacket tight against the cold. "And that's why he left Damien's body...he had to take the risk and take over Cole because he wanted Phoenix on Bird Island...Cole was the only person who'd be able to get a Grey sister back on Bird Island..."

Logan made a face. "Why did he want Phoenix on—"

I shrugged with a doubtful wince. "Aubrey said he needed her blood to break the curse."

A quiet fell over us. The only sound was the soft murmur of voices at the back of the van and the hush of wind as it pressed through the trees.

"Don't lose that." Logan passed the locket back to me. "You keep it in a lockbox...but you don't lose it."

"Right." I nodded, happy to think about anything other than my sister being stuck like a pig. I slipped the locket inside my jean pocket. I didn't bother asking how he knew about lockboxes, lead boxes etched with enchantments. I nibbled my lower lip as my thoughts wandered. Maybe the locket was similar... I shook myself and squinted up at Logan through the weak glow of a cold new day.

"He said he needed Grey's blood to break the curse?" Logan's brow furrowed.

I nodded as my stomach churned at the thought.

Logan jutted his jaw to the side as he considered something.

"What?" I asked him tentatively.

Logan met my eye with a thoughtful frown. He shook his head. "Why did he think he needed her blood? And why Bird Island? I thought Alice Grey had a shed in the woods?"

I hesitated.

"I mean...Debil was scum even by demon standards...like, low-level moron...an idiot. How would he know how to break such a hardcore curse?"

I rubbed my hand along the hollow of my throat. Then I remembered. "I don't know why Bird Island was necessary, but..." I looked up at Logan. "Aubrey said he reached out to another demon for help. She wouldn't help him. But maybe she told him what to do?"

"*She*?" Logan asked pointedly.

I nodded slowly as the memory came back. "Aubrey said the demon threatened to come here if Debil messed up again."

At the back of the van, Phoenix gasped and cursed loudly.

I flinched.

Logan put a hand on my shoulder. "You okay?"

Before I could lie, LaValley and Phoenix came back around the van. Phoenix was pulling her hoodie gingerly over her head, but she wasn't fast enough to hide her shirt. It was stained reddish brown with dried blood. The entire bottom half. My stomach lurched, and I looked at her, horrified, as her head popped through the hoodie with a scowl. "Okay, now that I'm all—"

I grabbed her arm and pulled her to a stop. Then I yanked up her shirt to see her stomach.

"Hey!"

Ignoring her protests, I moved my hand over her belly. There wasn't a mark on her. I pulled at the bottom of her shirt still stained brown with pints of her blood. My eyes flew to Phoenix's face. "Are you okay?"

Phoenix rolled her eyes and shoved me back, straightening her shirt and tugging her hoodie back in place. "I'm fine, Phin. Let's just go." She turned on her heel and marched around the other side of the van without bothering to say goodbye to LaValley.

I stared after her, mouth gaping. Then I twisted back to stare at LaValley. "Is she okay?" I demanded, pointing a finger through the back seat window.

LaValley nodded grimly. "I was able to mend the cuts...luckily, they were shallow. No scarring."

"Luckily," I muttered in disgust. "He must have cut into her a lot to cause her to bleed that much!"

LaValley nodded again. "Yes." He pressed a bottle into my hands. "This is miraculum. It'll help if you two decide to take up monster hunting as a hobby."

I popped the top and took a tentative sniff. "Bungleweed?"

LaValley raised his eyebrows and then his face relaxed into a soft smile, pleased and impressed. "It is. But with a few extras...I have a feeling you'd be able to deconstruct it and replicate it within a few days. But I'll save you the trouble and text Logan the instructions...it takes months to brew, but it heals most wounds and prevents scarring like magic." Father LaValley winked.

I stuffed the bottle into my pocket without a word. All I could think of was Phoenix. How she was hurt...*had been* hurting...and she hadn't told me. I mean, I knew it. She knew I knew it. But... there was so much blood. My heart hurt for her. For what she'd gone through.

Logan shoved off the van and shook LaValley's hand. "Thanks, Father. Again. I owe you."

LaValley held up a hand and waved away Logan's words. "This is just the start of things to come...you keep your eyes open. This is just the start."

LaValley shook Logan's hand, gave Cole and Phoenix a silent salute, clasped my hands in his, and bid us goodnight and God bless.

"God...right," Logan muttered.

Logan followed me around to the passenger side of the van. He climbed in the front, and I slid into the back beside Phoenix.

"Mama has a lot of explaining to do when she gets back," Phoenix muttered.

I tried to smile, but I couldn't. I felt empty. Hollow. Like all the hope and triumph I'd felt before had been carried off in the van along with Aubrey.

"Anyone want to go trick-or-treating?" Phoenix quipped. No one laughed. And then, Phoenix's voice came low and soft beside me, reminding me of Fawn when it's past her bedtime. "Can we go home now, Phin?"

I opened my mouth but shut it on all of my unasked questions. I forced a smile and pulled her into the crook of my arm. "There's nowhere I'd rather be."

Cole spent the entire drive back to the island in a somber silence. Logan tried to make a comment about the van, but Cole only nodded wordlessly. I kept glancing at his dark eyes in the rearview mirror, illuminated occasionally by the passing headlights. He wouldn't even look at Phoenix. I suspected he couldn't. The guilt of what the demon, Debil, had done to her...had made *Cole* do to her...was probably more than he could bear. Dread seeped into my stomach. What if their friendship didn't survive this?

And what about Mama? How could she have kept so much from me...Mama was a *twin*. Her sister had been magicless, too, and yet she'd kept it from me. Everyone had. I watched the lake, gray in the light of the new day, as we boarded the ferry. The whole family had known except me and my sisters. Or, had Mama trusted Phoenix with that information, too? Maybe it was just me whom Mama didn't trust? Maybe she'd felt I'd go dark, the same way as Alice? I bit my lip. Well, hadn't I almost...considered it?

I frowned as the ferry rocked grimly against the waves. No. I wouldn't believe it. Mama trusted me. If she didn't, she wouldn't have let me go to school. And she always had a reason for keeping us in the dark. I had to trust in her. I *had* to. Mama would make sense of it. As soon as she came home. But where was she right now? My eyes shifted to Logan in the passenger seat in front of me. I leaned forward and whispered in his ear, "What is my mother doing with your brother right now?"

Startled, he flinched. Then Logan hesitated.

I scrunched up my face and gave him an impatient tug on the ear.

Logan yelped and grabbed my hand, holding it fast in his. "You'll have to ask *her* that whenever she gets back because I don't know."

I scoffed. "You have to know something!"

Logan sighed. "Fine. What I do know is that it's a big deal. And according to my jerkface big brother, 'above my pay grade'... which means it's *way* above yours."

I groaned, pushed off his seat, and plopped back into mine.

Phoenix snickered. "He's annoying, isn't he?"

"Extremely," I snapped loudly.

By the time we reached the cottage, Cole was practically falling asleep at the wheel.

"He's going to need to sleep it off." Logan eyed him warily. "Like LaValley said, he gets a day of sleep, he'll be back to normal. Possession takes its toll on you...they don't usually let you rest..." Logan stepped out of the van, gripping the door as he watched Cole struggle to pull the keys out of the ignition. "Once he crashes, he could be out for days."

Phoenix hopped out, marched to the driver's side door, and wrenched it open for Cole. She jutted her thumb toward the house. "Out, St. Claire."

Cole muttered something about being okay, needing to go home, but Phoenix seized him by the jacket and practically shoved him inside the cottage as she shouted over her shoulder, "Get the keys, Phin."

I took the keys out of the ignition. Logan held his hand out expectantly. I gave him a dubious smirk. "Are you really that much of a bigot that you'd rather stay at that nasty motel than in a witch's cottage?"

Logan opened his mouth but closed it again. He dropped his hand back at his side and shrugged. "I didn't think—"

I grabbed his arm and turned him toward Grey Cottage. By the time we reached the top step, Icarus jumped down from the railing.

"Your mother will not be pleased..."

Logan yelled out in alarm at the sound of the cat speaking. Icarus hissed at Logan's boots as he backed out of the way, then padded swiftly inside.

Logan stared, wide-eyed, after Icarus as I guided him in the house. "All your monster hunting, and you've never met a talking cat before?"

Phoenix was in the kitchen, filling four mugs with hot cider. Cole was at the table, his head in his hands.

"Phoenix, shouldn't he get some rest? Like, lay down?" I asked tentatively.

"No." Phoenix dropped a mug in front of Cole; the cider spilled down the sides. "Not until he looks at me."

She sat across from him, her own mug dripping sticky foam down her hand as she gripped it. Her amber eyes glared at Cole.

Logan shifted awkwardly beside me in the doorway. With a roll of my eyes, I put my hand on his back, pushed him all the way in the kitchen, and passed him a mug.

"Well?" Phoenix demanded. Her hard eyes never left Cole as both Logan and I took seats on either side of her.

Cole clenched his fingers, grabbing thick tufts of dark hair in each hand as though he might rip it out.

I watched him nervously. "Uh, Nix—"

"Nope. He's not going anywhere until we move past this."

I frowned, biting my tongue, not wanting to fight with Phoenix so soon after finally making up.

"Look at me, Cole," Phoenix snapped.

Cole groaned, pulling his hair in agonized frustration.

"I said—"

Cole's head shot up. "I know what you said!" His dark eyes were rimmed red, swollen from tears, and his face was anguished. "And I know what I did."

"You?" Phoenix blinked, taken aback by Cole's outburst. "*You* didn't—"

"Maybe we should..." Logan muttered to no one in particular.

"Yes!" Cole shook his head violently up and down. "Yes, I did! I—"

"Outside?" I whispered to Logan over the top of Phoenix's head. Logan gave a curt nod, and the two of us pushed back in our chairs, mugs in hand, and I led him out the back door as their shouts followed us outside.

The cold air stung my face as I sat on the steps and stared up at the quarter moon fading in the bright blue sky. Logan sat down on the opposite side of the same step, as though he wanted to keep his distance from me.

I smiled slightly. "I don't bite, you know..." I flinched as the shouts from the kitchen punctuated the early morning.

Logan scoffed but didn't say anything. Instead, he gulped from his mug.

"So, what will you do now?" I asked softly. My face heated. For some reason, I dreaded the answer.

"Move onto the next monster." Logan shrugged over the top of his mug. "Hopefully, finally track down our demon."

"Right, the big bad one you've been hunting since you were three?" I smiled.

"Ten," Logan corrected me with a grin. Then his face fell, and he cleared his throat. "As soon as Traven gets back...whenever that is..."

My brow furrowed at the bitterness in his voice.

"If he takes much longer, maybe I'll head down toward Bolton and help Hannah Green with that closet critter..." He shrugged then as he leaned over his knees and stared down at the mug cupped in his hands.

A soft silence blanketed us in the quiet of the new morning. It was calm and peaceful, and filled my heart with warmth. The trees were silhouetted against the swirl of blue and white sky. Off in the distance, the top of the field glowed a gentle yellow, sparkling with frost; farther beyond, steam rose slowly off the top of the gray lake. And we sat together, sipping Mama's cider, huddled in our jackets against the cold of a dead October.

Before I could ask another question, Logan surprised me by speaking again. "I hate having to wait around for him all the time, you know?" He shook his head. "If it was up to me..." Logan scowled, then drank deeply from his mug.

I turned toward him on the porch so my back was against the railing and my knees were angled at him. "What?"

Logan sighed as he ran a hand through his cropped sandy hair. "Sometimes, I wish I could just go out on my own, you know? I mean, I've done solo hunts, here and there. But it's always on Traven's terms, you know? I mean, my dad...my dad died when I was a kid. Traven was like—what, twenty? Since then, Trav called the shots, kept me out of trouble...but—whatever, I don't know why I'm saying all this stuff..." Logan glanced down at his mug and quipped, "What's in this cider?"

"Veritas."

Logan sputtered, choking on a mouthful.

I giggled. "*Kidding*. It doesn't work that way, anyhow."

Logan gave me a small smile that made me grin. My face burned despite the cold, and I took a quick sip, hiding my blush behind my mug. "That wouldn't be my question, either."

"Oh, yeah?" Logan grinned. His green speckled eyes glittered mischievously in the golden sunlight. "What would your question be?"

I lowered my mug and looked him straight in the eye, emerald to silver. "Why do you hate witches?"

Logan didn't look away. He held my gaze, his face serious. He took a deep breath, but before he could answer, the kitchen door banged open and Phoenix stomped outside onto the deck, her wand fizzing in her hand like a sparkler. Logan and I flinched and jumped farther apart, as though we'd been caught doing something we shouldn't have as Phoenix plopped down between us.

She pointed her wand at the fire pit in the distance and sent a blast of fire into the wood. She dropped her chin in her hand and glared moodily out at the fire.

I put a gentle hand on her shoulder. "Are you okay?"

Phoenix snorted.

Logan slapped a hand on his leg and stood quickly. "Whelp, I'm going to get Guitar Hero into a bed and crash on the couch, if that's okay?"

I stood almost as fast. "We have two guest rooms. I can—"

"Nah, I'll just take the couch..." Logan gave an awkward wave and ducked inside without another word.

I sighed and sank back down on the step beside Phoenix.

We were silent on the porch for a long time, me watching the lake churning in the distance and Phoenix watching the fire.

NILE IS FOR LOVERS

The next morning, I woke up to the light *pat, pat, pat* of Icarus's paw on my face.

"The House Elders are here."

I shot straight up in my bed, sending Icarus dropping to the floor with an indignant meow. I tossed my pillow at the black and orange tangle of hair hiding Phoenix from view. She grunted in response.

"Grammy's here!" I didn't bother to wait for Phoenix to tumble out of bed. Instead, I ran from the bedroom, down the hall, and halted just outside the kitchen. Whispers murmured just beyond the doorway. I angled my head and strained to hear.

"They jinxed the doorway." Logan's words tickled my ear.

I jumped, my face flushed with embarrassment at having been caught eavesdropping. I peeked over my shoulder with a guilty smile. "I forgot you were sleeping on the couch..."

I pulled at my oversized nightshirt that stopped just above my knees, suddenly very aware that I wasn't wearing pants.

Logan smirked, and his green eyes glittered. "They showed up about a half hour ago."

"Sorry." Phoenix came up behind us, her hair sticking up in all directions, rubbing the sleep from her eyes. "I wanted to check on Cole." She yawned. "He's still sleeping—jeez, Phin, you couldn't put some pants on?"

My face burned. "I was in a hurry..."

Logan tried to hide a grin but failed. "Like I said, I think your grandmother put a spell on the kitchen, because I haven't been able to hear anything."

"Jinx it," I muttered. "Did you tell them what happened?"

"Why don't you tell us yourself, Seraphina," Grammy's voice murmured.

I closed my eyes briefly and took a deep breath, before heading into the kitchen. Logan didn't make a move to follow, so I grabbed his hand and tugged him inside after me.

Grammy, Uncle Richard, and Aunt Cordelia sat around the table, each with Mama's best teacups set beside them. Icarus sat in the center of the table, his eyes on the elders. As soon as I came in the room, Aunt Cordelia flicked her finger at the teapot and it floated up and poured more tea in her already full cup.

Instinctively, I bent in a low bow, highly aware of my naked legs. But Phoenix didn't bother to bow, much less curtsey. Instead, she dropped into a seat, an apple cider donut in her hand. Logan hung back, and took to leaning against the counter, rather than joining the group at the table. I stood, awkwardly, almost defiantly, in front of a chair, my fingers curling around the back of it for support.

Aunt Cordelia took her cup from the air as it hovered beside her and sipped through pursed lips, her cold eyes staring rudely at Logan behind me. Then her eyes flicked to rest on me. "Well? What do you have to say for yourself?" Aunt Cordelia demanded shrilly.

"Cordelia..." Grammy cautioned in a calm, steady voice.

Aunt Cordelia slammed her cup into the saucer, and Icarus hissed. Aunt Cordelia turned to Grammy with eyes wide and scandalized. "I heard everything. The *head* of the psychiatric ward in Maple Leaf House is a personal friend," she sniffed, her words runny with self-importance. "Demonic possession! Torture!"

Uncle Richard cleared his throat and spoke in his soft, gentle way. "Why don't we let the girls explain..."

Grammy nodded at me encouragingly.

I stared back at Grammy, studying this woman, whom I loved and respected above all people, yet who had lied and left me unguarded and ill prepared. Weighed down by disappointment, I couldn't return Grammy's smile. I spoke the only words I could manage, my voice almost a whisper. "Where's Mama?"

Grammy sighed heavily. "Seraphina..."

Phoenix mumbled around a big bit of donut. "That's not an answer..."

Grammy hesitated, opening her mouth and shutting it tight again.

My hands gripped the back of the chair so tightly the wood creaked beneath my palms. My anger flared. No. They had come into my home, uninvited, demanding answers from me? No...just no. "We deserve to know what's happening!" I shouted. Grammy winced at my words, Uncle Richard looked down at his teacup, Aunt Cordelia squealed in outrage, but I kept going. "Just like we deserved to know there were monsters roaming around! Just like we deserved to know about Alice Grey!"

Grammy blinked at her name.

"*You ungrateful little vastus*!" Aunt Cordelia hissed. I flinched at the slur, but Aunt Cordelia didn't stop. "I've never seen such disrespect in all my—"

Phoenix rolled her eyes as she scoffed, spraying bits of donut on the table. "Why are you even here?" Phoenix mumbled through her donut.

Aunt Cordelia shrieked. Uncle Richard hid a half smile behind his teacup.

"Icarus—" I snapped furiously. "*Show her out!*"

Aunt Cordelia's eyes bulged with rage, but before she could let out a roar of protest, she vanished in a puff of black smoke.

Uncle Richard's mouth twitched as he regarded the cat, who blinked slowly back. Uncle Richard's eyes crinkled over his bushy beard.

Grammy took a breath, but I cut her off as I pointed a finger at Phoenix. "Nix was tortured!" I jammed my thumb into my chest. "I was shot at!" I threw my hands up. "My friend was murdered! My *best* friend—" My voice broke. I couldn't think about Aubrey. "Cole was—" An arm wrapped around my shoulders as Logan came up behind me in a half hug. I shook my head in disbelief. "Kids are dead! And you have nothing to say?"

Grammy took a deep breath. "Seraphina—"

"What? What can you possibly tell me that will make any of this okay?" I demanded, my voice thick with emotion.

Uncle Richard glanced at Grammy. "Nancy, maybe you should—"

Logan's arm dropped back down to his side. He edged toward the door.

Ordinarily, I would have been embarrassed by the scene I was causing, but after everything that happened, I didn't care.

Grammy looked back at me with a rueful smile. "I'm so sorry, Seraphina." Her eyes shined. Her voice was brittle with her sincerity. "Perhaps we should've told you about the horrific reality of the world...and Alice..." Grammy took a shaky breath and closed her eyes for a moment. "Charlotte had her reasons...and every single one of them was to protect you three girls."

I remained silent, unforgivingly quiet. "Well, it didn't work, did it? *Now, where is Mama?*"

Grammy pursed her lips, as though holding back her words. Finally, she said in a calm, even voice, "There is a dark witch, known only as—"

"The Dark One...we've heard this already."

"Yes. She is an ancient power that has been lurking in the

shadows for centuries, searching for a way to raise the Devil from the depths of Hell."

"Mama said the Devil doesn't exist," I snapped loyally.

Uncle Richard and Grammy exchanged a glance. Then Grammy looked at me, sympathy shining in her silver eyes. "He doesn't exist in this realm...not now. Because he is in Hell."

I did a double take, my eyebrow cocked suspiciously. I looked down at Phoenix, then back at Grammy. "So, Mama lied."

Grammy inhaled deeply. "She didn't lie, but—"

"Not telling the truth is lying, Grammy," Phoenix mumbled angrily around her mouthful.

Grammy closed her eyes briefly but didn't bother to argue. Then she continued, her gaze flickering between the two of us. "He isn't an ordinary demon. Because the Devil wasn't ever human, he was an angel...and he fell—"

"Yes, Grammy," I cut in impatiently. "We remember our theology lessons, but what—"

Grammy continued, unfazed by my rudeness. "When we say that he fell...he didn't literally fall from Heaven. He was sent to Earth by God to learn lessons of humanity. When we say he 'fell,' we mean he fell from grace—became corrupted by the worst of human nature. He became so evil that God created a new realm to contain him. Keep him away from humanity, Heaven, and Earth."

"He's the first demon, essentially," Logan muttered at my back.

Grammy eyes flickered to Logan, and she smiled warmly. "Exactly, Logan." Then she looked back at me. "So, can you imagine the power, the evil, of a demonic force born of an angel instead of a human? Hell...the realm itself...was created with the sole purpose of caging him." Grammy glanced at Phoenix and then back at me. "Now, I've told Phoenix, and now I'm telling you, just before you were born, the Dark One almost freed him—there was a horrific battle, and she was stopped, trapped away until now. But what I haven't told Phoenix, and what I am telling you both now, is that your mother was the one who locked the Dark One away."

My brow furrowed as Phoenix coughed on her donut and gulped at her cider. "Mama married Daddy when she was eighteen," I snapped incredulously. "You're trying to tell us that Mama defeated the female equivalent of Lord Voldemort as a *teenager*?"

Phoenix nudged me. "Phin...Harry did it at seventeen...try Palpatine..."

I glared down at Phoenix. "*Whatever!*" My eyes darted back to Grammy. "How is that even possible?"

Grammy bowed her head in deference. "Which is why the High Council requested an audience with her...because the Dark One has been freed and is amassing a following of the most powerful demons to help her. She's gathering what she needs, and she will set the Devil free if she isn't stopped."

A heavy silence permeated the kitchen.

Then the back door banged open, blasting us with a gust of cold wind and showering us with icy lake spray, as Fawn stalked through the portal. She slammed the door behind her and stomped into the kitchen, her hair drenched and her nose rosy from the cold. She tossed the old passage candle onto the table. It rolled across the tabletop and came to a stop in front of Grammy, who regarded Fawn with a calm interest, as though the sight of the little girl bursting inside the cottage from Blackwell Manor was commonplace.

I stared at Fawn, still recovering from my shock. Then my heart stumbled in my chest. But before I could pull her into a hug, she snatched my hand, her honey-hued eyes on Grammy.

She spoke in a low, cool voice. "I told you: I need to talk to Seraphina." Then, without another word, she tugged me into the living room.

She walked me past the built-in bookcases to the closest corner of the room. Then Fawn stood in front of me, staring straight up into my eyes. She took a deep breath. "You hurt my feelings when you left."

I took her hands in mine and squeezed them. "I'm so sorry, Fawn. I was a hag."

Tears shined in her warm brown eyes, and she bit her lip as she held my gaze. Although her lower lip trembled, her voice was steady and strong. "Phoenix said you needed time to learn a lesson. Have you learned it yet?"

I smiled as a tear slid down my cheek. I shook Fawn's big little hands. I couldn't speak. Instead, I nodded vigorously. I took a breath. "I love you, Fawn." I pulled her into a fierce hug. "So much."

As I held her to me, I mumbled down into her hair, "How did you leave Blackwell Manor with Hermes lurking about?"

"I had to see you." Fawn glanced up at me. "And please, you really think a *cat* can keep up with me in the woods?"

I burst out laughing. The idea was ridiculous. And before all this, I wouldn't have believed her, for there was *no way* Fawn could've gotten past a familiar's magic on a direct order from his mistress. And yet, here she was...a rare talent, indeed. I tweaked her nose, smoothed her hair, and I hugged her tight.

Icarus jumped up on the back of the couch. "Traven DeVarney is here."

My hold on Fawn tightened, and I shouted, "Logan, he's back!" I pulled Fawn with me to the window beside the front door. We peeked through the windows. Logan's truck was parked in the driveway. There was a knock at the door. Before I could open it, Logan was there beside me. He swung the door wide and yanked his brother inside.

They embraced in the way boys do: a hard hug, a tight squeeze, a back slap, and a shove. I hung back a bit, my arm around Fawn, a small smile in the corner of my mouth as I watched the scene. I gave Fawn a little shake. The familial love was infectious.

Traven raked a hand through his sandy hair, and Logan gestured toward me. "Trav...Seraphina, and her little sister, Fawn."

Traven looked remarkably like his little brother, or rather Logan looked like him, except where Logan's face was all sharp angles, Traven's was softer. But he was clearly older. And clearly exhausted and disheveled. Like he'd just returned from battle. He gave us a warm smile as he stifled a yawn. Then he did a double take, his eyes wide as he studied my face. He rubbed the back of his neck and looked from Logan back to me. "Sorry, for a second, I thought I saw the ghost of Charlotte Past." Then he laughed, a nice, jovial sound that made me smile, however hesitantly and bemused. Traven stepped back and shook his head. "God. You look just like your mom. Not her eyes, though...those are yours."

Fawn crossed her arms over her chest and regarded him coolly. "You knew Mama?"

Traven grinned down at her and nodded. "That I did. When I met her, I was about your age...what are you, twelve? Thirteen?"

Fawn dropped her hands to her hips and giggled despite herself. "No, I'm only eight!"

"No way!" Traven's eyebrows raised as he feigned surprise. "You're so tall!"

Phoenix appeared and sidled up to me, her eyes on Traven. "Where's Mama?"

Traven hesitated in the face of Phoenix's cool demeanor.

I elbowed her. "Nix!"

She shrugged.

Traven glanced around at all of us. "Maybe we should sit down?"

Phoenix turned on her heel and marched toward the far couch. She crisscrossed her legs on top of the cushion, bouncing a little as she got comfy. I sat beside her, with Fawn slumped between us. Logan stood off to the side, lingering beside the mantel with his arms crossed. Traven took a seat on the opposite couch and leaned over his knees as he regarded each of us in turn. He opened his mouth, but Phoenix interrupted, "We know she met with the High Council—so how about you start with the part where you come in..." She waved an impatient hand.

A smirk twitched in the corner of Traven's mouth. "Right. Okay, so—"

"And don't leave anything out," Fawn added, mimicking Phoenix's curt tone.

Phoenix snickered.

Traven nodded his understanding and cleared his throat. "So, that Monday after I left Grey Cottage...I brought Logan to the motel and headed straight for Cassandra Sawyer."

"Who?" I prompted impatiently.

"She's a psychic who lives in Nile."

"A psychic?" Phoenix scoffed. "There aren't any other witches in Nile—"

Traven smiled. "She isn't a witch. Psychics are humans...but not. Just like witches."

Phoenix crinkled her nose and made a face. "How could some random psychic lady know where Mama is? She's Unreachable."

Traven nodded at the question with an indulgent grin. "Now that was the trick of it. How would I find her when she was, by definition, unable to be found. You see, Cassandra wasn't able to *locate* her. Instead, she was able to—"

"The psychic doesn't matter." I waved away the explanation. My cheeks burned at my rudeness, but I didn't care. "What did she tell you?"

Traven didn't seem to mind. Instead, he answered with a kind smile. "To head for the mountains."

"The mountains?" I repeated. Unease twisted in my stomach.

Traven's eyes moved over us, almost uncertainly. "How much do you know about your father?"

"Nothing," Fawn piped up, eager for information.

"Well—"

Icarus suddenly pounced onto the coffee table between us. His back was to us girls as he stared at Traven, who sat back instinctively.

"Hey, Icarus..." He smiled a cheesy grin as Icarus's tail flicked back and forth.

"He left before Fawn was born." Phoenix shrugged, as though it didn't hurt. "What does he have to do with anything?"

I leaned forward and pulled the cat into my lap. I stroked him in all his favorite places, and Icarus relaxed and began to purr, his eyes still glaring at Traven.

Traven cleared his throat. He eyed the cat in my lap and licked his lips as though tasting each word carefully. "Well, I've never met him, but—"

"I haven't either," Fawn chirped in the brutal honesty of a kid.

Traven flashed a smirk her way. "Nobody has, girlie. But, according to Charlotte, er—your mom—he's a pretty impressive demon hunter. And I knew as soon as Phoenix told me the High Council had called her that she'd head after him next." Traven's eyes rested gently on me. "Which is where Cassandra came in.

"Although, he wasn't really any easier to find. Cassandra reached out to the spirit world and was able to get a few vague answers. Cassandra found his last known location...from almost ten years ago. Rumor had it, he was retired and living up in the mountains somewhere..."

"Like the Unabomber?" Phoenix scoffed.

Traven shrugged. "But I ran into your mother, and we spent three weeks tracking him down."

"Did you find him?" I asked, my voice high and breathless.

Traven shook his head with a downturned smile. "Nope. But she's still looking. She sent me back to check on you three...and to tell you she probably won't be back for a few weeks more..."

Phoenix snorted. "She just happened to send you back right after we dealt with a demon?"

"A few weeks?" Fawn cried out.

I took her hand in mine and squeezed.

Traven's eyebrows raised. He looked over at Logan. "Demon? What demon?"

Logan shrugged. "Seraphina handled it."

"Wait!" Fawn twisted in her seat to stare at me. "*You did what? A demon?*"

My cheeks burned as Traven eyed me, impressed. "Congratulations. That's huge." He smiled warmly at me. "Your first exorcism...you never forget it..." His smile faltered and a shadow cast over his face. He rubbed his forehead and then said quickly, "Is everyone okay? You good?"

"Sure," Phoenix muttered dryly. "Fantastic."

Before anyone could say more, there was a burst of flame in the air between us and a scroll dropped onto the coffee table. Logan cursed as he straightened off the mantel in surprise.

Traven scooted back on the couch with a nervous chuckle. "I'll never get used to that."

Phoenix and I exchanged a glance, but Fawn snatched it before we could make a move. She popped the High Council seal and started to unroll it, but Phoenix yanked it out of her hands.

"Hey!" Fawn whined.

Phoenix pushed her head down as her eyes moved over the scroll, widening as she read. Then she slapped it into my outstretched hand, jumped off the couch, and marched toward the kitchen.

Fawn looked at me expectantly. "What? What is it?"

Icarus slipped off my lap and padded after Phoenix. As I read, my heart dropped into the pit of my stomach, and I headed for the kitchen without another word to the guys.

Grammy and Uncle Richard were sipping cider together, waiting for us at the table. They both looked up in surprise at our furious expressions as we stormed into the room. Phoenix snatched the box of donuts from the cabinet and leaned against the counter as I slapped the letter onto the table in front of them.

"Is this why you came here?" I demanded. "Because you knew they were going to send this summons?"

The two of them exchanged a glance, and then Grammy's eyes met mine. Silver to silver. She nodded slowly. "We did. And we'd hoped to discuss it with you, prepare you both, before it arrived... but Miss Fawn..." Grammy's gaze slid to the doorway, where Fawn peeked around the corner, her golden curls spilling past the frame. "Arrived before we could approach the subject..."

I tossed my hands up, slapping them back down at my sides. "So, what does this mean? Are they going to drag me out of here? Because I don't care what they say, I'm not going."

"Me either," Phoenix snapped as she snatched a donut and tossed the now-empty box back onto the counter behind her. "I'd rather go to Phin's high school than go to Stone Point." She made a face.

I nodded furiously. "I said it weeks ago at the Forging, and I'm telling you for the final time. And I don't care how much they butter me up with junk like 'extraordinary knowledge of craft' and 'masterful level of potion chemistry.'" I scoffed in disgust. "I'm not going to be sworn into any mage 'Order.'" Then I waved my hand at the letter. "And what does this even mean, 'having taken Charlotte Elizabeth Grey's answer into consideration'? What answer?"

"They asked her to help them. Work for them." Phoenix spoke around her mouthful. She pointed her half-eaten donut at Grammy. "Right, Grammy? So, Mama must've told them no."

I blinked. "So, she refuses to be...what, drafted?...and so they are kidnapping her kids?" I looked from Uncle Richard to Grammy, eyes wide. "That's what this is—they want to take us hostage...some kind of leverage to use against her?"

Grammy took a deep breath. "I spent all morning discussing this with Icarus. Considering the state of the witching world...and the threat we all are faced with...I don't think it would be a bad idea to at least consider the—"

"No." I shook my head furiously, my eyes burning at the suggestion. "They'll have to curse me first, because I'm not—"

"The boys are leaving," Fawn singsonged from the doorway.

My heart lodged in my throat. I couldn't breathe. I ran from the kitchen without hesitation. I slipped past Fawn, ran through the living room, and I didn't stop. A car door slammed outside. I yanked open the front door. The truck was leaving. I ran out into the gravel driveway, wincing as the rocks ripped up my feet. "Logan!"

The truck came to an abrupt halt, its brake lights bright in the gray autumn afternoon, just before it could make the first turn through the winding road leading back through the woods. I stopped where I was in the middle of the driveway, panting more from nerves than exertion.

The passenger door kicked open and Logan hopped out, jogging to meet me. He put a hand on my shoulder. The emerald found the silver. "Are you okay?"

I shook my head, my hair blowing in the wind, swirling around my head. "Take me with you."

"What?" Logan's hand fell to his side as though I'd burned him. He frowned, his eyes narrowed, completely taken aback.

"Take me with you," I repeated breathlessly. "I want to...I want to do what you do."

A smirk snuck onto his face. "A monster stalker?"

I shoved his shoulder, my impatience getting the better of me. "No, Logan, I want to help people, like Maddie, and Aubrey, and —" I stopped. I couldn't say Alice's name. I shook my head, struggling for the right words. "I want to save them—I want to stop them before they go dark. I want to help people."

The smirk vanished, replaced by a look of genuine curiosity. As though he were looking at me for the first time. Then he frowned. "That's not the whole reason..."

This time, it was my turn to pause. It shook me how he seemed to read me so well. My feet shifted in the stones, and I hugged myself against the cold, squeezing my legs together as the wind blew icy against my nightshirt. I didn't say anything more, only looked into his eyes with hope in mine.

"Listen, Seraphina..." Logan rubbed the back of his neck and squinted up into the cloudy sky like he was checking for rain.

My heart slowed and slipped down into my stomach. My hair tickled my face as another icy breeze streamed through the clearing. I held the hem of my shirt down against the wind.

How ridiculous I must look.

How childish of me to think...

Of course he wouldn't want me to come along. I was just a naive little girl compared to him and all he'd done. Why would he want to have to deal with me 24/7?

I swallowed and took a shaky breath, looking away from him and staring into the tangle of barren, ashy trees. I nodded. I tried to speak, but nothing came to me. Instead, I nodded once more, and turned away from him and ran back inside.

I didn't go back to the kitchen. I shut myself up in my room and didn't come out for the rest of the day. Grammy and Uncle Richard left shortly after the DeVarney boys did, at least that's what Phoenix said...but Fawn hadn't wanted to leave, so Grammy had to bind Fawn to her passage candle and float her out the back door. I couldn't even manage a smile. Then Phoenix, finally having enough of my sulking, dragged me out of bed to see Cole. The two of us sat on either side of the bed, staring at Cole's sleeping, peaceful face.

"Grammy woke him up before she left and gave him a brew she said should have him back on his feet within a few hours," Phoenix said softly. "She said she'll request an audience with the High Council...see what she can do about delaying the summons. I mean, it's Grammy. High Priestess of the House of Grey. They can't make us go anywhere if she doesn't allow it." Phoenix snickered. "And Icarus would banish them before they even set foot down Grey Lane."

I nodded, jaw tight.

It was quiet. Then Phoenix blurted, "Fawn doesn't blame you for being gone, you know...she actually wants the same thing..."

I looked at her in alarm.

"No, no...I mean...unlike me, she actually *wants* to enroll in Stone Point, you know—the academy...when she's older..."

"What?" I made a face. "Why?"

"She wants to study therianthropy."

"Shapeshifting? They teach that there?" I asked, impressed.

Phoenix nodded as the quiet settled around us again.

Phoenix glanced at me. "Do you want to talk about it?"

I continued to study Cole's face. Normally, I would've snapped at Phoenix. But I didn't. Maybe, this time, things could be different. *I* could be different.

I took a deep breath and let it out. "I asked to go with him."

Phoenix's eyes widened. "You—"

I groaned. "Yes, I know...insane idea. It's just—"

"No!" Phoenix grinned. "I think it's an awesome idea!"

I glanced sideways at her. "Really?"

Phoenix's smile set her caramel eyes sparkling, bright like amber gems. "How cool would that be—*saving the world*? What'd he say?"

I chuckled darkly. "Nothing...he's too good a guy to tell me no, so I took the hint."

"'Too good'?! That pickled potion?"

I laughed at her sour face. "What happened between you two anyways?"

Phoenix rolled her eyes. "Don't ask. Ever."

I bit my lip on a grin. "All right, so he's a bit hard around the edges, but he truly is sweet on the inside..."

Phoenix stared at me, her eyes half closed. "You just described a lollipop."

I scoffed, still fighting the smile that tugged at my lips. "*Anyways*, it doesn't matter. He's leaving. Probably packed up the second they got back to the motel. Heading off to hunt something else."

Phoenix gave me a sympathetic frown as she nodded and squeezed my hand. "Sorry, Phin. I know you liked him."

"No, it's not that." My face burned. "I just feel like a jerk. I was so embarrassed, I didn't even say goodbye."

"He didn't either, did he?" Phoenix pointed out.

I tucked my hair behind my ears as my face continued to heat. "Well, I think he was trying to, but I sort of ran away."

"You what?" Phoenix tried to stifle a smirk.

I buried my face in my hands. "I know. I know."

"Classic, Phin. Running away at the mere hint of interpersonal conflict." Phoenix tsked.

My hands slowly dropped from my face. "You're right."

Phoenix gave me a sly, sideways glance. "You know...the van is here...you could catch him before he leaves."

I stared at Phoenix. She was right. "Where are the keys?"

33

THE ADVENTURE

In less than ten minutes, I parked in the rocky motel parking lot. The truck's doors were wide open and the engine was running. My arms prickled, and my stomach twisted. The old pickup shuddered as the motor rumbled, the exhaust puffing out in cold clouds behind it.

I turned off the van and pocketed the keys. Something wasn't right. My eyes darted to the motel room. The door was open. Slowly, my breath catching in my chest, I slipped out of the van and shut the door, my eyes on the truck as I headed for the motel room. Cautiously, I crept toward the doorway and said in a voice too soft to be brave, "Logan?"

There was no answer.

I peered into the room. Logan sat on the far bed with a vacant expression on his face. He didn't even seem to notice when I walked into the room. Nothing seemed to be out of place. It looked just the same as when I'd been there last. Except now that meant something *was* missing, because just as before, Traven was gone.

I crossed the room and stopped in front of Logan. Like a child approaching a deer, I knelt in front of him, forcing his eyes to meet mine. Then, like the sight of me sparked life inside him, he blinked. His face was pale. His green and gold eyes were too wide.

"Logan?"

His eyelids fluttered, and he rubbed the back of his neck. He took a breath that rattled shakily in his chest. "Demons."

Before I could speak, he slapped his thighs and stood abruptly. "You need to leave."

I stood with him. "What happened?"

Logan moved back and forth around the room. He threaded his hands together behind his head, his fingers digging into his skull, as he paced.

"Logan..."

Logan faced the wall and crossed his arms over his chest. I hesitated. I took a tentative step forward and placed a gentle hand on his back. His broad shoulders rose as he took a deep breath, then he turned to face me. His face was grim and set. "The demon we've been hunting—she decided to pay us a visit. Traven's dead."

"Did they take him?" I demanded, my voice high and desperate. My eyes darted around every corner of the room, as though Traven might walk in at any moment. "How can you know he's—"

Logan shook his head and rolled his eyes to the ceiling. He moved away from me and inexplicably began to pack up his things.

"Logan..." I watched him slap shirts into a duffel bag. "Logan!"

He didn't bother to look up. "What? You want details?"

My mouth fell open. He could've slapped me.

Logan froze, his hand in the bag, and sighed heavily. He massaged his neck. "I'm sorry, Sam...I just—he's dead. They were waiting for us. I saw him—well...and then, yeah." He scoffed. "Yeah, they took him. Let's just leave it there."

Horrified and refusing to let my mind contemplate what might have happened, I closed my eyes. "What will you do?"

Logan snorted. "I'm going to kill the damn thing." Logan

dumped a pile of ratty old books into the bag. "But it'll take awhile. Unlike the demon on Bird Island, this demon is a beast. She has abilities that make her almost impossible to fight—and track..." He sighed, shaking his head. Logan pinched the bridge of his nose and squinted his eyes shut. Then he went back to packing.

I stared at him incredulously. "You...you're still leaving? *Now?*"

Logan scoffed and gave me an almost pained expression. "What else would I do?"

I blinked rapidly, my mouth agape. "Well, do you have any other family?"

Logan chuckled darkly. "My uncle is in California, hunting vampires. He doesn't mess with demons anymore."

I crossed the distance between us and pulled the book he was trying to pack out of his hands. "No...I meant someone you could stay with..."

Logan smiled ruefully at that. "No." He tugged the book out of my hands and went back to packing, muttering to himself.

My temper flared, and I snatched a CD case out of his hands. "You can't go off on your own."

Logan glanced at me sideways, his eyebrow cocked.

I nibbled my lower lip and shook my head. I backed up a step underneath the weight of his hard, stony stare. "You're, you're *traumatized* and—and *grieving*—Logan, you're not thinking clearly!"

He frowned and snatched at the CD.

I moved it out of his reach and held it behind my back. I took another small step back and shook my head again, blonde hair falling in my face, as I stammered over my words. "I'm not letting you run off like this. You're not thinking straight. How long have you been sitting here in shock? Logan, you'll get hurt!"

He scowled, his face lined with impatience. Then he took a slow step toward me as he spoke. "This isn't my first rodeo, Sam. Hunters are always losing people. Everybody's always dying." He shrugged dismissively as I recoiled at the heat of his words. The gold flecks in his eyes shined as he gritted his teeth. "It *happens*. Okay? I'm used to it. Part of the job." He took another step toward me, closing the distance.

"Fine." I backed up, holding the CD as collateral against the small of my back. "I'm coming with you."

"Like hell." Logan grabbed me, crushing me against him and yanking the CD from my hands.

I moved in front of the duffel bag. Jaw set in a determined look of defiance, I crossed my arms over my chest.

Logan stared at me, furious impatience hardening his eyes. "You're in the way."

"But I won't be," I retorted, chin high. "I can't cast, but I know my herbs and potions. I can help you. You know I can."

Logan's scowl deepened.

"At the very least, I can keep you from doing something stupid like this." I met his hard eyes with cold silver. "If I'm too much of a pain, you can send me back home to my grammy."

Logan's nostrils flared like a bad-tempered bull.

"Fine," he hissed through clenched teeth, then he grabbed me by the shoulders and lifted me off the ground and dropped me roughly back on my feet, out of his way. "If you get the okay from your grandmother, you can come with me."

My eyes flickered over his face. Overcome with emotion for his heartbreak, I jumped up and threw my arms around his neck. The sudden force knocked him back a few steps and instinctively, his arm came down on my back. He gripped me to him as he found his footing and steadied us both. His hand smoothed the back of my head, and then his hands gently untangled my arms from his neck.

I stepped back, and he looked away.

He needed help, whether he admitted it or not.

· · ·

Of course, I didn't need to ask Grammy. I needed to talk to Icarus. He was the closest thing I had to Mama right now. The cat regarded me with a coolness that made me shiver. His tail flicked with irritation. I bit my lip, my brow furrowed, waiting for his answer.

But he didn't give me one. "Have you asked anyone about the grim?"

I blinked. I hesitated. Had I heard him correctly? "I…"

"The grim you sent away."

I hadn't thought about it. There'd been so much going on…I frowned down at Icarus. "No…no one. How did you know about—?"

"Good." Icarus's ears twitched impatiently. "Seraphina, you need to promise me you won't tell anyone what happened with the grim."

"Why?" I cocked my eyebrow with a suspicious scowl.

"It is a rare witch who can command a creature such as a grim…and I think it in your best interest to keep that private until we speak to your mother. Agreed?"

I scoffed. "Fine, but—"

"Good." Icarus nodded his thanks.

"Sure." I smiled awkwardly. "Now, what about—"

"You would like to follow Logan DeVarney around on his homicidal monster rampage?" Icarus sighed heavily, his tail bristling. "As much as it pains me to say—I think your mother would approve of that, as long as I am permitted to accompany you. And your sister. You will have to ask her—" His ears twitched again. Then his eyelids lowered, heavy with annoyance. Then he slipped down and padded his way to the door. "Phoenix Grey, what has your mother told you about listening at keyholes?"

The door swung open as Phoenix stomped inside. "She's not asking me anything." She crossed her arms. "I'm coming too. And so is Cole. I already talked to him."

Icarus mewed indignantly as he disappeared through the doorway.

"He's awake?" I demanded. "When did he—"

Phoenix waved away my question as she began digging through her dresser. "As soon as you left the room. He was listening to us the whole time." Phoenix glanced sharply over her shoulder. "I'm not the only one with big ears." She turned back to her dresser as clothes started flying. "We'd decided before you even came back. We're taking the van. We've already packed most of the potions and crystals and magic stuff like that..."

"What about his dad?" I exclaimed.

Phoenix shrugged. "That's his problem."

"But I don't know if—"

"He'll get over it." Phoenix waved another hand dismissively, as though reading my mind.

I sat and watched Phoenix toss clothes onto my bed. Was *I* okay with it? I'd spent so much energy this past month trying to *get away* from Phoenix. Did I really want to be stuck on an endless road trip with her?

"You know..." Phoenix eyed the mess she'd made all over the room. She frowned thoughtfully and put her hands on her hips. "Maybe we should make a list?"

I forced a smile and pushed up from the bed to help her.

It didn't take long to pack, especially with Phoenix magically shrinking everything to fit neatly in our bags. Logan waited in the driveway, leaning against the truck with his arms crossed when Phoenix and I walked out onto the front porch, followed by a much steadier Cole. Icarus took up the rear, padding lightly behind Phoenix.

Logan pushed slowly off the truck, his arms falling to his sides.

Phoenix hopped down the steps, ignoring Logan altogether as

she tossed her bags into the van. Cole gave a little nod and salute to Logan, and hopped into the van's driver seat.

"Sam…" Logan walked up to me as I winced guiltily.

I shrugged. "They wouldn't take no for an answer…" I gave him a small nudge. "Seriously, is it okay if they come too?"

Logan stood, struggling with himself for a minute, and then a ghost of a smile flickered on his face. He inclined his head toward me and winced. "If I say yes, you promise not to jump on me again?"

I smirked and punched his arm. "Yes."

Phoenix walked over to us. Icarus was perched on her shoulder, peering through her hair. She looked up at Logan as she gave his arm a sympathetic squeeze. "I'm sorry about your brother, DeVarney. He was a good guy. I liked him a lot."

Logan's jaw tightened. He nodded curtly, and then jutted his chin toward the van. "Make sure Guitar Hero keeps up. I don't need you getting lost…" Then Logan looked down on her with a skeptical frown. "You're going to have to work at this…it's not all radio and road snacks…"

"Whatever you say, Master Qui-Gon." Phoenix grinned and gave a mock salute.

Logan's mouth twitched. Then he started for the truck, his hands in his pockets.

My heart sank as he headed to the passenger side and yanked open the door. Logan gripped the frame and stared into the truck, waiting.

I swallowed thickly. He was used to riding shotgun; he'd forgotten—

But then Logan glanced back at me, his eyebrow cocked. "You coming, Sam?"

I bit my lip on a smile and hurried forward, but Phoenix held me back.

"Wait." Phoenix lightly touched my arm, all humor gone from

her face as her amber eyes searched mine. "Are you sure you're okay with me coming, Seraphina?"

Was I?

I looked down at my sister, searching her anxious face. There was no question. "More than okay." A small smile warmed my face. "I need you, Nix."

I reached for her hand.

Thank you so much for reading.

This story is my heart.
It mirrors so much of my experiences growing up and holds the spirit of my daughters, their goodness and strength.

If you enjoyed *Seraphina Grey Summons a Demon*, let everyone know when you leave a review!
Share your thoughts on Goodreads and/or your preferred book seller.
And don't forget to post a picture!

This is the end of *Seraphina Grey Summons a Demon,* but the Grey sisters' journey into the supernatural world has just begun!

Pre-order book two in the series, *Phoenix Grey and the Blood Farm,* at cristinecourcy.com/books or your preferred book seller!

And if you send me a photo of your pre-order receipt to

cris@cristinecourcy.com

— you'll receive a sneak peek chapter e-mailed to you a week before release, and you'll be entered to win a signed paperback!

ABOUT THE AUTHOR

Hi, I'm Cristine!
I love old sitcoms and slasher films.
When I'm not writing, I'm playing Animal Crossing or Harvest Moon 64.
When I am writing, I like to write dark fantasy with a light heart. This means I want to disturb you without leaving you feeling yucky at the end of the story. In short, I'm inventing a new genre I like to call 'cozy dark fantasy.'
My books are heavily influenced by my experiences growing up wild on an island in the middle of the lake.
Almost all the things I write about are inspired by real life...but for legal purposes— that's a lie.
To read more lies and see photos of the things that *did not* inspire my writing, sign up for my newsletter at cristinecourcy.com/newsletter.

Connect with me online:
WWW.CRISTINECOURCY.COM

goodreads.com/cristinecourcy

facebook.com/cristinecourcy

instagram.com/cristinecourcy

threads.net/@cristinecourcy

youtube.com/@cristinecourcy

x.com/cristinecourcy

tiktok.com/@cristinecourcy

amazon.com/author/cristinecourcy